EARLY PRAISE F(

Wolf-Boy, David Fitzpatrick's hard-hitting YA novel, is by turns harrowing and heartbreaking yet, ultimately, hopeful. This is a book that deals honestly with real-life issues affecting adolescents, including drugs, suicide, violence, and self-harm, along with burgeoning and complex sexuality. It's a book that asks big questions about Art with a capital A, family, friendship, and the possibility of recovery from terrible trauma. Set mostly in 1979, when the acronym LBGTQ+ had yet to be created, the novel centers around Danny, a sixteen-year-old who, today, would probably place himself in the Q category: a boy Questioning his sexuality. But Danny is also Questing. Like a classic hero, he undertakes a perilous journey in search of truth and self-knowledge. Danny's voice is utterly compelling. He is so smart and funny, so real and touching in his vulnerability that readers will undertake this quest right alongside him, rooting for him every step of the way. *Wolf-Boy* is a powerful novel from a courageous, skillful and humane writer.

   ～ Hollis Seamon, author of *Somebody Up There Hates You*

Opening David Fitzpatrick's debut novel *Wolf-Boy*, the reader enters the story of a likeable but fragile sixteen-year-old named Danny who falls under the spell of a seductive but treacherous young photographer and her co-conspirator, a wild and unhinged local boy a few years older than Danny. In this harrowing and compelling tale, Fitzpatrick plumbs the depths of psychological, sexual, and chemical abuse in such a way that you root for the adolescent victim of this dangerous duo and worry that the damage inflicted on him will take him past the point of no return. I turned the pages of *Wolf-Boy* nervously and compulsively, in the grips of a frightening, unforgettable story.

~ Wally Lamb, author of *She's Come Undone* and *I Know This Much Is True*

WOLF-BOY

A NOVEL

DAVID FITZPATRICK

RUNNING
Wild
PRESS

Wolf-Boy, A Novel
text copyright © 2024 Reserved by David Fitzpatrick
Edited by Cody Sisco

All rights reserved.
Published in North America and Europe by Running Wild Press. Visit Running
Wild Press at www.runningwildpress.com Educators, librarians, book clubs
(as well as the eternally curious), go to www.runningwildpress.com.

Paperback ISBN: 978-1-960018-01-4
eBook ISBN: 978-1-960018-02-1

This novel is for my wife, Amy, and my father, Richard H. Fitzpatrick, Jr., Dr. Richard Kravitz, Dr. Tom Landino, and for my good friend, journalist Eric Boehlert. Five wonderful people in their own way that set me on firmer, dare I say higher ground?

There are some things
You learn best in calm,
And some in storm.

— WILLA CATHER, *THE SONG OF*
THE LARK

Many days you have lingered around my
Cabin door, oh, hard times come again no more.

— STEPHEN FOSTER, *HARD TIMES*

CONTENTS

A CREATION STORY

I am never *officially* introduced to Gracie, just immediately locked in her orbit, fascinated by the new, radiant, bald-headed cashier at my uncle Randy's photography studio Shoot! at the tip of Cape Cod. It's my first day of work the summer of 1979, and the world seems both infinitely huge and impossibly small all at once. Spotting her feels like a creation story—my silly, amateur world falls away, and my engines roar to life when she steps into the light that makes the old whaling village and artist colony attractive to photographers. Before Gracie, before Provincetown, before this wild, bittersweet season, there was only Whiffle ball, brine, and a nagging, primal fear of hairy palms.

"Randy told me to keep an eye out for a handsome young man," Gracie says, and my buddy steps forward to shake her hand. Everything about Liam Preston seems taut, from his shoulders and chest to the prominent veins on his hands and arms, *mini serpents, really,* which I find both terrifying and vaguely thrilling.

"I'm Liam," he says. "This other guy is Randy's kid nephew, Danny. Rumor has it he's got a huge crush on me."

"What?" I say, blushing before Gracie smiles, shaking Liam's hand, and slides her bizarre sunglasses down her face and winks at me. The glasses are black, bug-eyed, and make Gracie look like some cool space alien, as if the spectacles themselves have a life all their own.

"I find Randy's kid nephew sexy, Liam," she says. "And I adore Danny's doe eyes, and the funky, cool hollows of his collarbone."

I'm sold on her in a millisecond for that. Plus, I'm told she's an adopted child of Portuguese American descent, and most of my friends and family are Irish American, so to me she's a rare diamond—a dazzling thing to behold, and her body has the most wonderful, bronzed tan. "Sweet Ivy-League lady" is what Liam calls her, and part of that is his sarcasm, and the other part is pure, naked envy. Her bare head is round and smooth. When Gracie turns around, two dimples at the base of her skull remind me of resting cat eyes. Her neck is graceful and long and holds a hint of serpentine possibilities.

Most everyone's eyes follow her around the room. Even in Provincetown, a village where it takes quite a lot to stand out, Gracie shimmers. She has a sweet nose, although a little crooked, and the left nostril has a big safety pin through it. It's the shapely body, however, that nabs everyone, makes people *study* her. Her limbs appear coiled, as if she's prepared at any second to bounce up high, way above the jetliners, and zip back to the ground, squatting lower than a dime.

She smells different, too, like she rolls around on a bed of lilacs after going for a four-hundred-yard sprint, naked. I can still smell sweat, hail, whiskey, Coppertone, and fire. To a boy of sixteen, it's like the compressed bonfires of an entire Cape Cod summer—if a hundred of them were tossed and seasoned with all its collective lust, snow cones, crescent moons, half-finished poems, transcendent music, roman candles, and star gazing—if you sauté that with a case of unusually ripe narcissism and turn it to a liquid, what you'd get when that creation splashes down on a young woman is the one and only Gracie Rose.

One can't see her eyes much—they're covered by black, bug-eyed sunglasses that are unusually dark—she tells everyone she's overly sensitive to light. But her eyes are light green drops, and her lips are plump, almost fat. I never kissed a girl with lips like that before. I had French-kissed only two girls to begin with in my whole life, and my fingers had caressed just a handful of breasts.

Gracie calls me *angel* or *sugar so sweet*. Her endearments are like melodies—fresh, fluid vibrations that shimmy through every one of my bones. She also bounces when she walks, as if she gets the hiccups every other stride. I learn she made it through four semesters at Yale University before her adoptive parents went bankrupt in Middletown, Connecticut, forcing Gracie to drop out. She also speaks five languages fluently and says, "I bop around, doing this and that, but always pining to get back to the camera, where I am gifted and quite lethal with a lens."

Gracie lives in a tiny peach-colored cottage in Truro that she shares with a buddy of hers named Wart, who I later learn is a ball python. Gracie keeps fresh flowers around her at work and in her cottage and faithfully practices yoga too. Gracie enjoys Al Green tunes, recites Anne Sexton poems from memory, and sings only the second verse of "You Are My Sunshine" when she's lonesome.

On that first day, she pulls me aside and coos, "I see you and me copulating frequently in the near future and waking up the next morning with wildflowers sprouting from our various salty crevices."

"Yes, great... Right, please," I stammer when she knocks her hips into mine.

"The two of us, Danny," she says. "We'll probably have half a dozen kids and they'll be climbing all over us on Sunday mornings, raising holy hell."

On Monday, June 4—only a month away from my complete mental disintegration—we have our first *sanctified, sweaty date,* in Gracie's words. She phones me a day before and says, "I'm going to change your life with lobster rolls at Jill Mac's in East Dennis, a brand-new spot."

"What?" I ask.

"You'll sample-kiss my fat lips on our date, and we can have nasty, flirty fun," she says. "Eventually, there'll be dancing, pounding music, flashing lights, along with a giant turquoise eye studying your every move, plus a couple thousand photographs and a fair share of shenanigans taking place in your funky and wide tree fort. What does everyone call it again?"

"Palatial Palace of the Palpable Pines," I say.

"I love that so much," she says, clapping her hands twice. "Silly, corny, and goofy as hell, but so disarming."

"What should I wear on our date?" I ask.

"Black tie, tails, dress shoes, the whole ball of wax," she says, before she laughs. "*You're the guy, Danny,* you only need khaki shorts and a T-shirt and Nikes."

"Right," I say, before taking a shower the night before and another two the next morning. By the time I leave for the date at 11:15 a.m. on my trail bike, I get obsessed with my halitosis and body odor, so I devour three packages of Lifesavers and use two Dry Ideas bottles beforehand. In fact, I use so much antiperspirant my left underarm gets a rash for a day.

Gracie drives down in an older, poorly re-painted maroon Mercury Comet with a bumper sticker that reads, "Mother Earth *is* My God." We met at a dilapidated fried clam shack by the docks called Jill Mac's. Despite her singular skin and lack of hair, Gracie dresses mostly conservatively that day, at least for her. She has an Easter-egg-blue mini-sundress, a floppy, over-sized straw hat, and scuffed black military boots with pink toenail polish painted on at the tips.

Gracie has an old Pentax camera strung around her neck along with a new Nikon, and she takes shots as I arrive, crouching, leaning over some daisies and Queen Ann's lace, shooting up a trunk-shot of a funky, gnarled oak. Somehow, she makes it seem graceful, poised, a professional at work, stepping over stones, or leaping across a mostly dry creek bed.

"Ansel says, 'A good photograph is all about knowing where to stand,'" Gracie explains.

"Ansel?"

"Adams, goof-ball," she says. "Only one of the greatest in the history of cameras."

"Right," I say as she approaches and takes some close-ups of me. Many days later she showed me a few of the developed shots—I had no idea the pores on my nose were so *majestic*.

"I feel like I miss too many shots when I'm chatting, you know?" she says. "But you are one delectable treat for the peepers."

"Peepers?"

"Beacons, peepers," she says, smiling. "Windows to your deepest fears, my love."

"I see," I say, though I don't, *really*, as she kisses my cheek and I laugh nervously.

"Can't wait to gobble every bit of you up," she says.

The two of us walk over and sit at a table at Jill Mac's. Their porch overlooks the harbor. Red, white, and blue bunting is draped around the rails, and orange plastic candelabras are Krazy-Glued to the tables. There's a green tin roof that makes the coolest sound when rain is pelting down on it, but I can't imagine that roof will make it through the whole summer. The rest of the place consists of paper plates, plastic cutlery, and one diminutive lady as cook, cashier, waiter, and entertainment.

The owner is Jillian, and she whistles tunes only from *Fiddler on the Roof*, when she isn't chatting up customers. I order two lobster rolls, and Gracie pulls a silver flask out of her large bag, one of two she carries everywhere, and adds some whiskey to our sodas. The damp wooden planks beneath me feel warped, not very sturdy, but at that point I don't really care. We drink and watch young kids and their moms and dads fish off the jetties, with trawlers and gleaming yachts creeping out to sea between them.

I study two young women on the bow of a yacht in matching raspberry bikinis, raising their glasses to us, so Gracie does the same. At any other time, I would be mortified, but as the boat passes, we notice the name: *Serendipity*.

"I love that name," Gracie says.

"I don't know what it means," I say.

Gracie tousles my curly black hair.

"It's us, angel," she says. "By fate or chance, something dandy erupting out of nothing, that's what we're all about this summer."

Gracie knows everything. She is so damn experienced, or at least to me she is. I want to feel her kiss me or nibble on my neck. As I drink, I feel sophisticated and fancy, entitled even. There are many white-haired customers, and they ogle us, as if we are mirages, visions.

The lobster rolls arrive. Gracie examines them like a

conflicted ascetic, turning the plate around in a complete, clockwise circle, contemplating the meal before digging in.

"Helps me to remember my place in the cosmos and my dreamy good fortune," she says. Then she reaches across the table to stroke my forearms, hands, and fingers.

"What are you doing now?" I ask.

"Do you mind if I kiss you?" she says and then comes around the table and kisses me, her hand somehow brushing my erection so lightly I don't know if she meant it or not.

FOREVER TINY AND WILD

I am forever tiny. Undoubtedly, I'll grow fat from all the medications they're pumping me with at this mental health facility in the Green Mountains of Vermont. From my first seconds on earth to today, my vertically challenged self has always been gazing up at the world. Bright lights, pink fingers, doctors, nurses, Mom, Dad, Gramps, Randy, sunshine, stars, moon, a fancy tree fort at the Cape, Gracie, Liam, and so many jittery colors—memories and images float overhead. *Close to the ground I've always been,* as Yoda might say.

To take in the full breadth of the tale, it's important to know that I was born a preemie on Independence Day in 1962, the runt of triplets—my sisters, Molly and Eve, did not survive. After seven months together in the womb, I entered the world solo and spent significant time in the intensive care unit before going home. The ob-gyn who delivered me said my survival was a minor miracle, proof of a larger, beneficent force working in the universe.

My dad, Buck Halligan, referred to me as *the chosen one* after first hearing that, but a priest friend told him to *knock it off* after fifteen months. When the MD announced that I, alone, had survived, Dad phoned mom's dad, Gramps O'Riley in Dennis, Massachusetts, and told him he wanted to expand the original tree house for me. Gramps had built the tree fort two decades earlier for his fraternal twins, Randy and Miriam, the once inseparable brother and sister duo.

"I don't care about cost," Dad said, according to Gramps and Mom. "Turn that fort into a tree palace the likes of which the Cape and Islands have never seen." With Gramps's blessing and Buck's infusion of cash, construction started right away.

I spent my first birthday in Dennis surrounded by love as I was whisked down in my father's topaz Lincoln Continental and was the hit of the party at the first annual Wild Sands Road Day at Gramps's home. I remember frothy colors—blue skies, saffron balloons, bulbous white cumulous clouds, golden sun, chunks of so-very-vermilion watermelon, sweet lemon Italian ice, fresh red and green Bell peppers, and wide Irish noses with a fair amount of rosacea.

I recall Mom's carefree laugh, sweet and unassuming. Plus, there was Randy appearing so joyful, posing for pictures with Mom, clutching me in one arm atop the tree palace and christening a bottle of mid-priced champagne over its roof with the other. I adored those shots of Mom and Randy. My matriarch insisted from day one that I possessed a photographic memory —that every event in my life lurked somewhere deep inside me, waiting to be called up. She referred to me as *blessed sponge* until I was three and a half, old enough to realize how weird it sounded—true as it might be. So, on one side was Mom calling me a holy cleaning implement, and Dad on the other referring to me as the *chosen one.*

Mom died when I was four—she lost another baby before leaping off the roof of a large city hospital at dawn, crushing a local milk truck. She was captured on film by a passing Yale Divinity student who had stepped outside the hospital for a quick smoke. I didn't see that picture until I was nine, digging around in Gramps's attic at the Cape.

I became increasingly focused on mom's suicide photo. Once I had my breakdown in July of '79, when everything Gracie, Liam, and myself imploded, I brought the original pictures to Spruce Lodge Psychiatric Clinic, just outside Montpelier. I found myself guided by memories erupting from my own photos, my family's, and even by perfect strangers, like the Yale Divinity student, Rev. Walsh. There's a true fluidity about all those images in my life—it sometimes seems refreshing, other times so caustic it chokes me. Everything in my young life dealt with the power of pictures and their effect on memory.

I kept Mom's shot in my wallet, treating it akin to scripture. It may sound macabre, but Mom was radiant, and she had never looked so alive while she drew a breath. That shot helped me get through many anguished and harried days. Growing up with much love and attention, I pined to be singular, hoping my mark on the world would be substantial and lasting. So, it's cruelly bizarre to me that I'll probably be recalled for my adolescent physique—perfect tan and exquisite abs featured in one of the top-selling coffee-table photography books of the year known as *Transfiguration Photos*.

The details surrounding Gracie's classic pictures were, of course, not without sorrow, regret, and some abuse. Let's ponder the joy, though, since there was so little of it at the end. The last shot on the final page of *TP* is disarming. It was taken earlier in the summer, and so it ends up being a great solo print of Wolf-Boy. I was the only one left in the palace that day. Not even sure how that picture came to be—perhaps the corded remote Gracie used was jammed under some debris triggering the shutter even as the Nikon dangled precariously from the broken tripod.

Gracie stands only five feet, but she shoots massive works, aggressive and invasive images that pounce on you, demanding you swallow her subject whole. You can either turn the page or set her book down, but her prints have such an addictive quality, you keep coming back. You'll blush, grow aroused, and feel your spine tingle and burn, but it's near impossible to walk away.

Gracie's work, and the shots of my mom, not just the final, tragic one, stir memory and pack a significant wallop through this book of remembrance. On the last page of *Transfiguration Photos,* I hold a sculpture of an intertwined couple in my hand. Carved in cherry wood by Gracie's late mom, the eight-inch duo twirls and spins, and I appear to accelerate out the door, as if the piece of art was going home with me.

I glance back into the tree palace—home of wild, ecstatic grappling and all-out flesh wars. My defiant wolf mask appears to roar, *I'm the most ruined and obliterated soul around here, but I'm also young and resilient, so ignore me at your peril, insipid fools.*

FLAMBOYANCE

R andy's Shoot! studio takes up several storefronts just off
Commercial Street, and it's my job to keep it spotless.
The building is a refurbished gas station, and my father has
spent a substantial amount of money with Randy in fixing it up.
To be clear, my dad supplies only the funds—there's an under-
standing in our house that my father never crosses into
Provincetown. *Ever.*

Provincetown has one of the highest populations of
LGBTQ people in the country. And there are multitudes of
artists of every type; painters, poets, writers, dancers,
composers, sculptors, choreographers, editors, conductors, the
list goes on and on. The town bursts with creative energy, and
people come from around the world to visit and sample the
seafood and nightlife, wonderful galleries, whale watching or
some deep-sea fishing trips. Buck is comfortable with everything about Provincetown except the "B" in LGBTQ and it
drives him to extremes.

"Tough town," Dad says. "There's an abundance of flam-
boyance around here."

That's the funny-bizarre thing about Buck—he has no problem with lesbians, bisexual women, or homosexual men, but bisexual males really get his goat. He refers to them as waffle-boys, the lowest of the low on his totem pole—way down there beside defrocked Richard Nixon and other sub-par politicians. Buck loathes that *bisexual males* refuse to be one way or the other. He does distinguish the difference—a *huge one,* according to my dad—between a man one who is strictly homosexual and one who is a waffle-boy, incapable of making the choice, and standing up to be counted like everyone else when it matters. "Nothing gets into my craw more than that *indecision,*" Dad says. "Lack of decisiveness eats at me—irritates my gut like fingernails on a chalkboard."

Randy told me my mom knew Randy was gay since he was seven and that they were both very close throughout their lives. I have a huge collection of Randy and Mom's photos from school graduations and holidays and birthdays, once celebrating their sixteenth birthday atop the Empire State Building, a trip they won in a raffle at a church carnival the previous summer. My favorite is a first birthday party photograph with the three of us—Mom, Randy, and me—grinning like mad inside the palace.

Although Buck never specifically articulates it, the concept of Shoot! —having his brother-in-law Randy run his own business—was his attempt to have Randy embrace a proper vocation. Randy has tried to explain to Buck, as well, that employment discrimination was a massive problem in Provincetown and all over the Cape for decades, all over the United States, too, and in many ways my dad, to some eyes, is nothing short of a bigot. But Buck strenuously disagrees with that assessment, swears he loves Randy for being "fully gay," and supports him financially whenever the business falters.

My father is absolutely an odd duck; there's no doubt about that.

Buck Halligan, however, remains enormously uncomfortable with Randy's *hobby* of performing and crooning in ladies' clothes in the wee hours at gay bars and drag theaters, so he fronted the money for his brother-in-law, co-signed the loan in 1978, and helped Randy start the studio in the summer of 1979 in the hopes of steering Randy right if not straight.

Randy and the builders scrapped the two big garage doors from the former gas station, replacing them with large windows stretching nearly floor to ceiling, which was ridiculously expensive, but Buck was behind it all the way. My uncle has me do basic tasks: scrubbing toilets and waxing the hardwood floors, cleaning the windows and doors at the front, taking trash out, and keeping the dark room clean, locked, and stocked. I also run errands—picking up coffee, helping place ads in the local paper, handing out fliers during the busy season.

For day-to-day stuff, Randy has Gracie handling funds, setting up appointments, and dealing with customers. She's charming, so charismatic that people come in just to be near her. Little kids approach her daily to rub her tanned head.

"No fear," she tells them. "I may look different, but I'm the same as you."

"Are you sick?" one four-year-old girl asks.

"I got alopecia, which for me, at least, means hair won't grow anywhere on me—but it's a different experience for everyone. You asked me questions, sweetie, so that will cost you."

"How much?" the girl asks, smiling.

"Two big kisses on my head," Gracie says, squatting down so the child can kiss her. "Your smooches help keep me warm and safe through the long chilly nights."

Sometimes when Randy and Liam go out on a shoot, Gracie takes portraits of kids with an extra camera from the studio, making additional cash for herself. To me, it doesn't really seem like Gracie does anything resembling work, except flirting with deliverymen or chatting with tourists or neighboring merchants. It pisses me off a bit, but I take it in stride, for she's special, anyone can see that. Plus, as she points out numerous times: "You're the only man who owns my heart, Danny—and in that deal, you get everything that's attached." I was never sure what the hell that meant, but it sounded impressive, and I got to sleep with Gracie frequently, so I stayed quiet, thanking God that I had landed this wonderfully wild deal of the century.

Liam and Randy drive the company van to different gigs— baptisms, Christenings, anniversaries, weddings, bat and bar mitzvahs, retirement bashes, and other soirees. Randy takes care of the photography, which is odd since my uncle isn't known for his spectacular skills with a lens. He's a competent photographer, just not superb, is what I mean.

Randy is handsome in an interior designer-kind-of-way with a blast of long, red curls and green eyes forever hidden by Ray Bans. I have black curls, but still, both of us are quite short, and people insist we look like twins. I consider him the coolest, smartest adult in the world—ever since my mom checked out of the whole life thing, I've turned to him for my advice.

"It's great that I'm with Gracie, don't you think so, Randy?" I ask. "I'm *really attracted* to her, too. Like some hot magnet. Pretty wild stuff."

Randy tousles my hair and says, "What about Liam, though? You still spend a lot of time together, true?"

"Buck loathes waffle-boys, Rand," I say. "Imagine if that was me? No way in hell. Dad always told me to stick with girls."

"Don't be so afraid of your dad's prejudice that you miss a

chance to explore your own fascinating universe waiting out there, okay?"

"Why say that to me now?" I ask.

"Have you ever heard of a pansexual?"

"Of course," I say. "Um, well, no, not really... What is it again?"

"It refers to the sexual orientation of someone who is romantically, emotionally, or sexually attracted to people of any gender identity, gender, or biological sex."

"Like how?"

"When it comes to attraction," Randy says, "some people don't see gender, male or female. They find all that business irrelevant."

"*Sexually, I'm good with girls,*" I say. "I can't say it enough, apparently."

"Keep your mind open, that's all I'd advise going forward."

"Why stress all this to me now?" I ask Randy.

"I want to help you embrace your universe with gusto," he says. "Try everything on the menu while you still can, for our life clock is forever ticking away."

"Okay, but like I said, I'm good. I won't need to hear any more of this topic, okay?" I say.

"I won't bring it up again."

One family-secret side of Randy's life—at least, until he turned professional and started his *other* career—is that he enjoys dressing in ladies' lingerie and gowns and performing. It's one of my earliest and favorite memories: Me, sitting in a fastened highchair beside my mom, and Dandy Randy O'Riley prancing around in full chiffon, a long blue wig, heels, and a peach gown, singing "Cats in the Cradle" and "Peace Train" and "Black Bird" all while strumming and spinning around as he played his acoustic guitar.

When he's not dressed in women's lingerie or gowns for his

shows, though, Randy goes to the opposite side of the spectrum and dons strictly black, men's clothing. Even in the heat of summer, black khakis, socks, jeans, shorts, polos, or a short-sleeve, black linen shirt, baseball cap, black penny loafers, and a watch—a Rolex, of course, with a black band.

When he's playing tennis, Randy wears all black as well. He's an amateur in tennis but takes it all quite seriously. He's a big drinker, too, adores Ardberg Scotch—he tells folks he has *unusually* expensive tastes.

The black clothing is Johnny Cash homage, I believe, though I don't know precisely when that obsession began. He always loved the legend's music—specifically, the *Folsom Prison Record* in 1968. He's got a framed copy of that album hanging over his bedroom in his place in Provincetown—he's been whistling the tunes from that live album as long as I can remember. One interesting aside is Randy performs a slow, raspy version of Cash's "I Walk the Line" in his shows that brings down the house.

Despite Buck's scowls, Randy was a burgeoning star on the tip of the Cape and some clubs in Boston, Long Island, and Miami. *Dandy Randy* had a killer voice, high and far away. *The Boston Globe* even wrote a "Getting-To-Know Dandy Randy O'Riley" piece, highlighting his transformation from a black-clothed tennis player by day into a flamboyant, brightly colored-lingerie- and dress-wearing jazzy show performer at night.

Randy also let me attend one of his shows as a thirteen-year-old boy. My dad threw a shit-fit when he found out, but it was worth it, to see Randy in his glory, in the lights, twirling, crooning. I took it in from backstage, feeling so grown up. Randy tap-danced and spun, at one point calling up two drunken young men and tying them up in chairs on the stage. Shredded papers were set on fire around them and Randy dashed through flames to save them. He rushed off stage for a few moments and returned in a glittering cape and black firemen's boots.

The show ended with Randy shooting fire extinguisher foam between his legs onto the flames and over the two men. I told my uncle he didn't need raunchy comedy—his voice was wonderful and lovely enough. Randy only smiled, shook his head, and kissed my forehead. The show was later shut down by the fire department when there were reports of smoke in the theater.

Liam Preston drives me to work four days a week in The Lucky 7, his souped-up forest-green Chevy van. A Cape native, Liam's older than me by two years and without a mom. Rumor has it she went out for expensive toilet paper, Devil Dogs, Pinot Noir, and *TV Guide* one February night eight years ago and never returned. Phoned her boy on his next birthday and told him not to take things so damn personally.

He's handsome and tall with blond hair, almost black eyes, and a narrow, angular face. He rattles on about either weightlifting or porn—the latter being his most cherished contribution to the neighborhood. Piles of dirty magazines and tapes spill out of his first-floor double closet downstairs.

Not just *Hustler* and *Screw*, but hardcore stuff too. S&M, a massive collection of genitals and depravity, straight, gay, transgender, leather, latex, interracial, little people, and every kind of kink you can imagine. One grainy tape Liam never stops lecturing on are two naked, emaciated women in bright orange boots attempting to have relations with a miniature pony in a pea-green shower stall.

Liam says he wants to find the women in the orange boots,

hold them close, give them a soapy, hyacinth-scented bubble bath, a safe place to stay, new clothes, comfortable shoes, and good office jobs. Liam is peculiar like that, a horn-dog teen most of the time, but a vigilant big brother the rest.

From one extreme to the next, Liam keeps me guessing about his motives, and so remains forever intriguing. Like a large iridescent viper, he both repels and fascinates me, which annoys me too. If I had to make a declaration, I'd say Liam messes with my sexual identity—he discombobulates me. I would've preferred Liam not join Gracie and me in her sexy summer photo extravaganzas, but Liam kept harassing me, so I gave in, although in truth, I eventually welcomed his presence.

If it weren't for his Aunt Regina supplying groceries once a week, he and his father would have undoubtedly starved. The Preston's home has a constant, buzzy energy from the daily throngs of adolescent kids flipping through the magazines and watching dirty movies downstairs on one of Liam's many TV's.

Their home, a Cape on an acre, also features the under-lying sticky scent of sweat, mold, come, cat piss, Clorox bleach, and feces emanating down from Mr. Preston's upstairs lair. Kids swear Liam's pop is headed downhill fast, no longer both-ering with bathrooms. Says Liam must clean up after him daily, which explains the bleach.

Once I get a wave from Mr. Preston in his second-story bedroom window as I approach Liam's house. Liam assures me that the gesture is a sign of respect, and that I should feel incredibly lucky I don't have to live with the *biggest frigging headcase on the East Coast as my pop!*

PSYCHOTIC ELEPHANTS
ROARING

I 'm Danny Peter Halligan and my seventeenth year has not been a banner one—a harsh experience, to be true. I spent the last 364 days on the adolescent wing at Spruce Lodge in Vermont, a private mental hospital. It's now Wednesday, July 2, 1980, at 10:39 a.m., and I was moved to the young adult ward early this morning—the new unit is called PEAR, which a young lady with a giraffe tattoo on her throat told me stands for *Psychotic Elephants Are Roaring.*

Let me say that while I won't turn eighteen for two whole days, the administration sent me over early, for overcrowding issues, I was told. A year earlier in the Cape tree fort, the psychotic break was rising within me, waiting to erupt like some anguished orgasm, or perhaps Old Faithful.

My doctor and psychic guide so far are one Dr. Les Gingerman, or Dr. G. He says taking better care of myself should be my highest priority—namely, stopping the assault on my skull with fists, objects, or walls. That may sound simplistic, but I have berating, churning voices inside me, putting me down, insulting my intelligence, along with drug-induced flashbacks, and without warning I clobber myself, anything to silence the blaring boom box playing between my ears. It's usually punching or banging, but whatever it is, as Dr. G puts it, *must stop*.

Thankfully, Dr. G is a pragmatic, even-keeled force, and he calms me. A rugged, six-foot-three and white-bearded man who turns sixty-five in October, he wears purple spectacles and has a smoker's cough. He has multiple Matisse prints and ten orange lava lamps spread throughout his office. Dr. G was something of a hippie back in the day, and so his daughters and granddaughters never let him forget it.

Suzy, Dr. G tells me, is nine and adores hammerhead sharks and Greta is a budding zoologist at seven and loves water buffalos, so he has a few buffalo magnets on his cabinets and hammerheads on his bulletin board. He's gone right now, off for the holiday weekend visiting his daughters in Burlington, Vermont, I believe. So, I'm on the adult unit, just trying to be relaxed and placid.

"Package for Danny Halligan waiting in the conference room," a female staff member says, offering a quick knock-knock as she enters my single room. "I'm Josie and we'll need to open your gift in the other room, so follow me please."

"Certainly, thanks, Josie," I say and head out the door. Josie is an African American staff member, maybe thirty-four, with close-cropped bright red hair, and she moves like a gymnast. I try not to stare at her perfectly taut, muscular behind, but I can't help it.

When we arrive at the conference room, I know immediately who sent my gift. It's not the scent of wood smoke, nor freshly cut grass—no, no, what's flying off this package is Coppertone Coconut Tanning Lotion, Cape Cod, and the magic and horror I experienced there over a year ago. The scent contains the most elusive and prized words in my lexicon—

summer and boyhood—endless horizons, so much possibility, and a wildly *twistable* sense of time.

A month that stretched, shrunk, and meandered along through the cool nights and early afternoon thunderstorms, with memories so soaked in my psyche that nothing could save them from the cloying, tenacious hand of nostalgia. And, inevitably, my nemesis and heart-crusher herself, Gracie Rose.

"You okay, Danny?" Josie asks, and I nod, not wanting to give anything away. I open the slightly dented Macy's department store box and find yellow tissue paper beneath it.

Underneath that, I see a cobalt-blue business card with a quote by Oscar Wilde in black type.

Man is least himself when he talks in his own person— give him a mask and he will tell you the truth.

Kiss my ass, Gracie, I think, and I feel myself begin to perspire.

"Everything fine, Danny?" Josie asks.

"Sure," I say.

"Do you know whom this is from?" she asks.

"No," I lie, hands trembling. There's more tissue paper and a postcard of a lovely Provincetown sunset shot off the Pilgrim Monument looking out toward the harbor. Gracie was always going on about the unique light at the tip of the Cape, unlike anywhere else on earth, she'd boast, like she created the sun herself.

"You familiar with the Oscar Wilde quote?"

I shake my head. "Vaguely—I was supposed to read his play for school once, I think, but never did."

"Which one?" Josie asks.

"*The Importance of Being Earnest,*" I say.

"Ah, a classic farce," Josie says. "Why not plan to read it while you're here? Just set your mind to it, and get it done. Start with maybe five pages a day, you know."

"My concentration currently sucks, though," I say.

"Well, I realize you're not eighteen for a few days, so I'm probably—"

"I'm good," I say, holding up my hand. "Happy to get mail is all, Josie, and I appreciate your help this morning."

I'm breaking a rule that Dr. G set down months ago. *If Gracie contacts you in any manner, go to the staff immediately.* Until now, though, it seemed Gracie was never going to bother me. No letters, no phone calls. Nothing for a long year. I had discussed Gracie frequently with Dr. G early on—how I fell under her mesmeric spell and her charismatic, freewheeling style.

Periodically, Gracie told Liam and me *to act naturally as we shake and dance* or when to start doing back flips off the Truro dunes, all set to pulsing music blasting out of my stereo in the tree palace, or with her own portable boom box anywhere on the Cape. The varied songs were all over the place, sometimes a jazzy Nina Simone, other times George Clinton's Parliament Funkadelic or even Tina Turner.

Gracie was my agent provocateur, my queen bee, and she claimed her "harmless, magical, top-secret potions" would *holistically expand* my mind and Liam's too. She explained it would make psychic room for heavenly Grace to enter the milieu and perhaps even some *Divine Visitation.* Granted, Jesus Christ and his rowdy band of angels never did show up like Gracie swore they would, but she still put on a ferocious and singular show. Fittingly, Gracie dubbed all her photography shoots, *Extravaganzas with a Capital E.*

I figured that crazy, unhinged Gracie Rose business was ancient history, something not to concern myself with anymore.

I was wrong.

"You're still badly torn up about Gracie, Danny," Dr. G has said more than once, "and what she did to you over that awful summer. Even your voice goes up an octave when you recount your tales of debauchery with her, for she was exciting, wildly sexual, and unlike any woman you'd ever met. But—*and this is essential—she nearly killed you.* Don't forget that, or your pal, Liam—he wasn't exactly oozing kindness, either."

Underneath Gracie's Oscar Wilde quote are two magazines, *Film* and *Newsflash*, from a few days ago. They feature a black-and-white cover shot taken from the book and headlines about critics saying *Transfiguration Photos* will leave a permanent indentation on our culture and a substantial bruise on America's psyche.

It features two male teens leaning into one another, both half-aroused, with their teeth bared, like they were about to rip into one another's flesh. There's one in a Wolf-Boy mask (compact, muscular, sixteen-year-old me, Danny Halligan), the other in a Lone Ranger mask (a ripped, six-foot, eighteen-year-old Liam Preston). Seated between them is the irrepressible Gracie Rose, their charismatic leader, photographer, and dream weaver extraordinaire, and she's a nude, curvy twenty-one-year-old-sophomore-dropout from Yale, and wherever she goes, so goes this modern-day trinity.

I had to adjust myself as I absorbed the shots because I was afraid Josie would notice my hard-on. In the cover shot, a bare-assed Gracie gazes at the camera in her skewed, off-kilter way with her warped, sentient sunglasses, sitting cross-legged with her sinewy arms outstretched, as if she were delivering an incantation of great import.

The photo seizes readers; you can nearly hear folks asking,

are those naked guys going to punch each other? Or maybe fuck? And what's with that smooth-headed lady down in front? Does she use mind control on the two naked men behind her? So, she gets in on the action, too?

"Pretty racy material, huh?" Josie says. "I heard about this book—it's being released in Europe and America today. One critic I admire said ogling the photos was like striking a match on dry tinder, nothing but raw, potent sex set free, or like a mile-wide twister touching down in your neighborhood."

"Pretty wicked shots," I say.

"Did you ask for someone to send it to you?" Josie asks.

"I guess" is all I manage as I study myself in the photos. I'm sixteen in the pictures and my whole life is waiting for me on a perfectly sculpted sandbar, one huge opportunity soon to be ruined by a curvy, driven young lady who cast me as naive and corruptible Wolf-Boy, which ended up sucking out my very soul. Her manipulations were cruel, toxic, and brutal as hell. I know all that stuff, but examining our fired-up trio in that precise moment—*Jesus Christ Almighty*—didn't we each look so frigging raw and brilliantly alive?

"Can I read the magazines now?" I ask Josie.

"Peruse both of them in the privacy of your room," she says. "When you finish, return them to me at the front desk—too provocative for the unit as a whole, agreed?"

"Agreed," I say, and Josie finally disappears so I rapidly get myself off twice, reliving potent memories before I can slow myself down enough to absorb the tale.

The *Film* article begins: Transfiguration Photos by the photographer Gracie Rose was released today by an East London publishing house, and copies of her book of photos sold out in three hours. Gracie appeared on a new British chat show, holding court, confident as a well-seasoned pro.

"For myself right now," Frankie Wilbur, the show's host said, "I feel like I'm dangling on the far edge between fascination and all-out fanaticism. Now I'm a professional broadcaster and everything, so I try hard not to be too impressed, but this Gracie Rose woman blew me right out of the water with her photographs."

"I'm not interested in taking photos of any freaks, myself," Gracie said. "I like to stick with rage, sex, and a fair amount of allure. Plus, my big lips and lovely curves tend to scare the hell out of most Americans back home. Some of them can't handle a modern, independent woman like me who's up front with her needs —intellectually, spiritually, and sexually."

"Anyone else you want to insult on national TV?" Frankie asked.

"These photos will change you on numerous levels, so buy it now," she said. "You won't regret the move."

"What did your mom possess that was so helpful to you growing up?"

"A rock-solid faith, kindness, and a dry wit," Gracie said.

"Sounds sweet to me," Frankie Wilbur said. "How do you top something like that?"

"Mom would quote someone impressive and knock you flat on your ass."

"Like whom?"

"'We're not human beings having a spiritual experience, we are spiritual beings having a human experience.'"

"Who said that one, Gracie?"

"Pierre Teilhard de Chardin, who lived from 1881 to 1955, a famous Jesuit priest and philosopher."

"My brain is percolating with all these incredible quotes, wild facades, and nude bodies. Good luck, Gracie, but before we break away, let's go into the studio audience and get more response from everyday Londoners... first to the young woman in the back row there... Tell us your name, and if you'd purchase this book of photos."

"I'm Maddy, a student, just twenty and I love Gracie Rose and her feistiness, and the rawness of the pictures truly levels me."

"So, you plan to purchase it?"

"Straight away, three copies, two for me, one for my boyfriend so he'll learn to be a bit more adventurous in the sack. Now I know my mum will hate it. She'll lecture and say, 'It's way too lurid, lurid, lurid... and she'll ask me whatever happened to old-fashioned romance and love?'"

"Thanks, Maddy, and how about that everyman down in front wearing the denim jacket and brown cords, what was your take on the book, sir?"

"I'm Mike and I'm a tube operator," he said. "A real pragmatic soul and I only like my Beatles, that's my constant comfort food. My job is to keep everything running smoothly at work and in my family. I say *Transfiguration Photos* is nothing but cat turds, and it manipulates our children into spending all their cash. But mark my words now... my sweet and lovely bride will gobble it all up and be singing the praises of one American superstar Gracie Rose for the next decade or so, buying everything she produces."

"That's all we have time for, but I'm a massive fan forever." Frankie Wilbur smiled and offered a thumbs-up.

Random House and its cousin across the pond released *TP* in Europe and America simultaneously and critics raved. To purchase the black-and-white book of photos in bookstores and magazine shops across this country, one needs an ID, proving eighteen years of age, plus there is a plastic casing with a purple strip that keeps those not of age from perusing nudity.

The public and politicians debated the book furiously, free speech advocates supported it, and *New York* magazine's cover story on Independence Day asked: **Is *Transfiguration Photos* Art? Or Porn? And Is Gracie Rose Some Kind of Radical Genius? Or Just a Deviant Pervert?**

The Archbishop of New York even penned a letter to "Good

Moms and Dads of America" in *The Daily News* and *New York Post*, warning practicing families not to buy *Transfiguration Photos,* which only made it more popular, of course, fanning the flames, and the book will soon appear on the *New York Times Bestsellers* list, a rarity for a coffee-table book.

Later, Gracie's testimony at congressional hearings on obscenity charges against her book featured the talented lady butting heads with then Republican Senator and conservative fire-brand from North Carolina, Jesse Helms, who called the book of photos, "Nothing short of gussied-up trash."

"Wake up, sir," Gracie said. "They weren't created for you."

"Oh, is that right, Ms. Rose?" Senator Helms said. "I had no idea, thanks for clearing that mystery up for me."

"I like to help my country in any way I can, Senator," Gracie said.

Following that testy exchange, death threats followed the charismatic photographer wherever she went. So many were called in to Gracie's apartment in Greenwich Village that the NYPD complained about the burden of protecting Gracie Rose right along with the other eight million plus lonely souls in the Big Apple. Gracie left New York forever and returned to Provincetown where she bought a sizable barn on five acres west of town and renovated it, adding a darkroom and an indoor, saltwater pool.

All this Gracie and *Transfiguration Photos* advertisement in England and America and across this dangerous world is wearing me down. Gracie isn't some lofty, far away concept. She's a huge threat to me currently, right now, and the threat is immediate and dangerous, and I'm afraid what I might do to myself!

She's back to the tip of the Cape, I think, my palms sweaty, right foot tapping like crazy after I return the two magazines to Josie and go back to see the postcard again. I feel anxious and depressed most of the time around here and wonder if my attempts at recovery are futile—like when I lay on my bed and must concentrate so damn hard on *not* striking myself. It seems like it's *infantile behavior,* really.

I wake up some mornings and I only want to fly away to freedom, but then other days, I have these brutal anxiety attacks and am terrified of the world. I get furious at myself for being so passive, so milquetoast, understand? I can't even walk into the hallway of the PEAR unit without worry chewing me up, shredding me. All the intense fluctuations of mood—up, down, enraged, disgusted, hyper-aroused, self-harming thoughts—the whole roller coaster ride only feeds my self-loathing.

Don't be ganging up on Danny Hal too much now, I can hear Dr. G saying to me. *It's almost your birthday, celebrate a bit. Eighteen is a big deal.*

My nightmares scare the piss out of me too. I see 1000-pound puppies flying around the world, bringing love and tenderness to the populace, landing in wide-open fields, where people come running to cuddle and pet them. My night terrors overtake the scene, and soon giant canines freak out and devour whole villages. Massive Yorkshire Terriers and Cocker Spaniels turn rabid, slaughtering women, children, and everyone—a terrifying and bloody scene. Nothing out of the ordinary, though, for my scrambled brain.

I try some breathing exercises and check out the brochure on my desk filled with photos of the 125-acre New England-prep-school-like campus known as Spruce Lodge with redbrick buildings, a pool, six tennis courts, indoor bowling alley and a gym, hiking trails, and sculpted, fragrant gardens and towering trees with impressive foliage.

I learned PEAR stands for Psychiatric Education and Rehabilitation. Inside the pamphlet, I see photos of handsome, concerned doctors and staff in earth-toned cardigan sweaters, bright muumuus, and Birkenstocks without white coats, ties, or nursing hats. The model patients look pleasantly diverse, comely, slim, and chipper, ready to burst into show tunes. *This place is like an ad for a college, country club, or a gated community.*

And me, I'm not a model patient. I'm a groggy teenager trying to shake off flashbacks, psychosis, and sticky mental health tendrils from last year's wild summer. So, I'm called Wolf-Boy, and at moments I wish to bark and howl like mad at these doctors and nurses, for they have no idea of the psychic hell I've been through. I want to growl and rip into some bare flesh!

Intensive psychotherapy at Spruce Lodge, *Dr. G assures me*, will lead to an anguish-reduced life, and I only need to make proactive, lucid choices to chase delusions, rage, and shadows from my skull. Take my targeted meds daily, share in group therapy, stop punching myself, hike the trails on campus, and place the swirling, psychic garbage on the sidewalk, and voila—*Presto*—I'll be back in the normal world in a jiffy.

Ha!

The most pragmatic and wise words I've ever heard in my months of battling demons and sorting through my psyche isn't anything from Freud, Jung, Dr. G, Dr. Seuss, Maurice Sendak, Judy Blume, Shel Silverstein, Salinger, Cormier, Maya, or even Mathew, Mark, Luke, or John. Didn't come from Beethoven, Bach, Lennon-McCartney, Miles, Dylan, Aretha, Bruce, Stevie, Freddie, Carly, or Paul Simon either.

Instead, it's what Buck Halligan stresses. My dad, who runs a discounted hardware chain of sixteen super-stores stretching throughout New England, has a credo, of sorts. The gist is to stay active and go hard every day, just keep moving no matter what. Basic bread and butter stuff, I know, nothing overly profound. But I still gather strength from it. I keep the quote taped on the bottom left corner of my bedroom mirror on the PEAR unit. It was taken from a long missive my dad brought me during his last visit here. Sappy? Perhaps, but it has helped me in a general sort of way.

"If you sit and overanalyze existence, Boss, you'll probably end up finding the closest ledge and committing the irreversible, so be wise and humble and never quit. Just pray and love, and help others around you as you climb, but for Christ's sake, Danny, always go forward."

Dr. G told me it was bizarre that my dad, who's usually evasive with emotional, self-revelatory info, would write about *finding the closest ledge*, a reference to my mother's suicide. But I really like that line. Dad appears to be evolving rapidly and I enjoy being with him. He's becoming a lot more emotive and accessible. Mom would be proud of Buck, and all of us, I think.

I crunch up Gracie's Oscar Wilde quote in my palm, which is, I realize, a veiled threat, and ponder putting it through the shredder at the nurse's station. Instead, I shoot it at the Nerf hoop set up above my new desk, but it misses, falling short of the rim.

"Are you ever going to let me go, Gracie?" I ask my empty room before looking at a Polaroid of Mom, Dad, and Randy, and a two-foot-long wooden plaque Mom had bought for me in Wellfleet to celebrate my first birthday:

"Don't Just Survive in the World, Danny Hal, But Thrive."

"Miss you so bad, Ma," I say, knowing she would be in her thirty-fourth year if she had stuck around. "Why'd you have to go and jump like that?"

CRUEL COUSINS

It was the summer before Gracie, the year before Randy's photography studio opened its doors in Provincetown, when I took a quick bike ride to Liam Preston's house to say my goodbyes for the winter. Their home was only three football fields away from Gramps's Cape, but I still liked riding my bike there, taking it for a spin. It felt freeing, invigorating. I could have easily walked there, but I wanted to go fast one last time down our dirt lane known as 64 Wild Sands Road, for soon my dad and I would drive home to Connecticut for the school year.

I spotted Liam and his taller cousin Tommy crouched at the end of the street, studying a mound of dirt near his gravel driveway. Tommy was two years older than Liam, had coarse hair with a buzz cut, stubborn acne, and gray-blue eyes that never blinked. I had met him twice and didn't like him—he always seemed to be punching something or someone. Aggressive would be an understatement—plus, he had rancid breath.

As I got closer, I saw they were setting fire to a hill of ants, frying them with lighter fluid and matches, singing The Doors' "Come On, Baby, Light My Fire." I studied them for five minutes, left my bike leaning against the side of Liam's house, and foolishly followed them inside to bullshit together in the kitchen. We drank lemonade and ate oatmeal cookies, listening to Liam's favorite band, Led Zeppelin, while Tommy leafed through Liam's ever-present porn magazines on the Prestons' ugly olive, slip-covered couch.

In a corner of the room, four televisions, each balanced on a VCR underneath, displayed a quartet of porn tapes, with a variety of humans going at it with all they had. One was in English, another in Spanish, and the last two were Dutch, I believe. They all looked old and dated. Two were in black and white. The progression of the scenes was stilted, not smooth, like they were antiques, barely holding together. The whole thing was so cheap and sleazy, and the volume was turned down, but, still, their violence leapt off the screen, and I realized I didn't want to be hanging out with these creeps for one second longer.

I wanted to go for a long run or maybe dive deep in Cape Cod Bay, before I said so long to my favorite spot in the world, Bay View Beach in Dennis. I wanted to feel the pressure against my lungs as I swam as deep as I could, but as I placed my empty lemonade glass into the sink, the two cousins wrestled me to the ground, tugging my T-shirt and shorts and underwear off so quick I knew they'd planned it.

"Get off of me, you are lousy, slimy *shits*," I said, trying to kick my legs free.

"Don't touch Danny's sacred phallus, Tommy," Liam said in a stage whisper as they carried me deeper into the house. "No contact allowed, for that would be a raunchy mortal sin on his part. Only grinding when Danny Hal feels horny."

"That true, Danny?" Tommy asked. "You like the forbidden stuff?"

"Go to hell," I said.

Tommy cackled, and the two cousins moved me into the bedroom—Liam grabbing my hands, and Tommy towing my feet. There was a malodorous mix of mothballs, lighter fluid, sweat, sour milk, mildew, and cat piss in Liam's room. There were dirty socks and soiled clothes strewn all about, rotting fruit, and used tissues spilling out of a halfway-turned over beige trash basket.

On the wall was the famous Farrah Fawcett poster in her All-American red swimsuit, gazing down at me helplessly. I could almost hear her say, "Why would you ever hang out with these lame idiots, Danny?"

"You don't like my breath much, huh, Danny?" Tommy said. "It offends you?"

"*Liam,*" I said, now not only incensed but ashamed.

"Tommy's family," Liam said. "Not nice to say mean things about someone's extended family."

"Wasn't *meant* in a mean—"

"*Bite me,*" Tommy said, near growling. "Things will begin to hurt now."

Tommy wound a red rubber extension cord around my body, and it chafed against my thighs, groin, belly, and neck, and I freaked out, trying to wiggle free. *Where the hell does this crap end?* I thought.

Liam's cousin fastened the cord tighter, like a cowboy roping a calf in front of a rowdy crowd at the Big E State Fair. Tommy dropped me on my back on the dust-layered wooden floor next to Liam's bed, and I lost my breath when I landed and felt terror, a fright that comes with knowing a stronger, bigger adult male intends to damage me, as I had when something heinous occurred years earlier to me as a young boy. At the corner of Tommy's lips were white clumps of spittle, as if he were set to froth.

"*Liam,* help, *do something now.*"

I recall the next seconds in minute detail as they trudged past painfully slowly. I see Liam's childlike affect, stunned by his older cousin's rage. His black eyes seemed to recede inside the sockets, as if he was shutting down any of the responsibility factor, getting ready to slip out of town fast.

At that point, Tommy whipped out a page of porn and tried stuffing it into my mouth. I felt his fingers bunch around the magazine stock, driving against my teeth, lips, and jaw, with the salty, disgusting taste of his dirty nails and knuckles.

"*Help me, man,*" was all I could manage.

Liam spoke up then: "Knock it off, Tommy," and, "Back away, cousin, leave him be, okay?"

"All this can be yours if the price is right, Liam," Tommy said. "Do you want to make a bid on this pathetic, God forsaken shrimp?"

"Stop, cousin," Liam said.

"What is it with you?" Tommy asked. "*In a rush to get your turn?*"

"You're both pigs, nasty sows," I said to the cousins as my tears fell.

A horrific noise burst forth from above, and it took me eight long seconds to realize it was Liam's father screeching from upstairs like a dying wolf and banging on the floor with a heavy bat. I felt pure terror, hair rising on the back of my neck.

"What is it, Pop?" Liam called out after the noise stopped, his own voice quivering.

"LEAVE THE HALLIGAN BOY ALONE," Mr. Preston yelled. "STOP IT NOW!"

"You're lucky shit," Tommy whispered, before punching my sternum, stealing my breath. A car horn sounded outside as Liam's Aunt Regina arrived back from Purity Supreme Market, and her Chevy station wagon came into the gravel drive.

Tommy headed out to help his mom, and Liam soon ran out too.

"You're okay, we're okay, Danny, that's all over, we're done with every last bit of it," I said, tears falling, and, eventually, I got untangled and escaped the cord and dressed. I trembled getting back into my underwear and shorts and flip-flops, but I couldn't find my damn T-shirt. I stopped at the front door, noticing the mildewed living room was empty save for the buzzing of the cheesy, low-volume sex films, and twenty-five or so porn magazines spilling off the olive sofa onto the cheap linoleum. An orange tabby called Sherlock was bunting against my left calf as I banged awkwardly on the bottom stairs.

"Thanks, Mr. Preston," I said, looking up the stairwell. "You rescued me, sir, saved my ass big-time, in fact, so I appreciate that."

I heard the man sliding across the floor in his vinyl chair on wheels and cursing above me so when the door finally opened, the smell of human waste and Clorox overwhelmed me, nearly knocking me down. He was in his late forties with a potbelly and wearing a Pawtucket Red Sox cap and T-shirt and tattered blue boxers while puffing on a thin cigar.

"Watch out for my Liam," he said. "No one in this house is a decent soul, especially Tommy. Everyone's evil around here, Danny, you must remember that. Don't befriend him next year. My son is sub-par, understand me?"

"Yes, Mr. Preston," I said.

"What year are you going to be, son?" he asked.

"A sophomore," I said. "Tenth grade."

"Tenth graders are old enough to learn when to stay away from an evil kid," he said. "You understand me?"

"I hear you, sir."

"Pass along my regards to your Gramps and father, too."

"Will do… thanks," I said before he closed the door, and the

Clorox and waste odor slowly dissipated. And so that was how my summer of 1978 ended. An ugly assault, and some thoroughly singed ants. As Buck drove me home later that afternoon, I found myself still trembling.

As we passed through Buzzard's Bay, New Bedford, Fall River, and Providence, Mystic, New London and all the rest of the towns and cities, I set up precautionary ground rules going forward for next summer. If Tommy is ever there at Liam's house, just split. Runaway fast. And don't ever relax much beside Liam—try to always keep your back to the wall. *Be cautious, Danny*, I told myself. *That's not paranoia, just cold, hard truth.* Although if I pondered it, Tommy learned most of his behavior from studying hours of raw, violent porn, just one of Liam's many raunchy shows. *Is that a case of nature? Or nurture? You decide.*

A final parting fact blazed by my head—something Randy always said, like he knew I needed to hear it.

"I'm guessing around 10 percent of the American population isn't straight, Danny," Randy said. "Absorb that, take it in... That's a hell of a lot of bisexuals."

"What's your point, Randy?"

"I want you to know I'd never tell Buck."

PALATIAL PALACE OF THE PALPABLE PINES

Two days after our first date, Gracie shows up unannounced at my Gramps's Cape and whistles at me when I came to the screen door in only jean shorts.

"Hey," I say, looking around. "What are you doing here?"

She leans in and whispers, "I missed you so badly."

I can hear Gramps's partner, Eileen, doing dishes in the back of the kitchen, and then she stops. I step onto the porch and shut the door.

"And," Gracie says, "I wanted to see your tree fort..."

"It's a *palace*," I say, smiling. "Both Dad and Gramps helped out in funding this wild monstrosity."

"Who built it again?" Gracie asks.

"Gramps built it for my mom and Randy when they were kids," I say. "And Gramps and I have worked on it together ever since, funded by my dad."

"Who named it?" Gracie asks. "Palatial Palace of the Palpable Pines is a real tongue twister."

"Randy O'Riley came up with the title at my Christening,"

I say. "Gramps and Randy got drunk playing a marathon game of Scrabble and put the name together."

"Sounds like a good spot to make love," she says, looking around. "And art, so where is it?"

I feel heat on my cheeks and swear I can see Gracie's green eyes twinkle through her funky sunglasses. She steps closer and kisses me on my right cheek, cupping me through my shorts for a second, purring.

We walk out to the backyard, and she takes numerous photos of my palace. Truth is, the deluxe tree house is enormous—resting in the crotch of a huge oak tree, it's supported with the assistance of five flaring pines that twist into the sky like arthritic, triple-jointed fingers. With a case of beer in his system, Randy once said to a neighbor after Gramps and I had finished the last touches, "This is my old man's colossal, well-intentioned idea gone awry."

It has a winding, hemlock fir staircase that climbs nine feet into the air, cherry-colored bucket seats, and a black rubber steering wheel, along with an oblong skylight, a substantial stereo, and a mini-TV. There's even a rope bridge from one level to the next and a widow's walk at the top where a small weathered, red Adirondack chair sits.

Inside there's a big navy beanbag sofa and a framed poster of Wonder Woman herself, Lynda Carter, gazing down from the far wall, which has some exposed sheet rock. Floor to ceiling is eight feet high, with slanted shed roof, and the structure stretches forty feet wide in parts. There's gray and purple shag with solid Douglas fir roofing and even some gold-plated moldings and a well-lit, neon-orange plaque above the door that blinks, "Danny's Spot."

Gracie goes home after my Gramps calls me to dinner, but she returns the next day with a beaming smile. We have a brief thumb-wrestling match that I win handily, and since Gramps and his partner, Eileen, go to a late church service in Wellfleet, we know we only have a couple hours to work with. So, we quickly scarf down a shared egg and cheese sandwich and some cold apple juice.

Gracie looks cool and sexy leaning against the beanbag chair—her legs folded just so—military boots replaced with blue Keds on that day. She wears a sundress that barely covers her thighs, her style, I'm learning.

She has variations on the theme—peach, lemon, silver, white, and like on our first date at Jill Mac's, an Easter-egg-blue one. She wears the same one today—Gracie calls herself an eccentric contrarian and a Pagan—she's pound for pound a punk but likes to don brightly colored mini-sundresses and straw hats and gets off on confusing people, from her nose jewelry to the boots she wears occasionally, along with puffing away on her adoptive father's Dunhill pipe.

I never know which way she swings on any subject, and at first, I think this is only marvelous, an alluring sign of how substantial and true she is. Even sexually, she never commits— at one point, informing me she's famously heterosexual, not interested in *swinging*, saying, "All I need is one real man by my side." But then the next morning, cooing: "Sometimes, there's nothing like the suppleness and give of a woman beside you late at night." Before our summer ends, she whispers in my ear, "The idea of androgyny soaks me."

In the palace, Gracie isn't wearing a hat though her bug-eyed sunglasses are ever-present, as is the pinned nostril. Her dresses cover up most of her, and she's so sweet *and* intimidating that being around her feels like enough. At least, in the beginning it feels that way. Once I see what lies underneath her clothes I struggle.

"Tell me something I don't know about you," I say between bites.

"Well, I'm brilliant... *sometimes,* but then I screw up and get pissed at myself."

"Why?"

"I got some interesting facts of the world for you, Danny," she says. "Today is a school day—a ribald lesson plan. A symphonic sexual syllabus."

"Let's hear it," I say.

"The world we live in is increasingly race conscious," she says. "And both Americans and the globe will want to know everything about me, about all of us, I think."

"Yikes," I say. "No thanks."

"No worries," she says, smiling. "I'll get you through all that with flying colors. Even now, Americans gawk at me, and they're puzzled and get all mixed up. See, I'm racially ambiguous... Come on, look at me. I could be Latin, or Middle Eastern, or Indian, East Asian Indian, or anything, right?"

"I suppose," I say.

"I prefer being just another Rose girl getting through my days and nights," she says. "But when folks see my developed photos, my dazzling and pulsing shots of you, Liam, and me going wild, I don't want them to be slowed down, contemplating just what the hell my background is, understand?"

"Go on," I say.

"My birth mom left me on a US Postal truck with a box of Pampers, a mini-Portugal flag, a pacifier, twenty-five dollars, and one red and one white votive candle," she says.

"That's unique," I say.

"I made the local news in Palo Alto before we all moved to Middletown, Connecticut, home of the Wesleyan University Cardinals and where you find the most wonderful cookies, pies, and cakes at a bakery called Mozzicoto's."

"You were destined for the bright lights, huh?" I say.

"My mom was the first person to call the station," she says.

"And after a few hoops, interviews, and adoption forms signed, I blossomed into a sweet family Rose."

"You were tight with your adoptive ma, huh?" I ask.

"Yeah," Gracie says. "But don't sass me about it or you'll get detention."

"What's happens there?" I ask, and she purses her lips, wiping her hands on a napkin at her side.

"My detentions are odd but satisfying, Danny boy," she says.

"Neat," I say.

"You can't say *neat*," Gracie says. "You're not Bobby Brady. Say cool."

"Fine," I say, "that's cool."

"Better," she says, getting down on her hands and knees.

I watch Gracie prowl before me like a shapely young Eartha Kitt as Catwoman. My lover thrills me every second of every day, each step, every flex of her forearm, calf, or knuckle seems to touch me, pinch me, like one giant provocation. *And yet*, I think. *I feel this exact same attraction to Liam.*

"Is there a spot in the world for a twisted human like me?" I ask. "I mean I feel a pull toward Liam like I do with you—is that awful and stupid?"

"Of course not," she says. "Explore your nooks and caverns of your very-green psyche. I'd like to help you on your sex ed trip to find your rightful home."

"What about this thing with Liam?" I ask.

"In baseball they call it being a switch-hitter," Gracie says. "You swing well from both sides of the plate. You offer tremendous options and variety for yourself."

"I feel uncertainty, though," I say. "The topic leaves me reeling. I'm scared shitless."

"It's great to be open to every kind of body out there, Danny," she says. "To share the gifts of our pliant, nubile forms."

"I'm not sure what is right anymore."

"One option could be pan sexuality," she says. "It covers an attraction, regardless of gender, girls, boys, that doesn't factor into it. People can feel an attraction to anyone, including people who do not identify as a specific gender."

"The more I hear, Gracie, maybe I'm mostly straight?" I say.

"Don't banish yourself like a convict behind the words *mostly straight*," she says. "*Explore*. It's what our youthful bodies are created for."

"I'm afraid of what sort of young man I might be behind my curtain number one or two."

"With bisexuality, Danny," she says, "you'll discover life has two rivers, equally legitimate, essential, and fulfilling in God's wonderful eyes."

"So, I'm okay?"

"You told me about your father," she says. "How he uses words like waffle-boys. It's hateful, insidious stuff. Those words crucify young people, whether we're talking 1979 or 2029."

"So, you think I'm bisexual down deep, Gracie?" I ask.

"I know that word terrifies you, Danny," she says. "But with me and with Liam, we'll experiment, we'll show you how great and fun bisexuality can be this summer, okay?"

"I'm getting a headache with all these options," I say. "Can we get naked soon?"

"Patience, my dear boy," she says. "Let me simply point out that there exist many different sexual orientations and gender identities."

Gracie quickly rolls her Easter-egg-blue mini-sundress up

to her waist and smiles as I ogle her. "Don't be afraid of anything now, Danny."

I swallow audibly. "Very cool, you're bare—uptown and down."

"Yes," she says, smiling.

"You're so damn beautiful," I say, trembling suddenly.

She claps her hands, bringing her legs together quickly.

"Today is about only you, Danny Hal," she says.

"Why?" I ask. "I love what I saw in front of me three seconds ago."

Gracie moves toward me and coos: "Some lovely, soulful music to set the scene for us, perhaps?"

"Bob Seger, okay?" I say, and she kisses me on the cheek.

"This is your first fantastic and fried, flesh-filled undertaking," she says. "Music's got to be Lou Reed and 'Walk on the Wild Side,' released back in 1972."

Gracie kisses my cheek again, my neck, even my frigging underarm. For each of my sixteen years, I've been embarrassed about the spherical plum birthmark in my armpit. I don't like raising my hand. But this girl goes straight to the mark—she traces it with her index finger and says, "I think that mark is on fire, can't wait to capture it on film."

I tell her Liam calls it "God's Stain," and she smiles, stroking my face.

My hands are shaking uncontrollably.

"No need to fear, okay?" she says. "*You* are so beautiful, my dearest sweet."

I smile and blush.

"You're like my Clio," she says. "One of the nine ancient muses—you inspire me to perform superlative works of art, to create multiple photographic masterpieces."

I still don't have a clue what that means, but my eyes grow wet anyway. This girl speaks like no one I've ever come across—

her words don't just excite, but hold me aloft, keep me grinning for days, and twist me in all sorts of fanciful ways. Gracie's musings stone me more than any substance I ingest that summer.

I keep track of her language, writing a comment or word down in a notebook at home, and try to work it into my daily chatter. Liam sees through my pretensions, teases me about it. But I don't care if I'm near her, watching, interacting, and when we're separated, I picture what she's doing, running, tapping her flip-flops, maybe twirling around naked in her cottage, while her snake, Wart, absorbs the scene.

I'm also aware, faintly, of my brain morphing and transforming Gracie into this otherworldly, goddess-like status. But I don't question it. I recognize in a corner of my immature cerebrum that she's already a myth. She also has a crescent moon necklace on a chain that she places in her mouth and fools with. Just a nervous habit, but so erotic to a sixteen-year-old boy like me. And that silver anklet, a five-pointed star in sterling silver made by an artist friend of Gracie's at Yale.

"I like sacrificing virgins, Danny," she says. "Helping them on their fornication festivities."

"Sweet," I say.

"I dig you," she says, tickling my stomach. "And I want to feel you inside of me, but only if you stand erect, proud, like that wonderful part of you does."

I laugh, my face beet-red: "What?"

"You know exactly what I'm talking about," she says, grinning. "It's up to you, start walking tall and proud, or no sweet candy pour vous."

"I don't get it," I say, and she smiles.

"Be strong, show it off," she says. "Strut some for me and dance, okay?"

I laugh then, filled with a rush of momentum, and strut

around with my excitement tenting my shorts, nearly falling over. I spin around and walk with attitude before coming to a stop in front of her.

"Here, here, now that's what I'm saying," she says, applauding. "Give the ladies something to take hold of."

I feel dizzy, my knees buckling. "Holy shit," I say.

She's still in her Easter-egg-blue mini-sundress when she makes contact.

"Easy boy," she says.

"Oh, Christ," I say, barely containing myself.

"*No*, that's not Christ," Gracie says.

"Damn," I say, breathing quickly, gazing down. "Can you please just once put..."

I close my eyes, take two deep breaths. Then open them.

Gracie smiles.

"*Gracie*," I whisper.

"Will you be my wild superstar this summer?" she asks.

I nearly burst. "Yes, absolutely, most definitely."

"Sweaty, sexy poses for the camera?" she asks. "Will you do everything I ask?"

"Yes."

"You swear?" she says.

"Yep, yes," I say. "Anything, all of it. No question. Unequivocally."

"Danny Peter Halligan," she says. "Welcome to your *prime* time."

Ten seconds later, I erupt and attempt to keep my voice down, which is nearly impossible. My head fills with explosions of light, with butterflies dancing off my eyelids. Plus, my face burns and I feel a perspiration that becomes a glistening on me, not malodorous or damp, just a sheen that protects me from the world for a few minutes. Afterwards, Gracie hums "Sesame Street," and when she kisses me, I feel *reborn*.

YALE-HARVARD GAME

I loved going to Yale-Harvard football games in New Haven with my dad—then and now he walked on the balls of his feet like a kid, bobbing up and down, towering over most of the others around him at six-five, his shock of white hair up straight, like he's got a lot of gel in it. He had a great belly laugh, too, a roar that emerged from deep in his gut. When I was twelve at one freezing game at the Yale Bowl at halftime, I hovered at the urinal troughs in the men's room, finishing up beside my dad. I washed my hands and headed to the food vendors outside. The crowd hooted and hollered along with the Yale band playing away inside the stadium.

The air was bitter, and I bought a hot cocoa from a woman with a crooked smile under a lime-green, Knights of Columbus tent. There were grown-ups hustling past dressed in Harvard crimson and Yale blue, and a bunch of students with their university coats, scarves, hats, all bundled up, looking festive but frozen. I glanced away for a second, felt my nostril hair freeze, and met the eye of my dad, who was marching out of the men's room with a beet-red face. *Uh-oh,* I thought, *Dad's pissed off.*

"Deviant shits," my dad said, seething as he stormed past. "Bisexual assholes."

"What?" I asked, spilling the scalding cocoa on my fingers.

"A drunk waffle-boy," he said. "He snuck up behind me, stood too close... I told him to back off or he'd get a size fourteen shoe up his ass. Then I see him meet his girlfriend outside like everything is so damn wonderful." He nodded in the direction of the food vendors.

"Why does he do that, Dad?" I asked as two bare-chested males with blue Y's painted on their chests barked past, tossing a blue and white Nerf football around us before running back inside the Bowl, howling away in the tunnels leading to the field.

"Waffle-boys are scary, Danny," my dad said. "Like the one that got you five summers ago on the Cape."

I fell silent, stunned. My bowels seized up, and I thought I might tip over or faint. I sensed Dad was looking for me to respond, to say something, to fill the discomforting silence, so I offered a reply. As I spoke, I saw myself at seven on a white surfboard with the beast in a wet suit, curly black-and-white hair on his hands, with veins set to pierce my skin and shred me. He also had a silver wedding band on, and it shined my way, haunting me over the years.

"Why do they go *that* way, Dad?"

"Perversion, son," he said. "Bundles of it."

"Like they can't help it?" I asked. "Like Uncle Randy can't help it?"

"Christ, I don't know about that one," he said as I dumped the cocoa in the trash and caught up with him heading for his topaz Continental down the street.

"Yeah, but what about Randy, though?"

"Randy is a gay man," he said. "I respect that—he stays consistent, never wavers and I love that. He's as God created him. That's what I believe—he's a talented and blessed individual, too, the perfect twin of your mom, may she always rest in peace."

"Of course," I said. "But what exactly is a waffle-boy?"

"Someone inconsistent, I guess," he said. "Sexually speaking—they can't make up their mind whom they want to be with, sometimes men, other times, women."

Dad's eyes were wet, cheeks flushed from the cold, his breath on my face was warm but not unpleasant after he dispatched three tumblers of alcohol.

"Why do people *have* to decide one way or the other?" I asked. "Date a man, then a woman? Aren't there a lot worse things in the world to be doing with your life?"

"Life is about being responsible," he said. "Helping the team and assisting society as much as possible."

"Some folks never follow any rules, though, right, Dad?" I said. "They get away with murder out there, sleeping around left and right."

"You can't trust them," Dad said. "Waffle-boys go up or down, left and right, in or out. Can't make up their goddammed minds on anything. Life is about following through on your promises—it's imperative that you choose one side or the other. To me, waffle-boys are like duplicitously subtle monsters on the loose."

"But what if someone comes right out and says they're bisexual so they're never lying to anyone," I said. "Just speaking the honest truth."

"Ah, but see, they're still pulling the wool over everyone's eyes," Buck said. "Look at Tricky Dick Nixon. Our thirty-seventh president couldn't win fairly, so he gamed the system with Watergate, was impeached, and resigned."

"So, President Nixon was a waffle-boy, too?"

Dad shrugged and said: "Quite possibly."

My father held my face in his hands, kissed my forehead hard, and hugged me so damn close—I felt the itchiness of his black, Irish cable-knit sweater crush against my nose, and my eyes spilled. "All your mom and I ever wanted is for you is to have a wonderful and morally sound life."

"Right," I said as Buck gestured, his heavy arms, pink hands, and thick fingers reached up towards the cold, bruised sky.

"Be an airplane mechanic, a second baseman, a Latin teacher with savvy investments in Minneapolis, Cleveland, and Shreveport, Louisiana," he said. "But make it easy on yourself and the world—stick with young ladies, okay?"

"Absolutely," I said, but my cheeks flushed, and my chest tightened with... *what, exactly? Trepidation? Guilt? Dad can't mean silly wrestling with boys after school or last summer with Liam, right? I mean, that's nowhere near actual sex or love, correct?* I had more questions, but in my hesitant silence, Buck put the football game on the radio loudly when we got into his car with nine minutes left in the game.

Fifty minutes later, we pulled off the Limewood exit, and Buck nudged me awake.

"You and I disagree some—that's nothing but healthy," he told me. "I think you're going to be on the debate team."

"Why say that, Dad?" I asked.

"You're not afraid to ask me tough questions, to defend your principles," he said. "Not everyone can do that, so I'm real proud of you."

"Thanks," I said.

"Yale Bulldogs lost the battle today," he said. "Defense couldn't hold back Harvard's running game."

"Too damn cold out there, anyway, Dad," I said. "Let's go eat."

MOM'S LEAP

The startling black-and-white photograph of Mom's death wasn't printed until the early morning of April 2, 1966. Her actual leap took place at dawn on Friday, April Fool's Day, and the picture was taken by a Yale Divinity student who was visiting his ailing son at Yale-New Haven Hospital. The minister had stepped outside to smoke near the delivery entrance out back when Mom came hurtling down from above, only yards away, crushing a local milk truck.

The amateur shutterbug had his Nikon around his neck when he heard the crash, turned in shock, and reflexively took the shot of the deceased. "She looked oddly untouched like an angel visiting our Elm City," Rev. Walsh said to a nearby nurse. "One too lovely and fair for this cold, indifferent world."

Miriam O'Riley Halligan looked *relatively* at peace in her blue satin bathrobe, eyes closed, arms and legs turned away in a deferential pose, hair covering any unsightly blood with my clunky, papier-mache necklace snaked across her throat.

It's only her left ankle, splayed awkwardly, sans slipper, which signals anything remiss. Save for that bare foot, the delivery truck appeared like it absorbed most of the damage—its roof fully compressed, broken glass and shattered milk bottles everywhere, even a crushed pack of Lucky Strikes on the driver's side floor.

The milkman was inside making a delivery, so there was no other loss of life on that day. That photograph became the cover story on *Time* magazine with an article discussing the state of mental illness, depression, and suicide in America, circa 1966. The title read, "Why Is the World so Difficult for Some?"

The piece also touched briefly on post-partum depression and Mom's tragic arc of losing three babies before she finally gave up. It's that picture and article I found at nine years old in Gramps's attic after I had pestered him about my mysterious mom's life—something I folded up and kept safe in my wallet, treating it like rare gold coins.

As time rolled on, I laminated three copies of the photographs—I know that sounds macabre, but it's the most radiant shot of mom that I had ever seen, so I like to keep her near. I feel like a charlatan myself here in Spruce Lodge as I try to act like a mature, in control, almost-eighteen-year-old adult on the unit while struggling with ongoing *psychic difficulties*.

I still find myself running from my mother's suicide in conversation. I live a rather closeted life—my past is a postcard no one likes to turn over, least of all me. It's all so raw still. I mean, my breakdown only happened a year ago. Plus, the one time I confessed who I was to a patient here in the spring, a manic young woman named Ruth Brewster from Wellesley College, she rolled her eyes, saying: "Oh, so you're the anonymous Wolf-Boy from *Transfiguration Photos*? Well, perhaps you've heard of me then. I'm from the X-Men, people call me Storm, and my friend over there goes by Cyclops."

Death seizes my imagination, as well—the inescapable, rude fact of it, and the numerous ways we dance around, deny, or fight it. First with my mom's leap twelve years ago, and now with the number of struggling people I see around here. So far, I haven't thought of anything wise or comforting to offer those in despair, or even myself in the morning mirror—scary to witness how self-destruction and suicide can appear hip, the coolest, edgiest thing to a young, struggling mind.

I sometimes must push heinous, dark thoughts from own brain. A part of me wants to tell fellow patients here what Gracie told me, that we're all capable of so much deep, palpable love, and how if you have true friends, you can find a way to push through it all. Love and support. And I do believe that, but Gracie abandoned me. Without talented mentors like Dr. G in my life today or Randy or even my father, I could be gone, history, but sometimes loneliness can warp your sense of hope. It can ache and hurt, and certainly each of the clients around here knows that loneliness backward and forward and every other direction too.

Fact is, though, I believe it's always been among us—that dark, gnawing little seed. I'm sure at one time it was blamed on TV, and before that radio, and before that books, philosophy, and over-thinking. *It's just humanity*, I want to shout, or is that too scary a thought for a young man to have? I couldn't have said this last year, but I have faith in a God now, in a higher power and that certainly aids me a great deal. Is that too cheap and easy of an out on my part? Perhaps so, but I'm sticking with it.

"Danny, you got a phone call from Detroit," a twenty-year-old patient named Rochelle tells me then as I sit on my bed. "Says it's your aunt, *real friendly lady*."

"My aunt?" I say, popping up and heading to the first of the five patient phone booths down the hall. "Thanks, Rochelle."

I sit and close the clear-plastic door behind me and notice someone has scrawled in purple ink: *Parliament Funkadelic*

Lives, Zeppelin Rocks, Bruce is Boss, and Queen Rules, But Where Are the Beatles When You Need Them the Most?

I pick up the phone and before I speak, not even a hello, some subtle sound or breath must have alerted the caller because as I lift the receiver *that* voice says, "Hey, sweet angel," and immediately I freeze, and my bowels gurgle.

I'm mute for six seconds. "God, have I missed you, sugar sweet, know what I mean?" she says.

Just hang up, I hear Dr. G saying in my head. If Gracie ever phones you, hang up and go to the nurse's station and get anxiety meds and tell staff. Don't punch yourself, don't fall into that nasty habit, you can't afford any more concussions.

"You shouldn't have called," I manage to say, trembling, and Gracie carries on like we'd just left Cape Cod yesterday—as if we hadn't stuffed my mind with brain-eating, psychedelic maggots from her fancy words and nasty potions.

"I miss my angel," she says. "Especially your body—I want to kiss it all over."

I try so hard *not* to be turned on, but it's futile against her throaty, sexy voice, so now I'm fighting my arousal in a phone booth, and my traumatic past.

"Playing innocent again, huh?" I ask.

"I never wanted to hurt you," she says. "You know that."

"Stop," I say. "You destroyed me—my dad says you're a manipulative, controlling bitch on wheels."

"I *saved* you and brought much joy to your life," Gracie says. "Don't confuse the facts."

A lump sit in my throat and I fight off a sob.

"How'd you find me here?" I ask. "It's a big country, and this is a tiny place..."

"No one gets to hide from Gracie," she says. "Don't despair, though, I'll never tell a soul who Wolf-Boy is. Liam and I made a blood vow—you're safe forever."

"I don't feel safe," I say. "Feel like my head is spinning off right this minute."

"Guess who's on the cover of almost every magazine in the world nowadays?" she asks.

"Jesus Christ?"

"Close," she says. "Guess again."

"I can't even..."

"It's me, you, and Liam from my book," she says. "*Transfiguration Photos.*"

"Congrats, I guess," I say, hands trembling.

"Your love light led me to mega-success and fame," she says. "Our privates are blacked out, but that's Wolf-Boy, that's your body the world adores. What is to be done about all this heinous censorship?"

"I have to go now," I say without conviction, my hand refusing to release the receiver, my mouth dry, even as sweat slides into my eyes, or is that my tears? My mind races, thoughts zoom everywhere.

"You're a successful young man out in the world, Danny," she says. "Don't let any expensive, fancy shrink confuse you and tell you something different."

"Don't phone me anymore, Gracie, okay?"

"You still love me with everything you got, though, don't you, Danny?" she asks.

"You know I do, goddam it," I say. "*I wish I didn't*. But all these damn magazines and photos you send me threaten my life now... today. It's not something in the past, you brutal, nasty wench. I'm trying to function in the present, in the now, and each time you mention me on Johnny Carson, each time you phone me, I crumble. Bit by bit."

"I don't believe any of that horse manure," she says. "Doesn't sound like the Danny Halligan I've come to love and worship."

"Don't abuse me from a distance," I say. "Let me go. Be decent about it and release me from you, from us forever."

"Garbage, trash, that's what they got you thinking, all those crazy depressive doctors have you riled up…"

I hang up quickly, decisively, and think, *follow the rules, stand, and get your anxiety medications at the nurses' station. No funny stuff, simply turn and—*

I nod at a male staff member as I leave the booth, passing the nurses station and heading down the gray-blue carpet towards my room, the second on the left, men down one hallway, ladies down the other, though there's only me and another male, Harold C. from Baton Rouge, who keeps on using the word *commode* too often. ("Can't help but notice my commode is quite shiny," and five minutes later: "Almost dropped my electric razor into that wonderful commode," and, "Feel blue today, so I might just drown myself in the goddamn commode.")

So, it's just Harold C, me, all the *commodes*, and eighteen young women. His commode discussions are humorous, but everyone here is dangerous in their own way. He says *commodes*, but all the nurses know it's code for Harold C's musings on suicide.

Go back and tell a nurse, I think now. *Turn around now and tell one that you're feeling out of control, that you received a triggering phone call from Wonder Bitch.*

The large Day Room sits in the middle of the unit with light yellow couches and bright walls, colors, and festive themes. Right now, with July Fourth coming up in a couple days, everything is about red, white, and blue posters, and yet it strikes me as odd, false.

Independence and freedom for everyone on a locked mental ward, huh? I ask. *What a crock—I'm stuck here on this unit because my brain is malfunctioning and warped, because I can't stop beating the crap out of myself. But do have yourself a grand holiday, and grab a few hotdogs for me, will you?*

Along the hallways are also photos of benign, comforting images: rose gardens, fall foliage, a frozen waterfall, a few Degas prints: people skiing, sunflowers, and a stunning sunset over a blue-green ocean.

"Did you have a nice phone call with your friendly aunt?" a nurse asks me.

I turn and meet the gaze of Nurse Jen, a brown-haired lady who's shorter than me—a rarity—and I look into her face and notice honey-brown eyes with tiny flecks of black, perhaps too much mascara, but my first thought? *What does your bare body look like, Jen... and may I nibble upon it? Can I kiss your ruby red lips and whisper in your ear?*

Grow up, Danny, my brain says—*you're a hopeless, disgusting pervert.*

I feel shame as I look at Nurse Jen, can't hold her gaze for more than a second. I see her bouncing out of the shower or lounging in the bath.

Do you mind if I gently bite your wonderfully pink tongue? I hear in my head.

Don't stress over those natural and healthy thoughts, Danny, Dr. G tells me. *Relatively normal stuff for a cooped-up seventeen-going-on-eighteen-year-old young man.*

I absorb that Jen has a friendly smile, shoulder-length brown hair, a short-sleeve madras shirt with her nametag, khakis, and sandals. *Calm down,* I tell myself. *No more sex thoughts, easy does it, be mature and walk away, take a gentle stroll like it's just another run-of-the-mill, boring day at the local psychiatric hotspot.*

"I'm okay. Had a decent chat, thanks," I manage to say to Jen and mercifully move along the hallway to my room, taking a seat on my bed. *Victory, Danny,* I think. *That was a little victory, controlling the sex thoughts.* I try and practice some more of that deep breathing stuff and let all thoughts exit my mind, working on deep, cleansing meditation, but it's not working for me, so I give up on my mindfulness too rapidly. Sometimes I wear a mask of general sanity to cover up my internal misery.

Christ, I hope Gracie and Liam aren't laughing at me 24/7. "Gracie's trying to get inside my skull and disrupt any way she can," I say quietly, looking out the big window in my room. First, she magically tracks me down at this private hospital in the Green Mountains of Vermont, finds my confidential number, and phones me after a year of no contact—what the hell is that about? And then an annoying, teasing postcard to top everything off?

All those memories with Gracie and Liam still terrify me, I think. *I mean, some of it I miss—our laughter early on, sex, skinny-dipping, dancing on the beach, and fooling around in my tree palace, but with the booze, potions, and psychotic break, it would kill me to relive. I can't go back. I can't ever go back.*

Like a film in my skull, I see Gracie and me laughing, click, click goes the camera. We see Liam doing naked handstands in two feet of water, genitals bobbling all over the place. God how we laughed at the absurdity of it all. Sometimes Liam and I leaned against each other like little second-grade kids, catching our breaths, taking a mini-nap between extravaganzas.

At yesterday's session Dr. G implored me *not to do any more punching. You can't afford to sustain any more damage to your noggin. And don't hide in your room. Open to the adult staff around you. You only left the adolescent unit this morning, so introduce yourself, make the effort. Be the adult around here.*

Stubbornly, though, I remain on my blue New England Patriots comforter in my room. Dr. G wants me to socialize more, get out into the adult unit, and share hurts with my comrades, but all I do is deep breathe and stare out the window, seeing a horde of adolescents going to the cafeteria, unique in their gait. Some are gangly and awkward, others appear fierce, walking on their toes like predators, others pigeon-toed or bow-legged or stoop-shouldered, and the rest have blue, green, orange, purple, white, lavender, and neon-yellow hair, or some combination of those, to go along with their lithe, ripe bodies.

Although some have been here a long while, so they're bloated from the anti-psychotics. *Been only a handful of hours since I left them,* I think, where I saw from close that most had wounded wrists, bruised forearms, burnt necks, marked-up legs, scarred bellies, and melancholy faces, with the incriminating tracks of cigarettes, razors, knives, poisons, addictions, all of it occurring in their splintered, frenzied minds.

So damn hard to grow up, I think. *Especially when you mess with Gracie's Magical Potions, and your fists are so readily available to pound the skull.*

I think of the ancient kid's show *Romper Room,* and the soft and silky-voiced lady who would look into the magic mirror at show's end and say, "I see Henry, and Barbara, Richard, and Pamela and Susie and Gracie and Liam and Danny."

Those were the days, I think. *Problems were solved with a hug, a nap, a quick game of kickball, and peanut butter, graham crackers, and cold apple juice.*

I lay flat on the bed with my balled fists at my sides, flushing.

"Do some damn push-ups," I say. "You promised Dr. Gingerman you would try them if you got really stressed out and were losing your temper."

So, I roll onto the floor and do twenty-five of them, but even as I'm exercising, I lose heart and obsess instead about punching. I roll over on my back and examine the high ceiling and think *when I was tiny, I longed to live in an upside-down world*

—and had a fondness for high, fancy ceilings, imagining they'd be perfect to play on in a flipped over society. Yes, they'd be a bit uncomfortable for sleeping with the intricate woodwork and light fixtures getting in the way, but I was convinced I'd thrive there. Granted, stepping in and out of the doorways would be an awful challenge, but I felt I could learn to cope.

"You're turning eighteen in two lousy days, so grow up and stay cool."

But I walk over to my bureau, look at Mom's wooden plaque again. *The gift was made with deep love and affection from your favorite mom in the entire world, so why must you go immediately to the bad, to the evil, Danny? Don't ruin her gift, don't you dare stain her memory—don't rush to the cruel—why quit on yourself, you simpleton?* My doctor told me my internal dialogue seems to be mostly in second person.

"Don't just survive in the world, Danny Hal, but thrive," I say, reading the inscription. "Thrive, survive, jive, live, hive, dive—don't just survive, Danny, you are filthy, monstrous fool, but *dive, dive.*" *Don't, Danny,* I think. *Don't fall into a collapsing hole, it gets more difficult to climb out of, there's no guarantee you can keep getting out, as a matter of fact, no guarantees, it's nothing but a slippery slope, and you're twisting and falling again, simpleton.*

But I start sobbing, missing mom badly, and feel my whole mood tumble, like stepping off a cliff, and I can't get my balance back as I descend, and fall. Desperately, I reach out for the craggy, jagged mountains, and the rocks pound at me, and I fall so fast, I'm diving, *diving.* "I apologize for my lame weaknesses, Ma," I say, standing, and strike my mother's plaque against my left temple, as the tears rush out.

I feel loathing for myself as I crush it against my temple, plus the other side of my head, and quickly five times on my forehead. All of it ends up taking about nine minutes, and soon blood trickles down my cheeks. *At least I'm not falling anymore,* I think. *No more diving, we're all done with that awful diving business for now.*

A twenty-one-year-old from Santa Fe, a female patient who struggles with depression and bulimia named Sam, walks past my room, sees my bleeding face, and calls for staff.

I rise slowly, dizzily, and place Mom's wooden plaque back on my bureau, straightening it until it's just right, even though it's smeared in crimson.

"Damn you, Danny," I say and stumble slightly and sit on the bed as a few nurses run into my room and a button is pushed that warns patients to remain in the Day Room.

"Call for an ambulance," a nurse shouts. "He'll need some stitches."

I feel far away, but my head throbs like a son of a bitch, and the feelings that go along with it are an unsteady kind of nausea, anxiety, and melancholia, so I ask vague, semi-rhetorical questions to try and find my equilibrium.

"Why do we each give up so damn young?" and "What's happening to all our young boys out there in the world? Why are they faltering so frequently?"

"What'd you injure yourself with, Danny?" Nurse Jen asks, as a young doctor I don't know shows up in my room.

"My mother gifted a wooden plaque to me decades ago..."

"But you loved that thing, didn't you?" the young doctor asks.

"I did love it, Doctor," I say, crying harder, sensing his disappointment, disgust, and disdain. "I mean, I do, I love that plaque, it's important, it meant a lot, I adore it, I don't know why I would ever, I mean, I'm not sure, I adore it, I'm an asshole, a foolish, silly..."

"Try to be calm and breathe evenly now, Danny," Nurse Jen says, patting my back as others bandage my wounds. "I know it's hard. Sorry you couldn't share your pain with me earlier."

I want to be honest with Jen and tell her I would've shared with her, but she had that beautiful body, bouncing around, and it got me off topic quick.

"I almost did, Jen," I say. "Nearly did, but my mind is so damn sinful."

"Sinful?" she says, but at that point, I find myself floating way high on the ceiling, gazing at my bloody face way down below, shaking my head.

You fool, you're nothing but a melodramatic, screwed-up foolish fool of fools.

Caregivers' voices echo loudly in my room, ricocheting inside my brain—there's Jen, Josie, and the young doctor, and some supportive staff, but I feel far away and untouchable up here. I mean, certainly my head throbs, which may mean another concussion, but I'm on Saturn suddenly, rolling around in the rings, or *wait, am I on Pluto?*

I continue to whisper and ramble, leaving the planets far behind, and I am unsure if I'm speaking loud enough to have any of the staff comprehend me. I say something along the lines of it's not quite the same as if all this happened with people watching *Star Wars* in SENSURROUND screens in New York City, or on a large TV at some Friday night block party in Charlotte, North Carolina. Not as dramatic without the powerful film score, but also somehow more jarring and cruel.

It's not a famous actor in Oscar-winning makeup, nor does it feature mind-blowing special effects on a planet a billion light years from earth. It's a real human, a troubled, horny seventeen-year-old two days away from adulthood, one doing his best to live decently, sanely, trying so damn hard to be normal and present and to *not* self-harm. Can't we rewind the tape just a bit for him, five hours maybe? Or three? Or even a lousy four minutes? Can't we venture deep into the backrooms of this hospital, solve some mysteries, swap favors with the Gods, and bring the young soul back from his depths with a buoyant and sustaining hope?

Can't we just try?

MILES TO GO

It was late December in 1986 and I'd been loitering all day at this spooky, eight-story parking tower in New Haven, just licking my wounds, spiraling into a massive obsession on clinical depression and old-fashioned paranoia. It wasn't far from the hospital where I was born and where Mom had ended her life. When I wasn't spinning around, acting psychotic, I was trying to stay warm in my truck. But I kept lowering the window and listening intently, for I couldn't figure whether the echoing sounds I was hearing around me were normal or if I was growing paranoid.

It seemed like the whole world was on my case—I was bombarded with invasive sounds both big and small, dogs howling, sleet hitting my windshield and cab, and what sounded to me like a helicopter landing on my roof, which was in fact a Life-Star helicopter delivering a maimed teenager who'd been in a brutal highway accident to a nearby hospital.

I was on holiday from the group home in Montpelier. There were just ten of us living together in the supportive building, but around New Year's the staff takes a break, and the clients had to cope on their own for several days. Some clients stayed with their folks' states away, or maybe crashed at a friend's house. The wealthy clients stayed at a local bed & breakfast. My father was away for two nights—townies had vandalized one of his stores in Warwick, Rhode Island, and caused $20,000 worth of damage.

On top of all that harsh news, I felt suicidal, rotted out. I had recently been discharged as an inpatient from Spruce Lodge after almost five years, and I had another three years to go at the group home, and I felt lost, emotionally faltering. Whatever momentum I had from being discharged had wilted by then. Last I heard, Gracie was growing sicker from cancer and her vision was failing. All I had heard about Liam was that he had identified himself as Lone Ranger to the media and had joined a shitty band in Munich.

The lonely parking garage was vast and spilling over with haunting echoes—dress shoes tapping, engines revving, slamming doors, hip-hop music blasting, people yelling, and car alarms screeching away into the night. I had studied Yale-New Hospital earlier today, thinking, *it's time to quit your existence, Danny, go and sprint hard and leap into oblivion!* I was buzzing on some beer so I got out of my truck and spun around in the sleet like a whirling dervish, feeling toxic and broken. Around and round, I went.

Don't stop, Halligan, I thought, *it's for the best. The time to slip on out of this world has come, make it easier on Buck and your therapists, your number's up, pal. Keep spinning and then sprint hard and leap over the concrete wall, fly free and join Mom high above, see if you can spot her in the clouds.*

A car horn sounded so I stopped spinning, but I was unbalanced, and I fell over into a puddle, getting my khakis soaked. A stout security guard in a blue Ford SUV approached; I was confused, and I stumbled some more.

"Are you, drunk?"

"Just buzzing, officer."

"I'm not a cop," he said. "Are you okay?"

"I'm Danny."

"Why were you spinning around like that in the sleet?"

"Feeling giddy."

"Don't bullshit me, Danny."

"I'm an uncle today, sir."

"What's the baby's name?"

"A lovely girl named Gracie Rose."

"Like the famous photographer?" he asked. "She only seems to snap dirty pictures and make her many millions, right?"

"She ruined me, though, *demolished my heart some years ago, sir.*"

"I've heard three other young men this year claim they're anonymous Wolf-Boy, so forgive me if I don't believe you."

"Gracie ate me alive on Cape Cod in 1979," I said. "That's the plain truth."

"Do you maybe need a ride to the Psych ER instead?" he asked.

"No, no," I said.

"Babies are always good news, though, Danny."

"Right," I said. "Yes."

He shook my hand and got back into his Ford and drove off.

Two minutes later, he returned. "Let me give you a ride to the first floor, there's a good sandwich shop there. I'll buy you a ham and cheese sub celebration of Gracie, a holiday meal..."

"You don't have to do that, sir," I said.

"I insist," he said, and so my life was rescued by a stout, kind-hearted security guard by the name of Jonas Toll of Norwalk. He bought me a sandwich and a soda, and we spoke for fifteen minutes. He said he worked as an aide to a social worker in town, keeping suicidal citizens from parking lot towers and carting food to some homeless shelters and local soup kitchens.

"I like reaching out to people in their hour of need," he said, and by then I knew I would survive the night. "Plus, around the holidays and at New Year's people act so wacky and out of sorts."

"I was bullshitting about the baby, sir," I confessed. "Made all that stuff up, I apologize for saying that."

"No harm, no foul," he said and drove me back to my truck on the top floor. As I drove out of New Haven, I felt lucky to be alive.

When I finally got home to Limewood, I phoned Dr. G in Vermont and told him all I'd been hearing in my head that day was Robert Frost's "Stopping by Woods on a Snowy Evening." It had been recited by actor Morgan Freeman on NPR.

"You're far from being finished, Danny," Dr. G said. "You're just getting underway..."

"I lose my wind easily, Doc," I said. "I stumble, have trouble finding a purpose. Without that kind man who found me on top of an eight-story garage, I might not be here with you."

"Well, thank God for Jonas from Norwalk and that delicious sandwich," he said. "Don't be too discouraged, everyone falters, even me, even Christ."

"You're turning reverent on me in your old age, Doc?" I asked.

"A wee bit," Dr. G said. "It keeps me spry, gives my life added heft."

"I wish my life weren't filled with so many dramatic ups and downs," I said. "I'm tired of falling into every damn crack and crevice."

"Welcome to bipolar disorder, Danny," Dr. G said.

So, I wept, and Dr. G stayed on the line with me, patient

and kind as ever. We spoke until my hot cocoa was ready in Dad's kitchen. "Miles to go before I sleep," I repeated, and then we said goodnight.

Later, as I stared at Winnie-the-Pooh on my ceiling in my childhood bedroom, I pondered how no one believes that I'm Wolf-Boy, like I can't even claim or reject the truth of my own life. At times, it's excruciating. It'll be seven years this June. Is there anyone out there still waiting for Danny Hal? Pining for me to call them up? To take photographs with or go on a vacation with? Or see a movie, maybe? To share a life together?

Will I always be so alone?

HERE'S JOHNNY

The world can be very subdued in Vermont, even within an adolescent psychiatric unit. The change was good for me after the wild madness of my summer of 1979, and for a year there was little news about *Transfiguration Photos*. But when I walk into the PEAR Young Adult ward, a year after my disastrous summer, someone flicks the switch, the one that starts terrible things occurring inside and around me, like greyhound racers in the olden days chasing down electric rabbits on cruel racetracks. My emotions race around, veering from self-loathing to blah and back again. In the end, I can't seem to avoid Gracie Rose. As I enter this goddam unit, the world accelerates, the pace picks up.

From the moment I walk through the locked main door, Gracie and all things promotional for her book spread and catch like a spark, like a virus. Gracie is the center of the universe. Her face, body, and work appear everywhere I look. I can't sleep with the world buzzing about Gracie Rose and her masked duo. I develop bad insomnia and an older staff, a slim man in plaid slacks and blue turtlenecks named Herschel

Trucker, 61, with a bald head and a long red beard, befriends me. He doesn't ask many questions and often gives me home-made lemon cookies his wife bakes.

"Danny," he says. "There's nothing inside you or any of these other harried patients that can't be fixed with two excep-tional lemon cookies and almond milk."

One Wednesday night, after Johnny's monologue, I glance up and see Gracie Rose on *The Tonight Show's* couch, bare feet swinging to and fro, bare head, and those bug-eyed sunglasses in place. She looks stunning, tan as ever, wearing only a thin white skirt and purple T-shirt, sans any cameras. As the flirta-tious chat continues, Gracie climbs over his desk and onto Carson's lap as the audience hoots.

"Take it easy, sweetie," Carson says before she returns to her seat.

"You can't control me," Gracie says. "America should know this by now."

Carson and Gracie chat about her wild success for four more minutes until Johnny asks, "Are you ever gone to tell the world just who Wolf-Boy is?"

"No can do," she says. "Never."

"How old was that kid when you took the first masked pictures?" he asks. "Come on, be straight with America, okay? Was Wolf-Boy underage?"

"Those secrets go to the grave with me, Johnny," she says. "I made a vow."

"Why are you so damn protective of him?" Carson asks.

"Wolf-Boy is a lost soul *way* out in deep space," she says. "And yet he's a true f****** angel of light, my personal hero if you want to know the truth."

The censors beep her curse, the audience titters, and Carson scowls, and the show goes to a few commercials. When they return, Gracie Rose is long gone from the set and is never

71

mentioned or invited back to the program again until Johnny Carson retires.

A producer at Carson's show later admits no one knew how Gracie arrived on the set. TV actor Erik Estrada was set to go on first, followed by a comedian from Cleveland. A stagehand reports: "Gracie stepped out of a limo with her bare feet and hairless head. Claims she's only passing through, so I bring her to the green room, and she improvised from there."

I want to tell everyone at the hospital that they're talking about me on national TV. I can't fall asleep that night, I'm terrified that the world is going to discover who I truly am. And that Liam is an indispensable part of our love triangle, not just someone to dismiss when all the lights are back on.

Dr. G informs me the next day: "No more late-night TV watching, Danny—it's time to remove Gracie Rose and her toxic, devastating, and delusional grip on your psyche."

"She's killing me, Doc," I say.

MAGICAL POTIONS

Two days after Gracie brings wild and supreme joy to me in the tree palace, I hear my name being called in the middle of the night. Gramps had stayed at Eileen's place over in Dennisport so I stayed up real late at Gramps's home and played my records at nearly full blast until well after the talk shows signed off and the airwaves went dead. I couldn't sleep for more than an hour or two when I woke up with a start to someone whispering my name.

"Danny," a voice says. "*Halligan*, get up off your ass, up, up, up..."

"What?" I say, rolling over, sitting up.

"It's me, dummy," she says.

"Who?"

It's pitch black, I can't see a thing, no moonlight anywhere that night, so I get out of my bed, stumbling to the second-story window in my underwear.

"Gracie..."

"You left your damn fire ladder outside," she whispers. "I climbed it."

I shake my head and rub my eyes, trying to focus.

"I'll meet you out front, okay?" I say.

I dress and head downstairs, open the door, and we both run to Gracie's Comet parked in the road. When I climb in, I rub my right hand on Gracie's arm, back and forth. *So damn smooth and muscular, one wonderful, luscious frame.* The air's cool, but her skin is warm and smells of coconut oil, and it's so sweet to touch her.

"Hey," I say.

"Hey to you, angel," she says.

Gracie offers me a drink in a bottle after we'd been on the road for a while.

"Let's have a toast to your ecstatic and unceasing youth," she says.

But I just drink—at this point, I'm still half-asleep, dreaming of a moonless hour with nothing but the stars to guide us. The taste is sweet and sour. I had expected the taste of watery beer, maybe.

"What is it?" I ask.

"This stuff is better than Pop-Rocks, a dazzling secret potion with mystical-like power," she says. "It'll deliver you to hog heaven, which doesn't really mean anything, I guess."

"Huh?"

"An old family recipe."

"Really?"

"Straight from the laboratories of the CIA in Quantico, Virginia."

"What's the CIA again?"

"*Central Intelligence Agency,*" she says. "Spies and all that business."

"Why won't you tell me what the hell it is?"

"It's easier on you, on me, if you don't know," she says, caressing my left cheek for a moment. "*Understand?*"

"Guess so," I say, and fifteen minutes later, I'm bent over, giggling.

"That's it, my boy," she says, smiling. "Welcome home."

Before too long, the two of us admire the sunrise in Truro. The rising peach sphere paints the sky pink, silver, purple, strictly dynamic, wonderful hues. Gracie and I drink the potion, all before nine o'clock. We stumble through the dunes, and she kisses me and gently slides a wolf mask over my face, something cheap she picked up at a K-Mart in Hamden, Connecticut she tells me.

It's itchy at first, and I feel aroused, psyched, and I growl, howl, and feel like I can become anything or anyone with that mask on. I feel so excited, *so very pumped!* My layers disintegrate, most of my fears fall away, and hang-ups too. I find myself delighted with how far from my everyday life the secret potion takes me. With this magical witchy woman by my side, and the mask over my face, things blossom—life itself sparks, sizzles, and catches fire.

"You'll be safe behind this facade," Gracie whispers. "You can be whoever you want to be, my friend."

"You promise?"

"No one's going to stop you now, Danny," Gracie says. "Not even God."

It feels like new frontiers tear open within, and I hand my existence over to Gracie, let my new Wonder Woman take the keys. She has her cameras with her, as always, and she snaps photos of me lying naked on a blanket, or much later of me emerging from the outdoor shower at her cottage with a soppy wet wolf mask and excited as can be. What feels like a split-second later, she starts reciting an Anne Sexton poem to me, she tells me about her favorite one called "I Remember."

As Gracie recites part of the poem, we're back on the sand and she's spinning and dancing, shaking all over, taking photos of me, and she laughs and says, "And what I remember best is that the door to your room was the door to mine..."

"I love that, Gracie," I say.

"Nothing quite stings like a raw Anne Sexton verse," she says and spins around, laughing. It's so hot inside the mask now, and they're spectacular, too, the things I feel, see, and believe. I think of that term Randy likes to use frequently: *Transcendent.* I'm alive in a way I've never been, something like tiptoeing along the third rail of a subway, with electricity pricking my soul, and now I can spring into action, explode into this new world, my very own rapidly expanding Milky Way.

Gracie uses her old Pentax camera and a new Nikon that a Yale faculty sent to her. After a time, we get silly and laugh, and she poses me—flexing my biceps, sticking my tongue through the Wolf-Boy mouth hole, mooning the camera, and doing flips and cartwheels in the sand. She snaps away, one shot after the next. I'm a rather goofy wolf, she proclaims that morning, and so she announces the title of her photos as they occur: *Goofy Wolf-Boy Mooning and Giggling, Goofy Wolf-Boy Drunk,* and *Sated, Goofy, Super-Sexy Wolf-Boy Saluting the Universe.*

At one point, both of us shed our clothes, and she sits up high on my chest, her bare, nubile body thrust in my face.

"You dig this, sugar?" she says, smiling as she continues to snap her photos.

"Yeah, it's so damn perfect, sweet, and delicious," I say. By then we both are intoxicated on each other, along with various chemicals, secret and otherwise. Gracie stays on top of me, the sweat and smell of her filling my nostrils, my mouth, like a huge silky sheet wafting in the wind, and thrillingly, wonderfully melting on top of me. This is before it gets too stifling, and by that time we'd been on a roll for many hours.

"All right, gather round, listen up," I say.

"What are you doing?" she says.

"I admire your raw talent, your artistry," I say. "At work and everything, you've got a vision for this, and damn you, if it's not coming together like you predicted. Things are jelling just like you said they would."

"Thanks, I'm blushing, my lover," she says. "You make me happy."

"Right back at you," I say.

My forehead's damp, and it burns, and I like the heat, feel captured inside the mask. I feel sand fleas on my neck, more on my ankle, and I only shake them off. I go beyond any of the surface stuff, and I let Gracie pin my arms back in the sand, her two cameras now dangling around her neck like a fuzzy pair of dice.

It's dirty, kinky inside my churning mind, and I like how Gracie controls me. I give her that blessing—the right for the entire season—I want to go for the grandest, most spectacular journey a young man from Limewood, Connecticut has ever undertaken. Like from now on I sign myself away. It doesn't make sense to me, for I want to not only touch Gracie, but have her *do* me, too, somehow. I don't have the vocabulary, or the mental picture, exactly, so I whisper the first words that come to me.

"*Deliver me*, Gracie," I say, and she smiles and understands.

"Plenty of time for that later," she says. "Stay untouched, Wolf-Boy."

I giggle nervously, not understanding, not fully comprehending. But somehow, I know that's going to be my name this summer. I guess that's the most precise way of explaining Gracie Rose and my relationship with her—I didn't ever fully comprehend why she did anything. But I could never say no.

GRACIE, DANCING

Gracie invites me to her cottage and lights her pudgy red and white votive candles on her makeshift mantle and twists, spins around, dancing everywhere. She lets me witness her performance—Gracie loves incense, too, and shaking her body to the tunes of Lou Reed, Aretha Franklin, Etta James, and Nina Simone.

"Never mind your own angst, or distressing crime reports coming out of the big cities, or the fires out west, or tornadoes in Kansas and Oklahoma or Cat 4 Hurricanes in Florida and info about the brittle, vulnerable economy in our leading newspapers," Gracie said. "Be about light, life, youth, pulsing desire and imbibing all my magical potions, and try out some copulation for fun, but don't dwell on the mess, my friend. Together we may live forever."

So, I drink Gracie's witches brew like she suggests, and I grow bitchy and feel hyper-alert as it churns through my veins, and I hear words ricocheting around in my skull like *shining, shrieking, shocking, mocking, and talk-talk-talking.*

"Where did you go just now, angel?" Gracie asks me, but I

drift, half-dreaming, half-imagining I'm swinging on a trapeze inside a massive hockey arena in Winnipeg, Manitoba. Or perhaps I'm tethered to multicolored bras, imported scarves, cashmere socks, quilted jocks, and crotch-less panties forming a long swinging rope that is lassoed to a military satellite rotating in deep space?

I choke for a while, lose my breath, and feel there's no way for me to survive so I think, *this could be it...*

"Easy, babe," Gracie calls out to me as the dream speeds on, and huge crowds applaud with glee, with a dangerous and funky type of zeal. One moment it's jubilation with marching band music from trombones, oboes, and banjos, followed by thousands of folks chanting, "Banish that foolish young boy."

"I believe your death fixation is silly," Gracie says. "Sophomoric. That's my only point."

I pick at my thumbnail until it bleeds, and I stare at Gracie, unsure how I escaped but glad to be back in Winnipeg with the colorful socks, quilted smocks, breathing normally.

"Do you think we'll be together for many moons to come?" I ask.

"Who knows? Life passes so damn rapidly," Gracie says. "Although, I never have met a sexier teenager across this hallowed land."

I look at her toenails, painted rainbow colors, and her affect transforms into three distinct faces—one smiling, another scowling, and a third one, yawning. I feel a hostile spirit rip through my pre-frontal cortex, before I play handball against a talented and competitive scribe who teaches creative writing in the North Carolina woods, not far from Chapel Hill.

I ask her multiple times about her secret to a joyful life and producing such wonderful writing, but she only shrugs and asks if I want to play another game of handball. So, we compete for another hour, but she says little about writing or any thoughts on existence before wandering off like a phantom scribe onto a wooded trail, whistling an old Stevie Wonder tune.

Gracie makes a kissing sound and reaches up for a metal, eight-inch white dove on a shelf—the one her roommate made for her during her first year in New Haven. She strokes its beak, oddly colored silver and orange, and kisses it and places it back onto the shelf. Meanwhile, I take another drink of her potion. "You're cute," Gracie says. "Though at times like a toddler, so go take another swig of that stuff."

"Why?"

"It'll help your vitals see the good inside every person in our mad world," she says.

I swallow another sip, and she offers thumbs-up.

"You're way too smart for me, Gracie," I say, "but also a convincing bull-shitter."

"All about contradictions, that's my game," she says, rising and walking across the room to adjust her wooden sculptures, several of them carved by Gracie's own late mom in Middletown, Connecticut. Some of her pieces are dancing, shapely figures created from maple or cherry. Others are voluptuous art pieces of females reaching out, surrounded by roses and a blue and white scarf dangling off them.

"You called me a talented rock star once," I say. "Told me I was wise beyond my years."

"Magical rock star one day," Gracie says, tapping her temple. "Just a boy the next, you vary—don't sweat it so much."

We stay silent for a minute—Gracie remains standing, shaking her legs, like she was prepping for a 110-meter hurdles at the next Olympics.

"Are you a runner?"

She keeps her back to me, gazing out of her triangular window, which is being overtaken by photography books,

Walker Evans, Diane Arbus, Richard Avedon, Ansel Adams, plus jewelry, statues, and colorful trinkets—shells, sand dollars, pink and yellow polka-dotted necklaces, and rope bracelets, and a tiny replica of the Hindu God Ganesh. The view offers another window and more colorful cottages thirty feet away, and another fancy window beyond that, and more cottages.

Meanwhile, scents of the beach; brine, pizza, fudge, fried clams, cotton candy, and fried dough reach me. I realize it's already been a peculiar summer. I have been over to Gracie's home only twice so far, but I fancy the implication. Gracie is an adult, and so am I, or at least, she usually treats me like one, which is cool on her part. I'm like her lover, her man, her sly dude on the make.

"Doesn't everyone need to sweat and run around periodically?" I ask, feeling dizzy, and far away, still seeing multiple Gracie Rose's before me, those three faces in my mind's eye. I lean forward to kiss her full, succulent lips, but she's long gone, and I tumble through the trapdoor, falling through the sand, warm and dry on top, wet, and clammy deeper down, before I swish down a long metal pipe through the core of Middle Earth.

Somehow, my resilient brain eventually reorganizes and finds itself fully formed inside a balding chubby, fifty-eight-year-old man's body steering a Boston Whaler around Galveston Bay in Texas, listening to oldies tunes with his loyal pit bull, Ruby.

Gracie snickers. "What do you have against good health?"

"I'm afraid I can't match any of your brilliance," I say. "Or your Ivy-League wit."

"It's why I adore you, kiddo," she says, yawning. "Your lack thereof."

"Don't call me kiddo," I say before clearing my throat, wanting to strike out at her verbally, she who is transforming my summer vacation. *Or is she only ruining my future? Running me to the ground? Or am I completely wrong? Is she instead saving me?*

"Will we ever know the answer to that one?" I ask myself, trembling.

PATHWAY TO LIAM

L ouis was in a group of four pals, each of us around eleven or twelve. Louis frequently had a runny nose, and long, angular fingernails that he scratched his cheeks with until they grew patchy red. Louis's father liked to take his son and friends flying in a tiny Cessna airplane out of a municipal airfield near Fairfield, Connecticut.

Sometimes, the boys told me, Louis's dad would close his eyes high in the sky and pretend he was drunk, even attempting a spin or two, wiggling his neck like some nutty banana, and then an hour later, land the plane safely, effortlessly on the small tarmac.

The kids loved that man and his sense of fun, a not-quite-grown-up zipping around and flipping the world off from seven hundred feet up. I longed to soar and twist with my friends in the heavens, but Buck wouldn't allow it.

Though it's true I never flew in the plane, I found my own sense of danger with the buddies at Louis's house. There was something hovering, lurking in the Rilling's old brick place—funky smells of unwashed dishes, decay, wet dogs, secret poisons, or maybe even old demons. Louis was my first buddy who had divorced parents, and I was fascinated by that.

Louis saw his mother once every two months in Boston at a group home— "She has struggles, weepy-sad troubles like your mom used to have," Buck had told me, and so I was aware of needing to be kind. It was something we discussed in Catechism, compassion and sweetness and love towards those who ache, hurt, and are lonely. Sweetness and compassion to everyone, really, is how I heard it.

So that left us four boys with the run of the place while Louis's dad worked. After the religious lessons at a neighbor's house, we put our workbooks down in his front hall, ran to his back porch each Tuesday, locked it, and shook and shuddered to various bands of the time.

We listened to everything from E.L.O. to Journey to Aerosmith, and we pretended we were rock stars, giggling and shuffling around, then started tackling one another like boys tend to, banging on the invisible drum sets at the same time. Doing air guitar every now and then, swiveling our hips, and pretending we were going at it with pretty girls on the couch pillows.

Next, the energy of the scrum changed, and we howled and ground ourselves into one another, laughing tentatively about it at first, but then with conviction, with a guileless rage. Louis giggled, and the others started singing, "Hallelujah, ladies," and, "Can we get an amen over here?"

We each shouted back, "Yes, amen to that," feeling daring, spastic. Naughty. In our group, there was a kid named Lawrence, and he had kind of girlie lips, full and pouty, with lashes that mean kids teased him about. "Oh, here comes beauty pageant Lawrence," they said.

One time, I ground myself in Lawrence's face, into those plump lips. I felt the most spectacular friction and heat at that point, as if my whole body were about to burst into glow-in-the-dark confetti. At times, there was laughter, and the one time with Lawrence, when I finished doing my thing, I saw pure terror behind his thick lashes.

I hesitated, only to be tackled by another of the boys and smothered under one of them. When this occurred, when someone lay on top of me like that, I felt a complex range of emotions swirling, ringing inside me. Like Lawrence, I feared I might drown under the boys, that I would perish, just roll off and die. I would never be allowed to be free and stand up again, to breathe and shout out my own name. I also felt frozen in time, locked in there like some dinosaur fossil.

Mostly though, I felt intense arousal, mixed with the mad, terrifying possibility that we might get caught. We were young, so very naive, but not so much that we didn't grasp we were playing with fire. Screwing around with rules that older kids and adults had decided on long ago. That was, of course, boys go with girls, and girls with boys.

If that ancient pattern was interrupted for even a minute, if anybody found out, we'd be cast far away and known as that frightening term. *"Demolish the homos!"* was a phrase my Pop Warner football captain Oscar used to shout before every game—he said it half in jest, but, still, each of us got the message.

My first memory of Liam Preston involves grinding in the same way, and me nearly losing it over the sensation. The behavior stuns me when it crops up again: *Are kids doing this everywhere? I wonder. Or is it just me and my warped ways?*

We wander through the woods out back in Dennis or the high dunes at the beach. He pins me in the sand up there, grinding his hips into mine until it feels strangely fuzzy, but good, and we laugh, and later we swim way out into the ocean.

"Frisky mermaids and sailors of the world," he says. "There are naked and wildly conflicted and fallen angels everywhere in the surf. They're more dangerous to this nation's soul than Great White Sharks."

"Don't make a scene, Liam, come on," I say, and he laughs, bellows really.

"I am the newest ruler of this here horny Aqua Kingdom," he says and forces my head beneath the sea before releasing me. When I surface, he laughs, tousling my hair.

"Yeah, you know I love you and your family for how they look out for me."

It was true—my family had him over for lunch or dinner all the time. Gramps did his part, for Liam had no real guidance at home. A lot of other families in the neighborhood provided for him, too, making lunches, inviting him back for barbecues.

"I'm the juvenile delinquent everyone's family tries to rehabilitate," he would say, daring anyone to challenge him. "But it's futile, don't they know that?"

He was frequently talking about sex as well, so it forever interested me. One day, in the midst of our chats in the high dunes, Liam pulls my bathing suit off before sprawling back and displaying himself to me.

Eventually, the two of us tackle one another out in the sea, rolling sideways, laughing and wrestling under the sea, pushing together like predators. With a clear blue ocean and sky, we are far from any eyes on the beach. Each day, we do the grinding, and when we surface to catch our breath, we only want to push more, like two vipers incensed. I loathe it with all of my being, but I kind of love it too. The friction makes me feel like I might rip open with rage, a flammable, liquid fire.

As the wrestling continues, shame courses through me. I go to confession eight times one summer—this was before I was even confirmed. When I tell the priest I am sinning and don't know what to do or how to stop, he tells me to pray more fervently, and do 500 push-ups each morning, and try some

Hindu relaxation tapes. So, I have Gramps get tapes for me, and I stretch every which way, and listen to the calming voices, and at night, I whisper prayers on my knees.

"I'm not dirty," I say. "I'm no waffle-boy, no way, no how, Jesus."

But it's no use. In the daylight hours after my daily sets of push-ups and stretches, all I care for is grinding. I obsess, even make deals with the Divine, saying, *if I say 250 Hail Marys, and help ten old ladies cross the street, can mine triple in size by next Sunday?* One day I whisper, *come on, Jesus Christo, work a miracle here on the family jewels, loaves to fishes, baby.*

One time I share my truth with my oldest friend, the Cape Cod Bay, figuring I will shout it underwater, that way no one— not even the priest—can learn of the exact and specific nature of my sins. That afternoon I go under the sea, hold my breath, grinding against Liam's outlandish genitals, feel the fire and shout, "When we push, it feels beyond anything in the world."

It feels like there are hidden springs bursting within my nether regions, propelling me into the stratosphere and sending me thousands of miles away to the Black Sea, where I will twist, flip, and dive and have wild, subaquatic *relations* with three voluptuous mermaids named Samantha, Lilith, and Priscilla, and they will teach me every damn trick they know. That they will let me grind them so silly I will have no need of Liam, he'll be old news, nothing but a worthless antique, or an ugly bump in the road.

Despite my real lust for the mermaids and the intensity of my dreams and most of the relaxation tapes in the Dennis and Limewood libraries combined, things continue on as before. It is the following summer when I notice Liam's dramatic changes, physically and emotionally, from the previous year. He now has multiple hairs under his arms and five on his chest—he counts those out to me early on. And his weightlifting regimen begins, and so he seems rougher, tougher.

At certain times, he taunts me and says things like: "Don't be afraid of every new thing I bring up for discussion, okay?"

I abhor admitting it to myself, but what we do together feels immensely pleasurable. For all his energy, he can be a near invisible, silent person. Next second, though, he tries to grind with me.

I try to speak with him once about his AWOL mom and he only cackles: "The concept of a matriarchal figure no longer exists in me, and with you, I only take what is being offered."

"You think I'm giving myself to you?" I ask. "What a load of crap."

"I knew you'd deny it, because you're naive, green, and fear truth," he says.

"Horse shit," I say, and he giggles. At times, we take long bike rides into the woods on my mom's and dad's old bicycles and grapple atop pine needles.

One day, Liam suggests we go further than ever. "We can't *ever* do that, man," I yell, harder than I must. "We can only wrestle."

"What are you so fearful of?" he asks. "Afraid you're a gay-boy or something?"

"No, of course not."

"Don't worry, you like girls," he says. "You just dig this, too, exactly like me."

Though I denied it forever, I remember knowing he spoke the truth on that summer day. I was probably a waffle-boy, but the lame, pathetic kind who won't admit it until they've got one foot in the grave. One time, Gracie says, "I think Liam has helped teach you to explore your sexuality, Danny. I don't know if I get any of the credit for that evolution, myself, but I'm happy for you, nonetheless."

LATER, A PHONE IS RINGING

"Is Liam around?"

"Danny Halligan? Are *you* calling *me* for the first time ever in the history of the world? Did someone die? Did you put Gracie in the hospital?"

"No, nothing like that."

"Okay, then what?"

"I've got a short story I wrote, Liam," I say. "It's about you. A fictional kid named Lars Gills, who's a great photographer and has a dead sister."

"How'd his sister croak?"

"She walked in front of a New Haven transit bus."

"Jesus," he said. "So, it's not a comedy, then."

"No," I say.

"I'll come over to get it," he said.

Nine minutes later, I watch him from the widow's walk and think, *his muscles appear to be growing night and day.*

"Why write a story for little old me, Danny?" he asks. "Is it an Irish insult to write about a piece of white trash like me?"

"*What?*" I say. "No, and you're not trash, don't ever say that."

"Well, it oozes off of my cousin Tommy," Liam says. "And my Pop, too."

"There's a world of difference between you, Liam, and your cousin and Pop."

"Thanks for saying that," Liam adds. "But what if I hate your story? I want you to know I'm not a huge reader, okay?"

"It's a short story, ten pages or so, typed and double-spaced."

"Gracie is going to have a shit-fit over it, don't you think?" he asks.

"Probably, but just take it away and get back to me in the morning."

"You sure I don't have to write anything back?"

"Positive," I say.

"Would you mind if I read it up in the palace's widow walk right now? On that little red chair? I love it up there."

"Where do I go while you read?" I ask.

"Off for a brisk run," Liam says. "Jog down to Chapin Beach and back, it's probably only two miles or so, and you're right, it's short, so run around for twenty-five minutes."

"Fantastic, so away I go," I say and leave Gramp's house, go past the numerous Capes along Wild Sands Road and Liam's dad's cottage, and soon I find myself running in the direction of Chapin Beach.

GOOFY CHILD

BY DANNY HALLIGAN

L ars always towered over me—from the first time we met as boys to the last time I saw him in Provincetown. Lars had me by two and a half years and was nine inches taller than me, as well, and dominated the wrestling matches we had in the dunes behind our cottage. He was a gangly kid with curly red hair, icy gray eyes, freckles, and a runny nose.

We sometimes retreated to private spots and bashed each other with pillows, water balloons, and Nerf bats with an intensity that only the newly adolescent could muster. He was fun, quirky, and kind of belonged to me, like an overly aggressive and manic pet.

My mom had offered to help his sister, Abigail, when she was hospitalized with schizoaffective disorder, and had fallen into nasty self-harm. Abby had been a brilliant student of my mother at Yale until she had several breakdowns before eventually stepping in front of a New Haven transit bus a day before her 23rd birthday. My mom had met Lars during Abby's schooling and multiple hospitalizations.

When she heard he was left without a family after his sister's death—Mom offered to take Lars in for the summers. He stayed at foster homes in the fall and winter, so we took him from May through the end of August in Truro. My mom explained that the three of us were practicing tangible Christian love and compassion in dire times. "God appreciates this terrifically, Ethan," Mom said.

"Lars lost nearly everyone in his life, pal," my dad said on the first night. "We're inviting the boy up to spend ten weeks at the Cape—he'll be your friend, okay?"

"No problem, Dad," I said.

"He loves photos, is what I hear," my father said. "A true lensman."

***

"I am the rightful, holiest, and most gregarious kingfisher in our history," Lars shouted during the second summer, tackling me in the dunes. When I came up coughing, he smiled. "I love that you're like my professional babysitter, Ethan."

Lars and I periodically sprinted past my folks into the ocean and lost our bathing suits and did it some more. He threw my shorts across the water and shouted, "Attention, lads and lasses of every shape, there are mortally sinful souls treading water in our midst." This caused my dad to signal to us from the blanket.

"That's enough, Lars. Wrap that type of behavior up now," he shouted.

"Okay, sir," he whispered and blew bubbles at me, his gray eyes dancing. "I'll wrap everything up." And so, he wrestled me again in the waist-high water and coiled his hips around me. That was the summer I noticed his dramatic changes—both emotionally and height-wise from the previous year. He had shot up over half a foot.

At certain times, Lars said, "No records set for you yet, huh, Ethan?" and I knew what he meant, but I turned away, embarrassed. I didn't especially like what he did with me, but I didn't hate it either. I loathed admitting it, but it felt pleasurable when we pushed against each other. As if an expanding velvet bubble would soon burst.

Another time, Lars pranced about with a fierce erection in his Jockeys, and I was half-stunned, half-punchy so I burst out laughing, until my dad knocked on the door and said, "Everything fine, Ethan and Lars?"

"Wonderful and woolly," Lars said. "We're solid, sir."

"Is that true, Ethan?" my father said. "I need to hear it from you, as well."

"I'm fine, Dad," I said. "No problems in this jurisdiction."

"Okay," my dad said. "Carry on, I guess."

"This Lars character is a pretty frivolous human being," I said.

"As long as it's an entertaining brand of frivolity," Dad said. "That's fine, that's fun, just don't cross over the border into terrifying. Are we clear, gentlemen?"

"Absolutely crystal clear, sir," Lars said.

"I hear you, Dad," I said.

"Good to know," my father said.

Sometimes it was uncomfortable and semi-scary what went down between us, but it was Lars, so it was okay. For all his energy, he could be a near invisible, silent presence; his eyes glazed over, perhaps pondering the phases of the moon. I had tried to speak with him once about the death of his sister, Abby, during our wrestling matches, but he only replied, "She isn't in my cranium anymore—she's long gone, vanished from the solar system."

"Be real with me, for once."

"Abigail's now Sunday brunch for local termites and fire ants."

"Christ, don't say that kind of thing, Lars."

"Give me a break, Ethan," he said. "Stop analyzing me... I have no wisdom to offer you—plus, that's not your job. You're here to keep me laughing, footloose, and fancy-free."

"Whatever you say, Lars," I said. "Just trying to lend a hand."

"I know, I know," he said. "Let's go for a swim, though."

"Superb," I said, and off we dashed. I didn't know how to respond, how to assist him. Once, I called him *Lying and Lascivious Lars* for his head games, but he hated that shit, and so I ceased. When I was around Lars, my tongue felt thick and hairy—my hearing hyper-sensitive, each scent in the universe shot straight up my nostrils, it shook me, shocked me. Staggered me around like I'd been dosed with a secret, foreign herb.

There were days I felt enraged and wanted to run a half-marathon up and down Mount Kilimanjaro in Tanzania or fly first-class to a fancy Hollywood personal trainer until I was strong, toned, and stunning. One late July night, Lars said, "I'll show you the coolest tricks in the history of banging flesh."

"Nothing too horn-dog, please," I replied.

"Why won't you taste of life and its many splendored fruits?" Lars asked.

"I'm a neurotic, jittery teenager," I said. "There's a fever in my bustling cerebrum, like it's World War III, okay? Perfectly naked, and multi-sexed bodies diving, swimming, swirling, and crashing around me left and right."

"Yeah," he said. "I think I've been on that block before."

Lars usually had his camera and snapped tons of shots of my folks lying together at the beach or of me waking up in the morning, hair all askew. He had a beautiful Nikon my dad had gifted him one Christmas. We went for walks through the dunes, and he posed for me—flexing my biceps, wearing oversized teal sunglasses with wax lips and edible necklaces, giggling away.

Once I had seedless green grapes that my mom had packed for us in Tupperware. The two of us drove around on the tandem bike until Lars found the ideal shot in Truro. I was tired of his grinding and constantly trying to provoke me, so I pushed him off as he head-butted me hard, splitting my lip, and sat back and laughed, taking photos as I threw grapes at him. "Buzz off," I screamed and CLICK-CLICK he took a picture of my face sucking on the grapes, bloody lips covered in juice, my white teeth exposed like fangs. Those shots won Lars some awards.

Lars spent the weekend in a hula skirt, pink bikini top, Mardi Gras beads, and clown shoes and confessed he planned to join a traveling circus that winter. He liked to hold my arms back in the sand and say "Swear on every Holy Bible in America that you won't let the pretty girls ruin you, okay, Ethan? Will you promise me to stay untouched?"

So, I swore for him and *promised my fealty forever.* That seemed like the best way of explaining my odd pal, Lars, to the globe, to anyone out there observing us from afar. I rarely understood him, but I'd stand with him no matter what. I'd even take a bullet for the guy too, which is overstated and melodramatic, I know, but I meant it. *Or at least, I think I did.*

On brighter days, Lars and I used to take afternoon rides past the colorful cottages, the shops in Provincetown, the wonderful food like saltwater taffy and gigantic lollipops, penny candy, and all the touristy gizmos. We never got tired of that; giggling or throwing the ball around; volleyball, Whiffle ball, Frisbee, touch football, every game in the book. Lars's version of fun was mostly innocent, you know? There was so much goodness and creativity rolling around inside that wonderful red head of his.

Early on in our summers of exploration, Lars vowed to protect me from all the golden, long-limbed lacrosse-playing girls in the neighboring cottages. We played the same old games, *Spin the Bottle* or *Truth or Dare,* but all Lars would say is, "I've been selected by his parents to keep this boy, Ethan, sparkly clean from you developing young women with your filthy minds," Lars lectured. "That's how it must be."

"Lars," I said later in front of the TV (*Charlie's Angels*), "I'd like to kiss a lot of girls this summer—I want to French kiss them before

I go home. And I'd love to nibble on their breasts, too, and find their magic buttons deep within."

"Would you like you to French kiss me instead or grab my perky tits?" Lars asked. "I know so much more, a whole hell of a lot of tricks."

"But you're not girls," I replied.

He slapped my face twice. "You're a manimal now and you've got to learn more than French kissing, numb-nuts," he said. "You've got to FUCK, Ethan. Say it!"

"Mom…"

"Fuck your ma!" Lars yelled. "Can you say that?" When he saw that I was hurt he started tickling me and then stopped. "Do you know what intercourse is, boy?" he asked. "Do you know that's what everyone does everywhere on this heinous blue-green globe?"

"Of course, I know that," I said.

"Lars Gills is the only true man in this town with a raw passion, a pulsing cock, and balls of steel," he shouted. "The rest of the world is strictly satanic placenta ripped from suicidal sisters!"

Lars sobbed then, before sprinting up the stairs and slammed the door to the guest room. Then my father emerged in his bathrobe. He was a short stocky man of forty-eight with a narrow face and little hair and his bathrobe was too long. A life-long attorney and CPA, my dad now appeared like he was floating across the wooden floor to comfort me. I grinned at this thought before asking him what was wrong with my friend.

He sat down on our navy-striped ottoman, rubbing his tired eyes. "Lars is breaking a bit, his mind is splintering, going a hundred different ways," he said. "He's still twisted around about his sister's death."

"Why can't he be through being sad?" I said. "Why can't he heal quicker?"

"Lars went into a hospital in April for an incident of self-harm."

"Why would he do such a thing?" I asked. "He belongs with his

96

camera and me, you, and Mom—they should just leave him be."

My father grimaced. "Watch over him, will you, Ethan? Lars needs people to watch over him with care, with love."

"Absolutely," I promised. "I'll vow to keep him secure, Dad."

"Yes," my dad said, smiling slightly, and then stood up. He kissed the crown of my head quickly. "Keep him secure." I watched my father shuffle back towards the bedroom.

"Dad?"

"Yeah, pal?"

"How did Lars hurt himself?"

My dad stopped outside the bedroom door and looked at the ceiling before speaking. "He sliced off two of his fingers with a paper cutter after school," he said.

"Holy shit," I said.

I watched my father turn and study me for a reaction. I tried not to act too shocked. "Was it his focus and click fingers?" I asked.

"*What?*"

"The fingers he injured, were those the ones he uses to focus the lens and work the Nikon?"

My father smiled. "No," he said. "Lars severed two fingers on his left hand, but surgeons successfully reattached both, nerves and all."

"So, he still shoots fine?" I asked.

"Yes," he said. "He still shoots perfectly fine."

***

During the winters, Lars Gills used to call me from different psychiatric hospitals around the country. "I'm on a wild tour of this proud land," he'd explain with panache. "Back in the Bay Area, or the Berkshires, or Baltimore."

He said he knew when it was time for him to come in for *a tune-up*. "My obsessions are severe kicks to my failing limbic system," he said. "I know my thoughts and mania aren't going to settle down unless I get some ECT or am adequately sedated."

"Right," I said.

"The turning point was these visions of little kids that got me," he said. "I hung around a maternity ward in San Francisco and looked at all the teeming life—so serene and I got decent photos of women cuddling and rocking drug-addicted babies for a month. It brought me to tears—truthful ones."

"That's great," I said.

"That's what I felt, too," Lars said. "I used up most of my film on them. But when I took the bus ride home every evening, I saw these suspicious trash bags blowing and whipping all around in the street. I stopped and got off the bus and ran over to see if there were any babies inside."

"I don't get it," I said. "Why would there be?"

"I was positive that each trashcan was filled with dead infants," Lars said.

I paused and said, "Okay."

"Each time the city transit bus hit a manhole cover or a pothole," he said, "I thought there were more babies dying. I thought it was my fault—that I'd be arrested for mass-murder."

"Lars," I said. "Do you want to tell me why, man?"

"Hard to explain, Ethan," he said. "You don't know how many times I say that reply now. It's hard to articulate, Dr. Jude, Dr. Alicia, or Dr. Tim, blah, blah. OCD, schizoaffective disorder, my delusional and psychotic depression takes over. I was so sure that we were popping heads underneath the tires of city transit buses. One minute I was fine and next there were nothing but purple, bloated cadavers through my viewfinder."

"I'm so sorry, Lars," I said. "I wish it wasn't so rough on you."

"I can already tell what the shrinks are thinking—I'm a has-been before I'm even legally allowed to drink a beer. Plus, I'm running out of cash—administrators are going to suck out every penny I've got left. When I'm completely broke, they'll kick me out, boot me to some lousy state hospital."

"My parents will always help, Lars," I said.

"I can't take any more money from you or your parents," he said. "Plus, your folks sold their cottage—I know they're economically hurting. Everyone is in this economy. There's not much point to it, you know?"

He cleared his throat several times.

"What is it?" I asked.

He spoke quietly and kept coughing. I wasn't sure if he was whispering or crying. "My sister Abigail was a brilliant young woman, funny and hyper-aware of her surroundings."

"Yeah?" I said, stunned. He had never mentioned his deceased sister in years, not in a serious way, at least.

"That young lady wasn't some empty basket case who made a horrible decision on a rainy, tragic morning in New Haven," he continued. "She had standards, understand?"

"She was clinically depressed, Lars," I said.

"I say bullshit to all that, Ethan," he said. "She was analytical and planned it out like a mathematician. Made a list of pros and cons in her life and then stepped in front of the city bus."

"Abby was a gravely mentally ill young woman," I said.

Lars made a clucking noise. "I don't think that as much now," he said. "I believe Abby did what she had to do."

"She was delusional."

"I disagree," he said. "Abby used to tell me how agonized she was over putting me in a group home when she was struggling at Yale—I never understood it before and maybe now I do."

"And what's that, Lars?"

"Don't you see? Perhaps she did it for my... protection, my knowledge." He was quiet for a few seconds. "To save me from beating myself up too much now, like an encrypted message—a shadowy trail to follow when it came my time to go."

***

Lars has been gone from my life ever since. He never returned to the tip of the Cape, never phoned, not even sent a damn postcard to my parents. Sometimes I imagine meeting him again ten or fifteen years down the road, reconnecting, talking about our strange, intertwined lives. Trying to unearth our long-buried hurts, bonds, and joys. Somehow, no matter how many ways I shape the tale, my mind's eye can't recoup what was lost.

Maybe we will meet at the Provincetown ferry and awkwardly embrace, and perhaps he will ask me to pose for more photos in Truro. "Sorry, Lars, I can't," I tell him, voice quivering. "I can't spend my life being defined by your silly lens—I must concentrate on me now." I watch his face drop. "I'm trying to find a direction in life, okay?"

"Did you say *silly lens*?" Lars says. "You won't let me shoot you for three damn days? Fast, easy cash—I've got a great connection in Boston, and this is my chance to get back in the big-time."

"I don't think we can recapture the raw spirit," I say. "It was fleeting."

"Nothing's gone, man," Lars says, bristling. "It's all right here between us... so what if it's been several years? We've always got that special connection, right?"

No matter how I tell myself the story, I always end up discovering him the next morning. I weep as I phone 9-1-1. My first thought is that *this will follow me to my grave*. I feel guilty about that reaction, but what can be done about such rabid thoughts? The mind is a fragile and peculiar organ—you want it to go to the sublime photos of the split lip, green grapes, and blood or the laughter of friends on tandem bikes as we catch the dusk light ricocheting off the Pilgrim Tower.

Instead, you wind up elsewhere.

A PHONE RINGS AGAIN...

"Why'd you run home?" I ask when Liam will answer his phone later. "You were last seen reading my story on the roof."

"I freaked out," he says. "Your story blew me away, though, Danny."

"Yeah?"

"Knocked my frigging socks off," he says. "Do folks still say that?"

"You just did," I say.

"See you in three minutes," he says, and Liam soon shows up on his ten-speed bike, jumps off, and hustles up the stairs and into my tree fort.

"I'm beat," he says, collapsing on the navy beanbag chair. Shirtless, he only wears blue jeans, and his muscular frame fits them snug, along with his prominent-as-ever-veins. He watches me study him.

"Were you just lifting weights?" I ask, and he nods.

"I knew you'd appreciate the effort," he says.

"Old predictable Danny Halligan, that's me," I say, thinking, *what the hell do I do with myself now that he really likes me?*

"'Goofy Child' featured my raging hormones, but also my hurt," he says.

I nod.

"It also spoke of my kindness and a gentle understanding," he says. "Since my mom left ten years ago... Tommy buys me only a single beer at Christmas, Pop and I drink cheap scotch together."

"Bleak holiday traditions," I say.

"My point is Lars's story moved me greatly, touched me," he says, rising to his feet. "Which means of course, *you moved me*, Danny, *you touched me. It was the best gift I ever received.*"

"I'm flattered," I say.

"Let's get there this summer, okay?" Liam says. "Baby steps, incremental growth... *but somewhere.*"

I nod again.

"Thanks for not quitting on me," Liam says. "It'll get easier, I promise."

I smile.

"I'm ashamed by last Labor Day with Tommy," he says. "*Inexcusable what we did to you.*"

"A crime," I say with a bitter taste in my mouth. I want to hold on to some of this bitter, seething rage that I know I *should* own, but I also keep thinking, *I want to get closer and closer to this gentleman—he's been a wonderful surprise!*

"True," he says.

"But where the hell is my original ten typed pages of 'Goofy Child?'"

"Under my mattress," he says. "You'll get it tomorrow, although may I ask, do you really think I'll die tragically?"

"It's a story, pure fiction, Liam. Just pretend," I say.

"It was kind of cool to die metaphorically, though," he says, swooping in and kissing the crown of my head before exiting the tree fort.

"What's that for?" I ask.

"A proper appreciation of a talented Wolf-Boy," Liam shouts, and soon he's on his ten-speed bike, disappearing around Gramps's massive hydrangea bushes.

"So long, pal," I say to no one.

DETAILS, DETAILS...

I had my first manic episode when I read about Mom's death in *Time* magazine in Gramps's attic at nine years old one summer. Pure terror at first, of course, but as I sobbed about my dead, napping mom, I was soon dancing and laughing minutes later, shouting and clapping my hands. "Randy, Gramps," I called down the stairs. "Come to the attic, it's wonderful, Mom was a star, forever preserved on black-and-white film. She's only napping, just taking a short rest, I think."

"What'd you get into, buddy?" Randy called, running up the stairs.

"Do you think I'll be a star, too?" I asked. "They said nice things about my necklace I made for Mom when I was four."

"Oh, pal," Randy said. "They said it was a sweet and heart-breaking gift."

"Does that mean I'm not going to be a star?"

"Not exactly. You're too young right now, anyway," Randy said.

"What about Shirley Temple, though?" I asked.

Whatever the medical, religious, or scientific explanations

offered, the photo somehow retained Mom's charm and ethereal beauty. For me, who'd been kept in the dark about Mom's life and death ever since I was four, it was like my first Christmas. I tore into each maternal fact I unearthed as if it was gifted from Santa himself.

The next day, Randy drove me up to the Dennis Public Library across from the old cemetery and firehouse. "Why are we here?"

"Your Ma's photo, odd, Miriam," Randy said, voice hoarse. "Napping like, sister's affect, dead? No, you know? Was she in shock, her head, couldn't her face be out or figure, a brain sleep, days no luck for me, struck down, gone."

"Why are you acting so strangely?" I asked Randy. "Your voice is off too."

"Sometimes when I think or talk about your mom dying," he said. "It gets muddied in my brain, and I feel at a loss for words. I sound like a fool. I get mixed up."

"I get it, Randy," I said. "Same thing happens to me when I feel too sad."

"Yeah, see, I didn't understand why my lovely sister looked so damn content and perfect after she died on the cover of Time magazine," he said. "So, a shrink told me—"

"What's a shrink again?" I asked.

"Helpful but expensive doctors for your mind," Randy said. "I was told about an engaged, twenty-something-year-old bookkeeper in *Life* magazine named Evelyn McHale."

"She died?" I ask.

"On Monday, May 12, 1947, she leapt from the observation deck on the eighty-sixth floor of the Empire State Building. *Life* named her *most beautiful suicide*."

"You visited there with mom, right?" I asked.

"We had a minor sweet sixteen bash, Miriam and I," he said. "We won the raffle at a church carnival the summer before, so we stayed at a fancy hotel, and Eileen bought these snazzy, expensive cupcakes. Gramps and Eileen celebrated. It was so damn cold that we ran back inside, and later caught a Christmas Show with the Rockettes at Radio City Music Hall."

Inside the Dennis Public Library, it smelled of leather-bound books, dust, caramel candies, and too much vinegar. An older librarian in a cinnamon skirt with orange nail polish and tan lipstick passed the *Life* magazine to Randy and me. My hands were damp as I touched the librarian's palms, and my mouth, bone dry.

"Look how beautiful, Randy," I said, studying Evelyn McHale's body sprawled atop a crushed taxi, her string of pearls and long white gloves, her face lovely and untouched, like she was asleep. "All she needs is a kiss from a prince, right?"

"Whatever works, I guess," Randy said.

"Did the *Life* magazine lady's body fall apart?" I asked.

"Like everyone," Randy said. "Like Miriam, just like your mom."

"I wish I never saw the damn lady in *Life*," I told him. "Too much sadness."

"I'm so sorry," Randy said. "I hoped it would help you some, Danny."

"No, it does, it does a little... but it's a lonesome shot."

"Yes," Randy said. "Of course."

FINAL POLAROID OF THE
SEASON

G ramps loved to throw a huge bash at the end of each summer, and my father drives down and tries to be a good sport at it. The last fete of the season is the biggest and Gramps has a new title as Labor Day fast approaches. *The Absolute Final Shindig* is the hottest ticket, or so Buck claims the summer I turn ten. He announces the party on Bay View Beach with a bullhorn, claiming Gramps's annual soiree is as American as apple pie, Lincoln Continentals, and the Boston Red Sox.

Gramps says humans of every race, creed, political party, and sexual persuasion are welcome, but one must drink responsibly and leave $12 at the door, which gets passed around to teens in charge of parking and trash and waste disposal and a couple bartenders from a restaurant up the street.

"Everyone helps out everyone else" is one of Buck's favorite mantras. "Makes the world go round, lubricates the wheels of our big engine around here called life."

I'm prepubescent and singularly obsessed with a Polaroid Instamatic that Randy gifted me two years earlier, so I take photos hourly and seriously, trying to act like an artiste who exists above the fray. Which I define as being profoundly detached and oozing skill and wisdom from every damn pore on my little body. It's before Liam and I start hanging around, so I'm still green and naive as all get out.

Festivities begin early with a pancake contest between local dads in the neighborhood—blueberry, banana, chocolate, onion-boysenberry—every combination is welcome. One event tumbles into the next, and after lunch some play eighteen holes of golf up at Dennis Pines while others go home to take naps or borrow one of our couches for their siestas or try our hammocks in the backyard.

Before long, it's mid-afternoon, and people slowly develop their second wind, singing along to Jimmy Buffet tunes with their mellow mates. There are burger-eating contests prepared by local chefs at supper, volleyball and touch football in the front yard, games of hide and seek, kick the can, and truth or dare, and drink after tropical drink, including Shirley Temples and Virgin Pina Coladas for the kids.

There are sparklers and bottle rockets, and people ooh and ah as roman candles do their thing. Gramps welcomes a jazz quartet from Hyannis to play from our back porch starting around six. "Let's kick this thing into overdrive, ladies and gens," he says, as the band begins to swing. "The evening is still young."

At twilight, the perimeter of our property is draped in white, purple, and green miniature lights with strategically placed lanterns keeping the black flies and mosquitoes far away. Kids toast marshmallows in a fire pit out back, observing their moms, dads, aunts, and uncles stumbling and giddy with their favorite spirits. They hug one another, giggling, and wander into the kitchen to grab a glass and say, *"I'll have whatever she's having."*

Our place and pace are electric and throbbing, and it feels festive, and later my dad starts introducing himself to guests as the ghost of Mr. *Gatsby, visiting from out of town, investigating green lights spotted off the back porches.* Someone explains to Buck that it was green light off of Daisy's dock, and without the ocean, the story falls apart.

Other adults sway to the tunes, while older teens climb into my deluxe tree palace and guzzle beers, kiss, and pet with one another and sneak a joint. Near the end of the soiree, younger kids get cranky and tired, and I chase all the weed smokers out of my damn palace and grab my Polaroid Instamatic and prepare for the final Polaroid of the season. I watch my dad, Gramps, Eileen, and Randy shuffling around the bash down below, fanning out to find food, booze, or chatter like fire ants tracking prey.

I climb up high on the roof, balancing myself on the arms of the Adirondack chair, and take the Polaroid, shaking it on purpose, catching the electric colors and moonlight spilling into the lanterns, blurring into the fireworks, pooling into the chapped, sunburned faces, and on and on.

To others, it looks like an unfocused, throw-away shot, exactly what they'd expect from a diminutive and shy ten-year-old, but to me it's precisely what I was after. Randy told me I was the slyest dude on the globe for seeking out the unseen, the in-between, a photographic equivalent of a riddle.

I came to learn Gracie was skilled, her angles were precise, and she was gifted with both portraits and nature shots. Her peach cottage in Truro was always set for *Architectural Digest* to stroll right in and start snapping up complimentary shots, admiring everything about her, fawning left and right.

And yet, sometimes the most glaring truth about a force like Gracie was that when I did meet her, six years beyond this end-of-summer bash, which was created by Gramps and promoted by Buck, she was already a storm, a perpetual disturbance picking up speed and fuel and rage. Gracie Rose was like a big budget magician out of Las Vegas, skilled with sleight of hand and every sort of trickery. Perhaps if I had learned that lesson a lot earlier, I wouldn't have risked my life to impress her so much in 1979. To become so damn devoted to her cause, almost killing myself along the way.

FIRST EXTRAVAGANZA

In the early days of our relationship in '79, I was full steam ahead with Gracie and didn't want to hear anyone's gossip or dirt about her. Despite her and I having engaged in every type of intimacy save the final one, I'm so hyped up to *officially* lose my status as a virgin, so centered on that act, I go for a long run to drain energy. I shower and listen to Lou Reed. I'm still not sold on him, but I know Gracie will love that, and I watch a Red Sox-Yankee pregame on my tiny TV.

Randy gives his blessing, says he's willing to look the other way, and offers me a couple six-packs of Schlitz to enjoy. Although I try to behave as if nothing out of the ordinary is occurring in my young life, I feel my body and brain roiling, speeding about. I ooze need and absorb the universe with increased *everything*.

Racing thoughts, blurry faces, and images hurtling my way —melodies, birdsong, snarling car engines, booze, potions, wild twirling and bleeding shades of mustard, cobalt, chestnut, vermilion, and melon. Plus, the death of Dad's favorite actor, John Wayne, and the usual Hollywood fare, Liam's unceasing supply of porn, the myopic American political system, jiggling bikinis, barking dogs, hissing cats, spraying skunks, even sightings of great white sharks off Chatham.

All of it forms a great gob of energy and it blows against my body like a gale, and my response is to open wide and suck in every bit of it. Like a frenzied force released into my nervous system, it cannot be denied and demands to move forward, to assert. Soon, it takes over—sprinting, swimming, dancing, working, laughing, jabbing, punching, kissing, grinding, screwing, and embracing everything in its path. And when Gramps and Eileen head to Boston for a two-day high school reunion event, the palace is free.

We planned it the night before. I spend the early part of the day cleaning the tree fort, moving the beanbag chair to the corner and putting all of the other chairs and stools on the second level. Gracie shows up at noon. I'm two-beers in when I hear voices laughing outside, and soon Liam and Gracie stand in the doorway with a bulging white canvas bag on Liam's shoulder.

I wobble as I watch them, feeling anxious. Gracie has told me I need only a towel, which I've wrapped around me, though with Liam there, I feel awkward, stupid. Just when I'm ready to ask Liam to scram, Gracie says she wants to take photos of the two of us.

"I need you both naked," she says, "but with masks to protect your priceless youth—it'll carry you far, clear of any litigation for me, as well, I hope."

"That's cool," Liam says and slips off his T-shirt and bathing suit. Gracie grins, and Liam closes his eyes, and they share a joint. The whole thirty-second interaction seemed ridiculously rehearsed, so I backed away. I think, *no, whatever kind of show this is, she can forget it—*

"Listen, Danny," Gracie says, exhaling a lot of smoke my

way. "Hear me for a minute. This is what we spoke of, we'll have a blast, *plus* we had a deal—"

"Yeah, but—"

Gracie holds her palm up. "Don't waste time," she says, her breath tickling my ear and neck. "I know my damn lens will lead us home."

"I'm sort of afraid of your camera lens," I say. "What it'll do to my little life."

"No need to fear it," she says. "I mean, what type of camera do you like to use?"

"Polaroid Instamatic," I say." Randy got it for me several years ago."

"In a way, it's just like mine but more magical, too," Gracie says.

"Yeah?"

"Sure," she says. "You can zoom anywhere you wish with that camera around your neck, Danny. It's wildly sweet, like a tropical, wonderfully juicy treat from the rain forest to sink your teeth into whenever you feel the urge. And there's not much to fear with that private investigator at your side—it entertains, protects, and comforts you when lonely, it allows you to peer into other people's travesties without too much anguish. It steals souls and secrets, offers some distance if you wish, it solves age-old mysteries."

"Truly?"

"Utterly and completely—it aids those who need it," she says. "Frankly, it's one hell of an invention. And you can become so powerful, so in tune with all the living souls around you. I want you to feel the strength, the momentum, the power you possess with the lens around your neck."

"Still," I say. "I'd rather not become involved here with your trio."

Liam closes his eyes and walks towards me then as if on

cue, and I feel a churning in my gut, an awareness of my need, my inherent, riotous desire for him, like a freaking magnet. My shame is easing up. I want his electric body beside me, near me, on me.

It's at that point when Gracie says a few sentences I've played over in my mind a million times since.

"Will you get naked for me, my love?" she says, and then: "What if I undressed, too? Will you stay, Danny, and show me your *God Stain* on this lovely Friday, June 8, 1979?"

I blush, instantly aroused, and step toward her, pushing Liam out of the way.

Gracie slips out of her simple lemon sundress, and her body is ripe, her legs, muscular and so tan. Her breasts are the size of my palms, tiny delights.

"Divine!" I nearly shout.

She's tan, a coiled and lovely young lady at her best. Somehow, when I wasn't with her, she's grown more bronzed. It's only been two days since she took the photos of me in Truro, but she has somehow *improved*.

"Trust me, angel," she says. "It'll be so sweet and easy."

Soon she gives me more beer, unwraps the towel, and touches me, my belly and chest, before kissing my neck. I almost lose it, overwhelmed by the sensation of her lips. Somehow at the same time, Liam's pressing against her backside.

"I can only have alcohol," I say. "Can't do any drugs, understand?"

Gracie smiles peacefully at my comment, neither agreeing nor disagreeing. At the same time, she has Liam setting up a few lights, hooking up plugs and placing white canvas along the far wall of the palace as she kisses me. There's a drawing on the canvas of a giant turquoise eye staring at me, leering, seeing deep within. Gracie blows smoke in my face, and I giggle. I look around—the fort is wide so there's plenty of room, but I feel stretched out, as if my mind has sprung a wonderful, spastic leak. It's expanding, falling, even splintering, and *I feel supremely stretched and elongated,* I think.

"Easy, now, Danny," she says and takes her time kissing.

"My head is starting to relax," I say and laugh out loud. *How frigging weird.* My mind races. *How amazing she looks in this dappled sunlight.*

She kisses my belly. Liam wants to get involved and she whispers, "Not yet, not yet, Liam, be patient, wait, please wait a bit longer."

"You both look like Norse Gods today," Gracie whispers in a reverent manner. "And I always wanted to photograph Norse Gods."

I don't believe for a second I look like a Norse God, but if she wants to say that, in such a throaty, hungry manner, well then, that's cool. Today, there's a lovely naked Yale student feasting on me, and I'm a sixteen-year-old honorary Norse God.

At first, it's embarrassing to be naked around Liam, but I get used to it, not exactly gym class at the high school, but I roll with it. And the more I relax, the more I stretch out, listening to an old tune, Van Morrison's "Domino" on the stereo, the sweeter and richer I feel. The song was originally released in October of 1970, but it's like I'm hearing it for the first time.

It reminds me of rain falling, pouring, plunging, and streaming down into the mud, into a silvery-blue lake, covered with fat old lily pads. The chubby leaves are heavy, clotted with rain, with dew and with romance. Eventually, the water leads to the river, and days later, it rushes onto the swirling sea. It's raining deep, emerald drops into the turbulent and slamming wild blue-green ocean. A howling, magnificent storm is crashing around me with its plip-plop, drip-drop on a tin roof above me, the waves on the sea crash around us, and I guzzle more alcohol, unsure of exactly what I'm imbibing.

I'll never smoke any weed; I tell myself again. *I'll refuse it, just alcohol, that's it.*

That said, the smell and smoke of weed is everywhere in the palace, with Gracie and Liam blowing it back and forth, so I do end up getting some of it, *a contact high,* Gracie says. The *leftovers* is how Liam puts it, and that smoke singes my throat in the most wonderful way—the stench of it is fruity, rich, and I feel far away, numb, but also strong.

The wolf mask Gracie slips on me then is different from the first one we used in Truro—it's thicker with fur and eyes and mouth holes, and she says, "Let's play little Red Riding Hood, Danny," and "You're my growling Wolf-Boy." After a few minutes, she pushes her tongue through the mouth hole and climbs on me.

Gracie and I are laughing, enjoying every minute, and somehow, before long we bond. What did they call it in the olden days? Merging? Making whoopee, maybe? Belly bouncing? Boinking? Beast with two backs? The hunka-chunka? Horizontal mambo? *Who knows, I guess? Who truly cares?* But whatever the precise term is, we take part in it and excel.

Gracie's still taking pictures of both her and me, pointing the camera everywhere—up at the skylight, directly at my wolf head, swirling around the palace. Liam pushes himself against Gracie's neck, and occasionally, she turns her head and nuzzles him.

I have a general idea of what to do with Gracie, but she makes it seem easy, so musical, *lyrical, really,* and bathed in sunlight, with perspiration on her upper lip, the slope of her neck like some deep, sweet, smooth piece of mahogany, her magnificent flesh. A healing, rushing feeling pushes me

onward, something that if it could be spelled out would read
lovesweattearsromancejuice.

I get the hang of it before too long. Her belly is slick, and
she's growling, a humming, purring feline, a really happy one.
A noise that sounds like half yodel, half howl. And then,
quickly, the most luscious and wild finale rushes through me.

"Holy, holy crap," I say, and they both laugh. "Holy, holy,
Christ Almighty."

My heart roars in my chest, my heart pulses, and I want to
scream. I count my breaths, look around and smile. *Now, that
was fun,* I think, blinking my eyes. I swear I see pigeons flutter
in the corner of the palace, their gentle, graying wings teasing
my scalp as they rise and burst through the skylight. I put my
head down on the rug and watched Gracie shift towards Liam.

I feel drowsy, liquid, and light, but I also find it enormously
cool to watch two people merging, banging away. I'm so frigging close to the action, and it's unlike any of Liam's dirty, ugly
raunchy movies I've seen over the years. As I guzzle more alcohol, Liam makes a growling sound, and Gracie appears to
almost weep.

My earlier jealousies float away so fast. I watch transfixed
as Liam's considerable gifts disappear inside Gracie, and
quickly reappear, and disappear. The two of them seem more
practiced than me, but it doesn't ruffle my feathers too much.

The contrast of Liam's pale skin and her tan body is breathtak-
ing. A part of me feels I should be ashamed, but most of me soaks
up the scene—I soon find myself interested again. I want to touch
both but hold back. Yet, I can't stop studying, drooling, watching.
Eventually, maybe twenty minutes later, with deep, magnificent
sounds from both Gracie and Liam, they arrive at a stiller pace.

I think, *languid—somehow, this wild, funky afternoon has
turned languid.*

Four minutes later, Gracie pushes me back on the rug and starts taking pictures of Liam and myself. She takes photos of each of us with a brilliant flash. I realize I still have the humid wolf's mask on. She gets close and whispers, "I love your God's Stain, angel, it's so spacy and organic, and it pulses, just like you."

Next, her camera appears in her hand, but so does a remote for the one she sets up on the tripod across the way. Both cameras take shot after shot, and soon Liam and I are both on the rug, Liam smoking a joint. Our feet are touching, our bodies apart. I am guzzling away on Gracie's potion like some fabulously fatigued farmer after a long day shearing Shetland sheep.

I feel thirsty and hungry at the same time, and I look around at my transformed tree fort, the canvas walls dominated by the turquoise eye, a gigantic pupil and cornea. Everywhere I look, I see the eye studying me, measuring, gauging. *Cool, I think, slightly freaky, though mostly frigging cool, but wait, did the eye just blink? What does that mean? What does that eye want from me? Will there be payback down the line for these fleshy grooves and transgressions?*

The music changes and turns back into "Walk on the Wild Side." I want to complain to Gracie that I already have heard enough of this damn Lou Reed song and that it confuses me, I don't *quite get it*, but I know that will be the wrong comment, so I hum along instead.

I feel my head rushing off somewhere as Liam keeps reaching out. He keeps blowing his smoke at me and whispers something about these perfect days.

"We're enjoying this thanks to my father's magically sweet and decadent pharmaceutical habits," he says. Gracie shushes him.

"What?" I say, falling backwards, laughing, so far away, not caring, just feeling wonderfully pleased. Gracie has Liam slip into a cheap Lone Ranger mask she picked up from a K-Mart in Hamden, Connecticut, same place she bought the different Wolf-Boy facades. I see billowing smoke escape from Gracie's mouth in a pattern that seems like the most brilliant cloud of smoke ever. I see the shape of a tortoise and a partridge in a pear tree in the smoke—this made me giggly, free-floating, and I bask in the sensations.

My head spins and I see Gracie's most brilliant, gapped-toothed smile, and she blows me a giddy kiss, and I reach out for it. *It's not Christmas*, I think, *and I'm laughing at an astute and smoky partridge in a pear tree while weird stuff goes on all around me. How whacked is this wild-ass day?*

Liam gives me more liquid, and it's so good. I lay back. One part of my mind panics, thinking, *this is way out of bounds, people, this is way out of bounds,* but the other part welcomes everything flying my way. I feel far away, drifting off, floating into the sky, but I also sense heat, and can hear a drum roll, though it's not music exactly, and maybe it's way down, *within* me, submerged in my gut somewhere. I'm up on the ceiling like Spiderman, and yet I'm flat on the shag rug of my palace, the fabric is so soft, and it holds me, nearly cradles me. I close my eyes and listen to Gracie's whispers, which tickle my ear lobes.

"Don't be afraid, Danny Boy, don't be afraid to explore all this ever changing and evolving world we are born into," and soon she's touching us both, but shooting photos, as well. She's both in the shots and out of them. She's dancing, spinning, and crouching beside us, like a cool angel, or devil, can't really figure it all out right now, one thing I do learn is how Gracie can play a thousand roles, she's the best shapeshifter I ever meet.

What's happening with Liam and my body is new, and it lights a fire, and I fear it, mostly terrified, but curious about it, too, and so I welcome the naked need, the newness, the outstanding surprise of me touching him. It's like a surprise party in the hot sun, in late June, and the world is in a very giving mood, there is no angry Mother Nature today or tonight, sure, there's a handful of tragic DUI car accidents, or a few great white sharks spotted off Chatham, or trouble in Israel and Palestine, but our local world is damn calm and groovy. No twisters, no hurricanes, no spewing volcanoes or sink holes in the backyard. Nothing but fun for me, for us. I ask myself; do you want to touch that? Or have you ever kissed one of those? It's unique, it's wonderful, and it fills me up, so I swell with pride.

What does it all mean? I wonder. *What will it look like later? Will I be happy or sad? Up or down? I absorb Liam's phenomenal veins again, in his arms and hands, they are about to burst from his skin and seize me, take me down low where I don't want to go, but then I think why not? Life is one sizable flesh dance and it's our duty to embrace it, so bring on every goddamned vein in the book, big and small, thick or thin, and on or off.*

"Give me every vein you got," I imagine saying to Liam, but I blush, that's too much, I think to myself, but then I think of Carly Simon's "You're So Vain," and I realize I made a musical pun so I shake and dance and say to myself, "Why young man, aren't you the most clever and sexually promiscuous cat in town?"

"Seems like old times, don't it, boys?" Gracie observes, grinning, taking more photos. Gracie says something like, "I need to hear the growling inside Danny," and so I growl, I bark. I call out, "Gracie, Gracie Rose," and she laughs and starts crooning like she just got off the boat from Dublin, "*Oh, Danny boy, the pipes, the pipes are calling...*"

I want only to please this bundle of life, this wicked Yale dropout with the killer smile and lovely shape, and hands down, the most charismatic person I've ever met. I mean, *there's no doubt on that topic, no one has even come close to her, who in the world could ever top this super-sensuous lady?* Gracie's a divine, transplanted Palo Alto mystic chick, and she howls along to the music, but somehow, it's harmonic howling, a musical, rhapsodic kind of sound.

I feel like a dog in heat, a wild panther in a zoo escaping the clutches of an evil keeper and hurtling through a swath of cottony branches in a lush and golden rain forest. I see gigantic lady bugs with Kelly-green top hats and ruby slippers dancing on my nose, speaking with me, whispering, "Gosh, you really get around, Wolf-Boy." I want to do so many things as Gracie continues to dance and touch me, Liam, herself, everyone. A part of me wants to yell "Hip, hip, hooray" or "I'm so goddamned sorry, Daddy." But at that moment, the ladybug voices start to lecture me: *How could you let this happen, you trampy, loose skunk? You're the weakest link, Danny Hal, and don't doubt that your Buck will be furious.*

I think, *who cares? Who really cares?* I see more flashes of Gracie's dueling cameras, and it's like stars are bursting both inside and outside of my skull, and I'm swaying from all that's going on, and I feel like a movie star with the cameras flashing everywhere, so I sign a few autographs and pose for a picture with a beaming young fan.

Soon I feel a great amount of pressure on top of me, Liam somehow absorbs me into his wonderful frame, and as the cameras keep twinkling, and the voices pick up, the smoke, the booze, it eventually falls away, and starts to recede ever so slightly.

Pace eases at that point, and most of the movement, eventually, slows down. I'm exhausted, so I roll over and close my eyes, listening to my heart, my breath and feel my stomach groan and gurgle. I take fifty seconds, slowly counting them out in whispers. My body's filled with two main schools of thought —exhaustion and hunger.

God, I'm so damn hungry.

I study the ceiling through the wolf mask and feel partially safe, protected, and sheltered for the moment. It's sweaty, sticky, but I'm in a cocoon. I look up at the skylight and listen to the early afternoon sounds. I hear songbirds beyond the stereo. A chainsaw is groaning, some local carpenters are doing their best, hammers banging away, plus a helicopter zipping across the sky.

I feel panicked but sleepy. After what seems like a few days, Gracie crouches and kisses my neck, before slowly removing the wolf mask. I feel like I'm going to faint, so thirsty, and my body feels thick. *Dense.* My forehead burns, chafed by the mask. I even feel like sobbing, fully worn out.

"You're the top of the heap, my dearest angel," she says. "Most profound Wolf-Boy I've ever met in my young life."

I try to smile, but my whole frame feels *worn out.* Gracie's still taking shots of the light and the shadows, humming to the music, twisting, shaking left and right. The whole experience has hurt me terribly but grows to be a matter-of-fact kind of pain. If I saw an old-fashioned contract listing the various acts that our trio would be undertaking together that summer, would I repeat everything? Would I do it all again? If I were being honest, I'd say, "Yeah, sure... why not? I mean, really, who on earth does it hurt?

Eventually, Gracie stands eerily still, gazing down at Liam and myself with a sly grin. She hands us Dixie cups of iced tea, four orange slices a piece, and turns the music off. Gracie sneezes, giggles, rubs her bare left thigh and says: "Well, well, my wily wonder boys, that went a hell of a lot smoother than I thought it would."

LUMINOUS TANGERINE LIZARDS

The time I clobber myself with Mom's wooden plaque, I'm treated at a medical hospital for ten stitches, another concussion. It's only ten miles from Spruce Lodge.

"Time to smarten up, okay, bud," a resident says when he finishes the sutures on my head, "they told me about your history—psychosis, concussions, and flashbacks. The more you punch yourself, Danny, less of a decent life you'll have. Bottom line."

"Okay," I say.

"You'll be sent back in the morning to Spruce Lodge," he says.

"Thanks," I say.

"Life can't be that goddamned awful for you, can it?" he says and walks away, not waiting for my answer. But then the MD stops, pivots, and hurries back at me, his face real flushed now. "If I had one tenth of the chances you've had in your life, I'll tell you right now..."

"Sorry?" I said, pulling away from him slightly. "*What?*"

"You'll recuperate at The Lodge now, correct?" he asks.

I nod at him, head pounding.

"Anyone who can afford a stay at Spruce Lodge," he goes on, "has a lot more opportunities than most people in the entire world get, you should know that kid, okay?"

"Yes," I managed. "Right, whatever you say, sir..."

"All you do is drink, drink, drink and give yourself concussions, right?" he says. "You don't care, all you do is take, take, take, take, you poor little decrepit Danny..."

"*Doctor?*" a young nurse says. Amber Ruiz is a slim Latino woman with bright orange and blue fingernails, and she comes over to me. "Anything you'd like to share with me, the charge nurse tonight, Doctor? That is not how we treat or speak to our patients here, Doctor, are we clear on that?"

The doctor shakes his head, flushing.

"I'm finished with Danny, here, Nurse Amber Ruiz," he says. "*Done forever.*"

They offer me the oddest meal after that—a dry BLT sandwich, two radishes, green beans, grapefruit juice, spinach, a kiwi, butterscotch pudding, applesauce, and chocolate milk. It's like the dietitian couldn't decide between something good for you or a caloric feast.

Later, they let me phone my dad on a general line to speak with him for a few minutes. I hear his disappointment, fatigue, and fear.

"I thought you were doing better, Danny," Buck says. "Nearly your birthday, you'll be eighteen in a couple days. What's happening to you, son?"

"I don't know, Dad, I'm sorry. I won't do it again, promise"

"Sounds like hell on earth," Buck says when he gets on. "Don't know why you keep beating yourself up, we all love you to pieces around here. Everyone does..."

"I know," I say. "I appreciate that, Dad. I forgot. I just get so damn angry."

"The doctor mentioned that," Buck says. "Promise me you'll stop the self-harm, will you? I mean, can't you at least promise that for the sake of your ma?"

"Yes," I say. "Yes, Dad, thanks much. I love you a lot."

"No more punching, Danny, right? Can we agree on that?"

"I will, Dad," I say. "I'll do it for you and the memory of Mom, both."

I fell asleep watching the news, which featured a story about a train derailment in Georgia, a chemical spill. Some neighborhoods were being evacuated. An African American woman from the Red Cross in a red and white rain slicker was speaking to a collection of reporters when I shut it off and tumbled into a deep sleep.

I dreamt of being at a CVS purchasing items—shampoo, Q-tips, floss, deodorant, and mouthwash—and chatting with a purple-haired clerk at the register. Suddenly, I flinched because I heard a droning sound, a sign that evil was on its way.

On the wall was an FBI Most Wanted poster of me, and I felt a buzzing in my chest like pissed-off killer bees hovering, waiting to strike. I felt the humming inside and outside of me as well. Looking around, I spotted swirling purple-black twisters raging, ripping down the street with thousands of luminous tangerine lizards pelting the land, exploding into fiery pink and blue flames, setting the whole town ablaze.

The buzzing, the humming was deafening, and it came with the whack of vertigo. I stumbled, tearing off my clothes, running, yelling, and sprinting, chased by the twisters, begging them to pick me up and lift me to higher ground, to sacred and safe turf somewhere without too many medications. Far away from fires, from the high winds—Christ, how I begged and pleaded to be done with the thrashing, whipping flames.

The lizards burned like sulfuric acid on my skin as they struck me, exploding, leaving scars that throbbed. I thought of that Rolling Stones' classic tune, "Gimme Shelter," and how the pulsing beat and chorus encapsulated what my terror was about.

But, after the long droning faded, I looked around and realized there were never twisters, or exploding tangerine lizards, houses, or forests ablaze, everything was pretty settled and subdued. The pounding, driving music had fallen away, too. No burns were on my body, no rape or murder going on anywhere. Just a thoroughly damaged, trauma-riddled teen mind reliving a nightmare. I looked down at myself and realized my clothes were still on as well.

As I woke inside the vision, a seven-foot female reporter smoked a cigar in a black leather skirt, white T-shirt, white Stetson, pink tights, and a large, old-fashioned video-cam on her shoulder and interviewed other patients, doctors, and neighbors about me. Townspeople said they considered me harmless— just a troubled albeit bright special kid, wandering around, not hurting anyone.

One unhinged, loud, and rambunctious man insisted I was a terrible threat, though. He called me a communist and anarchic hippie with a shady, ugly past, and said I should be shot and volunteered to kill me if everyone agreed to it. The camera zoomed in on the one undecided citizen in the town, the pretty purple-haired young lady, the cashier from CVS, but she shook her head, wiping away real tears.

"Danny Halligan is probably just another hurting kid with his own hang-ups and enough baggage to sink the Titanic all over again," she said. "A part of me would like to get to know him, but I couldn't deal with his abundant sorrow... It's in his damn eyes. Way too much sadness I spot in there, along with hurt and melancholy swimming in those large peepers. When you get up close, the eyes are piercing, and you know inside he's wounded by something fierce. My mom would slap my head so hard if I ever brought him through our front door."

"There you have it," the reporter said. "Danny says that all he had were night terrors stampeding through his veins when he dreams about the trauma of his childhood. But everyone in town feels a bizarre, gnawing rage, and focuses their fire on Danny. They say he's too far gone for proper psychiatric help, plus it leaves a burden on the public who pay too many taxes to begin with."

I wake in a cold sweat and find Amber, the charge nurse with her yellow, orange, and violet fingernails painted with tiny smiley faces. She injected me with something, *a sedative,* she said.

"I have the worst nightmares, Amber," I tell her, and she shakes her head.

"Everyone heard you down the hall last night," she says. "And all the way through the double doors, and around another bend."

"What was I saying?" I ask.

She smiles as I notice her body wrapped up tight in a baby-blue cardigan sweater.

"Trash," she says. "For the most part, you were talking trash."

"Anything else?"

"You spoke a lot about talking cranes, those weird-looking skinny birds," she says. "Thousands of migrating cranes had come for you from so far away; Africa, South America, and all around the world."

"That's peculiar."

"You said several of them stopped by on their trek last night," she says. "Invited you to join them on their flight. Said you felt a bond with these brilliant birds."

"So, what happened?"

"You realized you couldn't fly," she says. "And they took off, left you behind and you were sad, pretty broken up about the whole thing."

"That's a real bummer, Amber," I say.

"Don't worry too much about it, though, honey," she says. "I can't fly, either."

I smile at her before I doze off again. Three hours on, I am back in Dr. G's office in Spruce Lodge, feeling calmer, at ease. We start talking about all my dreams, and Dr. G informs me what happens in my visions is a representation of Gracie exposing me, either purposely, or just accidentally in my role as Wolf-Boy. Or so that's what Dr. G tells me when I pressed him on the topic of reveries, fugues, visions, and dreams.

He told me he wasn't massively into analyzing visions, but I feel like they kept him quite alert and awake. My first fill-in psychiatrist at Spruce Lodge kept falling asleep on me, that's of course, when he wasn't twiddling his damn thumbs.

That was Dr. Bates—believe me, he was a real piece of work.

DREAM OR MEMORY?

I mmediately following the first extravaganza, Gracie, Liam, and I buy deli sandwiches and orange sodas at the Dennis Public Market in town and eat them outside on a bench in a park. It's a perfect, blue-sky regular kind of summer day, although I feel shitty about what just went on with everyone. I'm sure Gracie would say something along the lines of: "Sure it's *wildly different*, angel, but we're all experimenting. That's what you're supposed to do when you're so young, wild, and free."

Gracie wanders away from us to take a few shots of the pink roses in the local park fifty yards away. She is always busy, looking for the next killer shot, working toward her next book of photos.

My belly feels queasy, and my hands are trembling. I bend over, stretching my fingers toward the dirt, the dust.

"What's going on?" Liam asks, and I shrug.

"My gut aches," I say. "A bit nauseous, too."

"Try to take it easy," Liam says. "Breathe slower, pace yourself. What we do together, you and I, is natural... a progression. Try to leave the shame behind, okay?"

"I guess so."

"Not my business, I know," Liam says. "But don't allow your dad to rule you any longer. It's a true recipe for disaster, Danny. With my pop, he's brutal and loathes me. If I absorbed all his rage, I'd be dead, but I don't let his cynicism infect me."

"Simple as that, huh?" I ask.

"No, no, nothing is ever simple in life, Danny," he says. "You know that."

"Right... Sorry about your father, though," I say. "I don't know how you deal with him, talk about facing a daily burden."

"It definitely sucks," he says. "But you know what's cooler than all that? I loved your short story so much, it lifted me... sort of redeemed me."

"So, I hear," I say as Liam smiles, handing me the story folded in a business envelope. I put it in my back pocket.

"I'm no expert on creative writing, the *blues, musically or emotionally,* true friendship, or modern photography, but I enjoyed it. You and I have a lot more in common than you might first think."

"Yeah?"

"Where'd you come up with a character like Lars?" he asks.

"He just fell out of me," I say. "It was something that formed in my head as Gracie was shooting some initial shots of me as Wolf-Boy in Truro at dawn. They were very provocative and racy shots, so Lars started forming inside."

"That's cool," Liam says.

"Break it up," Gracie says, walking back to where Liam and I are sitting. "I don't want you guys getting too close, we must keep these quasi-lovers apart... so break it up, stand clear of each other forever."

"Too late now," Liam says, laughing. "Friskiness joins Wolf-Boy and Lone Ranger, from here on in, we're joined at the hip."

"Yeah," I say.

"We connect beyond the loins, making progress along the road to something more than friendship. Does that seem possible, at all?"

"Definitely," I say. "And thanks for addressing last Labor Day's fiasco."

"That was ridiculous, an ugly moment in my life," he says.

"Let's go back to Gramps's place, angel," Gracie says. "I've got a Valium for you that will settle you down. But don't listen to Liam's wisdom too much, Danny."

"Why not?"

Gracie says, "Every bit of your suffering and hurt makes for wonderful, delectable art... from Van Gogh to Anne Sexton to Kafka to Virginia Woolf. Those facts are impossible to ignore."

"Stay out of this, Gracie," Liam says. "We'll talk later, okay, Danny?"

"Sure," I say. "Glad you found my story moving, Liam."

"True to life in many ways."

"Great," I say.

"Danny," Gracie says, kissing my hands. "I can give you a pill."

"Sometimes you act like an insistent insect, Gracie, you really do," he says. "Maybe a common fruit fly."

"*Whatever*, Liam," she says.

Ten minutes later, Liam gets out of Gracie's car at his house. He kisses my right cheek, and I think, *Second kiss in a couple of days—cool!*

"What's that one for?" I ask, swallowing, feeling nervous, but a wide-awake kind of nervous.

"Sometimes you need to say, why the hell not?" Liam

exclaims and then he's up his front stoop and inside the house. Gracie drives by three more houses slowly on our dirt road silently and parks her Comet in our drive. I go inside with her, and she gets a sheet and pillow out of the closet, helps me lay on the couch, and gives me Valium with apple juice.

"What was all that with Liam?" Gracie asks. "The kiss and everything?"

"I wrote a short story about Liam called, 'Goofy Child.'"

"Like my *Goofy Boy* photos?"

"You inspired me partly," I say. "I just went off on a tangent... I had never written a story before, short or long, so it felt cool, natural to sit at a desk and create all these funky narratives."

"Yeah, well," she says and pulls a book of photos from her tote and begins flipping through it. "Be cautious with someone like Liam Preston."

"Why say that?"

"He can be domineering," she says. "And stubborn, and oddly radical."

"But couldn't someone say the exact same thing about Gracie?"

"No, they wouldn't dream of it," she says. "Because that would be rude, and the real Danny Halligan is never rude to anyone. It's why I love him so much."

"Ah," I say. "Interesting."

"Why's that interesting?"

"It's cruelly ironic, I know that much," I say.

"Can I read the story, please?" she asks.

"No, no, it's private," I say. "Respect that please, okay?"

"Fine, okay, okay," Gracie says. "Anyway, it's time for some sweet dreams, angel. Gracie will take you away from all that rough and tumble and offer the best care."

"What's the book?" I ask.

"*Diane Arbus: An Aperture Monograph*," she says.

"Who's she?"

"A gifted goddess who once lived among us mortals," Gracie says and passes me the book of black-and-white photos. I flip through it for several minutes. The photos are peculiar, even disturbing.

I come to a shot of an enormous, outsized man in a New York apartment with two regular-sized parents, who look like dwarfs in comparison.

"Odd," I say.

"It's Eddie Carmel, The Jewish Giant."

"Was he famous?"

"*Not exactly*," Gracie says. "Arbus wasn't interested much in celebrity."

There was a long pause between us as I studied the photo.

"Arbus once stated," Gracie explains, "'for me, the subject of the picture is always more important than the picture.'"

"Is that true for you, too, Gracie?" I ask.

"Not really," she says, making a sour face.

"Are you using me this summer, Gracie?" I ask. "Are Liam and I nothing but tools, handsome pawns in your bizarre game of chess on the Cape?"

"Stop," she says. "I love you more than anyone else, you know that."

"I could be a lot weirder if you wanted," I say.

She smiles and says, "You're the opposite of all that bullshit. My favorite triple scoop of vanilla bean on a sugar cone."

"You mean *boring* old, run-of-the-mill vanilla?"

"No," Gracie says, stroking my face. "You're pure and natural, my snow-white, perpetual virgin."

"You make me sound like a freak when you put it that way," I say.

"No, you're special, Danny," she says. "But Diane Arbus died in July of 1971, a suicide."

I watch her reach down to me on the couch and caress my face again.

"The best seem destined for trouble," she says.

"How old was Diane Arbus?"

"Forty-eight," she says. "Barbiturates and razors in a bathtub in New York."

"Jesus," I say. "Tragic story."

"Got some Arbus quotes here if you'd like to hear them," Gracie says.

"Go ahead," I say.

"'A picture is a secret about a secret. The more it tells, the less you know.'"

"And another?"

"'You see someone on the street, and essentially what you notice about them is the flaw.'"

"And one last Diane Arbus quote," I ask.

"'Ladies and gentlemen, take my advice, pull down your pants and slide on the ice.'"

"Cool," I say. "But now I've got a tough one for you, Gracie."

"Fire away."

"Why do people kill themselves?" I ask. "Like artists?"

She's quiet for a moment, tapping the bridge of her sunglasses twice with her right index finger like a wizened professor.

"Bleak winters, cruel springs, and toilets in airports, trains, and bus stations," she says. "Hard to withstand for any prolonged period."

I watch Gracie from the couch, my eyes heavy.

"I don't think it's something you know, pal," she says. "It's something *they* feel."

"But what about my mom?" I ask. "Why'd she jump?"

"Hopeless lady, feeling abandoned," Gracie says. "*Baby blues*, a real clinical type of thing that doctors didn't listen to women about for way too many decades."

"All my mom had was a four-year-old me and Buck," I say.

"Your mom got a raw deal," Gracie says. "It was how *most* of the world worked—they treated the mentally ill like outcasts."

My head feels like a ton of bricks—I want sleep, but I don't want to leave Gracie.

"But with Arbus," Gracie says. "Artists see truth, maybe, more clarity, less filter, leads to trouble."

"Like a long dormant bomb?" I ask. "Or tears hidden inside a wolf-boy's mask?"

Gracie barely smiles, rubbing my arms.

"Something close to that, yes," she says. "But let's get you eased and settled down. It's been a wild day for my favorite young man from Limewood."

Gramps won't return until the next morning, so Gracie says she'll watch TV in the den. She prepares iced tea and chicken salad in the meantime. I still feel afraid and tight in my belly, like there are scurvy rodents chewing on my lower GI. But after several minutes, I drift off to sleep, and find myself walking around at the Cape, though Gracie isn't there, and everything is a lot bigger. No, not exactly *bigger*, but I'm smaller, tiny, actually.

It's nearly dawn, and everyone's asleep, and I sneak out of the cottage and hustle the half-mile or so to Bay View Beach in Dennis, one of my favorite spots in the world. It's my seventh birthday, and there's no sunshine yet, but it's coming, I know it's coming. Only thing I want to do is swim upside down all day long, my back scraping the sandy bottom, and study the swirly, silly sunbeams through the clear blue sea. I've been coming here my entire life. There is nothing better than an early morning dip when the beach is oh so empty and I've got it all to myself.

I wear New England Patriots pajamas and K-Mart moccasins, but I'm thinking, *it's dark, no one will see, hurry up or you'll miss the sunrise!* Each year my father tells me about my *miracle* birth—saying I was born on July 4, 1962, at 3:27 a.m. My two sisters, Molly and Eve, didn't survive. They never drew a breath outside Mom's belly, and so I spent time alone in a warm hospital incubator, gaining weight and building strength.

When I arrive at the beach, I run to the shore, peeling off my Patriots pajamas and moccasin and dive into the water. Within a millisecond, I slam my head and sink deeper beneath the surface, only to be plucked out of the sea and shoved on a white surfboard by a huge figure in a black wetsuit. He's paddling on an oversized board, which I originally think is a killer whale or a Great White shark. I never see his face, only his taut shoulders, arms, and hands.

He never raises his voice, always whispering in my ears, offering subdued, prayer-like assurances. The unusually prominent veins on the back of his hands and forearms look like mini serpents threatening to burst through the skin. The hair on his body is curly and gray and black. *Like those SOS cleaning pads Gramps has in the kitchen,* I think.

"Easy, now, boy, easy, take it slow and easy," he says. "I'm here to make it so much better, to bless and comfort in this time of need, to show you some basic truths."

I stick my head off the surfboard and into the water, for below the ocean is subdued, safe, protected, no one knows, no one hears, no one has to understand anything below the sea. The man with the snake-veins and wetsuit, he lays me face down on the board while he rests on top of me and paddles us out, taking me from my usual beach, off Bay View down towards Sesuit Harbor.

My mind races: *Something's gone horribly wrong here, remember to breathe, don't forget to breathe, Danny. I made a mistake, why is all this happening on my birthday?*

High tide comes in fast, and the surf grows rougher as we go out, and the sun rises, and as I periodically glance back at the beach, I see lovers, walkers, and photographers doing their thing. They spread out, throw blankets down, one group already on their knees, digging sandcastles, taking in the enormous swath of sand, shells, and sea. I hear people shouting as the sun rises higher, some tossing a football around, or playing Whiffle ball. Others whistle and call their dogs or say silly things like "Frankie loves Johnny" and "Meghan loves the Cape more than anyone in the galaxy."

Voices float and bounce on the wind, shifting farther down the beach, over the water, and right past us and out to sea. It's probably a wonderful scene to revel in for most, the strengthening sun and almost-painfully clear blue skies, but, for me, it's all about the next ninety minutes, the dense, thick, in-your-face-so-you-can't-ignore-it kind of hurt. The deep voiced, veiny fellow never yells or grows angry, and yet I am exhausted by the intensity of our interactions.

"Where are we headed?" I finally asked, after a long time of his whispering.

"Sky's the limit, sky is the absolute limit this morning, my dear boy," he says.

"My head aches, it hurts so badly," I say, and he splashes salt water on my brow.

"There's a bad gash and a fair amount of blood loss," he says. "But salt water and air are best, it'll soothe you, and you'll learn a lot quickly. Trust me, son, I'm a teacher."

Oddly, I feel safer as he says that, though my eyes sting

from the briny sea, and a hoarse, chesty cough, the kind I always get from staying in the water too long, I feel it beginning beneath my ribs. I don't curse, but I feel enraged, and he encourages it.

"Yes, get everything out," he says. "Let the puss spill out of you like a bad pimple, I will make it better, and pop the acne, dear Denny. I will show you truth today."

I was confused by that slip—*why didn't he know my real name? He appears to care, I mean, he saved me, right? And what truth does he mean? I'm a kid—I don't have pimples yet.* I was drowning earlier, and the board smacked me, and he gathered me in like a pied piper.

"You're such a bad, stupid boy," I say, trying to shout but my voice cracks, weakening. "You let Gramps, Eileen, and Dad down today, why are you always messing up?"

As I speak, Teacher-Man keeps a constant, steady shushing sound, diluting it. He says: "No, hush now, deep breaths, things will improve, hush, it's going to be so sweet, my child, things pass, life moves on, we each learn hard lessons in the end, right?"

I come up for air occasionally, until I'm fatigued, so sick of the water, like I'm going to throw up. At the same time, if I don't dip my head under the cold sea off the side of the board, I fear I'll cry nonstop, so it's back and forth, ride the board, take a few breaths, and dip my face beneath the whitecaps. Teacher-Man *saves* me, after all, it's what he whispers in my ear as we approach a private empty beach about a mile down from Bay View beach.

"I rescued this boy from stress," he repeats. "I'll find Gramps, Eileen, and Dad and make everything better, and send Captain Crunch and Oreos. Would you like that, Denny?"

That's screwy, for the second time he calls me Denny. Granted, it's close to Danny, only a letter away, but could he have picked the *wrong* kid this morning? Yet he *is* on target about Captain Crunch and Oreos—I adore those snacks.

He proceeds to kiss my neck, lower back, and my ass, and it's terrifying. When he asks me to look back, he grins wildly and wears oversized swimming goggles and has my ass blood on his nose, mouth, and chin. He looks menacing, ferocious, and he's out of the wetsuit, too, and I can't remember when that happened. *How long has he been naked?*

"Where's your wetsuit?" I asked, panicked, my blue lips quivering.

"Hush," he says. "It's important to shed our skin every now and again, renewal is always a good thing, recall that in the coming years, my dear boy. Never forget it."

I'm suddenly terrified. *Why does he look like a bloody devil in the goggles?*

He leaves me without any more words in the shallows, where the water only covers my knees. I study the now-naked man sprinting away with the board. He hustles up the wooden stairs of a cliff and turns and gestures my way, so I wave back. He disappears, and after a few minutes, it's like he never existed.

I wake up groaning then, fighting for breath, reaching out for a person pressing on my belly, pushing them away, it's ninety minutes after taking the Valium, and Gracie kisses my face, but I have trouble returning to full consciousness. I'm panicking, trapped inside thick dry-mouth brine, as if some molasses grips my thighs to my toes. I smell fire, too, something burning like a bonfire, something that would blister me.

I feel under the ocean, too, and my eyes are heavy, as well, as if there's a thick film on them, and I hear Gracie soothing me, holding me tight, kissing me, but I can't escape Teacher-Man's manic grin, along with his horrible hushing.

"Easy," Gracie says. "I'm here, angel, you were dreaming."

"No," I say, then, "No, no. It was a memory, a real thing that took place on the beach. Something that happened when I was a boy, I think, it feels too clear to me, and I also smell something singed, like there was a bonfire, maybe?"

Gracie is still listening to me a half hour later as she wipes and kisses my tears. I tell her a lot about the memory, and after a time, she sings me a French lullaby I don't know, but it helps me, she eases me with her gentle timbre.

"I always knew there were deeper issues, angel," she says. "I'll try to soothe and heal, I'm on your side forever."

"You think it's true?" I ask. "The dream is memory?"

"I do—it feels real," she says. "No worries, sugar. I'll always keep watch."

"And the burning smell?"

"God, who knows?" she says with a hollow laugh. "Maybe neighbors are having roast duck?"

When I think back to that conversation with Gracie, I'm torn over it. My lover helped me wonderfully with the Teacher-Man trauma, comforted me, sang to me, eased me in a very loving and compassionate way for almost two hours. But then she started in with the lying and her world nearly caved in on her.

"Where's my story, Gracie?" I ask. "It was in the back pocket of my pants and now it's gone. You promised me you wouldn't read it. Did you?"

"You want brutal honesty?"

"Please."

"You stole my damn work, Danny," she says.

"*What?*"

"You twisted my idea around and made it into your lousy

fiction," Gracie says. "'Goofy Child' is an act of plagiarism, no two ways about it, no originality to it."

"Horseshit," I say. "Goofy Boy was like... conceptual photos. Several days later, I made up a story called 'Goofy Child.' I created the characters all on my own."

"I could sue your ass off," Gracie says.

"I was *influenced* by your work," I say. "Artists do it all the time. Is that what I smelled burning the whole time I was having the nightmare?"

"Okay, I did get a bit carried away and singed or burned it," she says.

"*Singed?*"

"Your prose was loaded with clunky, awkward terms," she says. "The sentences were way too florid to be taken seriously. You're not Proust, okay, champ?"

"Jealousy, huh?" I say, walking to the fireplace and squatting and finding charred bits of typing paper. "I can't believe you did this to me."

"You've let me down yourself, Danny," Gracie says. "Writing provocatively about your mortal enemy."

"Liam is *our friend*," I say. "Our colleague."

"He's not *my friend*," Gracie says. "No, I don't think so. He's anger and rage and all about inner fire. He's going to burn us all down at some point."

"He made a mistake with me last Labor Day," I say. "But we're cool now. He's apologized a few times, sincerely, I felt."

"You're too malleable, fickle, and silly, Danny," she says, "But be ready to work in the morning. Our photography show marches on."

"You destroyed my first attempt at art, Gracie, huh?" I say. "I'm pissed at you and disappointed. I thought you were going to be my mentor, a supporter, not a destroyer."

"Grow the hell up," she says. "And be ready in the morning."

"Fine," I say as Gracie hustles out of Gramps house, gets in her Comet, and drives away.

"Keep that part of the story to yourself, Danny," I say. "Don't tell Liam, try hard to contain it."

GUILT

One day after our first extravaganza, I still have the worst body aches and vomit several times. The hurt in every joint has Gramps thinking maybe I have a fever, plus my belly feels weirdly bloated so he thinks it's some sort of spider or tick bite, or possibly an appendix set to burst. He gives me aspirin and takes my temperature twice, but I'm perfect and steady at 98.6.

"A healthy young man," a sunburned doctor says after we spend some time in his Yarmouth office, going through a few tests.

"That's a relief, Doc," Gramps says.

"Are you under stress, Danny?" he asks. "Wrestling with anything at home?"

"He fancies an older girl from Yale University," Gramps tells the doctor. "Ivy League and all. No hair on this one, along with a safety pin in her left nostril."

It's the first time Gramps speaks of Gracie.

"She's decent for my soul, Doc," I say. "Plus, she's got a

143

disease, hair can't literally grow anywhere on her. Called alopecia."

"She's too sophisticated for you," Gramps says.

"Lots of those radical types hanging around," the doctor says. "It's a cyclical thing, you'll see, in a year, college kids will be mocking something more sacrosanct."

In private, the doctor asks me if I'm sexually active.

"Yeah," I say. "Several times so far."

"Is she cute?" he asks, and I blush, coughing.

"Yeah, of course," I say. "*Absolutely*."

He nods and tells me to use condoms and to always exercise.

"Good for the system," he says. "Nothing to fret over. It could also be drug use, but I know you'd probably never use them, right?"

"Never touch them," I say, blushing.

"I sure hope not, Danny," he says. "That crap can screw with your developing brain."

"Right," I say, before Gramps and I both shake off concern with the body aches and drive home, stopping for glazed donuts near Yarmouth. Next morning, still aching, Gramps suggested I not go to work again, so I called Liam.

"*Ha*," he says.

"What's that supposed to mean?"

"Wild pheromones floating inside your Tragically Phallus Palace."

"What?"

"Basic hunger often found deep in the loins of twisted adolescent boys."

I look around—Gramps is upstairs changing.

"You're not as clever as you think, Liam," I say.

"Forget *Palace of the Palpable Pines*, Danny," Liam says. "That's old news."

"How so?"

"Try *Tragically Phallus Palace* when it's just you and me," he says. "Dueling with our sleek and sinister schlongs."

"You're way too much," I say.

"Too much bad, *or too much good?*"

"I'm not sure yet," I say, laughing despite myself.

"See, when the action is focused on Gracie alone," Liam says, "it's *Kitty City.*"

"You're like a young Dr. Strange, huh?" I say. "Magical and everything."

"A sorcerer supreme, that's me," Liam says. "What a compliment."

"Voila," I say.

"I know you hanker for only me, Danny Hal," he says. "Clutch at me, wanting to take those repressed Catholic lips..."

"Quiet."

"I know that your need for me keeps you up at night..."

"Stop," I say.

"Everything okay?" Gramps says as he comes down the stairs in his swimsuit.

"Gotta go," I say, hanging up on Liam.

After Gramps leaves to go fishing, I rush down to the cellar and do a hundred push-ups and sit-ups. But Liam's chatter sends me into a rage. I fear I'll implode if I can't make Liam's erection fade from my mind. I go over to a metal pole next to the washer and dryer and slam my left temple against it, two, five, ten times.

I reach up, finding a little blood, and feel dizzy and have a bad headache. I shake my head and go out to the palace and crawl over to a pack of Marlboro Lights that Gracie left behind on the stereo. I take one out, unlit, and practice jamming it into my forehead, chest, chin, and nuts, before I crush it in my hand and toss them out the window.

"What's a young boy to do when he's trying so damn hard to behave?" I ask the palace, as I imagine Liam saying, *no matter if you're facing struggle or strife, Liam will be available at The Phallus Palace for the rest of your life!*

BUCK

My unique and God-fearing father, Buck Halligan, still bobs up and down like a fishing lure as he strolls all over town. At six-five, he sees more than others in the world. At least once each summer, my dad and I take a detour through Barnstable, and we visit a War Memorial for the Cape and Islands.

"Just gaze at the heroic statue, Danny," Dad says. "A sturdy hero, with thighs like a Heisman Trophy winner, and a tapered trunk and arms. They don't make guys like that these days."

The statue stands around nine feet high, oxidized green from wear.

"He's a symbol of raw determination," he says.

Dad will then ask any passing stranger to photograph us— father and son in front of the towering soldier. One time it was a traffic cop, another time tipsy graduate poets from Fairfield University, and another year it was a photographer from the *Cape Cod Times*, who put Dad and me on the front page, two Irish mugs grinning our butts off in front of our green hero.

Instead of saying *smile* or *cheese* when our photos are

taken, Dad and I say *fierce*. Buck told me it was something his college friends whispered when teasing him years ago, saying he was too corny and old fashioned for the modern business age, but Dad built his life around its principles—a romantic philosophy and ideal he embraced.

"A fierce family's love survives many storms," Dad explained. "Knocks down divisive walls, builds bridges, keeps us buoyant when we're flat and hopeless, holds people together when all that's left is sticky, tenuous fibers."

"Neat, Dad," I said.

"It's not that far from Judeo-Christian teachings, either," he said. "Just with my own twist, something I share with my one and only son. *Sacred and fierce*, understand?"

I know that may sound a bit goofy. Hell, it *was* a little goofy. Still though, I enjoy our visit each year, and when I make it back to the Cape down the road, I plan to visit the statue. I still have that front page of the *Cape Cod Times*, and photos of my dad and me packed away in an album somewhere. Five times we took that shot. It's fun to see me grow over the years, and watch Dad's hair turn thinner, his face more flushed with rosacea.

For the longest time, I thought my dad was infallible. Just figured he knew what to do, whom to call, what the correct, rational decision should be in every situation. When I used to see photos of my dad as a child, adorable, hanging on to his mom in the sea at Corporation Beach in Dennis, I assumed he could already understand everything. Looking at his little pudgy boy-face, I figured the kid was just inordinately wise. There was no doubt.

My dad possesses a wealth of pragmatic optimism, *and* he has a brutal dislike of those who don't follow the straight and narrow. However, it's not as simple as Dad being some malevolent monster.

After the death of my mom, he was aided financially by a great-aunt for several years. He continued raising me as he graduated school at Southern Connecticut University and became a successful discounted hardware chain-store owner, forever supporting Randy, his deceased wife's brother. And in 1978, Dad co-signed the bank loan for Randy's studio in Provincetown.

Randy was nervous but thrilled the day Shoot! opened. Buck dislikes that village, of course, but he felt obligated to keep an eye on his brother-in law.

"It's a complex and intricate thing, son," Dad said to me a few times. "It's a type of blood bond, a duty to care for a loved one no matter what goes on. Love is love."

"That sounds optimistic and hopeful from you, Dad," I said.

"Yeah, I'm coming around some," he said.

My father sounds radically conservative when he speaks about waffle-boys, but below the irascibility and knee-jerk bigotry is a warm and loving man. I do know he's determined to extinguish malaise—anguish is not welcome in his home.

When he speaks of his extended family and becomes melancholy, he mentions Mom, but he never touches on his father's athletic accolades at what is now Wilbur Cross High School in New Haven. Once my mom killed herself, Buck's father, Andrew, couldn't deal with any of his grief. He took off to Montreal, chasing some busty divorced pen pal who owned four hotels up in Montreal and played the trombone well.

It must be such an excruciating, aching emptiness inside Buck—the hollow missing pieces of his cancer-ravaged mom and his runaway father. Maybe cancer just sucked the life juice out of Andrew Halligan, maybe that's why he gave up and chased skirts for the rest of his life.

The only time Dad ever talks about Mom's suicide is in

Hyannis one Saturday morning, just after the second extravaganza. The summer was going by. I was exhausted. Gracie,
Liam, and I had been out late the night before. Buck is only
down for the weekend and so he and I wait on a bunch of keys
to be made at a hardware store. The two of us have to kill an
hour and head down a side street, me nibbling on a pastry and
orange juice, while Buck has a glazed donut and sucks down
one of his huge, piping-hot coffees.

Nearby is an empty park with an assortment of colorful
flowers and shrubs, some pear trees, and four benches, a baseball diamond, and a large open field. A hundred feet beyond it
on the other side is a U.S. Army recruiting station, and several
newbies are already in the lot, calling out their rhymes, voices
echoing like yelping dogs. It's only ten, but the sun is strong
already, and several recruits are looking worn out, ready for a
water break.

The Army recruiters are two tough and fit looking guys
with buzz cuts and aviator sunglasses. They bring out some
additional newbies to do calisthenics and sprint and grunt
around the park.

After watching the newbies work up a sweat for another
half hour, my father spits off to the side and shakes his head.

"Older I get, Danny," Buck says. "Less I know."

"How's that, Dad?"

"Like a crapshoot," he says. "Who'll last the longest, who'll
be victorious? The thing is, no one *really* wins, same goes for
everyone on this earth."

"Yeah?"

"Army, baseball, women, relationships, sales, discounted
hardware," he says. "No one earns the brass ring, only God,
understand?"

I nod. I think I understand him. You can try and pick out
who's the best at being a soldier, but you really have no idea.

Or at least *I* have no clue. Who knows how someone will perform in the clutch? Who'll fall apart when the bombs go off, who stays together when he sees his friends' bodies shredded? Who'll fragment early on and come back to life, maybe return like a ghost? And who disappears into a chasm and never breathes again?

Buck says, "The valedictorian in my high school class figured he'd be a movie star or a CEO somewhere. I mean, he seemed to have success, looks, and charm dribbling out of his ears back then, women everywhere, all over him."

"And he failed?"

"*We all fail,* Danny," Buck says, as he gazes down at me, his face looking puffier than I ever remember it being. "Guy couldn't get out of his own way," Buck went on. "Constantly tripped himself up—drank and drugged his twenties and thirties away, so damn troubled."

Dad clears his throat, coughs away from me for a moment, and spits again.

"He tried selling insurance for a number of years," he says. "Seemed to have settled down, married a sweet girl, raised a healthy daughter—we all thought our class's golden boy had finally figured it all out and found his path."

"What happened?" I ask.

"He hanged himself after he lost his daughter in a DUI accident," Dad says. "*He* was driving her home from sixth grade dance recital, drunk, and blacked out. She died instantly, he walked away unscathed, but he couldn't take the guilt."

"So how does one stay alive after such grief, Dad?" I ask. "How'd you do it?"

"Well, mine was a lot different situation," he says.

"Still," I say.

"Just pushed on through, I guess," he says. "Keep your head

up, pray, and remember to be kind, but don't ever get too cocky about life."

I nod, watching my father return to studying recruitment.

"I get stressed about things, too," I say. "Anxiety, pressures, all that kind of crap."

"Like with Gracie? And Liam?" he asks, looking over at me.

I shake my head. *What does he know?* I think, panicking. *Did Dad find my journal in the AC vent?*

"If it's not Gracie and Liam, what *do* you worry about?" he asks. "Almost seventeen, six months before a new decade? What's going on inside of my one and only son?"

"Well, what do you think is going on with Gracie and Liam?" I ask.

"Let's not bullshit each other, Danny," he says. "They're adults, and older, right?"

"I guess," I say.

"Gracie's through four semesters at Yale, speaks five languages, right?" Dad says.

"Yes," I say.

"Gracie's smart and knows numerous worlds, and Liam hasn't had it easy at home, tough kid, seen more things than you."

"So?"

"That leaves you at the bottom of their power structure," he says. "More peer pressure on you by a long shot, I think."

"That's true, Dad," I say, my face turning tight.

At that moment, I didn't want to go into Liam and Gracie, the booze, the bisexual pressures that are all over me, but then there's the molester, Teacher-Man, sitting in the corner of my brain, a big fat proverbial pink elephant no one ever likes to discuss. I certainly didn't want to bring it up, but I felt somewhat trapped with my increasing desires for males. Crushed up all inside of that stuff is the sexual abuse by this major tyrant in a wetsuit when I was seven.

As I mention this abuse to my dad, he rejects the confession, saying it's too much to deal with right now.

"Teacher-Man, I guess."

"Don't go there, Danny."

"Can't help it," I say. "Ever since the bastard raped me at seven."

"Too depressing a topic, son," Dad says. "Try to move on, if you can..."

"I'm sorry, but..."

It's at that point, when I find myself unable to reverse myself—I wander into the conversation in an odd way, or at least that's what my super-critical self says. I choke back real tears and feel enraged for reasons I don't fully grasp, namely Teacher-Man carries with it sludge, grime, shame, fright, TNT, and hurt that I never dealt with. I'm in quicksand.

"Not the time or place," Dad says, so I start shouting all of a sudden, cursing and throwing awkward punches into the air with this defeated, impotent rage. It erupts from me, like some personal volcano, and I even kick over a couple garbage cans in the park.

"Easy son," Dad says. "Come on, easy, Danny, let's get a hold of yourself."

A few people walking by stop and study me as if I'm an unusual flowering plant, and several army recruits gaze over at me from their drills in the park. Buck steps into the street toward the pedestrians and waves them away, like he's a large, angry traffic cop in the middle of New York City.

"Give us a minute, would you please, ladies and gents?" Dad bellows in a loud, peeved fashion. "Family business, clear the area, thanks much, not for public consumption. Go on about your own chores, please continue along your merry way."

All the pedestrians listen to Dad, though, and reverse their course, and the recruits return to sweating, not paying as much attention. My dad turns to me like I'm a wild boar that needs to be euthanized, but slowly, gently with tact, care, and privacy.

"Bastard ruined me, Dad," I say quieter, partially eased, though real tears are falling now. "Impossible to recover..."

"Too simple to fall into that mentality," Buck says. "I know you're a champion level fighter down deep so..."

"The bastard destroyed whatever..."

My dad stops speaking then and wanders over to sit on a green wooden bench five feet away, staying real hunched over. His face is pale, stricken, and I think he's having a stroke.

"*What is it, Dad?*" I ask, running to him.

Dad slowly looks up at me and says: "It's like when your mom leapt off the hospital roof twelve years ago."

I see his fists clenching and releasing.

"Felt ready to die when I got the call, understand?" he says, barely whispering, so I find myself beside him, leaning in to hear every bit. "Was so ticked off, I rushed to Miriam's hospital room and tore up her clothes."

I didn't dare breathe.

"How the hell could she do that to us?" he asks, shaking his head.

I see my dad at that moment in a way I never had before. Terrified, helplessly enraged, a lost man, adrift.

Not dissimilar to me now, I think.

"I sobbed," Dad continues. "Ripped up some of our wedding photos at home, tossed some of her wedding china at the walls."

"What'd you do then?" I ask.

"What could I do?" he asks. "I had to care for you and offer structure, try for some sort of life filled with love and some form of respect."

I watched my father spit to the side before continuing.

"Life rolls on, though," he says. "Death doesn't offer much, or at least that's what I believe down deep, just don't tell any of the local parish priests."

"I won't, Dad," I say. "So what did you do?"

"Figured I'd shape the news for you and me and Randy and Gramps—I didn't want everyone in Greater New Haven inserting themselves into our goddamned family affairs."

My father's thick hands and fingers gestured into the bone-white sky.

"Had some words changed for the next morning's paper."

"Which ones?"

"*Dementia* in place of *suicide*," he says. "Everyone knew she leapt off the damn roof, and I knew they planned to print a big frontpage photo of Ma on the collapsed milk truck. *Special Edition.* The editor phones me and says, 'I know it doesn't sound like a believable sentence, but she's beautiful in the photograph, Buck. She appears like a resting angel.'"

I nod.

"Editor promised me he would print cause of death as dementia," he says. "Seemed like a huge deal to me back then, now it seems silly, beside the point."

I see Buck look down at the ground, clasping hands.

"Miriam looked so damn peaceful on the front page," Dad says. "Like she was only sacked out for a nap."

"Yeah, Dad, you're right."

"You've seen the shots, Boss?"

"Gramps and Randy showed me it to me a while back," I say. "Got several laminated copies of it at home."

"People told me she looked like an angel on the crushed milk truck," Dad says, eyes wet. "At least, 75 people at the frigging wake said that exact thing, I swear to God, a resting angel."

"I believe it," I say. "She does, you know, Dad? She looks just like that."

"Whole event was awful, of course," he says. "Horrific. But God had done right by Mom on that one."

"Absolutely," I say.

"It got out of hand when *Time* magazine put her damn photo on the cover and wrote personal tidbits about her tragic life," he says. "Yahoos came out of the woodwork, asking for pieces of her hair, to touch her rosary beads and jewelry."

"Why'd they do that, Dad?"

"People said Mom might be a holy messenger," Dad says. "They claimed she appeared so alive-looking at her death, that she had this amazing, otherworldly glow."

"What'd you do?"

"I cleared out when that publicity was buzzing everywhere," Dad says. "I drove down to the Cape. Randy and Gramps really helped me, aided me for those days, I mean, they were mourning her, too. But we did it together. We went for long, long walks on the beach. Eileen kept a close eye on you back home."

"Why not bring me along to the Cape, Dad?" I ask. "I was a bright kid, right? I mean, I knew what was occurring the whole time I missed you not being there."

"Eileen said that you should come and share in the tragedy," Dad says. "She voted yes, Randy, too. But me and Gramps said no way."

"I wish I could've shared all that," I say.

"Big mistake by me," he says. "Sorry, I've made some doozies in my day."

"Right."

I watch my father study me before he says, "While we're talking about my epic mistakes, can I ask you something else?"

"Sure."

"It goes back to the Yale Bowl some years ago."

"Uh-oh," I say, swallowing audibly. "I think I might know this one."

"It was Yale-Harvard football in New Haven, a few weeks before Thanksgiving, you were eleven, twelve... I had had three beers, I was buzzing, work wasn't going well, plus some idiot crowded me at the urinal... I wanted to strangle the punk, drown him in piss."

"I remember," I say. "It was so cold, and you came flying out of the john, ticked off about bisexuals, spewing rage."

"A shaming day," Buck says. "I was rude to my only son. Danny, I don't know the first thing about bisexuality or where I first heard the term waffle-boy..."

"Okay," I say, my face beet-red, body trembling.

"Some warped Sister Franny in sixth or seventh grade, she didn't know jack-shit about life, she kept using that term to put people down. Like the theater teacher, or perhaps the hardware store owner, or an EMT in town."

"You learned the term *waffle-boy* from a mean nun, Dad?"

"Sixth grade," he says. "What a fool I was, I bought everything hook, line, and sinker from Sister Franny."

"Wow," I say.

"I listened to her like she was a prophet, and not some bigot influencing hundreds of these damn kids, each of us like sponges, soaking all her drivel up."

"Scary," I say.

"Are you bisexual, Danny?" Dad asks. "Or do you not want to say right now?"

"I don't know."

"It's okay if you want to wait," he says. "You don't ever have to say..."

"I mean... Dad, it's like walking through a one-way door. I wasn't sure when I or if I should say something to you, but then

I started, and I saw this might be the best time. Does that sound asinine?"

"Not at all," Dad says. "Takes a lot of balls what you just did. Gutsy."

"So anyway, I like girls and boys. That's it, that's the whole truth of it."

"So, you like *both?*" he says. "Equally attracted to both sexes?"

"Right, yes," I say. "*Both.*"

"What a massive life error by me, Danny," he says. "Looking back, I see that I tend to do that with sex or religious topics, obliterate nuance and sharing real truths because I don't want to listen and hear the entire, honest story."

"Right," I say.

"I've been doing some reading on the topic, believe it or not, and I'm so sorry that I hurt you," he says. "An ugly mistake."

"You're making up for it now, though, Dad," I say. "I'm impressed and proud of you, of my dad, and I know Mom would be, too."

"Thanks, but I'm no expert," he says. "You should tell me if I'm way off. I need your help and guidance with this stuff, okay?"

"It's impressive self-analysis, Dad," I say.

"Sorry it took me forever to say *sorry.*"

"That's okay," I say and so we sit, motionless, intimately together for another minute. I'd never felt so close to my father. There's a break in the clouds, and Buck stands, our time together seemingly over. He waits for me to rise and turns and kisses my forehead.

"Teacher-Man event was a hellish morning, but you must move on," Dad says.

"What do I do now?" I ask, voice breaking.

"Continue going to school, making friends," he says. "Show

more caution with Gracie and Liam—be aware of their sharp edges, okay? Get into therapy right away in September in Limewood, you need expert help with that material, maybe a few times a week. I don't know if it would help you at all, but if you wanted me to be there with you... That's okay, too."

"You're turning into Phil Donahue, Dad. You'll have a hit talk show soon."

"I don't think so," he says. "Do you forgive me for putting so much on your tiny shoulders? All that bisexual or tri-sexual stuff?"

"I forgive you, Dad," I say. "I never expected this kindness and openness from you. It's wonderful. However, I've never heard of this tri-sexuality... Is that something sweeping the nation?"

We both share a nervous belly laugh until my dad leans forward and kisses the top of my head and gives me his biggest bear hug. Hands down, my father gives the best embrace in New England.

"You *are* who I want you to be, Boss," he says. "You're actively *trying to live a better life*, it's all I need to know about my wonderful son who likes both girls and boys."

"Thanks..."

"You keep me on my toes, Danny," he says. "I like that."

RANDY AND DANNY

One day in mid-June, Liam doesn't pick me up for work—he cancels, says he's sick and badly hung over. So, I venture out with Randy—the concept is joyous and simple enough, a couple celebrating a thirty-ninth anniversary with a brunch at a restaurant in Brewster.

Pam and Roseanne Borski are comely and slim, and along with twenty family and friends they feast on French toast, bagels, eggs, and Mimosas, and this amazingly thick bacon. Initially, Randy's in a fantastic mood, charming the couple and the family and their imbibing friends, taking all kinds of photos, keeping the day rolling along seamlessly. The weather is cool, low humidity. Later, there's dancing to a DJ, gifts, and pictures, and so many toasts.

My job that day, essentially, is to carry Randy's various lenses and camera equipment around from the garden to the dance floor and back and to keep him away from the booze as much as possible. But he can't help flirting with a cousin of one of the brides, a hulking All-American high school sophomore swimmer named Gerard. After I excuse myself to use the facilities—my belly *still* aches—and return to the party, everyone is ticked off at Randy.

Where previously they heaped praise on him and his *control* of their party, they now approach me like I'm a powerful District Attorney hearing cases, listing all things that Randy has done wrong, including flirting with All-American Gerard and forgetting to tell the florist the correct time to show up so their portraits are lacking *true panache and color.*

In the end, they only pay Randy seventy-five percent of the fee that was agreed upon so as *I* start to drive away—I don't have a license, but Randy's trashed so I take the wheel—he flips them the bird out the passenger side window and yells how he loathes Poland and all its inhabitants. More carrying on back and forth as I peel out of the restaurant's gravel drive, and Randy shouts more insulting Polish jokes. Not the wisest way to drum up business for a new photography studio in town.

As I drive, we're both silent for fifteen minutes until he tells me to pull over around Orleans. Randy thinks he may get sick along the side of the road, so I pass him a bottle of water out the window, and he leans against the van, saying; "You got to watch yourself with the two wharf rats you hang out with, Danny."

"Excuse me?"

"Gracie's eating you alive, man," he says. "And that long-gone stoner Liam—"

"I wouldn't talk about bad behavior if I were you," I say.

"I'm already a mess, though," Randy says. "I'm a grown adult, but you're just a kid—your brain's still developing for God's sake... I want to make sure my nephew survives this summer intact."

I step out of the van, joining Randy on the shoulder, kicking my Nikes against the tires. He removes his Ray Bans, places them in the pocket of his black polo, and I take in his vivid, green, and bloodshot eyes. The wind has picked up since we started at 6:45 a.m. so his long, curly red hair is now blown about until he takes a few swipes at it with his right hand, and, somehow, it magically settles back in place.

"Lay it on me, pal," he says.

"What?"

"You're obviously troubled about something," he says. "I'm guessing it's about sex in some way, so ask me."

"Can't think of any..."

"Ask me the damn question, Danny."

"How do you know if you're definitely bisexual?" I say, and he looks at me.

"You and Liam, huh?" he says, elbowing me. *"You old dog."*

"I don't know who I am anymore," I say, picking at my sweaty left palm, until the hand falls away—*crumbles instantly* —and my fingers drop to the pavement and bounce on the road, and I think, *Oh, Christ, I've lost my fingers!*

"You okay?" Randy asks, and a second later, *I'm back,* gawking at my two beautiful hands with ten, lovely digits, moving every which way.

No more Gracie CIA potions, I tell myself. *Never ingest them again.*

"I feel shaky," I say to Randy, and he scowls as a truck roars past us.

"That's enough hallucinogens, okay?" Randy shouts, moving us to behind the van, away from the direct line of traffic.

"I just saw my left hand fall off," I say. "Fingers bouncing all around."

"Gracie and Liam are lethal," he shouts. "You're *too* damn young."

"It's been bizarre, Randy," I say, tearing up, as my uncle sighs, and his Mimosa breath feels warm but not unpleasant on my face. I feel a sudden burst of love, terror, and affection and want to embrace him and confess everything. How reckless I've behaved; how blindly arrogant and naive I've acted since day one of this summer.

For a second, I even feel like I could quit the whole season, end it there, and maybe retrieve my old, untouched brain, find it hanging deep in my closet upstairs somewhere, find a Narnia like kind of escape hatch into a more welcoming land, with a lot more love and possibility. I could return to Limewood and swear off Gracie, Liam, the Cape, wipe the slate clean, and never look back.

But I know that wouldn't solve my desires, I think. *I know it's a lot more complicated and intricate.*

Maybe run cross country in the autumn, take an SAT prep course, take better care of my body. But that tender, poignant moment speeds by, and as Randy starts slurring his words, I lose the chance, my opening, and I think, *Is Danny Hal trying to live a better life a futile act?*

"As far as bishexual stuff?" Randy says and stops. "Look, sorry, I'm really drunk, not the wisest man today to offer a quote."

"No problem," I say.

"Truest answer is there aren't any easy solutions," he says. "Do what feels right."

I study Randy, teetering against the back of the van.

He's a wounded soul with his drug and alcohol abuse, I think. *Perhaps a marked one if he doesn't quit now. Don't follow in his footsteps, Danny, wise up, and go to school on his drug habits. Watch, absorb, learn, but don't repeat his ways. Never repeat his alcohol and drug use.*

"Sounds corny, but if there's some trust involved and a great deal of love," Randy is saying, "and warmth, it can be worthwhile."

I nod.

"God knows, I'm no expert, so be really cautious out there, okay?" he says.

"Thanks, Randy," I say, and he touches my chin, and I feel I'll cry again, but Randy spits into the sand, and everything gets swept away in a gust, and most of the warmth vanishes too.

"*Condoms*," he says, and signals for both of us to climb back into the van. "Whatever you're doing with Gracie or Liam, make sure you're always wearing one, and for Christ's sake, no more drugs ever again. *Period*."

POWER OF WORDS

Gracie and I go to Scargo Tower in Dennis one day to take photos around the library, fire station, ice cream shop, cemetery, and the old Congregational Church.

"We're going to talk about power and process today," she says. "What the three of us are undertaking together," she says.

"Cool," I say. "I'm nothing but ears today."

The tower itself is way up the road on a steep incline and the structure is about thirty-feet high, is made of cobblestone, and was completed in 1901. Two earlier towers, both constructed of wood, could not withstand a gale, or a later fire, so cobblestone was decided to be the best choice.

We climb to the top of the tower with two cans of iced tea and Gracie describes how the origin of her photography project was her lover, Angie. The story of Gracie's unique lady friend isn't a shock, not really.

I know Gracie likes to surround herself with various characters—quirky, disturbed, or even downright weird and unsavory. I admire that about her, though. It shows her gravitas, her cryptic brand of kindness and verve—she never turns anyone away, not unlike a Lady Liberty in New York harbor: "Give me your tired, your weak, your poor and huddled masses..."

One story that impresses me the most also makes me terribly jealous at the same time. It's about a Yale graduate named Angie. She had a quirky, artsy Gram, who was frequently hospitalized with psychiatric issues. Once she spent twenty years in a hospital in upstate New York. Gram introduced Angie to vibrant colors as a girl. Angie's Gram played around with blue ink one day in an old claw-footed bathtub and explained to Angie how she dyes her blouses and willed the magical colors into the fabric.

Angie's Gram had thinning white hair, and a large mole in the center of her forehead that Angie swore worked like an on-off button for Gram's eccentricities. Tap it once and she'll speak in tongues, tap it again and she'll croon "Silent Night" in German at the top of her lungs. Tap it a third time and she'll bite you, tearing into your flesh like a Doberman.

Gram was severely hunched over as well, and only an educated ear would know her Austrian accent was actually Viennese. She couldn't hear a damn thing, but she showed Angie how the graying blue shades got squeezed into the clothing in the tub, with her gnarled hands and fingers kneading the shirts. Gram wasn't always lucid—she sang clearly to Angie on that morning, "I want to swim around inside the color blue, Angie, would you dive in, too?"

Angie was only four, but she hopped into the tub with an oversized white T-shirt and played amongst the blouses and colors with her funny and eccentric Gram all day. After the old woman passed on a few years later, Angie messed around with her hues, especially periwinkle, blueberry, and shades of indigo. Angie said she felt like those colors were deep within her now, that her Gram had left them there for a reason. *Implanted, almost.*

As Angie matured, she painted many impressive portraits of Gram on the walls of her bedroom with some spare paintbrushes she found in the attic. She created structure in her life by painting thirty-nine portraits of her Gram in variations of blue on her bedroom wall, and no one thought to stop her.

Angie's entire, once pale, and boring boudoir blossoms with more paintings, and by the time she leaves high school, she's damn good, and also out of room. She gets her undergraduate and graduate degree in Art at Yale University, graduates with many honors, but the day she starts working for real, she wakes to a harsh migraine throbbing behind her left eye.

Angie finds a significant number of dead hornets and ladybugs stuck in her paintbrushes. She picked up each of the dead hornets and surprised herself by smelling them. To Angie, they reeked of death, of rot, disease, and portent. She even listened to them, hoping they would explain to her why they are interfering with her artistic gifts and lineage, why the hornets are making Angie so damn uncomfortable with the concept of painting.

And from that second on, Angie was never the same woman—she never fully returns to the world. Every time she picks up her paints or brushes and tries to re-ignite her passion, her favorite thing in the world to do since she was a tiny girl, all she can smell is death. Painting became anathema to her.

Angie grew convinced that a larger, hovering force, perhaps an alien being, was sending her messages through the dead bugs, and the basic gist was she shouldn't ever paint, nor teach painting to one solitary soul, but instead writes her thoughts down constantly, only taking breaks for sleep, food, showers, and bathroom breaks.

Angie wrote term papers decently or filled out applications, but she had never felt any true interest or passion in writing. Suddenly, the young lady felt driven to write her words, her absolute truth. She started and hasn't stopped. Initially, it was only on paper sheets around the apartment—notebooks, index cards, scrap paper, motor vehicle paperwork, bills from insurance, cash receipts, credit card slips, newspapers, advertisements, or grocery lists.

Gracie watched her lover descend quickly into a severe and riotous case of *hypergraphia*, a compulsion that one must write, sometimes connected with bipolar disorder or even schizophrenia. Angie used old-fashioned quill pens, the expensive and rare kind, dipped in permanent ink, and one day, she left the paper behind in her home and wrote all over her body too.

Stripped naked in her kitchen, she wrote on her feet, breasts, arms, cheeks, belly, wrists, thighs, ankles, forehead, buttocks, soles of her feet, and ears, which she said was challenging, but if you use a mirror, it is do-able. Angie also wrote on her prized Mercedes Benz in her parking lot in New Haven —a vehicle her great-aunt purchased for her after graduation, a gorgeous four-door white sedan with an espresso-leather interior.

Angie wrote on her white-wall tires with her full spectrum collection of markers, with that ripe, strong smell that gave her a frequent high. Her vanilla hood and door panels were soon covered in neon-orange pens—she also wrote on the expensive leather steering wheel with black and purple marker, and the glove box, radio, and dashboard. Everywhere—she couldn't stop.

Gracie explained that Angie even wrote numerous haiku in her Mercedes's rear seats, especially the floor mats covering everything from her vague but persistent sexual fantasies to her weak and oblique short-short stories, to recurrent homicidal thoughts, to a beautiful, gut-wrenching piece about her gram and how she missed her so viscerally. Angie also wrote an essay on real and true art inside the hood in miniature print, maintaining that what she does must be an obsession or it shouldn't be considered "Art with a Capital A." People started to notice this driven, odd, and once epically successful young woman. She didn't hide her quirks—after a bad rain, sleet, or snowstorm, she got out her shovels or specially-made chamois towels out and dried her Mercedes off and started anew with her markers.

Neighbors and some of the homeless people liked to observe her writing so she always drew a crowd, faithfully listening to her portable radio playing Gershwin tunes. Gracie had to stop bringing Angie back to her own dorm when she woke to find Angie defacing the antique woodwork with a ballpoint pen. Physically, Angie grew thinner as time sped on, and her hair, always perfect in a short bob for decades, was now wild, blown-out and curly—Gracie watched her style it some days, twisting it with those big fat rollers of yesteryear, smoking, whispering about how fatiguing and peculiar her life had become.

The student paper, *Yale Daily News*, even called Angie "a fantastically original performance artist with boundless range" in one issue, and soon she was on local TV news as well. Quickly she became an eccentric artiste and even had a fan base in and around New Haven. Some undergraduates, in the cruel and obvious way that only undergraduates can pull off, wrote her name in for a local board of aldermen election. She didn't win, but she came in tied for third place with twenty votes.

Angie denied all the fame, didn't buy into it, explaining to her old friends, family, and therapist that it was a mission she had to undertake, a pilgrimage, an anarchic, spiritually taxing kind of journey. Gracie, however, fell head over heels for fame. Some octogenarian women gossiped in the Wooster Street section of New Haven that Angie was a prophetic scribe or perhaps a minor saint in the making.

In the spring, Angie did colorful chalk writings and sketching on the sidewalk, or in black ink on the stucco walls of her apartment, her tendencies spilling over everywhere. One day Gracie Rose finally read Angie's piece on *What Is Art?* inside the hood of the Mercedes Benz, which took her twenty minutes to read.

Gracie said it was the most singular definition of art she'd ever come across. It was also the first time Gracie thought of her own photography project on a grander, universal scale, something beyond the confines of Yale University. It felt almost like a vision to Gracie Rose, as she watched her former lover sink deeper into mental illness chasms and its obsessional miseries.

One day while Angie wrote—this time in black, pink, yellow, and red magic marker on the white walls of her apartment on College Street, her hard wood floors, her bathtub, ceiling, commode—everywhere—Gracie dropped by with fruit, pastries, and decaf-coffee for her distraught, hyper-manic friend. Gracie used the washroom at first, cleaning her hands in Angie's cluttered sink, with Angie's scribbles all over the place, though when she emerged, Gracie fell mute for several minutes.

Angie wrote, *"Transfiguration,"* eighteen times in tightly packed, block-lettering across the front wall and window. As Gracie looked at the whole scene, she could almost see the great mountain miracle from the Bible that her adoptive mother told her about numerous times in Middletown: Disciples Peter, James, and John witness the risen spirit of Jesus, now lit incredibly bright in his clothing, hovering along with the spirits of Moses and Elijah on Mount Tabor.

As Gracie's mind raced with ideas, Angie remained

entrenched in her work, only repeating the phrase, "Changing flesh to spirit, flesh to spirit, flesh to spirit..."

"What about it, Angie?" Gracie asked. "Why does that image fascinate you so?"

Angie pondered Gracie's query and placed her markers down on the print-filled kitchen counter for a minute, sipping her coffee and lit her cigarette. She kissed Gracie on her lips and took a huge drag. Angie was dressed in her usual attire—a blueberry slip and pale blue flip-flops, and was covered in tiny, scribbled words of navy. It was all over her face, throat, arms, legs, feet, hands, fingernails, head to toe.

Gracie knew Angie was rapidly spiraling down, that her former lover would soon be evicted from her current apartment, had already been booted out of a ritzy hotel in town, and forcibly removed from her stately Whitney Avenue pad for writing with black Magic Marker months earlier, causing tens of thousands of dollars in damage.

This was just days before Angie's family succeeded in obtaining power of attorney, simply because Angie didn't even try to fight it, and immediately they had her committed to an institution overseas. That day was the last time Gracie ever saw her.

"Don't know exactly why I love that word so much," Angie said, exhaling the smoke. "Only seems preternaturally cool—to unearth the photos of a man of flesh turning to spirit. Wouldn't that be a killer if you shot a hundred black-and-white shots of that transformation? Wouldn't it be so wild? Imagine the demand from the public? The massive crowds who'd come from everywhere to witness it? The ecstatic media and press? So damn wicked to be around that, don't you think so, babe?"

Gracie wasn't much of a believer, adamantly agnostic her entire life, but for the first time she saw the possibility of her concept, dream, and future success lay in Angie's torment, and the miracle itself. As the weeks went by, Gracie saw her book project of nude photos as a kind of allegorical triptych, featuring two naked young men, perhaps a smaller, innocent one with a wolf mask, the other mask something darker, right along the lines of the Lone Ranger and a nude Gracie in the middle.

Gracie saw herself sitting sans mask, with her bug-eyed sunglasses, with her bare head, and her arms, raised to the sky, all three figures shining so brilliantly in the light.

"So, you first got the idea for your book from Angie?" I ask Gracie, both of us leaning back against the cobblestone atop Scargo Tower, our butts sore, empty iced tea cans at our sides.

"Yeah," Gracie says. "And sometimes I still lose sleep over it."

"Why?"

"Only through my lover's torment and destruction did my idea form."

"You don't blame yourself for Angie's illness, though, do you, Gracie?"

"No, not exactly," she says. "Still, there is much guilt."

"Sorry," I say.

"No sweat," she says.

"You lead the coolest, most unique life in the world, Gracie," I say.

"I just go out there and try to blow my people away," she says.

"I can attest to that," I say, and we both smile.

Gracie kisses my forehead, and says Angie once explained to her, "I can't quit... I'd like to, love to, but I'm incapable of stopping. If I cease writing, I fear I'll keel over and die, just splinter into little bits of flesh."

"She was one messed-up young lady," I say.

"Yes," Gracie says. "Sometimes Art splits you and the ones you love—*the ones that inspire you*—into tiny pieces."

I watch Gracie closely, not sure what to say about the whole thing.

"Pieces, Danny Peter Halligan," she goes on. "Possible obliteration and fragmentation of a human being. You understand me fully right now?"

"I think so," I say. "But listen, what's Angie doing with herself today?"

"She's listening to her favorite music in a large art therapy room at a fancy mental hospital deep in a forest, fifty kilometers outside Zurich," Gracie says. "Scribbling the absolute truth down for no one."

"That's it?" I ask.

"Yeah, that's about it."

THE ODDITY OF GRACIE

I can't ever be enraged at Gracie Rose for too long or toy
with the idea of strolling away and leaving her for good.
First, I'd miss *us* too much, and second, I can't let Liam be with
Gracie when I'm not around. I simply cannot handle that
concept. It probably seems silly, but I think I'd miss the extravaganzas, the soaring, out of control feeling when I'm around her.
Or inside her.

So, when I'm not with her or Liam, instead of walking
away, I take out my rage and needs by rushing into our cellar
and doing push-ups and sit-ups. I go hard for thirty minutes
and count off fifty push-ups, fifty sit-ups, and then weights,
simple eight-pound barbells, curling from one arm to the next.
Count to ten left arm, then right arm. Repeat.

Just get it out, Dad tells me. *Go angry—imagine your
worst enemy, your worst pain—let your muscles take you far
away.*

For thirty minutes each day, barbells and sit-ups and push-
ups. Over and again. Repeat. Sometimes it's Liam's face I'm
trashing or maybe leaving it in the dirt. Sometimes I run, sprint

for a half a mile, jog for another mile, sprint for a half a mile and repeat. Other moments, it's Buck's mug.

I believe much of it gets set off by Gracie's aura, her some-times toxic vibe. Not a lot, but her burning up my story earlier in the week was an awful kind of cruelty. I had her high on a pedestal so maybe the fault lies with me there. She informs my every touch, or kiss, or suggestion on how to properly caress her, or Liam, or both.

Some acts are strictly testosterone doing its thing, I know, but my needs have grown odd, less proper, as if a mini-Gracie sits directly behind my eyes like a sophisticated truck driver with a special gear shift and a steering wheel in her hands. She maneuvers and manipulates me into feeling any emotion she thinks might be fascinating to witness. Rage. Ecstasy. Joy. Amazement. Obsession. Fear. Praise. Jealousy. Pain. Repeat.

She steers any way she sees fit. Like an evil, albeit alluring and erotic, puppet-master with an assist by Liam and his father's secret stash of pharmaceuticals. My regimented, under control, daily-activities-Danny-Halligan timbre is alive and proper with everyone I meet, and yet I feel quite fragmented. All the booze and CIA potions I absorb take a heavy toll on me —that's undeniable. On Sunday morning, July 1, after running five miles and doing a hundred sit-ups and push-ups, I take a hot shower.

I stand naked examining myself in the full-length mirror. There's something odd and freaky about the way the water drip-drops and plip-plops from the showerhead behind me. Like there's another wiser, unusually articulate aquatic force observing me, whispering through the water drops to my soul. I feel fuzzy in my mind, time twisting all about, the weather in my head is cloudy, a chance of afternoon thunderstorms.

You'll be alone forever, Danny Boy, the voice coos, *and everyone in the universe will perish too. But Gracie can be at your side, offering her gifts, her body, and she will rescue you, but you need to decide if she's worth eternal bondage. Are you up for the challenge of life-long servitude?*

There are loads of doubts in my head at that point, but I am also three short days from being seventeen, so I feel ballsy, immortal in the next moment. I step out of the shower and approach my reflection, stand a quarter of an inch away.

I stare into my irises, and they immediately morph into monster thunderstorms, careening from their usual hazel to gray-blue, and soon they flare up like lightning, more spectacular than ever: turquoise, yellow, light green, lavender, and cobalt. And, finally, deep purple with black bolts of lightning, like a hungry, coiled panther waiting to strike.

I wish to do something drastic, beyond the simple punching my head or banging it like earlier in the summer or frying myself with cigarettes that I do with Gracie's blessing and coaching. Maybe I can do something to enrage Gracie or impress her so much she will bow before me—*that* sounds cool.

I brush my teeth, and stick out my tongue at myself, knocking on the glass and say: "Perhaps Gracie and I shall get dressed up all frilly and fancy and have a sit down dinner in a cozy, well-lit restaurant. We'll get comfortable, listen to Stevie Wonder, and then I'll eat my left eye whole with salt and lemon rinds, and Gracie will swallow my right eye with a raw oyster, paprika, and we'll both have a couple of beers to wash it down."

Quickly, another of my selves is banging at the same damn mirror.

"You're not sounding like you're at the top of your lucid game, bud," Danny Part II pleads. "What happened to the concept and clarity of buying a lovely lady a basket of sunflowers and hydrangea, and making her a PB&J sandwich and cold milk?"

I can't say the entire summer is all Gracie or Liam's fault, and her stupid CIA Potions she mixes up for me. I feel it's more like some living, rat-like force messed with my circuit boards ever since I met them, ever since I first took a sip of Gracie's witches brew just before dawn a month ago. I think most experts will agree that my two *horny, preying colleagues* at the Cape left a large and powerful indentation on my brain, mostly negative.

I'm the one who pursued Gracie and Liam, and I'm the one who swallowed the damn potions and enjoyed pushing myself beyond the pale. That thought rarely comes, that I had some responsibility, I usually blame it all on my charismatic and druggie friends. *Reckoning, reckoning,* I feel that word dancing all around me, teasing me, looking for myself to own what is occurring to me, so I soar back to the greatest woman in the Commonwealth, Gracie Rose.

When I am upset at Gracie and feel ready to quit her, which I tell myself I can do at any moment, I get myself jacked-up, ready to confront her, and send her home weeping.

"You have pushed me too far," I'll say. "I don't need your crap in my life one second longer."

Next minute, though, she shows up at my screen door looking like a humble milkmaid with a countenance of both wanton need and blushing innocence—a bluebonnet sweetheart. She stands in bare feet and a black tuxedo jacket, a yellow beret, and a white bikini bottom. Yes, all of that wildly arouses me, but mostly I feel thankful Buck is back in Connecticut and Gramps is fishing, and the neighbors aren't around to witness everything.

My girl is one I both loathe and adore. Gracie has a knack for being lucky—she gets away with so much crap. Yes, I'm the Irishman, but that wild Portuguese spitfire steals all my luck, no two ways about it. Forgive me as my chronology gets a bit warped and twisted, just hold on tight for these rides and a wild, tumbling flight of fancy.

After I take the long hot shower and stare myself down that day, I find Gracie out front donning a pink wig and a tutu and bowing to me outside my home, and opening the passenger side door of her Mercury Comet, playing the role of the prima punk ballerina, I guess. She buys me what she calls "an early birthday lobster roll for my loveliest stud" before we go parking at Scargo Lake.

We eat, letting hours slip by—first, the traffic whooshing past on 6A, and local intoxicated lovers and skinny dippers giggling and singing and carrying on. Next, there are chubby skunks wobbling and shuffling, and cats and squirrels hissing and darting through the brush, thicket, poison ivy, and scrub pines.

We study the sunshine and the light fading, dissolving, and shadows and darkness roll right in, and we throw all our litter into the trash like good citizens and somehow, we end up in a small red canoe. My brain is skipping like a record now or an old movie sliding off its reel. Nothing is in order, and there are no transitions sometimes. Just hard stops and jarring starts.

We're on the boat (*stolen or borrowed or rented?* I never find out), and she shoots bottle rockets off the bow, some flare out, while others soar high, before dropping into the black, silent water. Gracie places tiny candles in diminutive holders around the canoe, there isn't much room, but she lights them like she's doing the most intimate, sacred thing ever, a true reverence about her on that night. She's quiet, whispering, cooing.

Would you like to merge with me, Danny?

Yes, but I have other thoughts.

Like what?

I want to please Liam like I please you.

Do you see that as evil or demented?

Not anymore, or as much.

You're no longer ashamed of your desires?

I'm a pragmatic American teen, still a bit paranoid about personal issues.

From now on, I will approve all intimate acts, with Liam, with me, by you, with anyone.

Isn't that ridiculously controlling?

Just the way it's got to be, my dear muse, I need to trust that you'll trust me.

Fine, I might get myself off later. Do I have your silly super-blessing?

Of course, but now mount me like dogs do.

On this little red canoe?

Yes, take me from behind, my love.

Won't people overhear us?

Yes, but our pleasure takes precedence over their petty slumber.

You confuse me.

How so?

Sometimes I hate you, and your thoughts and artsy-fartsy, egocentric ways.

And other times, Danny?

Other times, I'd die for you, and eat my eyes with paprika and lemon rinds.

You think about ingesting your eyes?

Yes, I think we could split the meal—I'll take one, you eat the other.

Like now?

Like right now.

Oh, you are so dear to me, Danny—I hope you absorb and remember that fact forever.

From that singular scene I go to a joyful moment—earlier in the season, just a few days after Gracie and I first fooled around. We drive and go skinny-dipping in a pond in Truro after our day at Randy's studio. Gracie dons a tweed jacket with rust-colored elbow patches that she removes from her trunk, and a pipe, and fins and wades in, wearing nothing else, giggling her ass off.

I think about that time frequently, it's simple, nothing *that* special, no heavy drugs, just a lot of dry white wine Gracie brings with her.

"I think you'll find it *very* dry, unusually tasty, especially if you have it with three Hostess Ho Hos," she says, and I'm not sure if she's mocking me, or herself, or our abundant ignorance of wine.

She saves me from my horrible memory of Teacher-Man a few days before, or was it thirty years in the future? Wild images of trauma and terror—and settles me down over what occurred with Liam too. She holds me and says it's perfectly natural to fear the unknown, but there's a lot of joy and plea-sure in exploring what was once thought of as taboo.

"Explore everything on this globe, my dear child," she says. "Don't be held back, only reach out wider and deeper." So, I try to absorb that advice as best as I can, and later we laugh, drinking wine as the sun fades, and eat a fair amount of Ho Hos, and drive along the water, and pull down a dirt road, and voila, we arrive. She ends up getting sloshed.

"You got plenty on June twenty," she says. "You can always say that to me now."

"Imagine that," I say, and she shakes her index finger.

"Don't mock your bronzed, bald, and brilliant Portuguese goddess of fire."

I salute her, smiling, as we undress, and she gets into her tweed jacket, and pipe and fins.

"You promise me, Danny, boy?" she says. "You and me and everything together forever until death rips us apart eighty years down the road?"

"I promise you forever, my dear," I say.

"Got a light, wolfie?" she asks, tilting her pipe at me.

Some people scowl and lecture me and say how awful Gracie was to me, and how she nearly destroyed me, but she was grand and spectacular in many ways, too. I know that sounds defeatist, sad, enabling, or pathetic, or whatever the latest term is, but you see she's very much a double-edged sword in my body, inside my psyche.

My dad and doctors think Gracie is nothing but trouble—I even heard Buck describe her as a *vile cunt* once, though he never used that term again in front of me. But having that one magical day, with the girl wearing fins, smoking in her Dunhill pipe and tweed jacket, it pleases me greatly.

For thirty days in the magical and potent summer of 1979, I believe that's the precise and actual number of days, there would be no stopping me—my short-term destiny is golden, set, and shimmery. Gracie lets me drive her maroon Comet, and I take my petite, sweet, and tender lady to a sandy-bottomed lake, a clear, blue oval down a winding path. Her far-away eyes, in her bizarre space goggles look wise, her body so curvy, and I think, *I am a time-warped, albeit joyous, boy from the Nutmeg State, and my girl teaches modern romance better than anyone on the planet.*

I light her pipe, and we shake and flirt and dive around one another, kissing and petting for a while, admiring the aquamarine fireflies and the fat orange, maize, and purple flowers, deep-green weeds, and ferns along the shore. And the delicate deliciously sandy floor, and the way the fading light still sparkles—sunbeams twirling, bending, twisting, and refracting all the way down. Or almost, I guess.

Like how that lake grows so cold at our tippy toes. And as we shove off together, Gracie leaves her pipe, tweed jacket, and her fine and frilly fins behind, underwater forever, and we shoot to the surface whirling, kicking, merging, taking deep breaths, imagining love, freedom and oh, yes, a true life to be lived at last!

EXTRAVAGANZA II

I obsessed a lot about what went down with Liam and me in the palace earlier in the week. To roll, groove, and bang with Gracie was sexy and raw and I didn't see a downside. Though I tried not to inherit Buck's bigotry with waffle-boys, I hadn't yet had our earth-shattering chat with my dad, so I was feeling low, out of gas, and ashamed. I woke early on that morning of the second extravaganza, showered, and went out to the tree palace.

Everything is a process, I thought as I climbed the spiral stairs, *a ritual cleansing to help redeem me. If necessary, Jesus, I will singe myself today, and I'll lift all my desperate blisters up to you.*

I took off my clothes and lay down on the soft shag of my palace. I put on Cat Stevens's record *Tea for the Tillerman* and lit a cigarette, but then Liam appeared out of nowhere, whistling the theme music to *The Odd Couple.*

"You smoke now, Danny Hal?" he asked, coming up the stairs. "And why are you naked? Not that I'm complaining, or anything..."

I looked at the lit cigarette in my hand, the soft shag carpet, and Wonder Woman on the wall, anywhere but at Liam. I could feel the heat of my blush from my ears down to my chest. I snatched my shorts up, pulling them on, and stubbing out the cigarette to prevent any embers from hitting the shag.

"Are you okay?" he asked in what was the kindest tone I had ever heard from him.

That gentle response inspired me to own the truth, so I said, "No, not really... I was all set to fry myself, Liam, to burn myself to blisters. I know I shouldn't do that, but I'm guilty as all get out for what occurs between us. Grappling or grinding, I guess."

"Ridiculous, Danny," Liam said. "Unnecessary—it sounds like something from the self-flagellation priests of the Dark Ages."

"Insane, right?"

"Yes, forget all that Catholic guilt crap," he said. "Let the bullshit go, I mean, what about celebrating our spirit? Our healthy, God-given attraction to one another, our youthful pull to each other? Just you and I—there's no need for any self-harm by you ever again."

"Sounds a lot more pleasant," I said. "But why'd you show up here so early?"

"Pop was being his usual asshole-self," he said. "So, I wanted to get away and I needed to escape his arrogance and stupidity."

"Right. You liked the story I wrote, huh?"

"'Goofy Child' was funny, sad, really lovely," Liam said. "It gave me some comfort, believe it or not."

"Thanks," I said, pondering telling Liam about the singed story, before thinking, *no, that would just destroy the trio!*

"I was touched by the gesture itself," he said. "Sweet. It

reads like my own life, the grinding in the water, the grinding in the dunes, and on and on."

"Yep," I said with a smile. "And soon, we'll go and have a wild second extravaganza..."

"Where we'll have more fun," he said.

"Yeah?"

"I'm glad I got here on time to stop your frying plans," he said. "And all those cruel, ugly voices rushing around inside your damn skull. Don't let them tear you down any longer, Danny. Try love for a change, please don't make me quote the Beatles right now, but I will if necessary."

"I hear you," I said. "All you need is..."

"Don't make me sing it, okay?" he said.

I smiled, nodding.

"Our differences should be celebrated," Liam said. "Not kicked and buried with shame deeper into your closet. Your life, my life, we're not destined to exist in some emotive trash heap near the dump, hiding behind the old railroad tracks in town."

"Right," I said. The early morning shadows and strengthening sun felt wonderful on me, on us as we sat beside each other on the roof, our bare feet dangling off. As Liam continued talking, I thought, *so this is what it's like to have a wise older brother*.

"How do you suddenly know everything?" I asked, and he smiled.

"A few winters back there was a cool kid, older," he said. "A lover, in fact, but he moved on... always seem to move on, those wiser souls."

"Why are wise people always older?" I asked.

"They're not. It varies with each individual."

I blushed and said, "I guess."

"Do you want to hear a cool word, though?" he said.

I nodded.

"*Friendship,*" he said. "You and me, we're blossoming into an ever-expanding friendship... and if treated right, nurtured with care and kindness, a friendship keeps growing into wonderful things. It's June 1979, and let's be thankful to the world that God or whomever put each of us in everyone else's lives."

I smiled and thought, *this is what it used to feel like with Randy, we were close, could talk about anything, nothing was off the table.*

"What I know for sure is our growing bond is not supposed to be some funeral march," Liam said. "This is 1979—we all have all types of voices now, this should be more like a baptism, a raising up."

I smiled.

"Let's go to the beach for a half hour before heading to work," he said. "Celebrate a little, okay?"

So we took his Lucky-7 Chevy van down to the beach—and Liam and I skinny-dipped. It was still early, so the beach was deserted save for windsurfers and people running with their dogs. The two of us were falling all over each other, laughing, partly shy. I couldn't stop smiling, though.

"I'd like to kiss you now," Liam said.

"Never heard that from a man," I said, and then he swooped in and it just happened. His lips were soft, and his tongue was probing but gentle, and the abrasiveness of his stubbly chin was wild, too. It tasted of cigarettes and maple syrup, which was weirdly cute. Truth was, he was a better kisser than Gracie Rose, but I knew I couldn't ever say that. But then I thought, *fuck it,* and told him anyway.

"Now I can die a happy man," he said.

"You can't ever tell Gracie, though," I said.

"Pinky swears," he said with a wink.

A few hours later, I was still a utility man at Randy's studio, helping wherever needed, carrying equipment to the vehicle, cleaning the floors and bathroom, picking up coffee. That rainy afternoon, though, Randy dismissed us early. So, our trio gathered again in Gracie's Mercury and off we went. I didn't want to drink too much, and I felt more devoted to Liam than ever before, but to Gracie, as well.

Everything felt brand new, like our trio had slipped into our human skins for the first time. I know that sounds insane, like eating your fingers for a snack, but I wanted to make more impressive kick-ass art with my summer buddies. A part of me wanted to do it forever, an endless summer and all that business, and I knew that would never work, but I thought about it, anyway.

"This is pretty wild, our connection, the trio, I mean," I say.

So, Gracie preached for a while about the new skin, how serpents shed theirs, and when the old skin falls away, the new skin is so fresh and ready for life."

"Cool," I said.

"Very true," Gracie said. "And sometimes snakes mate in a ball, all kinds of genders mixing, meshing, and rolling back and forth over each other. Twirling, moving left and right, shaking every which way. This *mating ball* is a version of what the three of us do here constantly—humans, reptiles, we are all mating, shooting for some delicious, bombastic shot for glory, for the photographic art and grace of it. Our shots here are pure, and each of us are grooving, writhing back and forth together, each of us, regardless of gender."

"That's pretty cool, Gracie," I said.

"Indeed," she said.

"You are exceptionally gifted at getting us all whipped up," Liam said.

I wanted to quit drinking forever and never get high again. But I also enjoyed being part of making history here with Gracie and Liam, celebrating three devoted young people doing their best, sometimes improvising, sometimes acting high, or just having an intense time.

It's not a word I would've used three days ago, but today I felt a great deal of respect and affection toward Liam, a newfound warmth. More than just a hankering, more than rowdy, kick-ass hormones buzzing all about. I wanted to say, *Liam, you're an amazing young man, and I like you more as the hours slip by.*

Liam offered Gracie some weed, and I drank whatever was available—I skipped some of the CIA punch as Gracie drove. Liam smoked a joint in the back seat, though Gracie wasn't having much of anything, said she wanted to be clear and lucid for this major photographic event. She was subdued for most of the ride, humming an Al Green tune I didn't know. The day was overwhelming me in a grand, positive way.

I pondered Buck, Gramps, and Eileen and wondered, *what would they say to me now?* There would probably be a tremendous amount of silence on their part. I blocked out each of the annoying questions they asked me the night before.

"What do the three of you do out in that palace?" Buck asked. "Do you use drugs?"

"No, just artsy photos, mostly," I said. "We laugh, dance, and twist around."

I said goodnight quickly before scooting upstairs.

"She's too old a soul for you," Buck called out. "I'm concerned. Plus, what happened to all the pretty girls at the beach from last summer?"

"This is my time, Dad," I said. "I'm swallowing all the colors of the palette."

"What the hell does that mean?" Buck asked. "Eileen, Gramps, do you have any clue what that implies?"

"No," they both said, and I closed my eyes and prayed they wouldn't follow me up the stairs.

"I just want you with a woman who is little less extreme—not some bald junior rebel at Yale University, understand?"

"We're soul mates, okay, Dad?" I shouted. "I finally got a cool girl, whom I love, and who loves me back. Don't threaten me for my happiness."

And that kept everyone quiet until I disappeared into my room.

As Gracie, Liam, and I drove that day into Truro, I realized I didn't care if Gramps or Buck found me with Liam and myself, both of us laughing. We were celebrating life, after all. *You know what would blow their minds. To have a photograph of you in his arms in Cape Cod Bay this morning.* Danny and Liam. It wouldn't have to be overtly sexual—just me getting kissed by Liam, something poignant, sweet. Would Buck get that? I hoped someday he would.

I used to fear my desire, I'd run from it, but now I believed with certainty that I was exploring the outer banks, the outer reaches of my cranium, and a large dose of joy was pulsing through me. What we were doing was revolutionary, one of a kind, so unique. Like Gracie forever preached, we were, "Unapologetically creating amazing and palpable Art with a Capital A to tremble and shake the world up, so they may see beauty, spirit, and a lasting love."

"We're each getting in tune with the world's depths and nuance," Liam said, and I thought, *Wow, how astute! I had not seen this guy for his depth and worth.*

On our ride, I touched Gracie's left breast through her white muscle shirt, and she said, "Easy, save it all for Truro."

"I do love being near you," I said, voice echoing around the vehicle. The pitch of it seemed extra deep, full. "I want to explode inside you repeatedly."

"I love being around you, too, sweetie," she said, which only caused a snicker from Liam.

"You're ridiculously kitty-whipped, Danny," he said, though his voice sounded meek, subdued, like he was unusually high.

"How's life going back there, Ace?" I asked.

"I am in a tremendously elevated mood," Liam said. "Not every day a boy you have a crush on writes a lovely short story for you."

"Our trio is such a delicate balance, people," Gracie said. "Do any of you begin to understand that?"

"What happened with us was no big deal in the long run, for we are all pursuing big-time art," I said.

Gracie's beat up Mercury Comet came to a screeching stop along a side road, and a hubcap fell off the left front tire, and rolled into a ditch.

"Learn to drive," Liam shouted as we all got thrown forward. Gracie hopped out of her car, spat at the windshield, slamming her fist against the hood three times and shouted, "Don't fuck with me, ass-wipes."

"We just kissed and rolled around," I said. "Nothing too wild, I swear."

"*Imbeciles*," she shouted. "It's a goddamned science to maintain our trio's chemistry we have here, don't you get it?"

"Sorry, Gracie," I said, and I noticed her whole affect had frozen, so the fancy glasses didn't hide a thing. She looked emotionally constipated, and she was still ranting.

"Any of you can be thrown the fuck out of our trio at any time. Do you understand, Liam?"

"Do I sense the green hue of jealousy, Gracie?" Liam asked.

"Try hard to be mature. I know that's a difficult task for you, Mr. Preston."

"I guess I'll just split with all my chemistry set ingredients," Liam said. "Go home and enjoy the rest of my summer by playing dominoes with my hateful, drooling Pop."

Gracie backpedaled then, taking three calming breaths. "We each must put a brave face on all of this business and then our show goes on, right?"

"Yes," I said. "I'll do a better job, and I'll run over to get your hubcap..."

"Let it rot," Gracie said. "It gives more character to this rusty vehicle."

"For all of us in the trio," Liam said. "Let's move forward as a unit."

"Right," Gracie said. "I concur."

Not long after, Gracie found the perfect dead-end with puddles and no traffic, so she pulled over and turned the radio up, rolling the windows down. She started whispering, psyching us boys up like Don Shula, Buck's favorite football coach for the Miami Dolphins. Gracie's voice rose as I slipped on the wolf mask: I downed some lemonade that Gracie brought with her, I felt an obligation, to Gracie, to our trio to drink a lot, to reach for the best Art we can create.

"Here we go," Gracie said. "Take a bigger swig of it, Danny. Guzzle everything you can, my dear boy, it's going to be a rambunctious, rude, and wild extravaganza on the Cape today."

"Fine," I said and gulped it until I choked. Gracie and Liam proceeded to secure the white canvas sheet with the familiar turquoise eye from several pines and a fence post, and they smoked more weed. I drank the potion as Gracie started clapping her hands, and that sound, along with her ragged, throaty voice, caused my head to feel as if I were bursting into colorful ribbons of liquid fire.

A part of me was still so thrilled and buoyant about what had happened with Liam and myself this morning, ecstatic, really, sitting together on the roof, splashing in the ocean, just shooting the shit, him and me, and our wonderful first kiss.

Our trio looked ready for duty, to celebrate our trio. Gracie turned up the stereo as we listened to a tape she made: Kiki Dee, Glen Campbell, John Denver, and Neil Sedaka.

"Oh, please help me, Mother Mary," Liam shouts. "Sappy music is slaughtering me as we live and breathe."

We found puddles, leaping and splashing. I felt so far away inside my wolf mask, but it was a safe, warm, and contented feeling, and when I saw Liam in the black Lone Ranger mask, I barked, I roared. I drank some more CIA potion and felt myself rise from Mother Earth, hovering, while thermonuclear missiles shot out my nostrils. My heart was beating so rapidly I imagined I was morphing into a human beat box.

I looked down at my tiny wolf-self and I bellowed, saluting my mortal jester, pleased to be buzzing, so damn clear and free. We did jumping jacks and opera-impersonations for a while, until Liam growled and splashed mud my way. I smiled and reached down inside myself, and we grappled with each other, pulling our swimsuits off, showing each other our taut, proud bodies.

We laughed and rolled around together in the soppy, cool mud puddles, knocked our heads together, and barked out loud like Rottweilers and purred like bobcats. We slowly danced, did a type of exaggerated waltz for Gracie, and we dipped, shimmied, and twisted all around and fell into the mud, laughing like wild kids, like manic feral kittens.

I got back on my feet and spat at him, and Liam scowled

and flipped me the bird. I felt playful colors splashing around my head, around my neck, like Saturn's rings that were wavy and vibrating, like fiery coils with wonderful, glowing colors and hues.

"Get angry at this chamber music, boys," Gracie sang. "Get furious out here in the harsh puddles of the downtrodden."

"Yes, indeed," I said as Liam pushed me off my feet and I splashed down in a puddle.

"Daniel, my dear lonesome boy," she said. "How's the anxiety going deep inside your wacky, stressed-out noggin'?"

"Whenever I get too tipsy like now, I feel a nasty paranoia," I said.

"Roll with it," Gracie said. "Ignore the paranoia."

"Sounds like a crock of a response, Gracie," Liam said.

Liam and I created new monikers: Liam's was *Rover Dover Grover*, and mine was *Prince of the Persian Police*. We pretended we were frisky, royal animals from the caged kingdom of the great Czar of Zeroworld in Cape Franken-fairy, USA. We howled like the angriest dogs, we swiveled and sniffed like vipers—other times we were sizable Komodo dragons with yellow, forked tongues that flickered and flashed.

I felt trapped inside Wolf-Boy, aroused, and was a bunch of things exactly at the same millisecond: acutely alive, brilliantly shrewd, shrunken, invisible, cowardly, and frozen inside my new, dizzy, ten-brained skull. I was so terrified of this new life, my old life, and somehow, I compartmentalized, a skill my dad shared with me as a boy: "Pack it away, Danny, just keep it low and away, pack every bit of the sad and scary crap under-ground, and move on to better and brighter things the next morning."

I nearly dropped to the ground—I felt immensely drowsy, weepy, and yearned to soar up, up and away, and play kickball as a third grader at the Charles Frank Elementary School playground in Limewood.

"Never mind your petty worries," Gracie said, but suddenly those damn bossy ladybugs were back on my nose with their Kelly-green top hats and ruby slippers, and they shouted ugly insults, and I had a difficult time listening, I couldn't figure out who was whom.

"You're a psychotic, raving fool," one bug said. "Like a lunatic on the astroturf in Houston."

"I'm not currently hearing people well," I said.

"Easy," Gracie cooed. "It's okay, everything will be fine around here. All that potion might be going a bit haywire in your impressionable brain right about now, so slow it down, hang in there, I always got your back, darling. I've always got control of everything. Never forget that fact."

Gracie opened her huge mouth, but all I heard were the high-pitched ladybugs. A moment later, her voice cut through the noise, saying, "I dig you all so much, I really do, we all explored a moment in time, and created this otherworldly artistic expression." At least, I *think* it was her mouth moving. The bugs danced, twirled, and shook on the end of my nose and screeched, "Oh, Danny child, my dear boy, it was so much simpler in third grade, wasn't it?" When I stayed silent the bugs screeched again: "Wasn't it all so much easier years before, young man?"

I screamed at the bugs that *it was a little better and simpler, I guess, though all in all, it really wasn't ever that easy for me.* But then I was back with the bugs stuck all over me suddenly, like locusts, too, they were both ladybugs sometimes, and locusts on my nose and Gracie grabbed and kissed me for five seconds, before pinching my ass, and then she psyched up Liam and me into a wired, whirling frenzy, and we cartwheeled through some deep mud puddles, doing handstands, and wild-assed flips.

"No, no, no. That's not how it's supposed to go," Gracie scolded me, shaking her right index finger. "You're supposed to slaughter Liam."

But then Liam leapt onto my back, going by his own rules and trying to pin my face into the puddles, and jabbed me in the belly, and I fought him. I felt overwhelmed, manic, enraged, in lust, certain of only one fact, I would run through brick walls for Gracie. I just wanted to please my lady—*I'll die for her; I'll kill for her. I will strangle Liam for the melodramatic show, just dance and prowl and shudder and pretend to tear both of his lovely heads off.* Gracie was there with her camera flashing, like the superb director and field marshal she was.

"Easy, easy, my dearest snazzy gents," she said. "It's a fanciful melodrama, remember, it's forever about having a good show here."

I didn't want to be aroused by wrestling with Liam, but I was, repeatedly. It was stupendous, outrageous, thrilling, shocking, confusing, appalling, intoxicating, eerie, and a little bit wonderful, but mostly exhausting. I heard words in my brain and spotted them as Gracie's music blasted and ricocheted all around my skeleton. Repeatedly I heard some scary locusts and ladybugs in a high-pitched screech crooning, *stag, shag, rag, lag, sag, bag, tag, bye, lie, bi, bi, bisexual, rock, sock, mock, clock, tick tock, tick tock, cock-a-doodle doo.*

I finally threw Liam off me and pinned his face into the puddle and slapped his forehead twice with my open hand. "Take that, you slimy useless and sometimes malevolent turd," I screamed.

I felt a rush of something new—was it sadistic, raw, more than pleasure? *What's the next step after pleasure?* Perhaps a manic glee at finally crushing Liam? I banged my chest and shouted, "Horrid and Ugly Bitchy Bastard, I Am Your Ever-Conquering King!"

Both Gracie and Liam laughed at my royal proclamation—Gracie bent over, putting the cameras down, and Liam rolled around, laughing. "Since when do you use words like *Horrid and Ugly Bitchy Bastard?*" Liam asked. "And how are you *The Ever-Conquering King?*"

I tried to smile, but instead lay down on the ground, feeling the cool of the damp mud against my back. My brain pounded, shook, steam blew through my nose, and inside, sparklers flared. "It's the new me, folks," I said, throwing my hands upwards in a dramatic fashion.

"I'm impressed," Gracie smiled. "You're slowly becoming... something nutty and unusual.

Liam snickered. "The wiser question is what the hell are you morphing into?"

"What do you think I am?" I asked, but then I heard Gracie's ladybugs, and they were mocking me and asking, *whom do you adore more, my child? You scoundrel, you nasty bitch of a whoremonger! Will it be Gracie or Liam who owns your captive heart?*

"Wellness is close at hand," Liam said, sneezing and somehow all the ladybugs and locusts vanished from his frame, and he danced and bowed before me. "You're transforming into a better sport, a greater mood for all of us today, Danny. If I were a brilliant, eccentric professor teaching winter intensive courses on needlepoint, crocheting, and macroeconomics, and Russian literature on the island of Tahiti, you'd get an A plus."

But Gracie was still smothered by locusts, and I didn't understand her, although Liam was now free and clear of the pests, and he said, "Today has been a magical day, from the beginning. You put down the cigarettes. You defeated the self-

sabotaging choruses in your head. You made my day, Danny—
saved me from my harsh and ugly father. So... Well done."

"Thanks," I said.

"You earned it, my friend," Liam said and kissed the crown
of my head.

"What's that for?" I asked.

"I find myself falling for you."

"Well, I hope so," I said. "That short story took a lot out
of me."

When Liam complimented me, all I wanted to do was
dance around and celebrate, but I knew Gracie was forever
watching, observing like a raven or crow, soaking up all the
personal info. Gracie stopped taking the photos, and we
removed our masks, put our swimsuits back on, and since
seventy-five minutes had passed, we quit, exhausted and
covered in mud. We packed the car and trunk with the
supplies, slipped into our sandals, and three of us went to have
pizzas and orange soda at a roadside restaurant and walked
along a pier.

We didn't say much of anything for twenty minutes, just
felt the day's weight and humidity, the itchiness of the dry mud
on our bodies, the buzz was still pulsing and clamoring through
our veins. We took a dip in the sea near Gracie's peach-colored
cottage, floated on our backs and studied a plane buzzing past
with a banner reading, "Protect Yourself Now with Trojans."

The three of us used the outdoor shower and ate some stale,
giant marshmallows—*the best kind*—and relaxed on her tiny
porch. Liam discovered without too much surprise that
Gracie's roommate was a ball python named Wart. We
watched her feed some dead mice to him, warming them up by
holding them between her wonderfully muscular thighs, and
then we split.

Gracie dropped Liam off at the Wharf and he said, "Have a great day, folks."

"You, too," I said, and a part of me wanted to leap again, to celebrate my fantastic new friend, Liam. So, I thought, *exceptionally well done, Danny!* But I knew Gracie was probably pissed off about how she had blown it all to hell by burning my story earlier in the week.

"Tuck it all away, Danny," I heard Buck say to me a hundred times as a boy. "Keep it hidden."

NOT TOO SHABBY

After dropping Liam off in town, Gracie shows me a photo gallery she adores in Wellfleet.

"How'd you think the second extravaganza went?" she asks.

"Pretty exhausting, really," I say.

"I'm sorry I burned your short story, Danny," she says. "I get jealous and sometimes lose control and act ridiculously."

"Right," I say. "We're all hard-headed, I guess."

"That's true of Liam and I," Gracie says. "But you're not hard-headed. More like kind and loving to a fault."

Later, as Gracie and I shuffle through the gallery, my lady turns reverent, almost like a child at her first communion. She and I hold hands, her thumbs twitching. She says things like, "Wow, not too shabby," at one photo and then, "Jesus, this is who I need to be competing with."

"What are you seeing?" I ask, whispering, as if we're in a chapel. I am acutely aware of the dust on the floor, the smudge on the window behind the shop owner, the awkward, thin man in a blue seersucker suit coughing behind us. I grow anxious for a few seconds that I have done something wrong, a grave mistake, but the feeling passes when Gracie squeezes my hand.

"Art washes away from the soul the dust of everyday life," Gracie says.

"Van Gogh?"

"Picasso," she says. "Art is transforming, people just need to give it a shot."

"Tell me," I say then. "How'd you get so smart?"

Gracie kisses my nose: "I could ask the same of you."

I smile at last, finally coming down from whatever was in the potent magical sauce she had given me earlier.

"We gotta improve and go beyond the daily grind," she says. "Stretch beyond comfortable, head to the land of our closed-eyes selves."

"Which is where?" I ask.

"Deep in our guts," she says. "Or maybe it's way up high in our psyches. I'm really not sure on that one, more research is needed ASAP."

I watch her with awe.

"You don't need the drugs to achieve the art, either," she says. "I once had a chat with a brilliantly wise young poet from Vermont named Baron Wormser, and he said, 'Imagination is the best way to tap into your unconscious without doing something illegal.'"

"Cool," I say.

"We don't need secret CIA potions at all, sugar," Gracie says.

"Then why do we use them so much?" I ask.

"It's the only way to get Liam involved," she says. "He needs them more than us, Liam offers balance... We can't ever lose his rage. He represents the fire. He lives in the beast's belly; all that war and kerosene is necessary. To balance us out."

I nod, watching her, not fully believing the truth of that comment, and think, *what would it be like if it was just Liam sans Gracie? Or Gracie without Liam? Somehow, I decided, they probably balance each other out.*

"No burns on the skin this morning, huh?" she says.

"Felt refreshing not to do it," I say.

"Earlier in the season scars, though," she says, grabbing my left wrist. "Seems like they're everywhere on you."

"Awful," I say, "but they used to help me cope."

"I understand," she says. "I had friends at Yale who did that."

"So?" I say, agitated.

"When Buck, Eileen, or Gramps discovers them," she says, "they might flip out and overreact, even send you to a mental hospital, I bet. It'll be a chaotic mess."

"And?"

"I love you too much now, sugar," she says. "Not ready for our summer to be ruined. Be strategic from now on, okay?"

"Strategic?"

"Hidden," she says, kissing my fingers. "Where the world won't find them, plus I can help you with placement of the burns, you know?"

"Like how?"

"Like watch or help you do it," Gracie says, magic fingers dancing over my groin, "make recommendations. Could be kinky and bizarre fun when you think about it."

I feel ashamed, aroused, pissed off, and weirdly bonded with Gracie at that precise second. A few minutes later, we buy pistachio ice cream in a sugar cone at a café with a jukebox of only Simon and Garfunkel tunes. I sit down inside and listen to "The Only Living Boy in New York"—I make Gracie sit with me and insist she listen to the entire tune, but she only says, "Not my cup of tea, babe."

"It's pure joy, though," I say.

"Too mellow for me, I'm already fast asleep," she says.

Gracie drives me back to Dennis, and we listen to John Coltrane's *A Love Supreme* on the stereo for the entire ride on 6A. Gracie tells me that the album can change one's life, eases pain, and so I pine for only that. I stick my head out the window and feel the wetness, the wind on my cheeks, even the sweat and moisture beading up on my forehead.

The music is hypnotizing, and I feel somehow silent within. The world feels at rest (*most definitely* not peaceful, but a compartmentalized kind of rest) and it becomes about the jazz, and I let the saxophone's sweetness filter and shuffle its way through my skin, my dimples, inside my frazzled body, and its rhythm offers me goose bumps. I shiver and the music flares up and down my spine.

I study the little cottages set back beyond some of the fruit and vegetable stands on 6A. In the back are two extraordinary grottos, dueling Virgin Marys, each surrounded with a blue shell and candles. The shells look impenetrable, and I wonder about God, what she thinks of me at this moment, if she is pleased or concerned at my downward, druggie spiral I seem to be taking. Hazy, numbing turns without much forethought. To avoid any further anguish, I concentrate on the grottos again.

The intricate designs remind me of Disney World, the first time I ever visited with Gramps. When I see the kitschy but stately Virgin Mary on a lawn, I think of a Disney character I spotted outside the Space Mountain roller coaster.

The female figure was a yellow and orange candle with a type of plastic halo, with arms and legs, and its poise and posture reminded me of a pensive Mary. As I rode on the roller coaster later, I thought oddly of her and took in the flitting, sparkly white, red, purple, and blue lights in the deep darkness, and the squealing young people. I loved the way the ride pushed my heart into my throat, and the force, the enormous speed as we flew around. It was nothing short of spectacular.

I recall wetting the bed at the 1776 Motel the night before, four miles outside of Disney World (the motel's sign was of a Patriot kneeling while he gripped his musket). Gramps waved his hand from across the room at me and said, "It's the damn mattresses, Danny, not your fault. The mattresses were all defective, broken, and cursed. Nothing wrong with you whatsoever, my good boy."

Earlier, we had both swam into the deep end of the motel pool, and the deep-green luminescent light of the water lamps gave it an eerie, haunted vibe. I dived down through the water, twisting, and brushed my chest against the rough concrete of the bottom, my ears pounding, closing in, and ready to implode. I pushed off the base and flew, kicking and laughing to myself and suddenly, WHOOSH, fresh air, deep-deep, huge, hungry breath, lungs opening, sucking in the oxygen.

A few minutes later, my belly hurt as I breathed so I sat on an old canvas lounge chair and studied my pruned fingers and toes while Gramps swam laps. Out beyond the walls of the pool, the neon lights partially lit the hotel along with billboards of huge, grinning women gulping pulpy orange juice.

I studied black telephone poles and wires, advertisements, streetlights, and beyond that some tiny propeller-planes soaring by. One large helicopter moves even closer and lower, maybe coming to land at the tiny airstrip a quarter mile down the road. Thoughts raced through me like: *Who comes to Disney World in a helicopter? Would they ever give me and Gramps a joy ride?*

The concrete of the pool area was damp but warm, the air felt thick, dense, like you could just reach out, grip it, and gorge on the night's blackness. I could see on top of the walls around the pool and the perimeter of the motel where broken glass and barbed wire waited for some intruder. I knew this couldn't keep me safe, though.

I loved being with Gramps, he was so playful, and goofy, like an extremely hip Captain Kangaroo, taking me for special rides in his brain. The afternoon with Gracie, Liam, and myself occurs only seven years after my time in Disney World, and I have already lost many things: my dog, Jagger, and quite a bit of innocence and stability, although Gramps is still around, hanging in there with me and Eileen.

Especially with Liam this morning, affirming me concerning my short story, getting me to skip those cigarette burns, goddamn, I think, I'd call it a wonderful day, a highlight of this funky summer of 1979. I hadn't thought of John Coltrane since that time, but with his music rushing through me, and Gracie's potions offering me an extra-sensory kind of groove, my eyes filled. To be true, I still don't know squat about life or anything really about jazz, but it was a freeing kind of day, a discovery to soak up during my summer of transformation. I was tired but so pleased to be alive, needed, and, *apparently*, important.

COLORFUL AND ON FIRE

G racie Rose drives me around to a bunch of galleries in Brewster and East Dennis on a Saturday, and we spend the afternoon searching for a medium-sized work to hang over her bed, something *colorful and on fire* is how Gracie puts it. I don't know a thing about the topic. My high school drawing and painting skills are rudimentary and influenced by study halls and how much time I need to kill and if I have a dull pencil or a bleeding pen on that day.

My drawings consist of basic doodles and weird faces, stretchy noses, scary teeth, and droopy chins on questionably shaped gentlemen with caps and voluptuous women in short shorts, and each has a cigarette dangling from their lips like an old-school fossilized pool hall hustler.

No, I was not the boy to ask for direction with artistic decisions—I tailed Gracie around, a pup along for the joy ride, my eyes by then already a little bloodshot, my mind reeling with a whiskey that Gracie keeps below the seat of her Comet.

My number one girl of the arts later settles on an eight-inch silver sculpture of a couple intertwined with one another. It costs her $70, which I think is outlandish, but she tells me she has a bond with the artist, an older man with a wheeze and a pipe—a cousin of her adoptive father from Middletown, Connecticut.

Not only the home of the Wesleyan University Cardinals, she proudly says, and her hometown for many years after arriving from Palo Alto as a toddler, it's also where she lost her virginity at sixteen to two attending physicians in the laundry room of Middlesex Hospital, where Gracie volunteered for a few years.

"Always loved doing things in groups of three," she whispers.

Her stories are both mythical and slightly fact-based. I follow them less and less as the summer goes on, but in mid-June I still hang on to each word. Of course, I'm decimated by her actions with "Goofy Child," but I was good at blocking facts out of my mind.

"We'll move on with our lives and shoot for excellence, right, Danny?"

"You said it, Gracie," I said.

"I think we've both made our mistakes in the recent past, but we're professionals, and will continue on with our day-to-day lives."

"Yes," I said.

Two days later Gracie discovers an indigo and gold watercolor in an old driftwood-like frame. It's a spherical sun-like piece at a tag sale in East Dennis, and it ends up looking cool above Gracie's bed.

I also cultivate an appreciation of sunshine thanks to Gracie's keen eye, and Liam's collection of hallucinogenic delicacies. But after seeing some scary images, like my left hand falling apart with Randy, I refuse to ingest anything too *spacey*. But I already feel a heavy whiskey buzz.

"Imagine you have a wide palette waiting at your finger-tips," Gracie says.

"Not sure what that is," I say, and she smiles, tousling my hair.

"A circular plate holding all the different colors in the spectrum."

"Gotcha," I say. "I see it now."

"Imagine the juices entering your system," she says. "Squint your eyes at the sun—known artists travel from all over to see this unique, delicate light, it's that rare."

"Okay," I say. "I don't think I need the drugs; the light is so—"

"Don't change the subject," she says. "*Fine,* you don't need them, but the fact is, I've already ingested the medicine, so now the light churns, watch pink turn dark purple..."

I nod.

"Watch the cobalt dance with black, or rust, or brown," Gracie goes on. "Watch the light bleed, Danny. Imagine it drip-ping and flowing and gushing like mad, feel it massage your soul, whispering into the cilia."

"Yes," I say.

"Do you feel it?"

"I think so," I say. "It's pretty cool."

"We'll ease off now," she says. "I'll take you inside to see a film."

We see a group of white-haired eighty-five-year-olds at the Cape Cinema, a movie house first constructed in 1930. I started to panic.

"Don't think I can go in," I say, my head light, body heavy.

"Hush, now, take it slow, deep, deep breaths," Gracie says, stroking my arm. "We'll go to the balcony, soak up the mellow vibe."

Gracie and I purchase tickets, popcorn and go upstairs to

the mezzanine to take in the wild fables on the ceiling: a massive, sweeping mural by artist and illustrator, Rockwell Kent. We glance down and find only a smattering of an audience, and no one, as yet, has joined us in the balcony. We finally focus on the screen minutes into an award-winning film.

The French film is subtitled, and I immediately stand a bit straighter, this being my first experience with a foreign film, and I feel a real panic about it, an expectation to pay attention, in case someone ever brings it up at a cocktail party, which is something I *also* haven't experienced before.

As the film plods on, Gracie and I quickly sour on it, climbing out of our seats and laying back in the center aisle. Though the carpet is worn and hard and sticky on our backs, the booze we shared earlier makes us feel more than buoyant, protected somehow, a magical cocoon that floats way up high. I slip my trusty golf jacket behind our heads for cushioning, and we take in the visuals together.

The ceiling holds varying shades of blue and orange and shows Taurus, a giant bull with wings, golden and ribbed, which flies effortlessly beside a ten-foot, orangey-red greyhound stretching out along with sculpted lovers soaring, golden hair and limbs intertwined. We study the light and shadow of flickering images dancing on the mythical scene above, and I'm suddenly overcome, eyes spilling.

"Time passes for all of us, Danny," Gracie whispers, kissing my cheek and squeezing my right hand. "Not just for you and me, sugar."

"I can feel the clock slipping and ticking by," I say. "Want to grip the day, keep it forever, and stay within it. Nothing more, just grip it so hard."

"Good luck with that one, babe," Gracie says.

There is every sort of constellation up on the ceiling—I figure I can find hundreds, maybe thousands more if my tears hang around long enough. There's a lot of wild times for me ahead and plenty of confusion. Lots of nagging questions await me.

But that day, early in the season, life feels simple—it's a basic attraction without subtraction, a wonderful rudimentary equation to figure out. The Cape is not yet brimming with a full summer crowd, so every ray of sunshine or gust of salt air feels gifted to me by the heavens. All I know is this wonderful, unique, and talented woman—pushing twenty-two—who's fascinated and turned on by a horn-dog sixteen-year-old boy is mine for the summer, and I'm hers. So, we kiss, and she holds my hand, and I cry happy tears.

But we heard the teenager usher shuffling down the aisle toward us, clearing his throat, so we awkwardly got to our feet, embarrassed for a few seconds. As I gather my jacket, the two of us slip past the usher's flashlight, go down the stairs out of the building, and make our way to her marvelously maroon Mercury Comet. With that singular and revered mural inside, I know summers will be forever safe, strung together like candied pearls for everyone to see, taste, and feel.

Forty-five minutes later, Gracie and I sit on a bench near the Provincetown Wharf watching tourists stream past. People return from whale watches and fishing trips, feasting on salt-water taffy, lobster rolls, and gelato. A handful of septuagenarians paint watercolors, doing their best to capture the remains of another sunset. It's a rare, sweet day, and I feel wonderful, brimming with life.

"I love the sunshine," I say.

"Me too," Gracie says. "But I like sunburns more."

I wander over to the other side of the street, purchasing a corn dog, and some chocolate marshmallow fudge among the crowds. The people I find there are a vast mix—some are pale and haggard, others young and toned, and several are adamantly straight, obese, or oblong. Others appear unsure, neurotic, and a bunch more are wonderfully bronzed but emotionally spent.

Some want to quit the whole life thing right this minute, maybe jump off a boat with cement in their pockets, or swan dive off the Provincetown Tower protesting a war taking place on another continent by wearing a high school lacrosse helmet and rusty corduroy shorts and some Wellington boots. There are also dancers, sculptors, and poets who are all set to start from scratch tomorrow—get to work at the crack of dawn so they can make the greatest works of their lives.

As I return to Gracie, I purchase a yellow smiley-faced balloon and funky olive-colored sunglasses, slipping them on, feeling the energy of the multicolored, multi-talented, multi-sexed humanity, the spectrum making me feel buoyant and thrilled.

"You look like a pathetic *tourist*," Gracie says, offering no smile.

"Sorry," I say, panicked suddenly, thinking, *wait, I thought things were cool between us, weren't they, some golden moments ago? How did I fuck this one up?*

Gracie pulls the yellow balloon down to her nose, sniffs it like it's coated in excrement, and lets it soar away. As I watch the balloon disappear, Gracie makes another noise of disgust and rapidly melts into the crowd. She vanishes like sunrise mist, and I lose her. At first, I think I'll find her around the next bend or in the next gallery, but she's nowhere to be found over an hour later. Had she ever been here or was all this a tragic vision from her ever-potent potions? Granted, Gracie fooled around with her CIA chemicals frequently, trying a little more vodka here, a bit of hallucinogen there. She doesn't seem to care all that much, but I don't allow myself to obsess about that fact.

Of course, I panic, grow frantic, and nearly accost someone

else's grandpa with a bald head and a purple polo shirt. In desperation, I run to the Shoot! studio down the street, but it's past closing time, so I hunch in the alley behind a dumpster. Sobbing away, I slip into a full-blown panic attack, nibbling away at each of my cuticles until they begin to bleed. When Gracie finally discovers me an hour later, my face is streaked with blood, sweat, and tears. My knees are roughed-up and scraped from tripping on the winding cobblestone streets.

"Oh, my dear angel," she says. "Where'd the hell you run off to?"

"I don't know anymore," I say, and her voice is soft, gentle, and I realize then that she loves me dearly, and I need her beside me forever. How could have I ever have ever doubted it? When her tan fingers lift my chin and her plump lips kiss away all my tears, I feel warm and safe. I mean, why did I ever run away from this Goddess of pleasure? Yeah, I mean, periodically she's cruel and selfish, but who the hell isn't? Why would I ever do something so foolish as to not fully rely on her?

LIAM'S RISE

After *Transfiguration Photos* was published to wild attention and acclaim, Liam Preston held his own press conference at his favorite saloon in Dennis, Massachusetts, called Joe Mac's and admitted he was the man behind the Lone Ranger mask and had a brief fling with fame. Liam always stayed silent about me, though, and I loved him for that.

"Wolf-Boy doesn't want any attention at this point in his life," Liam said. "He just wants to heal and get better, so please pray for him right now. He's one wonderful person, was that way from the beginning."

"Why do both you and Gracie protect him so much?" reporters asked.

"Not your business," he said. "And that's all I'll say."

Eventually, Liam somehow ended up in a new-wave band by the name of Tabs, where the entire ensemble had done enormous amounts of psychedelic mushrooms, and never ate meat or candy. Only problem was they couldn't sing, dance, or play anything, just released a seventy-eight minute, black-lit video of the quintet stumbling around, clapping hands, humming to an electric drum machine with their glow-in-the-dark jock straps and bright lime athletic socks.

They finger-painted anarchy and peace signs with psychedelic colors on a white wall, which was, in fact, a close-up of Ronald Reagan's teeth. They climbed ladders, played on swinging trapezes, did sit-ups with blinking neon ears on, sprinted on huge treadmills, and flexed near fog machines, mirrors, hugging a whole basket of two-faced kittens and plastic pythons.

Their video sales were dismal in America, though immensely popular in Western Europe. So, Liam also became a spokesman for the Humane Society in Berlin and Amsterdam and was a disc jockey in that part of the world for a time. Liam continued his public service announcements for homeless shelters and safe sex, and they became quite popular. Even after he passed on, they kept playing them.

One of the safe sex commercials showed Liam covered in fifteen puppies. In another one, little kittens climbed all over him. Another consisted of Liam dressed in a Lone Ranger mask inside a giant condom, walking in on different couples—straight, gay, lesbian—in a hotel room and reminding them to always use condoms.

"Protection ain't protection unless it's protection."

RANDY, TAKE TWO

Following our final extravaganzas, I recuperated for several days at the Psych unit, a holding area at Cape Cod Hospital. From a window there I studied all the tourist traffic going by. I saw some boats on trailers, multiple bikes on the back of a Subaru, some huge campers, and a Winnebago.

On July 12, 1979, Buck drives me up to Spruce Lodge, a leading psychiatric hospital in Montpelier, Vermont three hours away. I'm anxious and jittery about all I will see and learn. I wish Randy was with us, he was always so supportive of me. Dad tells me Randy continues to struggle with substances, and that his studio is *losing a lot of cash*, and he hasn't been heard from in a few days. *When was the last time I had a decent chat with Randy?*

"Are you alone, Danny?" Randy asks when he will finally call me a day later. "Can you get some privacy there?"

"I'm alone in the phone booth... No one's with me now," I say. "I'm safe, Randy."

"Buck's not there?" he says.

"Dad's down the other hall chatting with an ancient shrink about the discount hardware business," I say. "We're all alone."

"First and foremost, I wanted to begin by apologizing for letting you down when you reached out in Orleans," he says. "I was shitfaced, and you needed guidance on bisexuality, and I blew it—I choked. I barely mumbled, 'Always use condoms.'"

"No sweat, Randy, you can make it up to me," I say. "I'm not going anywhere, and neither are you, right?"

"Good point," Randy says. "I like the sound of hope in that answer, Danny."

"Not a death sentence for me at all," I say. "Or for you."

"Only temporary, thank God," he says.

"Are you at a rehab or a psych hospital, Randy?" I ask.

"Outside of Boston, near Natick," he says. "Part rehab, part psych, I guess, part Shangri-La."

"Cool, I guess," I say. "Can I gossip with you?"

"Please do," he says.

"Buck apologized about his waffle-boy comments he made when I was twelve at the Yale Bowl, the stuff he's been spewing for years."

"Did you about fall over?"

"Buck is like a new person, evolving all the time."

"Holy shit... Is this the same stubborn Buck Halligan I've known for decades? Closing in on fifty-three years old?"

"Bewildering, right?" I say. "I told him I was probably bisexual."

"That's extraordinary, Danny," Randy says. "Buck and you discussing bisexuality in a welcoming, loving manner."

"My mind was blown," I say. "Never been so proud of my dad, or of myself."

"That's so cool," Randy says. "Congrats..."

"Thanks."

"Can I, at least, ask some gossipy questions?"

"Fire away, Uncle."

"What the hell happened with Liam?"

"It was confusing and shocking, and I've still not figured any of it out yet," I say.

"You two always seemed so connected, but Buck says Liam ended up raping you?"

"Yeah," I say. "Horrible, apparently he was on some PCP..."

"Why would he take that shit?"

"It was insane," I say. "Days before all that, I had felt really close, bonded with him. And he helped me, even steered me away from self-harm. He was real affectionate, and I started thinking so positively about him and me. He kissed me for the first time at Bay View."

"How was that?"

"Sweet and weird and impressive," I say. "I thought maybe I could even have a relationship with the guy. I even gave him a goddamned blowjob."

"Wow, so how'd that one go?"

"Pretty good, but get this... I also wrote a short story for him a few days earlier."

"I would love to get a story from you, Danny," he says, and we both laugh. "But since when are you writing fiction?"

"Just woke up one day and put it all down," I say. "It ain't Hemingway, but it's not so awful, either. Just a beginner, nothing serious about it, so I just sat at my desk in my room and let it fly out of me."

"Can I get the next story?" he asks, and so we laugh some more. It's the first genuine laughter I've shared with Randy in months, really, maybe even a year.

"It sounds like you already forgave Liam?" Randy says. "Is that right?"

"No, no... I mean, *rape* is a huge, horrific word," I say. "I probably loved Liam before, but I hated him for the assault, still do. Obliteration is an accurate word for how Gracie and Liam left me on July Fourth. Dad saved me, though... Buck rescued me, the only thing I know for sure is Buck is the only true American hero in my life."

"Great," Randy says. "Stay positive and be gentler with yourself, okay?"

I hear him cough, hacking up a storm for thirty seconds.

"That doesn't sound too good," I say.

"Promise no more drugs," Randy says. "*Promise me right now.*"

"I promise, I promise, Randy," I say. "But are you getting legit help, Randy?"

"*Recovery Rehab*, they call it, but my roommate snores and farts like an old hag... I can't take much more of it to be honest... got another ten days to go, so..."

"Stick with it, okay?" I say. "Glad you're trying hard. You can always sing."

"My MD wants me to cut back on performing," he says. "Says my vocal cords are taking a beating, all that smoke in the clubs and theaters."

"You're my favorite singer ever in history..."

"Try David Bowie, now *there's* a star."

"I prefer Dandy Randy O'Riley at the top of my list," I say. "*Always.* The truth is, Randy, I truly don't feel like a together, contented human being unless you're involved in my life. You're such a steadying factor, so I'm so glad you called, and that you're shooting for sobriety."

"Merci, Nephew, that means a lot to me, but I have to get off the phone, my snoring, flatulent roommate is waiting to call someone wise."

"Phone me in a few days, okay?" I ask.

"I love you like crazy, Danny," he says. "Congrats for all the changes you're trying hard to make. You're on your way."

"Thanks, Randy," I say.

A HARD RAIN

Gracie pulls up near Gramps's cottage, whistling like one happy woman. Her windows are down, and rushes of cool air slip through her Mercury. Neighborhood kids are playing Whiffle ball on the Geller's well-manicured lawn across the way, but they dash inside as the thunder and heavy rain rolls in. Gracie rolls up her windows as we thumb wrestle before she illegally pins my thumb with her index finger.

"You cheat at this game all the time now," I say, and she shrugs and hands me a thermos.

I fought the temptations for a while, or *at least six days*. I said no to any of Gracie's magical potions, any mixes that would mess with my mind, with my perceptions. I had shared with her the incident of the crumbling, bouncing fingers on 6A in Orleans with Randy, and she balked: "My potions would *never* do that," she said. "I swear on my mother's name."

So, I listen to her and start coming around to her side again, to her way. Gracie works on me with her wiles, suggesting: "A true muse gives all of himself—I care for you, I will watch over you forever, but you must trust me, okay? Drink this and enjoy."

Admittedly, I don't know what the magical potion is made of, but after I take a big swig, I feel freer, more relaxed, and the sky growls a little louder, a teasing bark, but I'm not sure if that's my mind creating the sound, or the actual thunder. My trust in Gracie is almost complete—I rarely question what she hands me anymore. I take the medicine like a good boy because it's what my new Mama instructs. Perhaps that sounds pathetic, but she's a highly effective bully, wrapped in lovely sexual disguise. I find her so hard to resist.

Gracie is my universe, and the world doesn't exist without her. Even with Dad, or Gramps, or Randy, their conversation is debris, unimportant, trash-like and very much on the periphery. I know that kind of trust can be dangerous, and it's my fault, of course, I can't blame my family—they've each warned me of the femme fatale and yet I still celebrate and worship her. Dad is the most obvious, calling Gracie a harlot. She supplants everyone in my life. She dominates and rules my kingdom, and you know what is so cool and heady and bizarrely on target? *Danny Hal* is her kingdom! *Me*, or as she puts it—*MOI*—I am what she rules. Sure, Liam has his role, and I admit I like him and his muscular electricity, but being with Gracie is like a shining and glowing brightness at the center of the Earth, at the very core.

And that's my point about being with her, or near her, it's a powerful thing. Being the center, the focus of things, it's tremendously heady stuff. One time it was just me and Gracie and she had me write down any unusual sexual thoughts or fantasies. I tell her all about my second-grade teacher years ago, a naked, wonderfully bosomy Miss Bailey covered in Crisco oil.

Gracie says, "Give me something else, a really way out there nugget."

She wants to hear about messed-up dirt and gossip. She gets inspired by the pain of others, the struggles, and if that's me, *by God*, even better. I share with her what I wrestled with the previous year, my first year of high school and she's taken with it. I tell her: I mimed the act of cutting off my genitals—taking a very sharp scissors and placing my penis in between the blades and daring myself, spending hours pretending to slice the damn thing off, like a twisted version of Russian Roulette.

I like my penis, but I also enjoy this behavior—it became addictive with me last year, a game of obsession and chance. Something very trance-like about it lulls me into a kind of teasing, singsong groove: Like the scissors croon into my ears, the sharp blades harmonizing, like we have a heart-to-heart chat about castration and its wonderful and lasting benefits. *Just play the game, and study a clock, and be cautious, or we'll slice off your cock.*

Of course, it wasn't something I ever truly did, or considered, and yet I sat there, goading myself to get rid of it, one big slice. Come on, you silly bastard, I thought, live a little, I dare you, do it for the hell of it—unite all American eunuchs around this disturbed globe, show your support with a quick snip-snip and away we go.

The idea dominated my life for a significant amount of time in my first year of high school—I stayed home from school sick for three days in a row and watched silly game shows in the family room while sitting in my father's leather chair, naked, with scissors pressing onto my penis. Sometimes when I was really bored, I used two scissors, and I leaned back, those four blades cutting into me slightly. I mimed the castration, knowing a passing Mormon or a stray Maytag Repairman or anyone could show up at the front door at any moment.

I must commit this act, or pretend too, more like an intense compulsion, *a need*. Who knows? Maybe I saw it first in one of Liam's wild pornos a few summers before, or in some twisted, bloody horror flick. I went to see a therapist about my obsession, informed my dad high school was too overwhelming, and so I needed someone to unload on, to chat with.

"Whatever it takes, Danny," Buck said. "Get all the help you need."

"Thanks, Dad," I said.

But when I saw the shrink waiting in his office, he leaned inappropriately forward out of his leather chair in his khakis, loafers, and chocolate Izod sweater, trying to show a welcoming posture, but I saw he was dying to know my dirty laundry, to mess around with my little secret. He gazed at me like I was a frog about to be dissected. He was hungry for it, famished for my naked anguish.

I could already feel the doctor's incisors chewing my flesh, my pain, ready to take all the itty-bitty parts of me and lay them out on the kitchen counter, fixing to make a three-course meal out of my horrors, worries, and obsessions. He wanted to take my remains and fry me up with some extra-virgin olive oil, and peppers and sauce, and crunch, crunch, crunch, what a delicious and nutritious feast I would become.

So, I said, screw it, forget it, pal, and left the damn MD in his fancy, low-to-the-ground leather chair, just walked right out. And again, I did what my dad suggested and did three hundred push-ups against the cold concrete floor of the cellar, got the rage and confusion out and went hard and strong for a long while. *Feel the secret bursting out, wanting to escape, wanting to surface, out, out, get it out, Danny, get that goddamned ugly secret set free, share it with someone, you just got too, or you'll burst a seam.*

But I bit down even harder and tucked it away, packed it away like Buck always said, swallowed that bastard. Kept it hidden, swallowed that damn secret, kept it so far away, even if it hurt, even if it ached and the acid burned through the lining of my belly. *It's too twisted and bizarre, Danny, people will think you're too frigging whacked, they'll think you're the most insane cat in the clowder.*

I kept the secret hush-hushed, kept it down, swallowed it all. So many swallowed secrets, they were like stones in my pockets, I was afraid to go swimming. Stones of pain and sorrow would pull me under so damn fast and everything would be over. Done. Kaput.

Adios.

I ended up keeping my mouth shut and somehow, some-way, I never told anyone that year about my secret. The funny thing is, when I do finally reveal the truth to Gracie in the summer of '79, she drools. Her mouth opens and an actual, certified, flame-broiled artistic drool shows up. Even though my confession to Gracie is strange and embarrassing, it's also an invigorating and heady experience, a massive adrenaline rush.

My favorite goddess ever in the history of the world is fasci-nated by me even more than usual for another week, and through Gracie's sunglasses I can see that look of, "What the hell is this all about?" She's just like that shrink I saw many months earlier—Gracie wants to dissect me, too—I see it in how her lips grow moist, she wants to fry me up in a pan, throw herbs and spices on me and crunch me, crunch, crunch, crunch with her gapped pearly whites, and swallow me down. But, first, ah sweet Jesus, first, she wants to get the black-and-white photos shot.

"Sugar, so sweet," she says. "You gotta let me get some shots of that, okay?"

Of course, I say no, *never ever will that happen,* but as soon as the confession falls from my mouth, I know she will get the photos taken. And she does. She shoots about 235 pictures of me on a stormy early evening, me, naked in my Wolf-Boy mask on her bed at her peach-colored cottage, leaning against her fat, downy pillows while she moves around me, shooting from a standing, shifting position while Nina Simone sings to both of us, and a hungry ball python, Wart, in his glass cage studies us.

The serpent tastes our sweat on the air with lightning flickers of his tongue. And the rain keeps pounding at the windows, slamming against the roof, pelting the shingles, and the thunder roars and the wind howls, and I feel really unsafe, like my arteries are going to be sliced open. I'm terrified that Gracie's bouncing around the bed will shake my hand, and I'll be cut, or the worst thing, that she'll stumble and fall on top of me and accidentally fulfill the threat.

By the time she finishes ninety minutes later, I'm trembling with fear and arousal. At that point the most poignant and tender moment occurs—sweetest one I ever had with Gracie. For one brief interlude, she takes her glasses off and gets fully nude—she never had done that before, not once, and there is something so damn gorgeous about it—I know she legitimately loves me, that's the example I use, what I tell the doctors when I arrive at Spruce Lodge.

Gracie places her cameras down after our photo session and has me put the scissors away. She removes my wolf mask and sets it on the pillow. She strokes both of my cheeks with her soft, warm hands, and then embraces me while I sob into her chest. It explodes from me—ugly hurt, despair, shame, and fear.

The weeping goes on for fifteen minutes straight, full guttural cries. I have no idea how Gracie knew I needed to cry, or unload, but she just does. And then a little while later, Nina Simone gets turned back on the stereo, and Gracie and I make a strong, insistent kind of love. Real tender and sweet, and old Wart watches the whole damn thing, absorbing it, absorbing us.

This time we make love with deep feeling. Gracie is one

smooth, loving, and tactical operator—she does compassion and warmth better than anyone, but then she goes cruel, cold, and bitter so fast too. She always goes cruel, only a matter of time. But for the moment, Christ, for that small gap of thirty minutes she holds me, and we come together, it feels downright divine.

"Why can't it always be this way?" I asked her, snuggling close, holding on to her so tight.

"The Universe is too cruel for words, angel," Gracie said. "Society would devour us, destroy us, wouldn't even debate it. Right down the gullet and we'd perish."

"Can I say something to you?"

"Of course," she said. "Open up."

"Whenever I ask you, or anyone challenges you on your behavior, you blame it on the world."

"So?" she said.

"I don't know why I noticed that, but I guess I did, huh?"

"I don't like it when you think independently," she laughed.

"That's an awful thing to say," I told her, but she only grinned.

I felt bound to Gracie at that moment, an umbilicus tethered our hearts and souls. Like life support, almost—I think I would die if it were ever severed. It sustained even as we dressed and descended the stairs from her place to the Mercury Comet in her parking space. As she drove me home through the pelting rain and blackness back to the town of Dennis, Gracie started doing a type of play-by-play of our ride, a dramatic actor.

"The sheets of water pour down onto us on Route 6, every window minimizing and blurring away the rest of the world despite the heartbeat-like thump-thump-thump of the wiper blades."

"Yes," I said.

"I'm talking or praying or preaching as I drive and think, 'This water is like our greater womb, Danny—protecting us from the toxicity of the outer world, the hush, slip, and whir of my Goodyear tires over wet asphalt like rushing blood in our veins. The ride home seems to last forever, huh, Danny?'"

"It does, it does," I said.

I looked into her eyes—she'd kept her dark glasses off for the whole rainy trip. Her gumdrop emeralds gazed into mine, and I sensed it, too. Gracie's soul was within me now, and I felt the distant sensation of mine in hers. Our love is legit, correct? I mean, this is true love I'm experiencing with Gracie—sure, maybe Buck, Gramps, Eileen, and Randy don't agree, but I know her best, *I know the true, authentic Gracie.* Buck spoke about his deep love for my mom at the Cape War Memorial in Barnstable recently. He said Miriam was like a delicate, stunning flower. Maybe that's Gracie and myself, too, you know?

We left the Mercury outside Gramps's cottage. As we shut the heavy steel doors of the car, the resounding thuds were like thunderclaps. I looked up, a smile on my face, seeking our bond of love—the connection—but Gracie's dark, bug-eyed glasses were back in place. I drew a sharp breath as I felt the cord between us snap, severed by her calculated grin, and the bug-eyes.

A day later, I was still disoriented when I asked Gracie, "Don't we have enough illicit stuff inside us right now?"

"Don't be a party pooper," as she handed me a canteen.

"What's in it?" I asked.

"A magical potion especially designed for my favorite man in the world."

"Wonderful," I said. "But can we pull back a bit?"

"Never, sweetie," she said. "Tonight, we're going in deep."

I shook my head, confused, suddenly, and dizzy. I stopped and leaned against the back of Gramps's house.

"Are you okay?" she asked.

"I feel turned around. Was it tonight that you shot those photos of me on the bed with the scissors?"

"That was last night, angel."

"At times, I see myself in my head nearly slicing off my precious bat and balls forever."

"Intense experience, right?" she asked.

"Definitely," I said. "Odd that time can speed up, or floats backwards, or bounces all the way on top of itself? Or crawls in super slow mo, correct?"

My queen bee looked at me in an odd manner.

"What?" I asked.

She grabbed my shoulders: "You're talking to yourself way too often again, Danny, mumbling. It's strange, okay?"

"Are you serious?" I asked.

"You're mumbling like a real sick man."

"That's troubling," I said. "Maybe it's a sign we should slow the hell down?"

"No, just talk less, and we'll go for a rainy run in the woods."

There's a trail two hundred feet beyond my palace, covered in pine needles, twigs, and leaves, leading to still-undeveloped land. Many times, I ran on the trails during the early mornings, but the nights were something else. They scared me. I heard teenagers shouting on the paths on late evenings, rumors of animal sacrifices, conjuring spirits, but all I can do with Gracie that day is howl like a hyena, like I howled with Liam in the Truro dunes.

I sprinted in the pouring rain with my mind spilling over with wild ideas and fears and needs, like, for no reason, I wanted to run far away from Gracie, maybe climb up the tree palace and hide from her. Maybe I'll write another story for

Liam, and the two of us will go laugh and swim, or just hang out. I just want to be past Gracie forever.

But my legs pumped, my thighs reached up to my belly, toes touching only the pine needles as I ran in the rain. I kicked off my Nikes after two minutes of sprinting, it was as if I was soaring through the woods, like my feet weren't involved. I heard Gracie behind me shouting, "Wait up, angel," but all I felt was hunger and rage, and I only wanted speed, to run and somehow lift from the earth, fly away from my wounds.

I yelled, *"Why are all these nasty feelings exploding inside me right now?"*

I find myself enamored of the dirt suddenly, the mud—I see Mother Earth beckoning, I want to take her apart, so I fall to my knees and cup and dig at the pine needles, mud, rocks, and pebbles with my fingers. I remember a young four-year-old boy growing up who ate tons of dirt pies in Lavonia, Michigan, named Murphy Calla—he made these nasty mud sandwiches for a nickel. My hands ache as I dig up the dirt, the grime, the mud and bugs and stuff it into my face, into my craw. My mouth tries to chew, but I vomit. I force myself to stop, because I choke, I gag, and soon I'm spitting up bark, twigs, and bugs.

I scream into the dark as the torrents of rain pound into me.

"Why can't one thought belong to me and only me?"

I feel my psyche being twisted around—a mental structure made of bones and skin, stretching and breaking. My mind sends me for loops and twirls, sending ice-cold zingers up my backbone like electric jabs of current. As if there's an open sore, a large hatch on my skull that's become unfastened, and every-thing zooming past gets stuck inside my brain pan: Sarcasm, desire, derision, rage, love, hate, *Three Stooges*, death, *Bugs Bunny*, life, humor, and old-fashioned angst.

My mind races. "Why can't someone find my old skull?" I yell, just to hear my own voice disappear into the woods.

"That's what I need, okay? Why can't anyone find my old, untouched brain and return it to me, fresh, without any poison? Give me back my mind before I started drinking and drugging, that's all I ask."

I repeat the lines multiple times, but I only hear whispers, tiny voices, a combination of timbres joining together in a singsong way. I am rattled by my thoughts and by my actions in the dirt, and it's scary, but I am also intoxicated from the magical potion. I imagine rationalizing it all away tomorrow over a turkey burger with Gracie, saying, "It was just the silly liquid, wasn't me, right? Eating Mother Earth—that was nothing. The real part of Danny Halligan? Oh, I'm so fine, never felt finer than to be in Carolina in the morning... I'm a very high functioning and sane young man, everyone knows that."

But I panic as darkness moves in, and the silence takes over.

"I'm faltering," I say. "Feel myself fragmenting."

"You don't require me much longer, do you?" Gracie says, appearing at my side.

"I needed you earlier, Gracie," I say. "Where the hell have you been hiding?"

"You're an adventurous teenybopper, Danny," she says, gesturing like an old-fashioned street preacher on a soapbox in Time Square. "You'll go anywhere I say, you're so open I blush, gives me wild gooseflesh all over my nubile body."

I know I have a right to be ticked at her for treating me like a freaking chemistry experiment, but something crawls over me at that second. Is it a family of centipedes, or garter snakes? Or is it just the awful, cold rain?

"You're absolutely soaring above everyone now, angel," she comments, gesticulating. "You're like a space shot. I got the greatest, most intimate photographs of you eating the mud, stuffing your face, running and shouting and acting like a first-class clown."

"Oh, wonderful, that's all I need," I say.

She confuses me when she speaks like that, so we sit in the dark, mud, and rain, and Gracie puts her camera away and holds me as I cry, as I ooze out everything onto her shoulder. I seemed to be doing way too much crying. Frankly, I thought everything was *already* out of me—hurts, anguish, ego, all that scissor business I didn't understand, *still* don't, really. *Mixed up about everything.*

Below my ribs, a riptide shifts, bubbling and starts to spread within, fermenting, too. I picture a tar pit containing spiritual and physical decay—it jostles next to my pancreas. A rotted core that will, eventually, infect my entire system.

I must get control of my psyche or I'm in trouble, I tell myself. *Nervous breakdown-times-a hundred.* Gracie helps me stand and carries my wet clothes and keeps me walking so I forget most of her coldness. I push the angrier thoughts away for the time being. It takes us an hour to find our way back in the dark. Every now and then she kisses my neck, my mouth, and swirls her tongue with mine, removes pine, sand, and spit.

Reminds me of a PBS special I saw on Thanksgiving about birds feeding their young, regurgitating into their beaks for nutrition, but here Gracie's doing the opposite. Cleaning me out, draining me of all I once knew, removing what little wisdom I may have picked up in my sixteen years. She said it a long time ago—earlier in the summer, first time we fooled around; "I'm going to suck you dry."

A documentary of our adventures that summer would show three folks who posed and jumped and shook and twirled and banged away, we three amigos of black-and-white film adventures, the lovely angels of *Transfiguration Photos,* captured by those artistic pictures of our faces, bodies, genitals, navels, tongues, toes, teeth, tits, ears, and noses. *What did it mean to us though?*

For Liam, I think it was fun, a joyride, and a wild sexual month in 1979. For Gracie, she looks at all the wonderful shots like a trip into the bush or even Sherwood Forest, maybe. It was nothing but wild, fascinating art with a Capital A. Gracie loves to say that part, too. I'm sure when it comes time for her to do selling and publicity about *TP*, she'll use that line frequently. *Art with a big A, she'll toss that line around her like some cowboy showing off his new boots and lasso and ten-gallon hat.*

Now, I don't want to piss on anyone's parade, but it's been sheer hell for me, and yet, and yet, there have been spectacular relationships forged. Me and Gracie, for example, that wild, charismatic showboat or succubus, whatever your favorite term is. Gracie has been exhausting but spectacular. If she was a standup comedian for a few weeks she'd start by saying, "A troubled rose is a scented rose is a demented rose is a flirty rose is a whacked-out rose is a nubile, belligerent, and bellicose rose is a hollowed and miraculous and emasculated rose for all the marbles-kind of rose."

But with Liam, something opened in my heart to him this summer. I'm working hard to not put myself down for wanting him, for flirting away, for penning a provocative short story about him and handing it over to my friend like he was a little schoolgirl with a lunch box in third grade. I mean, I got a crush on him. Do you know what I mean?

I'm thrilled that somehow, I've made substantial progress in leaving Buck's antique views on bisexuals behind. I was blown away when my dad asked about what his only son, me, Danny, desired sexually. Dad apologized for ever putting down bisexuals. I'm proud of myself and him for the open lines of communication. And, though I'm exhausted, I've still got a few more weeks. Maybe time for another short story for Liam?

Who the hell knows?

But to bounce back, I think the PBS documentary on our

trio would steal a page from old Gracie and say, "Liam, Danny, and the shapeshifter herself, Gracie Rose, are talented and Unique with a capital U. But will they last? Or are they like dew in spring and summer, gone in a flash."

As far as Gracie and her treatment of me, I get it loud and clear—a creative being like her will slice its inspiration to bits if need be. If the work gets done, and her photos developed in time, there are no ethics to consider. Gracie is proving she takes and steals all the marrow from me. Yes, it's fun and grand to have a lovely Ivy-League college student hanging around naked, taking wild photos, staying out late and laughing too loud, but when that stuff is delivered with a poisoned tongue, it deadens sensation.

I wouldn't want our PBS special to be too depressing, though, but maybe make it a bit sobering. A warning shot for anyone out there who bets everything on the constellations each Friday night, to perhaps have a backup plan to rescue any loved ones who believe in Santa with everything they got.

Now on the path heading home, the rain slows. As we walk, my mentor, Gracie, speaks of the photos she's developing at Randy's studio in Provincetown and assures me I'm still the most gorgeous and innocent Wolf-Boy ever.

"Why am I still so damn *innocent*?" I asked her. "Aren't wolves brutal and fierce? Aren't they supposed to be true predators? Ripping at flesh?"

"Expectations trampled, traditions discarded," Gracie replied. "Lone Ranger is no hero, only a bully, and Wolf-Boy hasn't learned how to live with himself yet, never mind kill."

For Gracie, though, I believe the experience is going to be a success, you can just feel everything coming together, Liam, me, and her. The process of being photographed has been like a shredding, an evisceration, deteriorating more each day, each night. I see her in the studio and in the darkroom, but I'm shocked at the shots she's taken of me.

I'm naked—we all are, of course, or at least, Liam, Gracie, and me. But emotionally, psychologically, it felt like an open-heart surgery kind of procedure. I asked her once what's the best shutter-speed to capture a sunset on Chapin Beach in Dennis with the tide out a few miles, or when folks are riding horses on the sand bars come October or Thanksgiving, but she only shrugs and goes to bed. Consistently, she tore my ribs apart and found such a wild and funky mess inside. A real shit show, I'm sure.

When we finally reached Gramps cottage, my feet were marked up, and my hands and lips had abrasions, and there was swelling within my mouth, possibly from some bug bite. I threw my clothes in the washer and took a hot bath in the downstairs tub. While soaking, I feel the hatch on my brain that unfastened in the hard rain close, or at least, scab over.

I want to curl into my bed without any CIA potion *ever again*. I practice sharing my soul with the bathroom mirror: *Gracie, leave me alone for a few weeks now, okay? Give me some space.* When I come out in shorts and a sweatshirt thirty minutes later, Gracie's singing the second verse of, "You Are My Sunshine..."

"The other night, dear, as I lay sleeping, I dreamt I held you in my arms, when I awakened, I was mistaken, so I held my head and cried..."

Gracie makes grilled cheese and iced tea like the happiest homemaker in the Western world. I notice a calendar on the wall by Gramps's yellow refrigerator—a color photo of a Siamese kitten rolling around in yarn with three tiny ducklings. *Still only June 27, I think, summer hasn't even officially begun yet—and I don't think I can survive a full season with Gracie beside me. No exaggeration—she's a killer, an assassin.*

We sit at the table with ginger candlelight dancing. We eat sandwiches and drink the iced tea, studying the backyard, as I have the melancholiest thought: *Palatial Palace of the Palpable Pines or Phallus Palace or Kitty City or whatever the hell you want to call it—the fort is just not what I'm about now. A tree fort is for girls and boys, for happy kids who want to share smaller, pure golden secrets. But Mom's long dead and gone, and Randy hasn't been behaving in a healthy way either. Everyone has outgrown it by now.*

"What's the title for your book again?" I ask.

"*Our* photographs," Gracie says. "Not just mine, they belong to the trio, plus I recently told you a long story atop Scargo Tower, right?"

"Transylvania Something, right?" I say. "Based on a Biblical miracle, yes?"

"Not Dracula, you fool. *Transfiguration Photos*," she says. "A changing of flesh to spirit, death to life—a shining miracle of Jesus Christ's reborn spirit appearing on Mt. Tabor with Elijah and Moses to three apostles, Peter, James, and John."

"You'll piss off so many religious folks with that one," I say.

"That's my modus operandi."

"What does that mean again?" I ask.

"I enjoy pissing people off," Gracie says, so I kiss her head. "More than a hobby for me, which you probably already know by now."

"Slumber time has arrived for everyone in this wild kingdom," I say, walking her to the door and watching her go. I lock the door, and then go upstairs to bed.

SLIPPING AWAY

The comely nurse, Sara Maria, and Dr. Bates escorted Buck and me into his dimly lit office—the space smelled of antiseptic, vanilla, apples, and cinnamon and had framed diplomas on the wall along with overfilled bookcases and a corkboard filled with multicolored pushpins with notes and mediocre watercolors of Grizzly bears and their cubs. My father grew teary speaking of Randy.

"So where is Randy now, Dad?" I asked.

"Went on a bender, I'm afraid," he said. "Ran off again and boom, everything blew the hell up..."

"He's not at the rehab outside of Boston?" I asked. "We just had a great chat a day ago, he mentioned it was in Natick, I believe, or was it Salem?"

"Yeah, Natick, I think," Dad said. "He also told me he would like to visit you when he gets out. An administrator said Randy was AWOL, though, but Randy said his snoring and excessively flatulent roommate destroyed his positive momentum."

"Is he safe now, Dad?"

"He's hurt, Danny..."

"Another rehab?"

"No, no," Dad said. "For now, let's settle on the word *away.* He's *away.*"

Dad coughed for a long time.

"Or disappeared, I guess."

"Disappeared?"

Dr. Bates cleared his throat. "Important to say what you mean here, Buck."

"Don't lecture me on proper chats with my son, Doc."

"Truth is hard," the doctor said. "It's the surest way to healing, though."

Buck rose to his feet unsteadily and embraced my head as I sat slumped on the other hard plastic chair, my face jammed in his belly. I smelled sweat and Right Guard.

"Our only wish at the Spruce Lodge Clinic is to aid in the healing of a troubled young mind," the doctor said.

"Tell me he's still alive, Dad."

Buck didn't respond so I asked again.

"Dad?"

"He's in a medical hospital, barely breathing..."

"What?"

"He tried to drown himself..."

"Why, Dad?" I said, trying to punch my face, to strike my temples with my fists, but Sara Maria, the nurse, rushed over and held me back.

"Stop it, Danny," she said. "Randy's still alive, Danny, he's still breathing, functioning on his own... You can't hurt yourself here, though. We'll help you, but positively no self-harm is allowed. Consider this your final warning."

"Why wasn't I told *earlier?*" I hollered at my dad, stopping the punching, and held my head in my hands. "By you or Gramps?"

"We figured it would destroy you," he said. "Put you over the edge."

"It's like what you did with Mom's suicide—can't keep me away from the truth, can't keep burying people's unpleasant histories, Dad."

"I know," Buck said. "I'm so sorry, I was thinking on the fly."

"Was Randy drunk on that last night?" I asked.

"Yes," Buck said. "A mess—vodka, cocaine, and everything else in his blood."

Everyone was silent for three minutes while I sniffled and sipped from a plastic cup of water that Sara Maria passed to me.

"Did Randy strike another car that night?" I asked through tears.

Dad shook his head.

"Did he kill another person in the car crash?" I asked. "Or a pedestrian, maybe?"

Dad shook his head again.

"What happened, Dad?"

"He was all alone, obsessing about his many failures," he said. "There was a deep pond, and Randy got overwhelmed and drove into it."

"Fuck," I said as tears spill.

"A good Samaritan saved him, a retired marine, apparently," he said. "She left a note saying, 'This man wanted to die tonight but was saved by a former lifeguard.'"

"Thank God. How is he doing today?" I asked. "And why'd he do it?"

"His life was... *is* a wreck. He was teetering, Danny, you know that, boozing it up. Gramps said the same thing. Worse news, he lost the photography studio. He had to admit he couldn't keep it going."

"Does that mean you get soaked in the deal, Dad?" I asked, and my father shrugged.

"There are worse things, apparently," Buck said. "We'll be fine. It's still a wonderful piece of real estate, no doubt about that, folks are already making inquiries about it."

Eventually, I found myself out of questions, drained, and it grew quiet in the room for about fifteen minutes, everyone breathing, assessing the situation, save for the sniffling of Buck and me. Then I became profoundly aware of the number of times Dr. Bates's thumbs were twiddling around on his desk.

It was nothing at first, just a fleeting thought in my head, but soon I felt I'd die if the shrink didn't stop the manic thumb movement, it was crazy, they were going so damn fast, like he was holding a contest between the left and right thumb, which one could pin the other one down *faster*. How was this antique bastard with the crazy thumbs going to ever settle down and help me?

I looked up at the doctor that I'd known for a week, and instead of asking him about Grizzly bears, and the manic, ugly, disgusting, stupid, and masturbatory crossing of his whacked-out thumbs, I started weeping.

"Why won't my family stop destroying themselves?" I asked. "Why are all of us so damn afraid to live?"

"Fine question," Dad replied. "Excellent and astute, actually."

"Yes," Dr. Bates said. "Clarity of thought—it's a good sign for you, Danny."

"Welcome to Vermont, I guess," I said quietly as Sara Maria stood by with cups of water, Buck embraced me, and Dr. Bates looked grim on the other side of the desk, thumbs all a twitter.

NOT ALL TEARS

I t's not all anguish and tears on the young adult PEAR unit at Spruce Lodge, of course—the patients are bonded, and we feel close and share many dark and silly laughs. The ward is mostly female, and they feely share their snacks, books, art, and favorite music. They teach me a lot, help me learn how to cry without too much guilt and try to help me not punch myself so goddamned much for being human, for *absorbing the interior blows of daily life.*

In August of 1980, we listen to Queen frequently, and each of the young ladies sing with a passion absent from every other corner of their lives. We're inside a screened-in porch, and their wailing voices make me want to sob so I walk in place to keep from doing that.

The young women's eyes are half-closed, and their heads bop and groove to the yearning inside Freddie Mercury and his amazing vocal range. Cigarettes droop from their mouths like candied props. The wind picks up one weekend, and eventually we all throw on sweatshirts and jackets and stay out in the unseasonably cool air. Soon, three staff members join us on the porch and twist around with us, giggling, shaking their heads, swiveling their hips, like our own psychically blessed dance party in the Vermont sticks.

Buck drives up to have a family session, and we go on a quick day pass into Montpelier, grab some deli sandwiches, and I pick up *Sam Cooke's Greatest Hits* and James Taylor's *Flag* at a local record shop. My father is in a pleasant mood, and he smiles and nods when Dr. G tells him in a few years I may live in a group home near Spruce Lodge but would remain his client for outpatient therapy.

"It's a steady climb, an incremental growth occurring," Dr. G explains. "Danny's trying hard, really working in our therapy after that self-destructive setback around his birthday."

It's been seven weeks since I injured myself with Mom's plaque, so I'm feeling tentative, antsy. Even on the day trip into town with Buck I don't feel so steady. The only thing that's keeping me smiling is the young patient on the unit, specifically a wickedly wry lady I'm obsessed with who's been around the hospital for three years.

Elo is Peruvian and West Indian on her mother's side and South African on her father's side, and she has long fingers, fathomlessly deep black eyes, and high, sexy legs covered with bright flowing robes and skirts. Elo's regal and magnetic in a pathological way—she is undoubtedly a *morbidly melodramatic young lady*, which is how she likes to refer to herself.

Fire is her specialty. She says it's her *favorite, most exquisite way to leave the warped, conniving world we exist in*. She tells me on her bedroom wall at home in Philly she has a poster-sized reprint of the Buddhist monk in Saigon in 1963, protesting oppression by being doused in gasoline and setting himself on fire. One night, Elo waves me into her room, showing me a small, wallet-sized black-and-white photo of the monk's burnt body.

"I carry it with me everywhere," she says. "It's my core, my very essence."

She leans in and kisses me for twenty seconds, and it's a tender thing, and I find myself responding to her darting tongue, but as I move in, she retreats, steps back.

"Now I've got you inside me, too," she says, smiling. "So, thanks for that."

"Oh," I say. "Okay, sure."

"My monk photo isn't as stellar as your mom's picture though," she says. "She's a true pioneer—Miriam O'Riley Halligan meant business, didn't pull any punches, right?"

"What?"

"Your mama stared the abyss in the eye and never blinked," Elo says, smiling. "She said no thanks, not interested, and slipped on out of life like a true professional."

"No, no," I say. "That's not even remotely the truth..."

"The photo you got of her, Danny," Elo says. "The one of her sprawled on the crushed milk truck in the newspaper, it's so damn gorgeous—"

"Stop it—"

"I love it," Elo says. "Your mama deserves martyrdom, I'll never think of April Fool's Day, 1966, in the same way again."

"Her death was a horrid waste of humanity, though, Elo," I say. "Randy never saw his twin sister again; I never saw or hugged my mom again. It's a tragedy—a young life was taken too early. She was gravely mentally ill."

"Now don't go believing too much of the BS they serve here at this wacky psychiatric zoo," Elo says, kissing my forehead. "What your mama did was a grand achievement, so don't go soft on me now, Danny."

I was stunned by her cold, hurtful comments and went back to my room and sobbed. Not out of fear, but out of hurt, and a stilted heartbreak, realizing I could never feel comfortable with someone as cynical, negative, and cruel as Elo. She'd extinguish what was left of me in a blink of an eye, and I was working too damn hard to make that splintered part of me healthy and whole again. Nurse Jen passes me in my room and hears me crying so I share with her some of Elo's cruelty.

"She sounds like another important person in your past," Jen says.

"I'm not sure anymore..."

"She sounds a bit like Gracie Rose to me, Danny," Jen says. "A powerful seductive force who oozed cynicism, negativity, and even cruelty, to throw that word in there."

"That's a very wise observation, Jen," I say.

"Watch out for us psychiatric nurses," she laughs. "We've been known to help all kinds of people."

Five minutes later, just before my family session, I see Elo rushed out the door to an ambulance, and she waves as if she's heading out for a nightly walk, and I miss my opportunity to say goodbye to her. So, I'm scatterbrained before meeting with Dr. G and Buck, biting my nails so severely that I need Band-Aids on both index fingers. I worry my father secretly loathes me because of how expensive my care is, and how I'll never be able to repay him, unless I hit the lottery for $10 million.

I know deep down Buck supports and loves me, but I still wrestle with striking flashbacks and some paranoia. I have nightmares I'll be set loose into the wilds of Vermont, a non-verbal, chubby alien getting chased through the Green Mountains by gargantuan government men with Ronald Reagan masks in fancy, souped-up jeeps and military attack helicopters who will capture me in huge netting and use long electric prods on my genitals, shatter my kneecaps, crack my shins, and pluck off my toenails just because they can.

"Go ahead now, Danny," Dr. G tells me as we start our

session in a conference room with framed photos of sunny cornfields, a snowy mountain, and a placid silver lake.

"You okay, son?" Buck asks. "You seem overly tense."

"I saw a friend get wheeled out the door to an ambulance, so I'm shaken."

"Try to focus back in here with us," Dr. G says. "Do it for your father."

"I want to project success for you, Dad," I say. "Inside, though, I feel like a mess, emotional jelly."

"Try to be more direct with your dad, Danny," Dr. G says.

"You've done so much for me, Dad," I say. "Emotionally, financially, an enormous amount of love, support, and funds, and I'm so grateful for that."

"No worries," Buck says. "I'm here beside you always."

"Gracie and Liam crap doesn't go away in my brain, though," I say. "Like poison ivy—finds me on TV, magazines, and patients talking about Wolf-Boy on the unit."

"Have you ever sat them down and told them that you're the actual, bona fide Wolf-Boy?" Buck asks. "I would think that would shut them all up real quick."

"No one believes me," I say. "Yesterday, two female patients said they already met the *real* guy at a clinic in Montana, and that he was nothing but a cocky asshole."

"They say that?" Dad asks.

"Yeah," I say. "So that messed with my skull—I mean, *who* the hell is this guy in Montana and what is he trying to pull off?"

"Phone, Danny," a twenty-year-old, Charlotte says, knocking on our door.

I looked to my father and Dr. G, and they let me take it.

"I want to talk to Buck alone for a few minutes, anyway, Danny," Dr. G says.

I walk down the hall, pick up the phone, and sit in the last booth—someone has scrawled on the wall in orange ink, **Therapy Fatigue Sets In.**

"Angel," *her* voice says, and I feel cold throughout my body. "My forever lover..."

"I thought they blocked you from ever calling me again," I say, thinking, *hang up immediately, Danny, follow the rules and hang up, don't mess around with this fool.*

"No escaping me, babe," Gracie says. "My tentacles extend around the globe."

"I can't talk with you..."

"*Liam's gone*, Danny," she says. "*Dead* in Amsterdam two nights ago."

"*What?*" I say, my stomach lurching.

"Died at a fancy brothel," she says. "A heart attack, apparently, just days before his twenty-first birthday."

"Jesus," I say, my body trembling, thinking, *don't you cry, Danny, he was so horrible to you.*

"Liam told me he loved you last I saw him," Gracie says.

I'm silent for five seconds, thinking, *don't take her bait—don't even argue, she's only trying to ensnare you, catch you in one of her enticing but fatal cobwebs.*

"Angel," she says.

"He left me with real scars," I say. "In case you've forgotten the final extravaganza, Gracie, both of you manipulated and threw me around like I was trash..."

"*Angel dust* was horrific," Gracie says. "Finale was terrible, I know that, but..."

"But *what?*"

"Perhaps the rest was *nearly* love," Gracie says. "You and Liam had a true bond."

I bite my right index finger until the Band-Aid falls off, and it starts bleeding all over again.

"I'm supposed to hang up on you now, Gracie."

"Don't," she says. "Just a bit longer, okay? So wonderful to sit here and talk together with you, isn't it?"

"I can't do this anymore, Gracie..."

"I'm sending you a money order for $3,500 in the mail tomorrow," she says. "For your incredible, groundbreaking work on *Transfiguration Photos*."

"*What?*"

"More royalties will follow soon," she says. "Sorry it's taken so damn long..."

"You can't expect me to forget your wickedness just like that," I say. "You can't turn around and be all lovey-dovey best friends forever now."

"Hush, hush, doll," she says, and I slam the phone down, noticing in smaller red ink someone wrote on the wall, **ERIC CLAPTON AND HALDOL ARE MY NEW GODS.** I remain in the booth for a minute, trembling, thinking, *Liam, dust to dust, I have no male pals left, just ladies around me now, they're all I got...*

The same phone starts ringing again—one, two, three, four—

I pick up on the fifth ring and hold it a few inches from my ear as if Gracie's voice itself carries disease, rot, an aural, flesh-eating fungus I need to avoid at all costs.

She coos, "I have nothing but the most deep and abiding respect for..."

I quietly hung the phone up, proud of myself for not making a scene. *Easy does it now, Danny*, I think. *No violence, no punches, don't fall into any more holes, no diving, no falling, simply walk it off, just walk it off, don't even turn around if she phones again, don't even think about it, she's nothing, he's nothing, they're nothing, everyone's nothing.*

After I spoke to Gracie last time, I gave myself stitches and a concussion. Now five minutes on the line with her, and my mouth feels bone dry, and I'm trembling. I bend over and gulp water from the bubbler.

I think, *Liam hurt me bad, raped me, in fact, so why do I feel so crushed?*

The same phone rings again, and I ponder going back, but then I recall my dad is waiting with Dr. G in the conference room.

Don't tell them a thing, I think. *Stroll in calmly and say it was a wrong number—*

"It was *her,* wasn't it?" Buck says immediately as I walk in the room.

"No..."

"*Don't lie,*" Buck says, and my eyes fill, and I curse, but my dad grabs my hands so I can't punch myself, embracing me tight. My face is stuffed into my dad's shirt and left armpit; Old Spice, sweat, and Right Guard.

Some odors never change, I think.

"We're okay," Dr. G says, striding over to Dad and me. "You didn't hurt yourself, Danny, you may want to, but you haven't yet. Decent, small victories tonight."

"It's because I grabbed his hands, for Christ's sake," Buck says.

"*Still,*" Dr. G says. "Let's take the wins wherever we can find them."

"Why can't this hospital keep Gracie-the-witch-bitch off the phone?" Dad shouts at Dr. G. "You professional quacks keep failing my son big-time."

"Danny's doing his very best here, Buck," Dr. G says, getting up in my father's face. "I'm doing my best, as well— don't know what else to offer you."

"Easy, everyone," I say, stepping in between them for a moment. "Let's exhale and take a few breaths and try to act civilized for fun."

I take a seat while they continue arguing and I hear points and counterpoints, but mostly what I feel is exhausted; my body, dense, my mind, mush, my heart, crushed. After a few minutes they notice my silence and posture and look down at me, crying.

"What is it, Danny?" Dad asks.

"Liam's dead," I say in the awkward silence. "Gracie told me. Liam Preston's gone. He had a heart attack in Amsterdam."

"Heard it on the news a few days ago, Boss," Buck says. "Didn't know if I should bring it up or not."

After an additional thirty-five minutes of patching up the holes, insults, and bruised feelings, we promise to meet again in three months. I say goodbye to my father—get a bear hug from him, and he slumps out to the parking lot and drives off in his Ford truck, taillights fading into the blackness of a Vermont night.

"Don't feel too defeated," Dr. G says to me before he exits for the night. "It's difficult, and you didn't hurt yourself. That's a victory. Give yourself some credit, Danny."

I write about it in a journal Dr. G gives me:

Liam damaged me both mentally and physically that brutal summer of '79. But that doesn't seem to matter to my insides, to my heart. I feel stunned by his passing, and am stuck in a thick, sludgy kind of despair—an ugly naked pain that sits low within. It burns and feasts on me, and has my brain coursing with questions: When was I being most true and real as a person? Was it when I was with Gracie or Liam? Whom did I love more?

And is it a cop-out to say both?

DANNY'S EMOTIONAL LOCKJAW

It is June 29th, 1979—only days from my seventeenth birthday and one early morning before the sun is up, I find that I can't form words, experiencing a form of emotional lockjaw. I struggled with some clenched, grinding teeth earlier in the summer, but this time I can breathe, move, walk, go to the bathroom, and drink water, but no words emerge. I go to the kitchen, my footsteps creaking on the stairs as I descend, and grab iced tea out of the fridge and pour myself a large glass.

I stretch my mouth with yawns, trying to loosen up the jaw, lips, and throat, and I twist my tongue every which way. Eventually, I sit at the kitchen table in the dark and finish a second glass of tea. After more silence, and my mouth still not producing words, I strike a book of matches and light a stubby, ginger-smelling candle in a metal cup on the table.

I rub my palms together hard for ten minutes, something I did as a boy. Each day after elementary school I came home and visited the bathroom, rubbing my palms against each other with force, with determination. Eventually, small lines of soot or dirt or sweat rolled up on my palms, and I found the evidence of scum on me the most vile and disgusting thing.

But here I am now, sixteen, and I'm still taken with the palm-on-palm business. As I get rolling, my palms burn, and I see lines of dirt in the candlelight, and what appear to be mites marching up and down my hands, their mouths with sharp teeth chomping on the scum, the soil of me. I am determined to fight that thought, to *not* admit bugs are devouring me, but when they rise, zipping around my head like hornets, they are as fat as plums. All I can do is swipe at them wildly.

"Get away, you slimy bastards" quickly spills from my mouth, and I can't shut up at that point, words tumbling out of me. Not in a high-volume way, just conversationally, like I'm having an interview with Barbara Walters, as if she's sitting beside me in the candlelight in a white blouse and a long paisley skirt with cherry-red sandals.

"I'm starting to struggle with all the CIA potions I've ingested, Barbara," I say, still slapping at the mites. "And I don't think it's so fantastic what's happening to my psyche, you understand?"

I imagine her nodding kindly and sharing with me her own deeply repressed secrets, so I politely hold my left hand over the flame until she finishes her confessions, and I end up with a fat blister in the center of my palm. It hurts, but I also think it's cool, like a *Logan's Run* palm crystal. It is at that point when the sizable mites subside and melt away into the 11 p.m. kitchen gloom.

Next up is de-frocked Richard Nixon, whom I don't know much about but feel sorry for—it's like he can't figure out how to do anything well, forever guilty, sweaty, and anxious. He wears khaki shorts, a navy button down, and these awful black socks with black sandals, and I offer him iced tea, but he refuses. As he starts speaking on Chinese American relationships and political integrity, I do my best not to self-harm. *Not anymore burns, Danny, no more blisters are allowed. You're done with all that crap.*

Gracie would understand right away if she was here, I think, my brain speeding about. *She whispered a few times to me this season, "I burn for you, you burn for me, a trade-off, a romantic treaty between two horny factions."*

She is funny like that, witty, acerbically so, an SAT word I picked up by listening to her. I wonder how I'm ever going to get used to dating high school girls, or boys, for that matter. I feel like Gracie and Liam have got me more confused than ever about where I belong in the world of desire and want. Or maybe I do know, and I am just afraid of embracing bisexuality in the Nutmeg State. *Seriously, what on earth will I be? Whomever will I belong to? Once you've tongued the very hot sun with a sensual priestess of the highest skills, what is left back in the old world? The antiquated, stupid, inane, comparably flesh-less world?*

I whisper: "No one can steal this secret from me, Mr. President, it's all mine."

"You've entered a dangerous stage in your life, my boy," he says. "I suggest using great caution."

"I worry terribly," I confess to Mr. Nixon. "For if this is what every American teenager does, we're going to have a load of unstable, whacked-out kids come fall."

After thirty more minutes of my bizarre fireside chats with Barbara and the thirty-seventh president of the United States, they disappear into my basement, and I never see them again. I look at my blistered palm as I hear Dad's footsteps on the stairs, and soon he's beside me, tapping my shoulder.

"Hey, Boss," he says. "Can't sleep again, huh?"

"No," I say, "not a wink."

He sits beside me and eats some cookies and places his

huge palm over the top of my left hand. He squeezes the top of it but doesn't speak, and I almost weep, nearly burst out crying. I know he wants to say something wise, to reach me and pierce the bubble of stoned-lost-boy thoughts, but in the end we only drink more iced tea, watching the stubby candle's flame shift and dance. My father had come up the night before after Gramps had mentioned to him that I'd been behaving *a bit strangely*, just a little "off-kilter." Gramps was spending the evening at Eileen's home in Dennisport.

"Why light a candle and not use the lights down here, son?" he asks.

"I don't know, Dad," I say, thinking of Gracie and the way she leaves stubby candles around our extravaganzas, whispering in my ear as she touches me, taking hundreds of photos, bouncing this way and that and saying, "Oh, Danny Halligan, you angel of my dreams, let there be light!"

"Figure I should give mood lighting a spin," I say, telling myself to *concentrate, stay alert, don't let Dad discover the painful burns.*

"Are you okay?" he finally asks when he finished gulping his tea.

"I'm pretty good, I guess," I say.

"Are you sure Gracie Rose is okay for you?" my father asks, his voice breaking. "Is she siphoning away the best parts out of my one and only son?"

I nearly collapse when Buck asks that, but I try to stay calm, not let him find out how messed up I *am.*

"No, she's great," I say. "It's been a real special summer, unique, but a good one, I'd say, Dad."

"Okay, Boss," he says. "Well, let's head upstairs then."

And so, I blow out the candle and we do just that. Dad heads to the guest room upstairs, and me into my room, though it takes me a while to find slumber. I kept hearing Dad's questions repeated in my ears.

"Is Gracie siphoning the best parts out of my one and only son, Danny?"

What exactly is a young man to do, I think, when he's tempted by the wildest girl on the Cape? Cautious people might get off at the next subway or the next highway exit, escaping her rage and fire. But when you get the chance to dance and twirl with the devil herself, you take a breath, bless yourself, and you find that girl with the bare head, lovely curves, and funky sunglasses, and you dance with her every way you dreamt about, backwards, forwards, upside down, inside out, until you and her can't breathe, until you're both exhausted, already dreaming of the next waltz.

"Gracie's scary, but it's the big leagues now, Danny, boy," I whisper into the bathroom mirror, slapping myself hard on my face twice. "Stay sharp and don't whine, it's not becoming of a true gentleman."

TO WANT OR NOT

L iam phones and asks me to take a ride for steak and eggs
at his favorite spot, overlooking the marsh in East
Dennis. I decline, but he insists, suggesting we meet for a meal
at Beachy Café.

"Treating me to a late lunch, huh?" I ask.

"We'll call it an early birthday gift."

Thirty minutes later we sit in the mostly deserted restaurant. The exterior is worn, weather-battered shingles, gray and
wet, navy shutters, paint peeling. A sign reads **BEaCHY** with
the *A* light bulb burned out. Even the porch looks warped and
saggy, as if it could give at any moment. But they serve delicious
giant blueberry muffins with eggs and huge glasses of juice.
Breakfast every hour, and the customers keep returning.

They have an oversized cuckoo clock over an oil painting of
a clipper ship near the entrance, and the wallpaper is red,
white, and blue, with tiny patriots holding muskets along with
yellow roses in their teeth. Plus, they supply crayons in a tin
cup and thin drawing-paper tablecloths for their customers.

The restaurant offers a hippy-trippy kind of milieu, but the food is first-rate.

Liam's blond hair is still wet. He smells clean and wears jeans and a black T-shirt that reads: "Jimmy Page is God." His black eyes look heavy, exhausted, still a tad bloodshot, and a local, curvy, and tanned waitress flirts with him as we order. When she returns to the kitchen, he smiles at me.

"Would Gracie approve of our meeting?" he asks, yawning and stretching.

"She'd want to hear every detail," I say, picking up a crayon in the cup, and start doodling.

"Ever think of dumping her in the sea?"

I look at him and shrug.

"Blame it on a great white shark?" I ask. "What would cops do, though?"

"Mercy killing," Liam says. "No charges would be filed—we'd be scot-free."

We watch two senior citizens heading out the door with doggie bags in their hands, one laughing with a chesty, deep cough, another waves goodbye to the cook.

"Things going okay at home?" I ask.

He shakes his head, rubbing his left ear.

"Not like at Gramps's place," he says. "Pop and I got only silence, porn, and old movies, not a lot of love between us, pretty pathetic material."

"Does he cuss you out?" I ask and notice Liam's silence. *I'd like to help him,* I think. *I wish I could support him more, but I don't really know how to do that.*

"Pop doesn't think I'm a worthwhile human being," he says. "Says I'm scum, not salvageable flesh."

Liam starts coughing then, as if he has something stuck in his throat.

"Drink up, Liam," I say, passing the water.

His chin is down, and his arms and left hand cover his flushed face, and he trembles, and I stare, *stunned, really,* to realize Liam is crying, and when three full sobs fall out of him onto our table like moon rocks, neither of us want to acknowledge them. Feels like way too much. *What can I do?* I think. *The feelings, the emotions are so raw. Where do I start? I'm terrified, but he needs to be comforted.*

"I'd like to help you if I can," I say.

"Thanks, but today my Pop said he wants to trade you for me," he whispers. "And I *totally* get it, I understand, but it's a lonely cold smack in the face."

I swallow, self-conscious, and watch several waitresses look our way.

"Hey, it'll get better, man," I say.

Liam slams his fist down on the table, and I knock over my ice water and think, *beware of that rage, but you must help him today.*

"Sorry I've been so violent," he says, helping to wipe up the water.

"Don't be silly..."

"*Please,*" he says, teeth clenching. "Don't be false with me—let me say my shit."

Our food arrives.

"Thanks," I say to the waitress.

Liam keeps his eyes down as he speaks, and the waitress retreats.

I dig into the muffin and corn beef hash, and Liam has steak and eggs. I watch a purple and orange delivery truck pass a window behind his head and back up slowly, awkwardly. Starts and stops. Beep. Beep. Beep.

"Didn't mean to," he hesitates, words fighting him. "Be so damn *rough.*"

I blush and my head feels stuffed, bloated, and I think, *I want to support this kid. Not quit on him like his dad and mother always did for so damn long. I know he's got me by two years, but Christ, right now he appears so green.*

"I'm sorry it's been so harsh," I say. "Can I help somehow?"

"I don't know, I mean, during the first extravaganza, you were long gone in the tree palace, and Gracie planned it all," Liam says. "She told me to get you soused, what was to occur first, how we'd shift from one thing to the next, blow all the weed smoke your way, etc."

"I can't believe she goes behind my back like that," I say.

"Those are facts."

"A part of me doesn't want to believe it," I say. I wish to push back against it in my head, so I think, *must be a damn lie, she adores me, she'd never do such an awful thing!*

"You had tons of her *CIA punch* the first couple of times," he says.

"Which is what *exactly?*" I ask, and he shakes his head.

"Little bit of everything," Liam says. "She doesn't care—she's like a mad scientist, a lady with a vulture's soul, telling me to take advantage of an innocent boy."

"I wish I wasn't so naive," I say. "That I didn't I gobble her stuff up so easily."

"Don't ever say that Danny," Liam says. "I think if you were older, you would not have written the wonderful story for me—it was such a kick-ass thing. You don't understand how much that saved me. I mean, my pop was such a dipshit and asshole to me—real cruel and ugly, but your story lifted me, saved me from beating myself up too much."

"Wow, that's great," I say. "I was afraid it was so damn goofy and silly..."

Liam gazes at me, face sunburned, and I realize a part of him is still a boy. And that makes me feel stronger and at ease.

"Why aren't you allowed to like both ways like every other human on Planet Earth?" he asks. "Gramps seems a lot more mellow. He's cooler, saner, no?"

"Gramps is good, but my dad is coming around, believe it or not," I say. "He's working hard to change his feelings, his thinking process."

"That's huge," Liam says.

"But you, Mr. Preston," I say, "with your words about the story, the second extravaganza, how you rescued me from self-harm the other day... That was incredible, it was sweet."

Liam says, "My pleasure, Danny."

So, we eat the rest of our meal silently, and he leaves a good tip behind for the young waitress and we exit the restaurant ten minutes later. When we get into his Chevy van, he lights a Marlboro and, eventually, pulls out onto Route 6A.

He speaks without looking my way. "Again, we got an obvious attraction there, but it doesn't mean you have to embrace some new lifestyle."

"Okay," I say. "Tell me again about the other day."

"It was just after the first extravaganza," he says. "I mentioned about your meditation skills, about your breath... and how to try and stay mindful. We connected on some deeper level, I think."

"Yeah," I say. "I remember that, and Gracie charged right in and interrupted me and gave me a Valium."

"And then off you went," Liam says.

"Right."

"But your whole story just blew me away," he says. "The second part is quite good. I mean, I'm no literary critic, but that moved me."

"Thanks," I say and laugh before letting my right hand ride the wind out the open window—up and down, twisting, sailing, and pulling my hand back inside the van before a big branch goes flying by on 6A. Feeling the wind on my hand frees me up, like the way I had always wanted it to be with Liam.

Him and I together, no secrets, I think. *If only life were that simple.*

"Gracie can be a bitch," he says.

"Gracie only wants full steam ahead for me, and never worries about what her stuff does to me."

"Bingo," Liam says. "Look, we're each young, but you're only sixteen. Crazy."

We are both silent for about a minute, and I look over at Liam.

"Do you ever get visuals when you indulge?"

"Nothing too radical—why, have you?" he asks.

"A while ago, I saw my left hand fall apart before my eyes," I say. "I studied my fingers tumble down and bounce on 6A. It scared the shit out of me, and I was sober."

"Watch yourself with her," he says.

"Gracie told me her stuff would never cause that," I say. "That she would never allow bad concoctions put inside me."

"Yeah," he says. "And I want to sell you the Cape Cod Canal."

"Did your father ever talk about Gracie to you?" I ask.

"Like how?"

"Asking questions," I say. "Buck's attracted to Gracie, mentioned it a few times, her curves, 'got an attractive mate, son,' he said at one point."

Liam laughs. "No shit?"

"Buck's got a hankering," I say.

"Pop sits all day watching classic films," Liam says. "Jimmy Cagney, Robert Mitchum in *Cape Fear*, and Spencer Tracy, and then he watches porn for hours, drinking gin, eating dry bologna sandwiches, hard to tell what moves him."

"Gracie tells me she doesn't ever remain still but then jabbers on and on about how great her yoga practice is. I never understood that."

Liam looks over at me.

"Watch yourself with her, Danny, okay?" he says. "She's ferocious and devours souls."

"How so?"

"Her bug-eyed sunglasses keep it hidden," Liam says. "She's fierce, her Yale camera gig is life and death, so don't be so sold on her that you lose your charm."

"What's my charm?" I ask him.

He smiles, bites his lower lip. "I can't tell you that, or it'll go straight to your head."

"Of course," I say, looking over at Liam again, swallowing, my pulse pounding through my whole body, my ears, my head, my conscience saying, *not right now, save it for another day.*

"Are you feeling, okay?" he asks me.

"Pull into this little road up here."

"Where are we going, man?" he asks as he drives through and pulls into the lane.

"Felt I needed this," I say, my mouth bone dry. "Or wanted, I guess."

Gracie told me to just reach out and touch, but how do I know he won't reject me and laugh in my face?

"You okay, man?" Liam asks, and so I lean over and grasp Liam through his jeans, and he makes a unique growling sound, like something a leopard might make when pleased. I unzip him, and he pops out like a prize. It's the first time I ever touch him there, causing Liam to groan and curse. My heart slam-slam-slams in my chest as I push Liam down as he releases his seat in the van, leaning way back with a half-shocked grin.

"You're kidding, right?" he says, his breath short. "Is this some joke?"

I had seen him tons of times—but the damn thing appears almost perfect in the late afternoon shadow and light. The most prominent vein running up him appears angry, ticked off, and so I hold it, bringing myself down, hearing hundreds of dissenting voices but going for it anyway. *Ignore the negatives and all the shaming voices. This is good, it's only good.*

"You don't bullshit around, huh, Danny Hal?" Liam says.

I concentrate on what I'm doing. It's a challenge, but it only makes me more determined. I taste everything on the earth for a time: salt, piss, soap, beer, nicotine, corned beef hash, too, but *that was probably just me.* My manic brain chants negativity, but I ignore it, and wipe my mouth.

Liam eventually pulls back onto the main road. Silently we study the scenery as if we entered a remote, foreign land at dawn, maybe Greenland, nothing but vast glaciers for miles. No communication necessary, at least for the first ten minutes as we drive along, my heart and brain pounding against my chest and ears. I just keep breathing, become aware of my breath. Over and again like Liam says. *Deep breaths, back and forth, like riding a bike, ignore the bullshit voices, you don't need them anymore, you are home free now...*

I worry, of course, but there's still a sense of pressure being released within. Liam looks sweet, genuinely happy, wearing a goofy smile. I feel it, too. Like a huge and healing wave breaks over me, water rinses me clean. It cascades down on me, a real sense of renewal.

Liam speaks in a cracked voice, eyes wet. "That's the coolest thing anyone ever did for me, man," he says. "Ever."

"Yeah," I say. "One for the ages, I guess."

The greatest thing is I haven't been immediately seized by too much negative self-talk bullshit. My whole body and soul have survived. As a matter of fact, I feel a weird type of glee and affection for Liam. My eyes are wet, but I cough and smile and think, *no crying today, one accomplishment at a time for Christ's sake! This is a wonderful day.*

"Danny," Liam says, minutes later as we approach the intersection near the Dennis Public Market, near our homes. "We'll continue taking Gracie's photos if you're okay with it. But if you're not, we can stop everything right now. We'll hustle away from Gracie's circus-life, you and me, we'll stroll away."

"Right, great," I say.

I'll forever remember his kindness, and that window of time, as we idle in traffic and make a turn onto Beach Street. *Now if you were really liberated, Danny,* I tell myself, *you'd tell him you love him right now.* We drive past a worn-down, rectangular park with a rotting wooden fence along the perimeter, surrounded in back with scrub pines, elms, hydrangea, pachysandra, and a few rose bushes, and children on the playground, with swings, and an orangey-brown jungle gym.

Next to the swings, four-year-old twin girls in Red Sox caps are doings spins and gymnastic-moves in their lime-green swimsuits and cherry-red oversized sunglasses, preening for their parents' Polaroid, getting dizzy as can be. It's a peculiar thing because I don't recall the twins' hair color, only the twirling and their cartwheels, and I know I didn't hear their giggles, either, because a bittersweet classic song was coming from a boom box set to the side, the Beach Boys' "Sloop John B." But in my head, I hear the girls giggling so light and carefree.

"Let me go home, I want to go home, I feel so broke, let me go home..."

On the far side of the park, two little boys in white Adidas cleats and knee-high yellow socks play soccer, kicking the ball into a miniature net, only slightly wider than the ball. And an old Italian-looking man with a cane, straw hat, and what looks like an undershirt, red shorts, and black sandals, relaxing on a bench, simultaneously smoking a thin cigar and eating a slice of cheesy pizza, absorbing the entirety of the dusky day.

I feel tense, so damn nervous, obsessed with everything that has occurred—about what Liam, Gracie, and me are truly all about. Whether we are as unique, singular, and blessed as Gracie promises and preaches each day. Are we truly gifted and bound for heavenly glory? The more the days course by, I doubt it heavily, doubt Gracie's boasting and claiming that our trio is divinely ordained.

I doubt her mystical gifts—like Gracie can walk on water or that she's some type of modern-day mystic and I doubt we'd all go into the fame stratosphere and make billions from her extravaganzas. All of that sounds like a crock.

And though being with Liam doesn't entirely register with me yet, I still think it through and am certain of one single, unwavering truth: The time on the wooded trail and passing the park with the whirling twins, Beach Boys singing their melancholy tune, the old man and his pizza, the soccer kids and their cleats and knee-high yellow socks, and Liam protecting me in his own way, remains the most distinct and poignant memory of the season.

"Understand one thing," Liam says. "Gracie wants to squeeze every bit of life from us. She's a sexy lady, but we're merely mighty handsome fruits in her evolving still life."

"Okay," I say.

He smirks. "*Mighty handsome fruits*—it'll be our word to quit. Say that to me, and we'll walk away. I'll stop, and we'll escape and never look back at her."

"*Mighty handsome fruits*—got it," I say. "Okay. Good. And Liam?"

"Yeah?" he says, looking over at me finally, one hand rubbing his stubbly chin.

"Thanks," I say. "For everything."

"Right back at you, man," he says. "This was a special day."

MARSHMALLOW THERAPY

Dr. G sits me down one frigid February 1983 morning in his office, Matisse prints dotting several of his walls, and there are some extravagant-looking lava lamps, some gold, some orange, and a few neon-pink jellyfish lamps. Outside his window, I see threatening gray-white clouds and two crows struggling across the sky.

"Gonna be more ambitious with you today, Danny."

"Have I been doing therapy wrong?" I ask.

"Not necessarily," he says. "But I'm going to push you."

"Can I push back?" I ask. "I should be allowed to push back, right?"

Dr. G ponders the comment, offering a shrug.

"We hit substantial roadblocks, Danny," he says. "We get deep, but *something* slows us down every time."

"Is it my mom?" I ask. "I feel like I'm owning the fact that it wasn't my fault, her suicide, I mean. I don't feel that weight as much as I once did."

"Yes, you're doing better with your mother's death," Dr. G says. "But your dad... We have some work to do there."

"Sounds like I *am* screwing up," I say, and he shakes his head.

"No, no," he says. "We have archly heterosexual Buck on one side of the room and Randy over there—two examples of masculinity for you growing up."

Dr. G sips his tea, adjusts his thin spectacles, and leans in.

"So where does that leave Danny Halligan in late February 1983?"

"Mixed up," I say. "But add some sweaty romance in my palace in Cape Cod, and since it's now in *Transfiguration Photos*, I feel trapped in amber."

"Why's that again?"

"The perception of who I am," I say, "*sexually* gets decided without me."

"So you didn't feel any of the desire shown with Liam in the photos?"

"I desire Gracie, of course," I say. "But I fear my desire of Liam."

"Do you think Liam felt anything else beyond desire?" he asks. "In that last phone call with Gracie, she intimated that Liam loved you. How do you feel about all that now?"

"I know the guy is dead," I say. "But he raped me, Doc."

"Feelings can be tremendously fickle, though, Danny," he says. "Malleable, changing constantly from one day to the next."

"So, you think I had a crush on the older kid, huh?"

"Definitely, I do," he says. "I think that's something you always push back against, as if it's some terrible scarlet mark on your resume."

"Right."

"Maybe it's time to let Liam into your life now—because he's gone, he's history. Maybe you could show empathy to your young self. When you wrote him the short story, I thought that was a profoundly moving gesture."

"Yes," I say.

"Is there a reason you're pushing back and *reaching* today?" Dr. G asks.

"I partly feel my back is up against the wall," I say.

"How so?"

"Don't know, maybe I feel afraid of what I might say," I state, my feet tapping manically on the floor.

"Try to remain calm in here, Danny," Dr. G says. "You're getting too revved up."

"You said you wanted to be more ambitious, right, Doc?" I ask. "Let's liven up therapy? Pick up the pace, hut, two, three..."

"I don't know where all your rage is coming from, Danny..."

"Want to go for a spin way out on a huge white surfboard, Doc?" I say, voice breaking. "Perhaps a ride in the ocean air? Come on, don't you want to dive in?"

"*Slow it down, Danny.*"

"Want to hurt me out at sea, *Oh Captain, My Captain?*" I ask, eyes wet.

"What's happening inside you now, Danny?"

"Go ahead, Doc," I say. "Saltwater helps heal every wound."

"Deep breaths, Danny," he says. "Hush, hush..."

"*DON'T EVER SAY HUSH TO ME,*" I stand, hollering, tears falling.

"*Why the hell not?*"

"Hushing me is exactly what *Teacher-Man* did."

"Who's Teacher-Man?"

"A tall guy in a wetsuit who raped me at seven years old on a surfboard," I say. "Said he was a teacher, and I only saw his bloody, maniacal smile and his swim goggles when it was over."

"Why'd you never share about this?" he asks.

"It churns inside me like poison, like if I revealed the topic to the world, my life would erupt, or burn down, or disintegrate," I say. "Plus, I guessed it might somehow be my fault."

"Why would it be *your* fault?" Dr. G asks. "You were seven."

"Maybe I'm nothing but a waffler myself," I say, restless, jumpy. "So, I deserved it, the breakdown, concussions, flashbacks, every bit of misery, okay?"

"God, no, Danny, no way," he says. "Tell me from the top, go slowly."

"Long story, Doc," I say.

"Tell me all about it," he says. "We got time."

"It was my seventh birthday," I say. "I only wanted to swim, watch the sunrise, and this guy showed up, paddled me out to sea, and raped me."

The doctor passes me water and tissues.

"Guy made me so homophobic, Dr. G," I say. "Straight, gay, bi, trans, androgynous, everyone, even though I knew the right word is pedophile."

"Glad you voiced that."

"Buck is a totally different man, a better father than ever," I say, rolling up my sleeves. "He used to think folks who weren't all gay or all straight abused kids, anyone in the middle was tarnished, rubbish."

Dr. G studies me as I grimace, fighting something toxic inside.

"I feel desire still raging," I say. "Want to yell like Buck and tell everyone to piss off..."

"*But what?*" Dr. G asks. "Don't dismiss it, *say it to me now.*"

"Don't you see?" I ask. "Buck has done the impossible—he's like a true renaissance man. I told him I'm bisexual and he didn't freak out. He instead hugged me and said he loves me. Amazing stuff, true?"

"And?"

"Mom dead, Randy continues to struggle, most everyone else is dead," I say. "And there's only me, afraid to truly change."

"Why?"

"I don't know how to be healthy."

There's silence as Dr. G leans back and sips his tea. I fight an ache, a familiar anguish, something like relief mixed with shame.

"How long do you plan to carry that nuclear warhead around your neck, Danny?"

"Got used to it, I suppose," I say. "It fits me."

"No one's yelling at you now, though, right?" Dr. G says. "Liam's dead, Randy's treading water, and Mom's dead, and Buck's evolving, he apologized to you before the final extravaganza. He spilled his guts, and you to him. Oedipus is no longer in the neighborhood for the Halligan clan, which is wonderful."

"So?"

"No one cares anymore, Danny," he says. "Kids don't give two shits about sexuality. Buck told me that you forgave him for all of the waffle-boy words, the bigotry."

"But I saw Buck's face when he caught Liam raping me in the palace," I say.

"Buck was *panicked*, Danny," he says. "Your Dad feared for your life."

I look up at him, shaking my head. My chest feels less tense, but my face is hot, and more tears fall.

"I love him dearly, though," I say. "My dad has given me so damn much."

"Whom you love the most," he says, "can piss you off more than anyone."

I see snow falling out his window, huge fat flakes accumulating, and two crows resting on a tree limb, studying Dr. G and me *closely,* like we've offended them.

"People bang heads politically, but they still love one another."

Dr. G sips his tea again and leans forward.

"You nearly got away there with some sleight of hand, Danny," Dr. G says. "You can't blame your homophobia on the old Buck Halligan, you know."

"What?"

"You still think of Liam as less than you because he's bisexual," Dr. G says. "You're measuring a man with the same belittling way Buck used to looked at males. If one is entirely gay, they get a break... They're off the hook, and not a threat."

"I know," I say.

"Why can't you accept that the part of you that likes men also loved Liam?"

"He raped me, though, sir," I say. "And yet, I love him, I wanted him."

"That's okay," he says. "You must embrace that fact that you like women and men. No one way is better than the other. Understand?"

"Are you saying we should go over the allotted amount of time today, Dr. G?"

"I make my exceptions," he says, clearing his throat.

"Ready," I say.

"Let's move on to Gracie," he says.

"Yes."

"Think she's trying to make peace with all the money she's been sending?"

"It does appear that way," I say. "I feel torn up and wrecked over it."

"Do you think you could ever forgive her?" he asks.

"Used to think never, no frigging way in hell," I say. "Used to give myself concussions for even pondering such a nasty thought."

"I remember each," Dr. G says. "But now?"

"Gracie said she would destroy me once," I say. "We were atop Scargo Tower. She said art can shred people, leave you in tiny bits and pieces."

"And?"

"I was having too much fun getting laid, partying, drinking," I say. "In one ear, out the next. Randy, Liam, Gramps, Eileen, each of them warned me, but I didn't listen for a minute to any of it, never did, not once."

"You've come a hell of a long way, Danny," Dr. G says. "Just to be here now, discussing this kind of intense conflict within..."

"I'm not finished."

"Tell me all of it then," Dr. G says.

"Used to be impossible to think any part of the abuse was *on* me," I say. "The responsibility, you know? Not avoiding what went on, just, what's the correct word?"

"No, no," Dr. G says. "*You tell me* the correct term."

"*Complicity*, maybe?" I say.

"Expand."

"I couldn't fathom it," I say. "Made me want to hurt myself even more, but now, it's like, okay, I know had a definite role—I had a part. And that's gotta be okay within me, or everything is for naught."

We sit quietly for a minute as I pick at a loose thread on my rag sweater and Dr. G sips his tea. We both watch the crows outside and listen to their calls as one jellyfish lava lamp steals my attention.

"Let's escape the molester's toxicity, okay?" Dr. G says. "Leave him behind and celebrate Danny's significant growth."

"Sounds good," I say. "What sort of party do you propose?"

Dr. G leans back toward his desk and opens a bottom drawer, removing a plastic bag, taking out six mini-marshmallows. He offers three to me.

"Ever use stale miniatures in your psychotherapy?" he asks.

"Think I'm ready for such radical therapy, Doc?" I say.

"*Oh, you earned every one of these bastards today, my friend,*" he says.

We both smile, agreeing on something silently and eat them together.

"So, I should just keep plugging away now?" I ask Dr. G, and he nods.

"Keep at it while you're here in Vermont," he says.

"Or at the group home?"

"Yes," Dr. G says. "But know that it won't ever be a cake walk, in your life I mean. Some hard times may still wait for you, but I know, and you know, that you're capable of so much now, Danny. That you can beat it, and you can ride out the difficult patches. And the more you accept yourself and stop pushing that part of you away, the part of you that loved Liam, you're going to be in superb shape."

"Yes," I say. "I think you may be right, sir."

DANNY, GRACIE IN THE CREEK

Tuesday is the last day of being sixteen, so Gracie drives me to a pharmacy near Yarmouth. The CVS is set back from the road. Beforehand, I write down Gracie's strengths and weaknesses and take a true, moral inventory of Gracie Rose. I put it on a small yellow legal pad, but it's not even a close call. Evil outweighs good by huge margins. *Domineering. Rude. Cold. Cruel. Antagonistic. Sadistic* and on and on—and those are just the main ones. I know she's a talented force of energy and creativity, but she never leaves room for me.

Truth is, being an object of her fancy sounded a lot cooler at the start of the summer. But when you have a gorgeous, shapely young woman focusing her lasers on you, it's difficult to think with any clarity. I'm only sixteen—seventeen tomorrow—and my need and ache for her is what rules me. I'm not alone in that—it goes with the hormones, I know, I get it. But even an unusually horny teen should know when his luck is turning. On that day as we come down the creek behind the pharmacy, Gracie goes on about the talent and unique essence oozing from my soul.

"Drowning in your BS today," I say. "Cut me some slack, okay?"

"No time to squabble, angel," she says. "Artists are demanding, get used to it."

"Not sure if you ever had any truth inside," I say. "Or integrity. I don't know if you have any legitimacy left."

"Been talking with Liam a bit too much, huh?" she says. "Darling, those are his words, he's manipulating you just as much as he contends, I twist you all around."

"I speak truth," I say.

"You spit back rubbish that Liam feeds you," she says.

"Give me a break," I say.

"Glad you're developing a backbone," she says. "It's a sign of growth. But don't ever threaten me—we're here to do a job, and your body is part of my work."

After that initial skirmish, I swallowed my rage and we both grabbed inner tubes I brought from home with built-in drink-holders and face-painting crafts we picked up at a cheap art store. Liam supplied Gracie with joints, and I told myself I'd only drink beer that day. I signal for her to walk over a small stone levee behind the pharmacy, and the closer we get, the louder the water becomes.

We both take a seat at the creek's edge. I paint yellow and purple stripes on my face, while Gracie hums, and snaps pictures of an empty chocolate milk carton and some candy wrappers downstream, getting stuck along the grassy banks.

Gracie tells me Randy had words with her, told her to use more caution with me.

"What Randy doesn't grasp is I'm forever gone on you, Danny," she says. "You seduced me—truth is, you'll be fine, and I'll be mortally wounded."

I nod, not getting it, not hearing. What is most bizarre is that some of her CIA potion is still within me, active as ever, but I feel a *nuanced* difference. Within my elevated height, there is another part of my skull working, whispering.

Don't be fooled too much, Danny. Underneath the sweetness, she's still calculating and maneuvering as ever. That realization makes me feel horribly sad. All Gracie Rose sees in me is a follower, I think. Someone to use and abuse. I'm so tired of being held down, limited because I'm not fitting her ideals. She sweeps me aside all the time—I'm only trash and debris.

Now I feel like my earlier-in-the-summer description of Gracie as a firework was way off base. Yes, she can appear like a roman candle or a zooming bottle rocket, and I admit, initially, I was sold on it and played along, but now I see there's no real hope in being with her. She's more of an explosive, yes, but with an awfully sour taste, like some combination of an M-80 and a fat, old stink bomb. One who implodes souls with glee, and whomever is hanging around near her.

To Gracie, I only inspire when I stand at attention, preferably naked, always ready to pose or dance or swing through her extravaganzas.

"How do you get your black-and-white photos to speak to the world?"

"Talent, I think," she says. "And a couple sexy models to join me."

Meanwhile, as I stay drunk but conscious of Gracie's misdeeds and manipulations, her body has found a way to soar high into the air. I know that sounds like a load of bullshit, but it *seems* quite true. I watch her hover over me like a peach, a sweet magical, mythical treat.

"Some of our fans will initially only see the nudity and wild trysts in our photos," she says. "And, no doubt, some will get off on it... but we've got numerous layers and depths presented. They're being offered art and stark beauty honestly. We're not bullshitting anyone."

I am crestfallen right then—I have discovered Gracie's a fraud. It's not a talent I possess so much as a clearer understanding—I finally see through her fancy layers. Much later, years on, I'll realize this was another example where I could have pulled out of the whole circus-life. Walked away from Gracie's abuse—but I did not, and that error lies within me. I knew what was happening and continued like it was just another slow summer day.

I watch Gracie float herself back to shore. My heart throbs through my chest and the fading light of late afternoon, along with birdsong, car horns, and children giggling and yelling nearby, tickles the cilia in my ears. We take a break, mostly because I'm exhausted and can't stand up anymore. We have sandwiches, lemonade, and of course Gracie's favorite, oatmeal cookies, as we sit on her hood.

Soon, with Gracie's star, Al Green himself, blaring from her stereo, a crowd of fifteen people gathers on the banks. Gracie takes over, pulling candles and sparklers from her trunk. She's like a prop designer for a frugal off-Broadway play, making something gorgeous out of nearly nothing.

She shapes floating pods that hold burning wicks, and I drift in my inner tube downstream while Gracie marches with a baton (my old yellow Whiffle bat) and sings the Notre Dame fight song, which I can't fathom how the hell she knows every damn word to that one. Funny thing is before the rent-a-cop stops us, before his whistle and siren ring out, and he charges us with disturbing the peace and public lewdness and nudity, I see it ending in my head. Our time together is closing—the grand finale is fast approaching. Not just the summer, but everything in my life. Will I stand up for myself? Or will I continue to hurl myself onto the fire that burns all around Gracie Rose? Will I continue dissolving into the whirling juggernaut of desire and obliteration? What's it going to be, young man?

"Enough BS," the rented cop yells. "Leave the inner tube behind, kiddo, we're writing you and Kojak a ticket."

After the ticket, a stoic, silent Randy drives down from Provincetown and picks us up at the pharmacy lot, then silently drops us off, one at a time, in silence and drives home.

FINAL EXTRAVAGANZA

JULY 4, 1979

To say I was merely drunk the morning of my seventeenth birthday wouldn't be accurate—it was more like everything *within me* fell apart, like that riptide or fermenting pit, the force I feared would soon infect and destroy me, finally got its way.

Gramps informs me he is gravely disappointed in my choice of friends and so he leaves at sunrise to drive to meet with Buck in Limewood, and before he goes, he tells me I have half a day to say goodbye to, in his words, "the dirt-bags." Gramps says Dad will arrive at three, and we'll have a birthday supper, drive home, and my summer will be kaput, finished.

I phone Gracie and Liam and say let's have one last rumble. I am pissed off and so fatigued of Gracie, thinking of how she pranced away at the creek behind the pharmacy the night before, but it's my *goddamned seventeenth birthday*. I want to beat up the world with my rage, and there isn't a human alive who celebrates and croons sugary-sweet crap and faux-love with more power than my wild Portuguese Princess.

I go into the palace and find a thermos of her punch that

Gracie had left behind on the turntable. I guzzle it and feel like I must escape the closed walls, like the ceiling is descending. *I can't breathe,* I think. *Literally can't breathe.* I wake up in the Adirondack chair on the roof an hour later and hear shouts and blaring music coming from below. I rise and wobble along the edge of the roof and make it inside where I find Liam choking Gracie with both hands.

"Easy, easy, Liam," I say, trying to peel Liam's fingers from her throat. When he releases her, Gracie falls onto the carpet, coughing. She spits, gives Liam the finger, and walks to the other end of the palace.

"What was that?" Gracie asks.

I shout, "You can't strangle people, Liam, you're not a savage, right? I mean, why would you do that?"

Paranoia rushes into my body, chest pounding, brain throbbing, and I find myself on my knees, crouching, unable to make up my mind about whether to get up, or how to stand, or how to breathe. Gracie adeptly slips on my wolf mask—and she steps back and takes more shots.

"What's wrong, angel?" Gracie asks. "You're trembling and kneeling."

"My summer was wonderful," I manage. "I'm too drunk— my heart's beating so rapidly—I cannot handle it... We've gone too far."

I'm silent for thirty seconds, and the rage and sudden caustic storm surrounding me feels intolerable, like a damp, itchy sock is stuffed down my throat.

"Should we bail, Danny?" Gracie asks. "You sure you're up for this?"

"Less than average, to be honest..."

"It's your B-day, sugar so sweet," Gracie shouts over me. "A splendiferous event—let's get it going and scream it from the rooftops."

"Turn the music up then, I guess," I say, my voice cracking, wishing *somebody, anybody, help me cease this bullshit parade.*

"I'm tired of playing third fiddle in this fraudulent soap opera," Liam says. "I'm the focus of everything starting right NOW."

"No chance," I say, my head expanding, and I feel pressure to not mess up the words. "We each have a supporting role here, together we're like one..."

"Get over yourself, dipshit," Liam says, nearly barking. "I give the orders now."

"They're not your expensive cameras, Liam," Gracie says. "Not your project."

"Not your Palatial Palace, either, dipshit," I say, surprised by the feeling behind my words. "*She's* the photographer, *I'm the muse,* that's how it's always been..."

"Listen to the dork," Liam says. "I want to be the muse for my lady to abuse, *I'm the feeble muse, or is it I'm a little tea pot, short and stout...*"

"Go to hell, Liam," I say. He pushes me to the carpet, climbing on top of me, sticking his forearm against my throat so I can't breathe.

"Let him go, Liam," Gracie says. "Gig is up, let's get this wrapped and finished."

I'm the goddamned muse, I think. *I'm the most essential person here.*

Liam's spit drips out of his mouth and nearly reaches my face, but he sucks it back in and stands up.

"Thought so," he says. "Both of you are nothing but pansies."

Liam and Gracie gaze at me still on the floor with the most intense and melancholy eyes. I rush up to Gracie and she helps me swallow more of her potions.

Liam is a different animal—caustic rage oozes from him. I

can see in his eyes he's like Gracie now, in it to manipulate and damage, though I don't know *exactly* if a part of that is from my newfound paranoia.

"Where's friendly Liam?" I ask. "We just had an incredible experience, unreal how good that day was. So who the hell is this barbaric guy that shows up now?"

"No friends with PCP," Liam says. "Dust is playing violent, devouring role. *Destroy Wolf-Boy*, that's what PCP says so I follow my orders."

"Why'd you take PCP, you fool?" I ask.

"No questions, I must destroy you toute suite," he says, and then The Kinks' "You Really Got Me" comes on the stereo, and I swear my face pulses, drums fill my cranium, guitars grind into my ears and mouth, spilling out of my pores.

Gracie is constantly moving, shooting picture after picture, bouncing around, and she says, "Reality is crowding in on something luscious, the end is near, folks, our world is failing, crystal floors imploding, fragmenting, dreams vanishing left and right."

I watch Gracie's hands gesture all about—has she always had so many? She's like a wild conductor out there, a Tasmanian devil.

"A final shot at rapturous glory," Gracie says. "A free ticket to oblivion."

"*Oblivion?*" Liam asks. "But you promised Divine Visitations!"

Gracie and I drink, and I try so hard to make it feel like it used to, I *want* that so badly. But I can't. I'll realize in a few months, with Dr. G's assistance, that Gracie fits the stereotype of an exceptional cult leader. Magnetic, talented, persuasive, but also a bully and a sadist of ferocious proportions.

I poke Liam in the eye accidentally.

"*You little shit,*" he says, swiveling violently, and punches me on the mouth, and my lip splits, which knocks my mask off. I stomp on it, destroying Wolf-Boy and a connection I should be aware of but am not. It was a dangerous sign from the Gods that I had waited too long to escape, like my whole summer was inexorably changed.

Gracie takes more quick photos of my fragmented mask like she's a celebrated war photographer, reporting from Palestine.

Liam grabs me. "Help me," I say to her. "Stop this, Gracie, would you please get him off?"

"Push him a bit farther now, Liam," Gracie says, voice higher, *like a child talking about Halloween, her voice an octave above.* In my head, I feel so damn betrayed, and I think, *you damn fool, you waited too damn long, it's over. You're going down big-time.*

"Help me, Gracie," I say. "He's lost control."

I can't help but ponder that heinous day when Liam and Tommy assaulted me the summer before, the red extension cord winding around and around. The punches, the fear, the shouting and banging from above, Mr. Preston and his screeching voice. My hair going up on the back of my neck, exactly like now. Liam's lost it—he's crossed over into savagery.

"We're so close to truth though, angel," she calls out, taking photos, bouncing around the palace with her Pentax and Nikon, capturing the brutality. "Rawness is right on top of us, we're creeping up on the animal, so hard to capture this beast on film."

"No stopping me, I got a lost boy in my sight," Liam says, growling.

"Walls crumbling on our once titillating trio," Gracie goes on. "Angels sob and Gods sharpen their knives. Keep pushing, Liam, we're straddling art, so close to it now."

Liam and I throw each other around the tree palace, our naked bodies reeking of sweat and my own fear.

"Still interested, sweet pea?" Liam shouts, his erection against my thigh. What once made me smile, now makes me terrified.

"*Never,* you lousy bastard," I say, and Liam punches my belly hard, and I feel something give way, something like my whole life slipping past, my future, all my hopes, now I just gotta try and survive. That's all that's left for me now.

"Push him more, Liam," Gracie shouts again. "Puncture the boundaries, art's creeping closer, it's apocalyptic, but I love the rage, I dig this kind of shit so much."

I lose my breath as Liam continues to damage me.

"YOU'RE NASTY, FOOLISH, AND SELFISH PRICKS," I yell as I get flipped over.

"Doesn't everyone destroy their first loves?" Liam yells. "It's who Gracie is…"

"*Mighty handsome fruits,* Liam," I say. "You said you'd stop if I said *mighty handsome fruits.*"

"Way too late for any of that, champ," he says. "Everything's rotten now—no more free passes for you, buttercup."

"What the hell did I ever do to you?" I shout.

"You let Gracie and me exploit you," Liam says. "Never fought back, you're a lame Pinocchio, a puppet, no one's ever allowed to get away with that crap."

"I never once lied to you," I manage.

"*Everyone lies, Danny,*" Liam says. "It's how people stay sane. You thought Gracie was a queen bee sent to rescue you from your petty angst and teenage doldrums."

"I thought you were my friend," I say, and Liam snorts.

"No one has friends anymore, pal," he says. "You live in a fantasy—your home is *The Brady-Bunch.* Friends are passé, a joke, old news, like some worthless antique."

The truth is a frigid thing. Instead of rescuing me, or at the very least trying to keep Liam from hurting me, Gracie shoots *all* the interaction. She gets up close.

It's at that point, when my mind tries to escape, but instead I find myself trapped on a huge white surfboard leaving the shore with the beast with the mini serpent-veins busting through his hands, curly gray and black hair, with that silver wedding ring, so shiny and mocking me through the years. There's also the smell of brine, and the palace's dirty shag reeks of a decaying black wetsuit.

The rest happens horrifyingly quick, and I gaze up to find Buck Halligan stepping through the door, in shock, like a dazed Grizzly bear.

"*Daddy,*" I say, his eyes glossy and bloodshot from the three-hour drive. Buck is heavier than ever, so to see him crowding in the palace with our trio, stooped slightly so he wouldn't bang his head, sweaty armpits staining his blue button down, which is un-tucked and wrinkled, it's a peculiar word to use for Dad, but it's *obscene*. What Gracie and Liam and I expose him to probably sucks years from his life.

Buck's mouth stays agape as he surveys our mess, bending over, hands on his knees like a high school baseball ump catching his breath after breaking up a bench-clearing brawl. Even from my vantage on the floor, I see Buck's dental work, and his bright pink uvula, as if that vulnerable piece of flesh awaits some sign, a message that decency will one day return to the world.

For me, this is the hardest part of *Transfiguration Photos* to see, the pictures, brutal, savage, really. My face and bloodied lips are swollen, one eye bruised and swelling, and welts rising on my body. Dad kicks Gracie hard in the ass, and she crashes into the stereo, which makes the volume blare way too loudly, so Dad rips out the plug and the sounds, the crying, the shouts, the insanity all comes back to me like a nightmare. It was a terror. Liam takes a swing, but my father clocks him.

"Anything but this, my boy," my father says, face stricken. *"How? Why?"*

"Dad," I say, curled on the floor. "Help me."

I crawl around on my hands and knees, I can't catch my breath, I'm yelling at everyone; at Liam, Gracie, and Dad, even for long dead Mom too. I feel they can hear me maybe, somehow, but then I think of my mother watching this savage assault. *I hope she can't see this,* I think. The palace is now whirling, spinning.

My father points to Gracie and Liam: "Never want to see either of you again or you'll be killed."

"You busted my jaw," Liam mumbles.

"And you raped my son," Buck says, "and if it ever gets out, you'll die."

"Danny adored me, sir," Liam says, on his knees. "And I, him. We had a great day not long ago, I swear to you..."

"Why did we ever help you?" my dad asks. "Gramps and Eileen and I fed you for a significant amount of time, many summers..."

Liam holds his jaw, crying. "Piss-poor decision on your part, man."

Gracie sneaks out just then with her camera equipment.

Wench deserted me, I think, my swirling, tumbling mind so full of rot. *My queen abandons, abuses, and destroys her once-favorite muse.*

Liam is on his knees, holding his jaw.

"OUT!" Buck hollers. "YOU NEVER KNEW, DANNY, GOT IT?"

"Yeah," Liam says, moving slowly, tripping over a table in front of the door, shaking his head. He signals from the stairs, saying, "Again, I'm so sorry about all this, Danny, truly..."

"*OUT!*" Dad yells, and Liam disappears forever.

"What is this?" I ask my dad and the almost empty fort. "Why did they sacrifice me like I was litter, debris, what kind of human beings do this to one another?"

I can't stand properly as my tree fort spins wildly, tipping way over to the right. One sheet rock wall has been dented by Gracie's skull. Several drops of blood form a grotesque jack-o'-lantern face with stretching and unhinging jaws that look set to devour me.

All that remains in the palace is a father and son shadowed within the branches of an oak tree and every one of the intersecting pines. My knees, ass, and lips are bleeding. I cling to the floor, and by then no Kinks or Lou Reed plays. No music whatsoever. Only Buck's labored and heavy breathing.

"Christ Almighty," my father says, bending over, and with a deep groan, he lifts me up and carries me to the exit. I smell his stale breath, sweat, and long ago splashes of Old Spice on his dirty collar. Right Guard.

"Love you, Dad," I mumble. "I mean it."

"Sons of bitches, they're nothing but vermin," Buck growls as we get stuck trying to leave. The exit is blocked. We can't get around the fallen table left behind by Liam.

Dad places me down for two seconds and throws the table out of the way then picks me up, and we maneuver our way down the winding stairs. Buck's breath is loud, ragged. My eyes see writhing, huge black and silver serpents with flickering and poisoned lavender tongues moving in to strike. I can't believe I didn't sprint away from all this shit weeks ago.

Looking back into the palace over Buck's shoulder, I notice a tattered Boston Red Sox banner on the floor, a half-empty pack of Gracie's Marlboro Lights, my broken, lime-green flip-flops, and a tiny television playing a game show without sound. Is it *Match Game*? Or *Price is Right*? I'm not certain which, but there are so many carefree smiles, people giggling in the studio audience, having too wonderful a time in Burbank or Hollywood or wherever the fuck they are.

I think, *they're all fake, we're each fake, no one in the world is legitimate any longer, nothing is real, holy, and good anywhere on this earth.*

The absolute last thing I see is the *Wonder Woman* poster, hands on her hips, looking brave. The magic rope, her bullet-repelling bracelets, and her magic tiara, plus the otherworldly breasts in the amazing, patriotic outfit. She gazes at me with profound disappointment. I can almost hear Lynda Carter addressing me: "Danny, what in God's name were you thinking hanging out with those rats?"

I have no answer. As a testament to my father's indomitable spirit, he offers a pep talk as we leave the winding stairs, but he trips on the soft grass, and we tumble onto the backyard awkwardly, falling over one another.

I'm giving Buck a coronary, I think. Buck picks me up again and we race for his topaz Continental, only sixty feet away, looking shiny and so glorious in the sun.

That was one of the oddest facts to reconcile—with the rage, contraband, nihilism, and destruction floating around my palace that day, it seems like the terror *should have* taken place in a hurricane at midnight or within a tornado at three in the morning. But there's only clear blue sky, radiant sunshine, and chubby white cumulous clouds, the breeze teasing the branches of the trees around the palace.

"Okay, Boss," Dad says. "We'll get you to a hospital, Danny, we'll get you to the best doctors in the world."

We approach the back porch, but I already feel many moons away from the Danny Hal that began the season a month earlier—*that* physique is sucked into the sky while a remote camera captures my tired frame, bones, fat, muscles, and sinewy tissue. Current Danny is disassociating from the linear, normal world forever, and he's floating and drifting so damn high.

A handful of photos remain in my subconscious, shot for posterity—saved memories for intensive psychotherapy down the road. My brain spots a Bugs Bunny beach towel on a red canvas chair, sandy, water-logged Nikes, a black grill Dad uses for our summer barbecues, a yellow Whiffle bat, two tennis racquets, and a deflated beach ball resting on a wicker table.

"Why'd they hurt me?" I ask, crying again, as I become aware of the neighbors gawking, the fathers with hands on their hips, and the moms and aunts cupping their hands over their mouths. Must have been twelve folks together, all witnessing my spiraling descent—even their annoying border collie stopped yapping for once.

"Can I help in any way, Buck?" a neighbor calls out, and my father frowns.

"We're okay here, Jerry," Dad says. "We'll go to the hospital; we'll rush him there."

"Nearly there, Dad," I say.

"We're going to get you in tip-top shape," Dad says, opening the passenger side door of the Continental, placing me in it, before kissing my forehead and running inside. It's a terrifying and awkward silence as Buck disappears.

"Dad?" I call out. "Daddy?"

"He'll be right back, son," the neighbor shouts to me. "It'll be okay, Danny."

No, no, no, sir, I wanted to scream at the imbecile. *This will not be okay.* I'm still panicking as serpents chew on my face, so I close the car door.

"Daddy?" I whisper again.

"We'll get you there," Dad answers. Somehow, he's back

beside me again in the flesh. "Everything's going to be just fine."

"Promise?" I ask.

"Yeah, yeah, settle down now," he says. "We'll shoot for it."

My mind races, *Dad, God, Jesus, Yahweh, Mary, Mother Goddess, Buddha, Krishna, Vishnu, Allah, Abraham, and whoever else is listening I believe in your wisdom, help me, comfort me. Mom wasn't here to warn me. Take me away to a safer spot, a healthier space. Deliver me to a better place, Daddy...*

VULTURES CIRCLING

There's a simple brown paper package waiting for me at the nurses' station at Spruce Lodge on the young adult PEAR Unit. The postmark reads Saturday, December 17, 1983, and beside my package is a current issue of *The Boston Globe*, and I briefly check out some headlines. President Ronald Reagan is rolling right along—already survived an assassination attempt a few years before—and one big film of the year is *Silkwood*, starring Meryl Streep and Cher. Paul McCartney and Michael Jackson had a big hit song with "Say, Say, Say," and Nazi War Criminal Klaus Barbie was captured in Bolivia.

"World's flying past all of us, huh, Danny?" Nurse Jen asks me.

"Yeah, seems like it," I say.

My name and address at the clinic are typed in compact font on my package, and it reeks of coconut oil and Coppertone.

"Something from Gracie again, right?" Nurse Jen asks.

"Certainly, smells that way," I say.

"Where should we open this package?"

"My room, okay?" I ask and meet her gaze.

Now I am stable, stronger, and I can appreciate her without the BS or my obscene radio boom box blaring.

"Your room sounds good," Jen says, and when we arrive, I remove the brown paper wrapping, discovering a white Macy's box. I open it to find a cobalt-blue business card inscribed with a quote in black font taken from Nathaniel Hawthorne's *The Scarlet Letter.*

No man, for any considerable period, can wear one face to himself and another to the multitude, without finally getting bewildered as to which may be true.

"Touché, Gracie," I say before removing the yellow tissue paper and unpacking two Wolf-Boy masks, each nearly five years old, the first, relatively undamaged, and the other, tattered. I pick the first.

The wolf face is still there as is the slight red fur on its cheeks, chin, and forehead. It kind of has an Eddie Munster groove to it now. I rise and walk over to my bureau mirror. I hold it out in front of me, hands trembling.

"Shall I wear it?" I ask quietly before pushing my face into it.

"How's it feel on, Danny?" Jen asks.

The scent is Coppertone mixed with mothballs, but I'm pleasantly surprised when screeching monsters don't rip through my amygdala. The mask chafes against my cheeks and forehead so I remove it and toss it onto my bed. Dr. G would say, *Process, Danny, talk it through now, let's get every last bit of that out of your system.*

"First mask feels pretty decent, okay," I say to Nurse Jen. "Feels like freedom—unlimited possibility, playing on the Truro dunes—it was fun, a lighthearted, sensual experience.

Like a whole new world was opening for me, showing its gifts."

I gingerly pick up the second disguise—it's mostly destroyed, thinking, *watch your step with this one, Danny.* There's not much left of the façade—Liam had punched me during the finale, and the mask had fallen off, and I'd stomped on it. Looks like nothing more than badly used pantyhose now. It had felt more enclosed, hairier, slipped over my whole head, made me feel claustrophobic by the finale.

"This second mask, Jen," I say. "It's where the horror sat for me. I walked into a horrific buzz-saw with this façade on."

"Let's steer clear of it then," Jen says.

"Say goodnight, Gracie," I say and hand them over to Jen. "Please keep them far away from me."

"Don't forget the attached note," Jen says so I pick it up and read it out loud:

I'm Falling Apart Rapidly Now Lover,
Liam's Long Dead, and Macular Degeneration Is Cruci-
fying My Vision. Cancer's Devouring My Once-Unlined,
Gorgeous Face. And if That's Not Horrid Enough,
There Are Too Many Nasty and Hungry Vultures of the
Press Swarming And Threatening to Expose My
Favorite Anonymous Wolf-Boy To The Wretched,
Whirling Earth. Pray for Both of Us, My Dear Sweet.
Hugs and Kisses, MOI

"What's all these scribbled lines on the other pages?" I ask Jen.

"Shorthand," Jen says. "I took it in high school. Gracie says it's the ten-page 'Goofy Child' story she wrote down before burning the original tale. Here is all of it."

"It was a cold, brutal thing to do to a friend, a lover," I say. "Just more manipulation by Gracie."

"She always has something up her sleeve," Jen says. "Trickery and mirrors, like some deviant magician."

"Bingo, Jen," I say.

FAREWELL

Dr. G and I had been discussing it for a long time—a final, symbolic separation from the largest ghost in my past. One morning, we took an extended stroll around the hospital, passing huge elm, oak, ash, birch, pine, spruce, and maple trees. Some are naked and bare now, black fingers twisting, intersecting, and reaching up into the bone-white sky. The only substantial brightness is found on the ground that day, plastered with brilliant red, orange, yellow, and rust-colored leaves.

"I feel bereft as autumn sets in," Dr. G says. "Same each year, I find."

"Because the colors fade so damn fast?"

"Yes," he says. "And getting ready for the long, brutal winter coming."

I stare down at my bluchers and kick a few damps orange leaves away. I notice the nets are all gone at the six tennis courts, and the outdoor pool has been drained and covered with a green tarp. Two squirrels dance on the surface of the cover, chasing one another as we approach and scurrying up the far side of an elm tree.

"But I also know that deep inside there's renewal on the way," Dr. G goes on. "Promise of spring will eventually show its green, sprouting, and wild face."

I smile as he talks, notice where he nicked his bearded neck shaving today.

"Ever think of trying a different part of the country, Dr. G?" I ask.

"I like Vermont too much," he says. "Plus, most of it has been covered—what I mean is young people always invent fresh, unique ways to harm themselves, but the anguish is steady, the hurt, constant and similar. Plus, I got my grand-daughters here, and they keep me spry."

"You might try Hawaii, though, Dr. G," I say, and he chuckles. "Lots of despairing, emotionally strained surfer boys and girls in need of an ass-kicking there."

"Is that what our team has done to you here?"

"Well, yeah," I say. "But in a wonderfully complete way. You guys set me back on course, Doc. It took me a huge amount of time, almost five years in total, but I eventually got the message."

"You've done very well here, Danny," he says. "I'm pleased with your arc."

"Didn't even know I had an arc for a few years."

"Think back to how lost you were on arrival," he says. "Struggling with the punching, the boom box blaring away inside your head. But you kept at the healing, stayed tenacious."

"True, but you helped me, guided me to see my rage at myself over my sexuality, too," I say. "Homophobic times ten— it shut me up for so long. Initially, I hated you for it—but you always score with the wisdom, Dr. G. Bit by bit, I find myself growing into it, becoming more comfortable. Does that sound stupid and lame?"

"No, not at all," he says. "You've been mindful all along of your journey, going from lost, bitter, and struggling to embracing a stronger, healthier Danny."

"What else was I going to do?" I ask.

"No, no," he says. "Don't diminish your victory now. It's a difficult business, self-care for a tattered brain and body that was once much maligned. Many clients are incapable of taking care of themselves for the long term. Not in their wiring, I'm afraid, but you were determined in the most glorious way, and hope became a big part of the story. It carried and drove you all along."

I watched him cough again, clearing his throat.

"Tell me about the young woman who misread your mom's suicide photograph?"

"She let me down when she insulted me, and the memory of my mom," I say. "That really blew me away, stung."

"Right," Dr. G says. "It was very cruel and selfish behavior."

It's quiet for a few minutes, and I hear Dr. G's smoker's cough as he turns his head, and adjusts his wedding band, a nervous habit he's had since day one.

"Gotta quit those cancer sticks, Doc," I say, and he laughs.

"Yes, I certainly do," he says and looks at me, waiting for me to speak, to continue along with our conversation.

"It's time I said so long to the death photograph."

"A photo of her living can be a great thing," he says.

"But it's creepy to hold on to her suicide photo, you mean?"

"Absolutely," he says. "*Eerie and disturbing and plain wrong.*"

"That's why we've arrived at the fire pit today," I say, looking at a charred, open clearing. There are concrete slabs, a grilling area for outdoor hospital receptions and barbecues, and some picnic tables. On the ground to our right, I see several rain-soaked books of destroyed matches.

"Can I bury the ashes of the photograph?" I ask.

"Bury them, or sprinkle them around the grounds," Dr. G says. "Bake a cake with it, if you wish, but release her, the obsession with her dead body is deeply troubling."

I take the photo out, and I get flummoxed, hands trembling.

"Should have done this a long while ago, I know," I say.

"That's why we have the here and now," Dr. G says. "*The today for today.*"

I borrow his silver Zippo lighter and burn the paper of my dead Mom on the local milk truck, April Fool's Day, 1966. All the despair and hurt encapsulated in her photo turns to ash.

"Take care now, Miriam," I say and watch the paper catch and burn—orange, yellow, and purple flames eating at her body, throat, everything vanishing in a matter of seconds. I'd like to be impressive and say I didn't choke up, but that wouldn't be accurate. I take the ashes and rub them onto my palms, the tips of my fingers.

I walk over to a brook nearby and I crouch down and wash my hands clean. The cold water feels bracing, invigorating.

"Nice touch," Dr. G says. "Does it feel good to have everything done now?"

"To be honest, I'm not quite done yet, Doc," I say as I stand.

"Why's that?"

I blush, taking out three more laminated photos of my mom on the collapsed milk truck out of my back pocket.

"Ah," Dr. G says. "The plastic backups, of course, one, two, and three."

I borrow his lighter again and burn the laminated trio until they each melt, gradually dripping into the brook, bits and pieces trickling downstream. After a few minutes, everything is gone, erased—there is nothing left of my mom, no backups, no secrets.

Zilch.

"Any more surprises up your sleeve today, Danny?" he asks me.

"*Finis,*" I say, handing him back his silver Zippo. "Thanks, Dr. G. I couldn't have done any of this without your expert guidance."

"That's why I'm here, my friend," he says as we embrace. "Been a pleasure, a real treat to see you recover."

A PHONE RINGS ONCE AGAIN

On Tuesday, July 10, 1979, Liam Preston's bedroom phone rang on Wild Sands Road in Dennis, Massachusetts at 8:57 in the morning. The call is from Cape Cod Hospital in Hyannis. The facility has a holding unit to keep psychiatric patients stabilized before they get sent out to different mental health facilities or discharged to their homes.

"Hello? Is it you, Danny?" Liam says. "Please speak and say something."

Silence.

"Danny Halligan?"

Silence.

"Danny Hal?"

"Why'd you rape me on my damn birthday, prick?"

"My jaw is fractured where your dad slugged me," he says.

"You deserved it, asshole," I say.

"Yes, I did. I'm so sorry," he says. "Huge mistake..."

"PCP... Why choose that drug in particular?"

"I'll come over right now and make it up to you, I promise I can explain everything perfectly."

"No, no, my father is driving me up to a Vermont mental hospital soon."

"I'm sorry," Liam says, crying now. "I want to fix it..."

"Why'd you have to go and mess it up in the first place?" I ask. "It was going so damn well, so smoothly between us."

"I'm not used to having things work out," Liam says. "Self-sabotage is my middle name, Danny."

"You were going to be the wise one, remember?" I say. "Our friendship was going to blossom forever, right? You charmed me, Liam, and then you eviscerated me."

"I'm so sorry."

"Buck's coming down the hall," I say. "I'm off to Vermont, I guess."

"Call me again from Vermont, okay?" he says. "We can rebuild this; I know we can. I love you so much, Danny Halligan."

"That's a first-class load of horseshit, Liam," I say. "We're over, we're done, you're history in my eyes, goodbye."

"Wait..."

"No, you're done," I say, hanging up the phone.

PROVINCETOWN

JULY 4, 1989

I visit Gracie at her rented, periwinkle-blue cottage not far
from Commercial Street on Tuesday, July 4, 1989, my
twenty-seventh birthday. I'm let in past her dented screen door
by a wide and tanned hospice nurse named Shelly, who tells
me she'll wait outside, and how it's "a blessed thing to come all
this way to forgive a dying friend."

"Not here to forgive, Shelly," I say, and she scowls, turning
away.

I stand alone in Gracie's living room with framed portraits
of Hollywood stars and Gracie's most recent work, a collection
of retired octogenarian fishermen called *Fish Folk* that was
published in 1985, sold impressively, and was critically lauded.
The familiar painted turquoise eye is over the mantle, hovering,
studying me along with a ceiling leaking into a Folgers can.

"Busy enjoying the many sights out there in my hallway,
huh, angel?" Gracie's voice creaks at me. *Like a dying mouse,* I
think.

Last time we spoke, I was in Spruce Lodge, working hard to
turn things around. Gracie had told me Liam was dead, and

three years later, she sent the note saying she had aggressive macular degeneration and was going blind, also had multiple cancers eating away at her body.

She survived against all odds for years, miraculously, but now her disease has spread to other internal organs. Liver. Pancreas. Even her mouth became badly infected, and she lost almost all her teeth. That's when her royalty checks increased in amount and frequency. My father refused to cash Gracie's checks initially, but eventually he came around. The money was good and started adding up, and it eased my dad greatly. Financial healing is a real thing, or at least that's what Buck claims today.

I spent five years in that Vermont hospital—followed by a group home in Vermont for another four plus years. Nowadays, people only stay at inpatient facilities for a few weeks, if that. Everything's changed, the world, Gracie, me. Psychiatric places like to get you back out into the world as rapidly as possible. Now, it's everyone for themself. Which is a scary thought, especially if you're struggling, treading water out there.

I have lived at my dad's house in Limewood ever since, and Gracie's nurse phoned me days ago—said she was fading fast, and I'd better hurry. A decade has passed since I've seen my old lover, which is curious—the time feels both shorter and longer. Gracie had sold her huge barn several years ago, and now rents a small cottage. *Downsizing,* the woman explained, and a local hospice nurse came in and took over for the final week of treatment.

"Almost there, keep coming in, angel," Gracie calls out. I meander down the hall, seeing several honorary degrees from Yale and Wesleyan University, and fancy postcards from Palo Alto, Middletown, New Haven, and Provincetown. On Gracie's bookshelf I see an eclectic combination of Walker Evans photos, Anne Sexton poems, a biography of Diane

Arbus, and an illustrated Bible. Beside the Bible is a framed quote from Gracie's mom's favorite Jesuit priest, Pierre Teilhard de Chardin: "Someday, after mastering the winds, the waves, the tides and gravity, we shall harness for God the energies of love, and then, for a second time in the history of the world, man will have discovered fire." Gracie had drawn a line through the word *man* and added *humanity* in magic marker.

"Have you forgotten all about me in here, my dear boy?" Gracie asks so I enter her wide bedroom as nonchalantly as possible. It's off-white and reeks of lemony Lysol and urine. Two large windows look out on a ferry carrying in-bound tourists and a tiger lily garden with two girls playing badminton. I think, *perhaps they are Molly and Eve, my two sisters, long gone but never forgotten.*

I keep my eyes from examining Gracie for five seconds, trying to get hold of myself, contain my trepidation, but it's a challenge. My breath gets short, and I find my balance is way off. When I do glance up, I see my old flame is shriveled, tiny, her jaundiced complexion scares me, and nearly half her lower face is gone. My first thought is to walk out, try it all over again. I had seen a photograph of her recently in *People*, but to be up close is jarring, and I try to look pleased, or at least, not so stunned.

"I may look like mangled death to you," she says. "But you're not appearing so svelte, either sweetie. I guess those antipsychotic medications really pack on the pounds, huh?"

It's been a long while since I last saw her in the palace, but I'd built her up into an enormous satanic sphinx of a force. Processing it all, I'm sure of nothing now. *This is the most charismatic force in the history of my own little world? Where the hell did she go?*

Gracie sits high in her bed with her trademark sunglasses, tucked in tight beneath a peach comforter, and behind her is an enlarged cover of our book. The trio, shoulder to shoulder, save for Gracie, sitting naked and cross-legged at our feet, her hands raised high, like she was calling out to the world, perhaps announcing our arrival.

I take in all the life-saving machines buzzing and beeping, and the many tubes running in and out of my old lover. Gracie's smile has been disrupted by the disease—destroyed, really. Her teeth aren't there. On the left side of her face, below her neck, there's a lavender pashmina covering up so much. *Like the curtain in Wizard of Oz,* I think. *Times ten.*

"Racking my brain on how best to greet you," Gracie says, her voice raspy. *A dying mouse,* I think again. She reaches out to shake my hand with both her damp ones. "I freed you up to explore zillions of galaxies, dear sir."

"You *stole* much of my life," I hear myself say. "Coerced me in hurtful ways."

"I *gave* you life, my good man," Gracie says, her posture straighter now. "Think intent, my love. I only wished you golden halcyon days—nothing but laughter, dancing, and peaceful fun."

"Never know what's coming next from you," I say.

"That's true, I guess, darling," she says as I watch her trembling right hand wipe the sweat away, and I reach my hand back and feel a stool behind me and sit. If it hadn't been there, I would've fallen. "You ever get the Wolf-Boy masks I sent you years ago?"

"I did," I say. "Always trying to get the upper hand, aren't you?"

"No, no, sugar," she says. "They're part of our famous relics —art history—mark my words... they'll be worth serious cash, an investment opportunity as years fly by. We're already at ten years—folks will care about our trio, I guarantee."

"Maybe," I say. "And you just had to include the 'Goofy Child' story in shorthand, right?"

"What was wrong with that?" she asks. "Just wanted you to see I'm not a brutal monster, that the story was lovely. Innocent."

"I guess," I say.

"Ideally, I wish the two of us could have made it to 2029," she says. "Which would have made it the fiftieth anniversary of *Transfiguration Photos*, but, alas, several cancers had other plans for my once luscious body."

Easy, I tell myself. *Keep it together, keep it together, she's the dying one, Danny. She's the dying one, just like riding a bike here, deep breaths, in and out, and repeat.*

"Not saying I wasn't partially at fault years ago," Gracie says. "You were a fawn, undoubtedly, but I, too, didn't know who I was. No clue, I made it up as we flew along."

"And..."

"Only mesmerized by this breathtakingly innocent kid," she says. "And his lusty allegiance to me, to the cause, to try anything with his whole body, mind, and soul."

"And you the most seductive thing on two feet a decade ago," I say, telling myself, *back and forth, back and forth, you can do this stuff, Danny.*

She bows my way from her bed.

"Hope you'll forgive me now for any transgressions that went down," Gracie says, and I shake my head.

"Why can't you keep Wolf-Boy's identity a secret?" I ask, my voice breaking. *She's dying, you're healthy, Danny,* I think. *Back and forth, like a good volley in tennis.*

"Out of my control, babe," Gracie says. "Gossip rags... They feed like parasites now. All the paparazzi chew up souls. They'll out you soon enough, with or without me, they just don't give a damn anymore."

"But you *vowed* to keep everything secret for me," I say, icily. "*Promised* me no matter what, I'd be safe and sound."

She shakes her head, holding her palms out, and the connecting tubes running through her make her look, at that second, like the melancholiest marionette.

"I'm so sorry, darling," she says.

"It *was* a tragedy, though," I say. "A nightmare. Why the hell were you so cruel to me?"

"I don't know," Gracie says. "Guess I have a meanness inside me somewhere."

"I guess so."

"Across the board muses never fare well throughout history, though," she says. "You were my one magical and spectacular phoenix for that summer, angel."

"Worked well for you."

"Is there something else eating at you, babe?" she asks. "*Tell me...* what is it?"

"Can you be honest for the next fifteen minutes with me?" I ask. "Can you at least offer me some clarity?"

"Why the hell not?" she says, snapping her fingers. "Fire away, I'll answer everything, I'll rise to the occasion like a fading Hollywood starlet bidding adieu."

Ladies and gents, I think, *welcome to Gracie's absolute final extravaganza.*

"Were you ever sincere with me?" I ask.

"Loved you profoundly," she says. "But your naiveté was exquisite, like dark chocolate. I survived on that alone."

I watch her gesture, like an old, rickety preacher warming up.

"I was at Yale," Gracie says. "People got me a camera, I won several awards, and one day I discovered you at the tip of the Cape, wanting me so fully."

"A true sucker," I say.

"No, but ideas and true magic fell into place when you were near," she says.

Her face brightens as she goes on.

"A conflicted teen," she says. "Hopeful about life, and willing to do everything in the book."

"Touching?" I ask.

"Beyond perfect to put you in a wolf mask," Gracie says. "Like an opera, and Liam adored you by the way, just lost it at the end, way too much PCP."

"I felt desire for both of you, actually," I say. "You guys played me like a sap."

"It's all perception, sugar," Gracie says. "Don't you see that yet?"

"See *what?*"

"I viewed our trio as art," Gracie says, gesturing with both hands. "You saw mostly abuses, and Liam saw only sexual conquests, notches on his belt buckle."

"I'd disagree," I say.

"How so?"

"Liam was coming around to my side, we were connecting, but then PCP arrived, and the rest, well, it was hellish... but we were on our way before that. Does that sound too ridiculous for words?"

"No, not at all," Gracie says. "You're changing as time goes by—never thought I'd hear that from you, babe. I'm pleased for you both."

"Bit by bit."

"What does Buck think about his twenty-seven-year-old son now?" she asks.

"Buck's coming around," I say. "We're closer than ever, to be honest."

She exhales and holds both her hands out to me.

"I never wanted anyone else, babe," she says. "Just my Danny Hal, you'll see in the end."

"See what?"

"No more worries ever again, angel," she says. "Understand?"

I don't, but I get distracted by kids' voices screaming outside, or *wait, are they only playing?* I study the poster above Gracie, and some other shots taken from Transfiguration Photos. The shots are all still impressive—the public called us *whores, druggies, miscreants, and pornographers.* Three youths in our glory—toned, tanned, and wild, set to take on the whole universe. In the shot above Gracie, we look hungrier than ever, famished, ready to pounce on one another.

Me and Liam, or Gracie, or everyone piling on. Gracie is holding on to my nuts, smiling, and Liam is looking down at both of us, sated. *Pleased.* What I mean is he's thrilled, which is exactly what went down most of the time. There's even a quieter shot of a pensive Gracie gazing at her two young men, never with those damn sunglasses off, though.

She wore them like a superhero shield.

A lawnmower starts up down the street, and seagulls cry, and their clashing sounds scrape against the sky. *Fingernails on a chalkboard,* I think.

"Why'd you show up here on your twenty-seventh birthday, Danny?"

"Wanted to see if you had mellowed," I say. "Or if we were ever something."

"You mean our love, or my news that you'll soon be revealed as Wolf-Boy?"

"I'm not sure," I say, shrugging, and study Gracie for fifteen seconds as she pats her forehead with a beige hand towel and places it aside. She's a shell, fading fast. I ponder shaking her hand as I rise to leave, feeling pity.

She was a nasty and brutal bitch, Danny, my gut says. *Ten years wasted and gone—never let her off the damn hook!*

"Want to skinny dip for old time's sake?" she calls out. "Plus, I believe you said you'd forgive me, right?"

I glance back at her from the doorway, a tiny soul now peering over the peach bedspread, with all the electronic machines keeping track of her dwindling life. As I exit the room, she cries out. Not a scream—only an exclamation.

"Truth is," she says, throwing her sunglasses off the bed. "I think God blinded me for what I did to you!"

My knees buckle as I come back inside and steady myself on the stool. I feel pity and clarity. It's the most honest she'll ever be. Not wanting to move toward her, nevertheless, my legs hurry me across the floor, and in one sweeping motion I kiss Gracie's damp eyes, and forehead.

"*Oh, lover,* I missed you, too," she says as I pull away. "Please say you forgive me."

I turn back to look at her from the doorway and hear that damn rain.

"Danny," Gracie cries out. "Say it now or so help me, God, I'll take my life."

I stride away, leaving her weeping, before I stop in the living room. *She still has you going in circles, Danny—you're waffling—make a damn decision for once!*

I stare at the ceiling and see that leak growing worse, and I watch the now overflowing Folgers can. *Walk out the door,* I think. *You owe her nothing—she ripped a decade off your life, tore it from your gut, don't let her off the hook.*

I hear her sobbing as I use the hallway bathroom. The rain is pounding down now, I finish, wash, and dry my hands, and I notice a fading, creased photo of a little girl in her First Holy Communion dress and bonnet. It's crammed upside down in the mirror, so I straighten the photo with both hands and study a tiny Gracie Rose—an innocent kid from long ago dressed up all in white. Her chin is slightly elevated, as if she knew *even then* how to draw the best light.

We are all ancient and fading fast, I think. *We are already so ancient.*

When I return minutes later Gracie is still cursing, spittle flying everywhere.

"Gracie?"

Her head pops up—face stricken and beading with sweat.

"Danny Hal?" she says. "My only true, sweet, and forever friend."

"*You* need to forgive *yourself* before you go," I say. "My words won't help."

"*Still,*" she says. "*Still,* my sweet angel, you do forgive me, right?"

I study her, not as she once was, not as a charismatic, sexual, and magnetic stealth predator, but as a feeble, rank, jaundiced creature, her body failing her in every way—dying, trembling, and nearly blind.

Won't kill you, I think.

"I forgive you, Gracie," I say quietly. "But I'm taking back my soul."

And in that moment, the massive, marbleized façade I had created and maintained around the creature crumbles, and what's left of her enchantment melts, falling away. I hear other sounds, several sobs as I move quickly through the house. Gracie calls out two more times, but I ignore her.

I go outside to the hospice nurse, who stuffs an envelope in my hands, and then I head down the street a few hundred feet, breathing heavy, as if there'd been little to no oxygen in Gracie's room. I sit on an unsteady wooden bench outside a deli, squeezing my eyes tight. The rain is only spitting now, and I hear a kid whistling the theme song to *The Flintstones,* but when I open my eyes, I see she has thinned white hair, a stoop, and a four-pronged cane. I take the envelope the nurse handed me and stuff it into my back pocket.

I walk to my car and drive to a secluded inn not far from Race Point. I park and move down the walkway. I take a turn and see a welcoming face on the veranda, lifting towards the clearing sky. I call out his name and he smiles crinkly at me, standing.

"Lunch?" Randy says.

LEGACY

G racie's withered frame gave out a day after I visited her in Provincetown. I try to feel somber when I hear about it on the news back home in Limewood, but instead I walk around my dad's neighborhood and people watch. Lots of kids are out, laughing and playing with their families—some returning from the beach, others dashing through sprinklers, or splashing in kiddie pools, while a group plays Whiffle ball. The joy bursting from them is palpable, and I find myself afloat, riding the wave like a mood surfer.

I did laundry that evening and saw Gracie's note still in my khakis. It explains what the world learns a week later—Gracie Rose left her entire fortune to the formerly anonymous Wolf-Boy, a man by the name of Daniel Peter Halligan, 27, of Limewood, Connecticut.

With help from my dad and several of his attorneys, I bequeathed all of Gracie's photography collection from *Transfiguration Photos* to the Cape Cod Museum of Art in Dennis. I will begin to receive substantial and steady income from sales of her images. I'm also informed by Gracie's attorney that a new book of rare color photos will be published next May, entitled: *Unmasked: Gracie Rose and Wolf-Boy.*

The cover photograph shows the two of us in the creek behind the pharmacy—*au flagrante.* It's exactly what Gracie wanted, it occurs to me now. Everlasting life—to be forever part of the buzz, steering and maneuvering the living from the grave.

Posing them, even.

TAKING FLIGHT

Eight hours after I hear about her death, I fall into a deep slumber in my boyhood bedroom in Limewood and dream of a young, renewed Gracie Rose. I see her approaching me in her Easter-egg-blue dress, wearing the same outfit she first seduced me in a decade ago, with her familiar black, bug-eyed sunglasses.

But now Gracie has tight blond and red curls like singer Annie Lennox. Gracie looks reborn, stunning, sexy, and strolls towards me with this insouciant bounce, as if she really knows me, and can envision exactly what I desire. I try to thank her for my inclusion in her will as she draws near, but Gracie reaches out her exceptionally long right index finger, closing my mouth. She takes off her glasses and winks—her eyes are a brilliant, wet turquoise.

"You're going to be free from me now, angel," she says, embracing my body, and leads me to a glass door off an elevated porch. Outside, a sheer cliff drops away to nothing. Gracie opens the door and shoves me out, and I fall into a cold, wild blue.

I tumble and fear I'll crash and burn, but I steady myself and begin to rise. I gain altitude, along with confidence, twirling, humming an old Van Morrison tune, soaring through storm clouds with my mouth wide open, gulping raindrops as if they were nectar.

MY LUCKY DAYS

BY DANNY HALLIGAN

Here's how I look at my current life, all the ups and downs, the many trembling joys and concerns. I see *forgiveness* as essential to understanding who I am now at thirty-five. I never wanted to speak all that much about absolution, or similar terms like pardon or clemency. But a year after Gracie died of cancer in '89, her first posthumous book, entitled *Unmasked: Gracie Rose and Wolf-Boy*, came out, and it stunned me. It was more of the same—a *Transfiguration Photos* kind of text with nude shots of a sixteen-year-old me and Gracie frolicking in a Cape Cod creek. But every shot showed me without a mask.

My name got released and I felt exposed. Initially, I was pissed at Gracie, but when I learned she signed over all her rights to her pictures and books to me, I realized it was gracious and kind, and now pads my wallet in the most wonderful way. And it leads me back to the word *forgiveness*. But that's not the type of forgiveness I sought. Being unmasked led me down a path of creating my own photos, moving in radical directions and following wild, elliptical ways of thinking. The prints that appear in my book are all Polaroids of Liam taken by me with an old Instamatic that Randy gifted me as a boy. I felt Liam got a raw deal from the press and was dismissed as a lowly addict, nothing but a third wheel in our famous trio.

To me, though, Liam was a lot more. Not only a solid friend and a lover—there were days that summer when I felt quite close to him. It was like being in a zone—as if every jump shot I took was automatic in a pickup game of hoops we were playing together, and we had dibs on an outdoor court by a beach. When twilight came, Liam and I and a few others flipped on our car headlights, and we played until midnight before the cops sent us home. It was as if we were nestled in the grooves of a hit record, dancing, zooming, and spinning around in wonderful synchronicity. Liam crooned from very low to falsetto and made me join in, too. We laughed and flirted about so much, although I was younger by two years and didn't know squat about American politics, Emily Dickinson, algebraic equations, or how birds fly so effortlessly, but it didn't matter, really. All I knew at sixteen was I couldn't NOT listen to my own throbbing pulse, and I had a sixth sense that I was a switch-hitter at heart—bisexual. Something I disliked admitting for the longest time.

My book of Polaroids is called *My Lucky Days* and its basic premise is Liam is the unsung hero of our summer of '79, when he, as the Lone Ranger, performed his wild twisting and leaping with me and Gracie. One shot I took shows Liam running in the Truro dunes, grinning like a thief while his sinewy arms are outstretched like a lithe, modern dancer set to lift off. Plus, he has a buoyant manner—it's infectious and it lifts me when I feel crushed.

Another shot of Liam is him laughing in the tree fort, wearing my Wolf-Boy mask on the bottom half of his face under his usual Lone Ranger façade. The shot still freaks me out. In an odd way, I'm touched by him donning two masks—it's like he gave me a rest for thirty minutes and let me snap my favorite Polaroid of my good friend. For a solid portion of the season, when we were alone, it was like me, Danny Hal, was the most talented lensman in town, observing my world with a steady, discerning eye.

Yes, Gracie Rose took her famous shots, but behind the scenes is Danny catching my muse, Liam, looking forlorn or thrilled or terrifically bored. It was wonderful, like I was a shadowy figure impersonating a maestro, a dashing documentarian stealing all of Gracie's best moves. Honestly, I aped every one of her steps, for I was nothing short of a sophisticated lens specialist.

There's even a photograph of a diminutive Liam in 1975, standing before his prized collection of miniature train engines in his dank cellar. A day on, he traded them all in and started buying his own porn collection that was eventually known all over the Mid-Cape. A part of Liam regretted being known for that fact, but he was too stubborn to admit it to anyone but me.

The final Polaroid was taken on Labor Day, 1978, with me crying after a bully named Tommy wound a red extension cord around me twice. In the self-portrait, I'm in the bathroom at Gramps's, having escaped and biked over from Liam's. I still get anxious when I think of Liam aiding his cousin with the assault, which brings up many excruciating memories. Like being raped on a surfboard at seven years old by a huge man in a wetsuit and a bloody smile and a haunting silver wedding band and, much later, of being assaulted by Liam during the final extravaganza. As I selected the final shots to be placed in *My Lucky Days*, I had to release every ounce of that pain. I left it on the gray and purple shag carpet of that damn tree fort.

Liam could be an inspiring young man, an underdog in his own odd and quirky way, but my God, did he have chutzpah spilling over everywhere. He was the antithesis of me—he never had a stable home life and worked a lot of shitty jobs to stay afloat. He was handsome and complex and offered the world a lot of peculiar and funky angles. He didn't seem to fit in anywhere. But then a bald, sexy, and charismatic Yale shutterbug named Gracie sauntered through Shoot! photo studio just off Commercial Street during the summer of '79 with a Pentax and a Nikon around her neck, boasting of *Transfiguration Photos* set to occur in a deluxe tree palace in Dennis, in Liam's neighborhood, so he was all in. The rest is history.

Although he whirled and shook like a zombie that season and dove into the shallow sea, performing silly, nervy handstands, showing off his bobbing junk to the world, he behaved like a rebel from another planet. Truth is, he changed me for the better.

Do you understand what I'm trying to communicate now? I mean, beyond the famous photos and various egos that sometimes bristled against each other like a sister or brother might, I felt we possessed something supreme and unique. We embraced the blessed and the defeated, the joyous mixing with the cruelty and searing grief of death, and we realized life is a sacred and remarkable gift. Everyone should be praying in thanks to the light for our families, found pals, friends, and peers still trying to find their way home.

Liam didn't believe much in God. Humans are unmitigated, bumbling disasters, he said. We can't be left alone for too long for loneliness will strangle us, just like heroin or excessive alcohol or an untreated mental illness. There are good days and then there's miracles going down all around us. Like when Liam dashed into my tree fort one early morning and stopped me from frying myself to blisters with a pack of cigarettes. That day was like one massive blessing, a holiday thrill-ride, as if Christmas, Kwanzaa, Hanukkah, and even Boxing Day had somehow morphed into one wild, two-week-long bash. Early in my life, I had a lot of pathetic hang-ups about every little move I made in the world.

After I gave Liam a blowjob, though, I realized what I did wasn't evil, but instead a positive and redemptive act, occurring in at least ninety million other lives. A joyous act of affirmation, of spirit. That said, I was still a neurotic teenager with lapsed Catholic guilt and waffle-boy bigotry swirling around inside. Randy had once told me that 10 percent of the American populace is LGBTQ, and that includes a large swath of bisexuals.

"Is that me?" I finally asked myself in the bathroom mirror. "Is that who I am deep in the marrow?"

I knocked on the mirror and said, "Yeah, that's me."

JOURNEYING ON

My new shrink in New Haven is a fan of traveling themes and metaphors—sailing, flying, or driving along the highway from one spot to the next from Limewood to the Cape to Vermont to New Haven and home again to Limewood. Dr. K says trekking up life's mountains is necessary, elemental, and he will help me do it well. It's fun to work with a younger doctor.

I was used to the slower, wiser groove of Dr. Les Gingerman with his Matisse prints and multiple lava lamps, but with Dr. K, he's not so much paternal as fraternal, the wise, confident brother I never had. I tell him I feel a sense of momentum, no longer trapped in the inertia and anguish of the mental health system, and with the sweet monetary boost of Gracie's estate, I'm off the hook, free to philosophize more than most.

It's startling to consider how vicious I used to be to myself, doling out frequent concussions. I mention it to Dr. K, asking why it took me so long to stop.

"What's your take on all of it?" he asks.

"I couldn't leave the hurting behind," I say.

"And?"

"All the magical CIA potions and secret sauce didn't help much either," I say.

Dr. K nods.

"But even at your lowest points, you clung to your life," he says. "When you carried your mother's suicide photo around, it was always about recovery and finding a new path, so that you wouldn't *end* up like her."

"You think?"

"I *know*," Dr. K says. "Like a prodigal son returning after many difficult years away—if no one has voiced it yet, welcome back to the world, Danny."

I also find myself on speaking terms with a word that is so damn hard to pin down when you don't have any in your life. Hope—what I feel is a great deal of hope. Which carries me to my most daring, radical act of mercy ever. Me, Danny Peter Halligan, forgiving myself—for not walking away sooner from the final extravaganza, and for not romantically pursuing Liam earlier in the summer and possibly rescuing him from his tragic death. It took much therapy and hard work by me, and three decades and change to arrive at this semi-comfortable spot with my own sexuality, with my whole life, *really*.

I'm now mercifully free.

ACKNOWLEDGMENTS

Many thanks to the wise Amy Holmes, and also the impeccable, even-keeled work of my Running Wild Press and RIZE Editor for *Wolf Boy* Cody Sisco, so calm and cool from the beginning. Also, thanks to my 3Arts Entertainment agents Richard Abate and Hannah Carande. And huge appreciation to Lisa Kastner for her team at Running Wild Press, from Kimberly Ligutan to Evangeline Estropia. From every sector of Running Wild or RIZE, excellence is the norm.

Thanks to everyone from my mom to my brother, Dennis, to Laura and Paul Fitzpatrick-Nager and Julie Fitzpatrick and Pete Palumbo and Fitz Pant and the mystery kiddo. Thanks also to Hollis Seamon several times over and to Wally Lamb, as well. I send out kudos to Bill Parisi and Dr. Barent Walsh, and the Namibia contingent of our family, Rick, Mary, Dominic, Christopher and Gabriel Fitzpatrick. Kudos to Ryker Holmes, a wonderful and kind nephew from North Carolina along with Juno, and Stella and Helen Holmes in New Hampshire, and Ruby, Scargo, and Beardsley Fitzmes out of Middletown, Connecticut.

Jan Hunt is the closest thing I've got to a truly holy Godmother, and thanks to Julie Levesque with her great work and focus with my website, David-Fitzpatrick.com, and also her art can be found at Rice Polak Gallery in Provincetown. Deb Goldstein, Julie Levesque's wife is another grand, nuanced artist from Rice Polak at the tip of the Cape, definitely well worth investigating. A deserved affirmation to all the Guilford boys out there who miss the laughter and presence of Eric Boehlert: Rich Abate, Tim Devaney, Kevin Healy, Bill Barnes, Gary Kaisen, Brian Rigney and Tony Walker.

For people who've helped along the way, from Ron and Tracey Holmes, to Joe Rutlin to Bette Sommo to Sue LaVoie to Rachel Basch to Baron Wormser to Lary Bloom, Suzanne Levine to the photography of Pete Duval, to Michael White for his writerly example, to talented copy editor Heather Zullinger, to the great work of Fairfield MFA Katie Schneider and Chris Belden, hosts of the best damn literary show online.

Running Wild Press publishes stories that cross genres with great stories and writing. RIZE publishes great genre stories written by people of color and by authors who identify with other marginalized groups. Our team consists of:

Lisa Diane Kastner, Founder and Executive Editor
Andrea Johnson, Acquisitions Editor, RIZE
Rebecca Dimyan, Editor
Andrew DiPrinzio, Editor
Cecilia Kennedy, Editor
Barbara Lockwood, Editor
Chris Major, Editor
Cody Sisco, Editor
Chih Wang, Editor
Benjamin White, Editor
Peter A. Wright, Editor
Lisa Montagne, Director of Education
Lara Macaione, Director of Marketing
Joelle Mitchell, Head of Licensing
Pulp Art Studios, Cover Design
Standout Books, Interior Design
Polgarus Studios, Interior Design

Learn more about us and our stories at www.runningwildpress.com

Loved this story and want more? Follow us at www.runningwildpress.com
www.facebook.com/runningwildpress,
on Twitter @lisadkastner @RunWildBooks